TEEN

VOLUME

BASS ACKWARDS
AND
BELLY UP

BASS ACKWARDS
AND
BELLY UP

A novel
by Elizabeth Craft and Sarah Fain

LITTLE, BROWN AND COMPANY
New York ✢ Boston ✢ London

Little, Brown and Company
Time Warner Book Group
1271 Avenue of the Americas, New York, NY 10020
Visit our Web site at www.lb-teens.com

First Edition: May 2006

The characters and events in this book are fictitious.
Any similarity to real persons, living or dead, is coincidental and not intended by the author.

ChapStick® is a registered trademark of Wyeth. Tinactin® is a registered trademark of Schering Corporation. Neosporin® is a registered trademark of Burroughs Wellcome & Co. Inc. Band-Aid® is a registered trademark of Johnson & Johnson. Tylenol® is a registered trademark of McNeil Laboratories, Inc.

Excerpt from "The Dreamer's Dictionary: The Complete Guide to Interpreting Your Dreams" copyright © 1974 by Stearn Robinson and Tom Corbett
Reprinted with permission from Taplinger Publishing Co., Inc.

Excerpt from *The Amy Vanderbilt Complete Book of Etiquette,* entirely rewritten and updated by Nancy Tuckerman and Nancy Dunnan. Copyright © 1978, 1995 by Curtis B. Kellar and Lincoln G. Clark, Trustees U/A dated March 10, 1980, and Doubleday, a division of Bantam Doubleday Dell Publishing Group, Inc.

"Nothing to Save" by DH Lawrence, from *The Complete Poems of DH Lawrence* by DH Lawrence, edited by V. de Sola Pinto & F. W. Roberts, copyright © 1964, 1971 by Angelo Ravagli and C. M. Weekley, Executors of the Estate of Frieda Lawrence Ravagli. Used by permission of Viking Penguin, a division of Penguin Group (USA) Inc.

Football cartoon on p. 138 is by Tracy Bellomo.

Excerpt on p. 382 from the poem "Bread and Wine," by Friedrich Holderlin.

Library of Congress Cataloging-in-Publication Data

Craft, Elizabeth.
  Bass ackwards and belly up : a novel / by Elizabeth Craft and Sarah Fain. — 1st ed.
    p. cm.
  Summary: When one of four best friends lies and says she will pursue her dream of writing a novel rather than start college, two others join in, one by going to Los Angeles to become an actress and one by back-packing through Europe to find herself, while the fourth goes to college, joins her hero's ski team, and tries to fall in love.
  ISBN-13: 978-0-316-05793-6 (hardcover)
  ISBN-10: 0-316-05793-2 (hardcover)
  [1. Best friends — Fiction.   2. Friendship — Fiction.   3. Self-actualization (Psychology) — Fiction.
4. Authorship — Fiction.   5. Actors and actresses — Fiction.   6. Voyages and travels — Fiction.
7. Colleges and universities — Fiction.]   I. Fain, Sarah. II. Title.
PZ7.C84318Bas 2006
[Fic] — dc22   2005029064

10 9 8 7 6 5 4 3 2 1

Q-FF

Printed in the United States of America

The text was set in Granjon, and the display type is JM Libris.

For every girl who's not afraid to dream.

And even more,
for those who are afraid but dream anyway.

PROLOGUE

"Mia, I have to take a shower," Becca Winsberg insisted, banging on the bathroom door for the third time in half an hour.

"Just a minute!" her stepsister snapped.

Becca raised her hand to bang harder, then thought better of it. Really, she decided, what was the point? Mia didn't care that this was Becca's last night with her friends, and that maybe she didn't want to spend it smelling like sweat and closet dust — the unfortunate result of hours of furious packing for college. All Mia cared about was vomiting up her doctor-regulated afternoon snack, brushing her teeth twelve times, and staring at herself in the mirror for an hour to make sure not a gram of fat made it to her butt.

Returning to her room — a tiny, gabled corner of the second floor that Becca's stepfather had called "a temporary solution" when Becca and her mom moved in seven years ago — Becca reminded herself that bulimia was a disease. Usually, it just felt like sixteen-year-old Mia's pathetic attempt to get attention from her father.

Becca sank onto her twin bed and half-slipped under her yellow down comforter. Everything was going to be fine. She could wait. She didn't exactly have a choice — so there was no point in getting upset. Especially when the inevitable explosion hadn't even happened yet.

As if on cue, her twelve-year-old stepbrother, Carter, started banging on the bathroom door.

"Open up!" he yelled.

"Screw you!" Mia screeched.

"Dad, she's puking again!" Carter bellowed.

Becca sighed. She knew what was coming next.

Within seconds, she could hear her stepdad, Martin, stomping up the stairs. Martin yelled at Mia, who yelled at Carter, who yelled back at Martin. Soon her mother's voice joined in the cacophony. Finally, Martin stormed off to get the screwdriver. The lock was coming off the door again.

Becca groaned and put her pillow over her head.

All she wanted was a shower.

Okay, and maybe some peace.

Sophie Bushell poured a third pack of Equal into her nonfat iced mocha latte and contemplated the bangs of her future roommate, Maggie Hendricks. They were unforgiving bangs. Dark brown and shiny, they cut across Maggie's forehead as if someone had been holding a ruler under the scissors to make sure not one strand escaped the slaughter.

The bangs, along with Maggie's buttoned-too-high J.Crew black oxford shirt and perfectly creased brand-new blue jeans contributed to Sophie's opinion that Maggie was as rigid as her haircut. Then again, they'd only met fifteen minutes ago, and Sophie had a tendency toward outrageously unfair snap judgments. If she ever tried therapy, it was definitely a character flaw she'd have to work on.

"You're so lucky you grew up here," Maggie was saying. Apparently, she'd run out of material on the debate team camp that had brought her from Des Moines to Boulder two weeks before classes started, her need for "quiet time," and what color duvets they should buy for their shoe box in the dorm. "I bet tons of your friends are going to CU."

Sophie crushed another pack of Equal in her hand, showering the Formica tabletop with tiny granules of faux sugar. *Three, two, one.* Yep. There it was. The hard ball of dread that formed in her stomach every time the subject of college and friends came up in the same sentence. Which was often.

"Yeah, it's going to be awesome," Sophie managed to respond. She didn't feel like delving into the topic of her three best friends — Harper, Becca, and Kate — leaving her alone in Boulder while they went off to lead fabulous lives on the East Coast.

Maggie was looking at Sophie like there was something really disgusting hanging from her nose. "What?" Sophie asked nervously.

"You're ... uh ... kind of ... teary," Maggie pointed out, averting her gaze. "Or something."

Sophie reached up. Her eyelashes were wet. Damn. She *was* teary. Keeping her emotions close to the surface was one of the hazards of being an actress, but usually Sophie left the actual bawling to Becca. It was only lately, as the countdown to losing her best friends had begun, that Sophie found herself having to swallow hard and blink back tears on a regular basis.

"It's an allergic reaction," Sophie replied quickly, dabbing away the evidence. "Probably something in the sweetener."

"Allergies suck," Maggie responded, equally quickly. Her obvious discomfort almost made Sophie like the girl. Almost. "You probably look good, even when you're bawling. My face totally puffs up."

Sophie nodded. Her African-American mom and white aging-hippy dad had managed to pass on primo genes to their only child before they decided to lead what they amicably called "divergent lives." The result — Sophie's creamy caramel skin, huge dark eyes, and high, striking cheekbones — meant she looked good doing just about anything.

The crisis averted, Maggie smiled and leaned in closer. "I should probably tell you now that I'm a little obsessive about practicing my pro and con speeches. I hope it won't be a problem."

Sophie forced herself to smile back. "Nope. No problem at all."

Tomorrow morning, she was definitely going to see about getting a single.

"You should think about Yale Law," Kate Foster's mother said, dusting a sterling silver condiment bowl with a starched linen dishcloth.

Kate, who was artfully arranging a tray of European cheeses and Carr's water crackers in preparation for her parents' impending party, glanced across the marble kitchen island at her father. Already dressed for the evening in a tweed blazer and navy-blue striped tie (a gift from Kate and her sister, Habiba), he nodded his graying head in silent agreement.

Not that Kate had expected anything else. Her parents *always* agreed. On everything. Including, apparently, on the fact that even though Kate hadn't yet *started* at Harvard, it wasn't too soon to begin planning what came next. Which, Kate had to admit, was probably a good idea. Her parents had never steered her wrong before. So she might as well go with it.

"You think Yale Law is better than Harvard?" she asked, creating a fan of green apple slices beside a bowl of Spanish membrillo.

"Not necessarily," her father said, stealing a cracker. "But if you want to clerk at the Supreme Court, the *Yale Law Journal* would look impressive on your résumé."

"Which one is the Supreme Court?" Kate's fourteen-year-old sister,

Habiba, asked, entering the kitchen with an iPod in one hand and a bottle of Fiji water in the other. Dressed in faded Gap shorts and a cornflower blue Max Azria tank, Habiba could not have looked more American. Even her accent was perfect now. The only traces of her sister's Ethiopian birth were her smooth, dark skin; her carved, patrician cheekbones; and the beaded brass necklace she always wore around her slender neck.

"The Supreme Court is the highest court in the nation," Kate's mother answered, filling the condiment bowl with almond-stuffed olives. "There are nine Supreme Court Justices. . . ."

Kate pushed up the sleeves of her Harvard sweatshirt and refocused her attention on the cheese tray as her mother went into what was sure to become a detailed lesson on the American judiciary. Habiba didn't seem to mind — she was interested in virtually everything. But lessons about the Supreme Court were hardly what Kate had expected three years ago when her parents, after many years of hoping to have more children, decided they were going to adopt from Ethiopia. The decision had been preceded by many long conversations about the complexities of international adoption and the idea of having a biracial family. Kate had been prepared for the challenges — even if she had been just the tiniest bit trepidatious. And she had respected her parents for living up to their deeply felt political and moral beliefs: that all children should have access to stable, loving homes, enjoy equal educational opportunity, and live free from racial and gender prejudices.

Mostly, though, she had simply been excited about her new big-sister responsibilities — lullabies, diaper changes, supervising of first steps and first words. All the good stuff. The fun stuff.

But her parents hadn't come home with a baby. They had come home with Habiba. And suddenly, Kate was sharing a bathroom with a twelve-year-old who spoke broken English and only knew how to tell time with a sundial.

5

Not that there was anything *wrong* with that. And Habiba was great. She was smart and funny and curious . . . a lot of good things. Just . . . different good things than Kate had expected. Habiba didn't want to be cuddled. She didn't need anyone to put her to bed or read her stories or take care of her. She was already grown. Or, a lot grown, anyway.

Habiba was too old to really be a sister . . . and too young to be a friend.

Not that Kate would ever, in a million years, have said that aloud. To anyone. *Ever.*

"But Kate hasn't even started college yet," Habiba was saying when Kate tuned back into the conversation. "Doesn't she have time before she thinks about the Supreme Court?"

"Yes," Kate's mother nodded. "But time flies. She'll be graduating before we know it."

"It's always best to have a plan," her father added. "And stick to it," he finished with an open-handed smack on the countertop for emphasis.

But tonight, Kate thought, wasn't about Yale Law or Habiba or her parents.

Tonight was about her friends.

And despite the fact that her mom and dad had chosen Becca's last night in town to throw a welcome party for a newly hired European History professor at UC Boulder, Kate, Sophie, Becca, and Harper were going to make the most of it.

Four best friends, she thought with a smile, a couple bottles of pilfered wine, all the cheese they could eat. . . .

Kate felt the flutterings of a sudden, rising panic. Becca was leaving for Middlebury tomorrow. High school was over. Really, over. She wasn't the president of the community service club anymore. Or the editor of the Fairview High yearbook. She was just Kate Foster, almost-Harvard-freshman. What if she wasn't ready? How had life after high school started so soon? What would she do without Sophie, Harper, and Becca?

Kate took a deep breath and forced herself to remember that she had a plan. And that meant that everything was going to be fine.

Because, as her father had said, it's always best to have a plan. . . . And stick to it.

Harper Waddle stared at her reflection and thought about blackheads. She had four of them, and no amount of poking, squeezing, or exfoliating had made them go away. She might as well accept them. Maybe she could even think of the little pockets of bacteria as family.

Harper pulled the belt of her white beat-up terry-cloth bathrobe tighter as a light knock on the bedroom door interrupted her rumination about the nature of blemishes. "What?" she called to her dad.

He was the only one in the house who bothered to knock, and that was just because of a mutually embarrassing incident involving a home bikini-waxing kit that had occurred in ninth grade. The door opened, and Mr. Waddle stuck his head into the room.

"Your mother wants us to help load mini quiches into the car." He grinned, his hazel-blue eyes glinting behind his drugstore-purchased reading glasses. "She said to expect certain death if you're not downstairs in five minutes."

Harper rolled her eyes. Threatening murder was one of her mom's favorite hobbies. "But you'd be mad if she killed me, right?"

"Are you kidding?" he deadpanned. "I'd cover it up for her."

They'd had the same exchange a thousand times, and its familiarity gave Harper a pang. Because after tonight, everything would be different.

"Five minutes," her dad repeated before he ducked out and shut the door. He was wearing his work boots, and Harper could hear him clomping down the stairs of their cozy two-story house.

Listening to her father's retreating footsteps, Harper decided there were worse things than being a seventeen-year-old girl with almost-hip black eyeglasses, almost-straight dirty blond hair, and four hideously ugly blackheads.

Worse things like secrets. One secret in particular.

Harper turned away from the mirror and headed to her cedar closet. She had to find something half-decent to wear tonight. It was the last time she, Sophie, Becca, and Kate would all be together before The College Years began, and she wanted to show up in something more inspired than a faded black Ann Taylor skirt and a sweat-stained tank top.

But it wasn't just the momentousness of the occasion that warranted Harper's abandoning her sloppy-writer persona. She felt it was imperative to look together, in control.

Because inside, she was a mess.

For over a hundred and thirty-eight days (not that she was counting), Harper had been lying. To her friends, to her family, to the mailman. For over a hundred and thirty-eight days, she'd been trying to find the courage to tell the truth.

So far, she hadn't. What she *had* managed to do was find a bright side to the grim truth she'd been hiding. It had taken all summer, but she'd found it.

Harper was going to drop the bombshell on her friends tonight. And hopefully, they would be happy for her. Hopefully, they would still love her. As for telling her parents the news — she'd worry about her mom killing her tomorrow.

Harper Waddle
5306 Canterbury Road
Boulder, CO 80302

Dear Harper Waddle:

We are sorry to tell you that New York University will be unable to offer you a position in next year's freshman class. We received thousands of applications and reviewed each one carefully. Although many applicants were qualified, we have a limited number of spots available.

We wish you the best of luck with all future endeavors and invite you to reapply in the future. Thank you for your interest in NYU.

Sincerely,

Phoebe Pettler

Phoebe Pettler
Dean of Admissions, New York University

ONE

Becca was not going to scream. Even if Sophie pulled every hair out of her head, one strand at a time . . . She. Would. Not. Scream.

There was one final, solid tug to the back of Becca's head. Then, suddenly, she was free. It was over. Becca released her white-knuckled grip on Kate's green Egyptian cotton duvet and opened her eyes.

"Thank God," she muttered weakly.

"Check it out," Sophie beamed, as Becca slid off the bed and crossed the hardwood floor to the full-length mirror mounted on the back of Kate's walk-in closet door. In fifteen minutes, Sophie had managed to turn the frizzy, auburn brown greaseball on Becca's head into a sleek, sophisticated ponytail. The girl was gifted.

"Wine for later," Kate announced, entering with two smuggled bottles of Chardonnay wrapped in a sweater.

She took in Becca's hair. "Much better," she commented, slipping the wine into a drawer in the long oak library table that lined one whole wall of her bedroom. The table was already covered with a Vaio laptop, printer, books, and papers with HARVARD UNIVERSITY emblazoned across the top — all of it neatly arranged and ordered.

"Thanks," Becca replied, trying to keep the wounded tone from her voice. She hadn't looked *that* awful before. Maybe her hair hadn't been perfect, but her khaki pants and lime-green button-down looked pretty damn good, thank you very much.

In her aquamarine cotton sundress, Kate, of course, looked perfect. Blond, blue-eyed, and beautiful. A sculpted nose, high cheekbones. Graceful, confident, not too tall, not too short, not too thin, definitely not too fat . . .

If Becca didn't love her, she'd hate her.

"Hey," Kate scrambled, seeing that her words had landed unintentionally hard. "You always look great. It's just —"

"Now you look slamming," Sophie finished, taking in her own slamming self in the mirror. The figure-hugging black pants and flowy, hot-pink tank she had on would have done any supermodel proud.

"Exactly," Kate nodded.

Becca felt her cheeks grow red. Leave it to her to hear an insult where none was intended. It was just that she always felt slightly . . . *less than* standing next to Kate. Brown hair, freckles, and muddy green eyes did not a beauty queen make. Not that she wanted to be a beauty queen. Just a beauty.

Unfortunately, her genetic ship had already sailed, and she'd been earmarked "cute." "Pretty" on a good day.

"Sorry," she sighed. "I'm a little . . . emotional today."

In the car on the way over, she'd actually started bawling listening to that Ryan Adams song about New York. She couldn't stop thinking that Harper was going to *be* a New Yorker soon — whatever that meant. Probably that she'd be carrying the requisite black messenger bag, shopping at Zabar's, and hanging out with all her cool new NYU friends in the East Village.

Harper would be a New Yorker, Kate could be a Bostonian, Sophie would be . . . well, still in Boulder. And Becca . . .

This time tomorrow she'd be on a plane.

The thought of finally being an actual freshman at Middlebury gave her a feeling of exhilaration and terror not unlike how she felt jumping off a ski lift to take on a black diamond. Only on this particular black diamond, the moguls were meeting new people, trying to get straight A's, making a concerted effort *not* to gain the freshman fifteen, and helping her new ski team keep its reputation as the best on the East Coast.

Sophie threw an arm over Becca's shoulder and planted a smooshy kiss on her cheek. "I'm gonna miss you, babe. And later, I predict some serious tears. But right now, we've got to rescue Harper from catering hell."

Becca grinned back. Sophie had an excellent point. Harper was downstairs somewhere with an armload of finger food, surrounded by hungry, semi-drunk academics. They had to take action.

"Have you talked to Harper today?" Kate asked as they descended the oak staircase into the crowded living room, where UC Boulder professors stood in packs of three and four, throwing around words like *semiotics, deconstruction,* and *post-modernism* between sips of Italian wine. The Fosters' two-story Cape Cod would have looked out of place in *Architectural Digest* — but only because of its comparatively diminutive size. Otherwise, it was a showplace, with antiques inherited from generations of Fosters in every room, and knickknacks collected on the Fosters' travels all over the world adorning the walls.

"Yeah," Becca answered. "She called to ask if I thought lying was a bigger sin than omission."

Sophie shook her head. "Our girl's been a big freak lately."

"Who's a freak?" Harper asked, coming out of the kitchen with a tray of her mother's bruschetta. She set the bruschetta down on the dining room buffet, then turned expectantly to Becca, Kate, and Sophie.

"Uh . . ." Becca began. Why did she have to be such a terrible liar?

"My mother," Kate explained, jumping in smoothly. "She's decided I should go to Yale Law."

"Oh." There was a weird pursed quality to Harper's face.

Yep, Becca decided. Something was up with her.

"Well," Harper continued, "I guess it's a done deal then."

Kate frowned. "Not necessarily."

Harper gave Kate a look. "Okay," she said, and walked back into the kitchen.

Becca turned to Kate. "Definitely a freak."

Kate considered a moment. "She's probably just upset you're leaving tomorrow."

Becca groaned as her eyes welled up.

Kate wrapped an arm around her shoulder. "Sophie's right. Don't start." Then she smiled. "You'll get me going."

"Yeah, right," Becca laughed.

In the five years Becca had known Kate, she'd never once seen her cry. Not at the end of *Jerry Maguire,* or when she'd broken her wrist playing field hockey, or even when her grandmother died. Becca always imagined Kate with an invisible force field around her. No matter what happened, she always seemed protected, safe. She just dealt with things and moved on.

Of all the things about Kate that made Becca just the slightest bit jealous, that was one of the big ones.

A sandy blond head appeared at the other side of the room. Becca's heart lurched. He's here, she thought, watching as he approached. She hadn't even known he was coming — the guy she'd loved since eighth grade, when he'd held her hand and given her her first kiss outside the boys locker room at the Valentine's Day dance. He was everything she could ever imagine wanting in a boyfriend — smart, funny, commandingly tall, boyishly handsome, with wind-tossed blond hair and gleaming ocean-blue eyes.

14

"Hey, Bec," he grinned. "Hey, Sophe."

Then he planted a gentle kiss on Kate's waiting lips.

"Hey, babe."

"What're you doing here?" Kate sounded not quite pleased.

"Your mom invited me," Jared Burke replied, pulling her close.

"I'm gonna see if Harper needs help," Becca said, and made her escape, leaving Sophie alone with the lovebirds.

Her smile didn't falter until she was in the kitchen. A girl couldn't spend seventeen years surrounded by a totally dysfunctional family without developing a certain skill at hiding her emotions. In her family, feelings were little more than ammunition for someone else's gun. The only way to stay safe was to hide the bullets.

So, for years, she had been hiding her feelings for Jared. When he'd broken up with her two weeks after the eighth-grade Valentine's dance, Becca had pretended to be fine. Admitting she was broken-hearted seemed silly, even childish. She hadn't wanted Kate, Sophie, and Harper to think she was some loser who couldn't get over her first crush. Then, a little more than a year later, Kate and Jared started dating. Kate had come to her, flushed with excitement, and asked if Becca would feel weird about it. She had of course said no. And after three years, Kate and Jared were still a phenomenal couple. They were happy together. And Becca was happy for them. Truly.

But, deep down, if pressed . . .

She had to admit, that of all the things about Kate that made her just the slightest bit jealous, being loved by Jared Burke was the biggest of all.

"It'll only take a minute," Kate said, leading Jared up the stairs to her bedroom.

"It'll take more than a minute," he grinned, grabbing her wrist. He pulled her into the bedroom and closed the door behind them.

"Jared —" Kate began as he wrapped his hands around her waist and walked her slowly backward toward the bed.

"Not now," he said in a low voice. The back of Kate's legs hit the mattress, and Jared gently pressed her down, until her shoulders landed softly on the comforter. Then he leaned over and kissed her.

Just for a minute, Kate told herself. If she didn't at least give him that, he'd be grumpy for hours. So she tilted her head back, giving Jared's lips better access to the curve of her neck. After almost three years, he knew just where to linger, just where to —

Chess in Mathematics, or Literature & Justice?

Jared's hand slid under her sundress and up, across the hollow of her stomach.

There's also the Bob Dylan seminar. That could be fun.

Jared's hands stopped. His lips left her neck.

Kate opened her eyes to find her boyfriend looking down at her. Whoops. Looked like he was going to be grumpy anyway.

"If you didn't want to do this, why'd you haul me up here?"

Kate blinked at him. If there had been a mood to break, that certainly would have broken it.

"Excuse me?" she said coldly.

Jared backpedaled. "I mean, my girlfriend grabs my hand and pulls me up to her bedroom, I just thought . . ."

"There's a party downstairs. It's Becca's last night. I just figured since you're here, we should talk a minute."

Jared's blue eyes were skeptical.

"About our class schedule," she admitted.

He sat up, adjusting his shirt.

"We don't leave for Cambridge for, like, four days."

"Freshman seminars fill up fast," Kate explained. "My mom didn't get the one she wanted her freshman year, and she ended up studying finches with some eighty-year-old professor emeritus."

"I'm sure he's dead by now," Jared retorted.

"It's our first chance to build a relationship with a professor —"

"You do know that college is supposed to be fun, right?"

Kate paused. Of *course* college was supposed to be fun. Why would he even say that? But that didn't mean they could just show up and hope for the best. They had to be prepared. Then, sure, fun fun fun.

But there was something in Jared's tone that gave her a tiny, anxious knot in her stomach

"Jared," Kate cajoled. "Are you saying I'm not fun?"

"You gotta relax, babe," he replied seriously. "I mean, cut the cord. That's the whole point of college. Getting *away* from parents, doing what we want."

"I know that." Of *course* she knew that.

Then Jared smiled, pulled her close.

"You know what I want to study right now?"

"What?" she replied cautiously. As he brushed her hair away from her face, Kate reassured herself. Jared loved her, and she loved him. This was just a transitional time. Of course there were going to be bumps, but they would get through it.

He kissed her, and pushed her back down against the pillow.

"Biology," he said. "Let's start with the basics. Top lip, bottom lip." He kissed each in turn.

Kate couldn't help smiling as she put a hand on his chest.

"Party downstairs," she said simply. "Parents. Friends."

Jared groaned and stood up.

"I'm going home."

"You're being silly —" Kate started to say, but Jared was already out the door.

Kate sighed.

He'd come around. And when he did, she'd be sure to let him

know that he could stop making these ridiculous assertions about cutting the cord. It wasn't like she listened to *everything* her parents said.

If she did, she'd still be a virgin, for God's sake.

"It's not fair." Sophie waved the enormous glass of Merlot she'd poured for herself when none of the adults were looking to emphasize her point. "Why am I the only one who has to stay in Boulder for college?"

Habiba toyed with the beads of her African brass-beaded necklace, considering the question. "Maybe because your grades weren't good enough to get in someplace like Harvard?"

With the party finally winding down, Sophie and Habiba were camped out at the black-and-white marble-topped island in the middle of the kitchen, waiting for the Fosters to usher out the last of the academic types.

Sophie rolled her eyes. "Is that *my* fault?"

"Well . . . yes." Habiba looked confused. "I mean, who else's fault would it be?"

Despite the fact that she never sugar-coated the truth, Beebs was usually a sympathetic ear. Habiba understood pain (even the relatively shallow kind) better than anyone Sophie knew. The story was a little hazy, but Sophie knew that Beebs's biological father had died in a war when she was a baby. Then, when she was three, her mother had gotten sick and was forced to take her to an orphanage. As far as the Fosters knew, Habiba's mother died a few months later, and aside from the nuns and the other kids in the orphanage, Habiba hadn't known what it was like to have an actual family until she came to the United States.

Usually, Habiba's story made Sophie realize her own life had been absurdly free of pain. But tonight Sophie was too caught up in her own drama to have even one iota of perspective.

"Never mind," Sophie complained miserably. "I'll just waste away in Colorado the rest of my life, playing bit parts in community theater productions of *A Christmas Carol*."

"I'll be in the front row," Habiba promised, reaching for a sesame cracker.

"Thanks, Beebs." Sophie gulped her Merlot, wishing she could go back in time. Even to three months ago, when the whole summer stretched out before her, and it seemed like Kate, Becca, and Harper would never leave.

Habiba nodded meaningfully toward the swinging door, where Mrs. Waddle was entering with a half-full tray of mini quiches. Sophie quickly slid her glass away from her and grabbed a nearby can of Diet Coke.

"I saw that, Sophie," Mrs. Waddle informed her, setting down the tray. "You might want to work on your 'innocent' face in acting class."

"Good one, Mrs. W." Sophie would miss her easy rapport with her friends' parents. Running into them at the Pearl Street Mall in downtown Boulder wouldn't be the same as hanging out in their kitchens.

Harper stomped into the kitchen, somehow managing to hold eight empty wine goblets between her fingers. "Becca and Kate already went upstairs, and I'm officially off duty," she announced to Sophie, setting down the glasses with a massive clatter. "Let's go."

"Someone's in a bad mood," Habiba observed to Sophie as Harper ripped off her apron and headed toward the Fosters' back stairs.

Sophie nodded. Harper sounded cranky. Really cranky. She'd been acting bizarre all week, and it was getting on Sophie's nerves. What did Harper have to be pissed off about?

In a week, she'd be moving to Manhattan, exactly like she'd planned since seventh grade. Sophie, on the other hand, would be moving three blocks from her mother's house, exactly like she'd always feared.

"Have fun, girls," Harper's mom said. "You'll remember tonight forever."

Sophie waved goodbye to Mrs. Waddle and Habiba as she trailed Harper up the narrow set of oriental-carpeted stairs that led to Kate's bedroom. It was true. They *would* remember tonight forever. They'd always be friends — best friends — but these were the last hours the girls would spend truly together, without their new separate lives getting in the way.

"I think tonight should be about me," Sophie told Harper as they entered Kate's room.

Harper gave her a look. "Becca's the one leaving tomorrow."

"Yes, I am," Becca agreed, popping her head out of the bay window that opened onto the flat section of roof outside of Kate's room. "And it's making me want to throw up."

"You're *all* leaving," Sophie complained. "I'm the only one staying behind to hang out with the other losers who couldn't get into a school good enough for their parents to fork over their life savings to pay for it."

Kate appeared next to Becca in the window, her long blond hair brushing against the sill. "Nobody forced you to stay up late watching *Inside the Actors Studio* reruns instead of doing your homework."

Naturally, Kate had to say something like that. Structure and discipline were like oxygen at the Foster household. Even Habiba had fallen in line, perfecting her English within nine months of her arrival in the United States. I should have hung out here more often, Sophie realized, a mere four years too late.

Sophie pulled off her tight black pants and gauzy tank, replacing them with a skintight lavender Juicy sweat suit. Then she followed Harper, who was climbing through the window to join Becca and Kate.

"There's no way I'm going to live in a room with gingham curtains," she announced to no one in particular as she made her way onto the roof, which Harper had dubbed The Death Trap sometime during ninth grade. The only thing between any one of them and six months in traction was a small stucco ledge that had a tendency to crumble anytime it was touched. "It's just not happening."

Kate handed her an open bottle of Chardonnay. "So tell Maggie Hendricks you've got your own stuff."

"I will!"

Sophie settled into her usual spot next to the long-forgotten papier-mâché volcano Kate had made for her eighth-grade science project. Harper plopped down under the window, and Becca and Kate got as comfortable as possible leaning against the delicate wall.

For several moments, they just sat there. The late August air was warm and sweet and filled Sophie with a longing for everything in her life to stay just as it was. She loved her friends . . . why did they have to leave?

Sophie closed her eyes, wondering how many times she, Becca, Harper, and Kate had sat here, laughing and arguing late into the night, until Mr. Foster finally banged on Kate's bedroom door to signal they had to go to sleep or suffer the consequences. A hundred? A thousand? Sometimes they'd even bundled up in parkas and come out during the middle of winter. . . .

"Remember the first time we roofed it?" Kate asked. She could always read Sophie's mind — not necessarily a good thing.

"Seventh grade, September eighteenth," Becca recited instantly. She'd been the loneliest of the four before they became best friends, and had therefore appointed herself the keeper of such historic details.

"I was still mourning the death of Storm Chase," Sophie recalled, referring to her favorite soap opera character.

"Lucky ole' Storm bit the dust in that suspicious parachuting accident," Harper commented. "Otherwise, Kate would be kicking it out here with Gina Percy."

There was a collective groan. Everyone hated Gina Percy, whose idea of a fun time was pointing out to teachers when her fellow students were passing notes in class. She'd been Kate's best friend until that fateful day in the second-floor girls' bathroom at Arapaho Middle School.

It was the first week at their new middle school, and Sophie had been crying over the untimely passing of Storm, rolling out toilet paper from one of the stalls to dry her tears. Kate had walked in, assessed the situation, and immediately pulled a travel-sized pack of Kleenex from her blue canvas backpack.

Kate had thought Sophie was insane when she found out the tears were over Storm Chase. But as Sophie went on and on about the lurid details of his TV demise, Kate couldn't help laughing. They were both giggling hysterically by the time Harper and Becca, who'd just bonded over their mutual love of cafeteria tater tots, had come into the bathroom to try Harper's new Stila lip gloss.

Worried that these two strangers would think she was a lunatic, Kate had launched into a rambling explanation of what was going on. Within minutes, the four girls had decided to go to Sophie's house after school to watch Storm's funeral. By the time Storm turned up unannounced and alive at a board meeting three months later, Sophie, Kate, Becca, and Harper had become best friends.

"Gina's not so bad," Kate still insisted. "She's just slightly anal."

"Sound like anyone else you know?" Harper asked, at which point they all pointed at Kate.

"Too bad Gina's not going to CU," Sophie said. "I'd take any friend I could get."

Sophie was bummed her friends didn't jump in with comforting words. Apparently, they felt they'd comforted her enough over the past few months.

"What if everyone at Middlebury hates me?" Becca asked suddenly and quietly, as if she'd been building up her nerve to pose the question. "What if I'm a total outcast?"

All of a sudden, Sophie felt small. Teeny, tiny small. Sure, it sucked that she didn't get to leave home like everyone else. But at least she knew where to buy her tampons. At least she'd already know people.

And it wasn't like Boulder was a *bad* place to live. Some people might even say it was idyllic. Located at the foot of the Flatirons of the Rocky Mountains, thirty miles from Denver, it was a beautiful town, full of artists, bohemians, and general lovers of the outdoors. There were also thousands of college students, one of whom would be Sophie.

"Everyone will love you, Bec," Sophie assured her, placing the bottle of Chardonnay in Harper's outstretched hand. "You're inherently lovable."

"And if they don't, Harper and I will take a road trip to Vermont and personally kick their asses," Kate added, without breaking a smile.

"Really?" Becca sounded slightly reassured.

"Definitely." Kate looked at Harper. "Right, Harp?"

Harper didn't answer right away. Then she shook her head. "No. We won't."

"Why not?" Becca asked, panic rising in her voice.

Harper stared down, apparently very interested in peeling the label off the bottle of Kendall Jackson.

"Because . . ." She looked up, her eyes wide behind the lenses of her glasses. "I'm not going to NYU. I'm not going to college at all."

Sophie's first thought was that Harper had lost her mind. Her second thought was that her prayers had been answered.

She wouldn't be alone after all.

Dove. White doves signify happy domestic affairs and/or a peaceful solution to any disagreements which may be troubling you. A flock of doves predicts sudden travel or the return of an old friend from a distance. The cooing of doves promises reciprocal love, but the voice of a turtledove heralds some approaching sadness.

Draft. Fluctuations in your fortunes from which you will learn useful lessons for the future are forecast in a dream of sitting or standing in a draft. See also *Soldiers*.

Dragon. You will get an enormous boost in your progress toward financial success from a powerful and influential personage if you dreamed of a dragon. And if you don't now know such a big wheel, you soon will.

Drain. A drain in a dream is a warning of low vitality; it would be wise to get a medical checkup and include a blood test.

Drake. See *Ducks*.

Draperies. Decorative draperies (as differentiated from curtains) predict coming luxury, and the more elaborate the draperies the greater will be the wealth, unless they were faded, torn, otherwise shabby, or obviously shoddy, in which case they signal possible losses through lack of attention to your own best interests. Stop taking the line of least resistance unless you're sure it also happens to be the right one.

Drawbridge. Your diary will soon be full of exciting engagements if your dream involved an opening drawbridge; if the bridge was closed, it signifies a satisfactory conclusion to one or more pending matters. If the bridge in your dream was being lowered, it was telling you that you may have to take a step backward in order to take two forward.

Drawers. A closed drawer means that you will have to outmaneuver an unsuspected rival for something you want. An open drawer signifies a new opportunity, and if the drawer is full it signals a propitious time for undertaking a new venture. An empty drawer indicates success but only after hard work. A locked drawer or trouble opening one suggests unforeseen obstacles in your path, but persevere, you can overcome them with patience.

Dreams. A dream within your dream portends a deferment of your highest hopes but nevertheless a definite improvement in your present circumstances.

Dress. To dream of having or seeing an attractive new dress augurs some imminent social satisfaction. An embroidered dress signifies casual sexual pleasures. See also *Clothes* and *Colors*.

Drift. The sensation of drifting experienced in your dream is reminding you that your problems won't disappear if you ignore them, so you'd better get down to some positive action to sort them out.

TWO

I'm going to move into my parents' basement and write the next Great American Novel," Harper continued. "I'm going to follow my Dream."

Seconds passed. Harper couldn't breathe. She couldn't see. If she started to smell burning toast, a stroke was definitely imminent.

But at least she'd said it out loud. For the first time, she'd put it out in the world that Harper Ellen Waddle — editor-in-chief of the high school newspaper, winner of the Alfred J. Prufrock teen fiction competition — was a college reject. Her friends would just have to deal with it.

Of course, they didn't know that part yet. Harper had decided to lead with the good news. Her Dream. That way, they wouldn't feel so bad for her when she told them her dream had been born out of necessity once she got rejected from the only university she'd applied to. Any second now, she would spill that little detail. Really. Any second.

"Somebody *say* something!" Harper finally yelled.

But they were all just staring at her. It was eerie.

"Pass the wine," Sophie offered finally.

"Your *dream*?" Kate demanded, as Harper handed over the bottle. "What the hell does that mean?"

Harper felt like the entire contents of a junk metal shop were grinding in her stomach. "I'm going to write a book."

She wasn't sure exactly when she'd decided that's what she was going to do. Maybe the idea had started to formulate as early as the day she'd gotten the letter from NYU. A nuclear bomb had gone off on her future, and she'd had to find some way to face it. So she'd gone to her passion. Writing. It was all she'd ever wanted to do anyway. And with NYU out of the way, there was nothing stopping her from doing it now.

If everything went according to plan — her new plan — this time next year her book would be hitting the shelves of Borders and Barnes & Nobles all over the country. Or at least be finished.

Kate shook her head. "Yeah. Right. You're going to write the next Great American Novel."

"That's so hard to believe?" Harper asked defensively. She knew her news was big — even earth-shattering in their cookie-cutter suburban world — but did Kate have to be so . . . *Kate*?

Sophie and Becca were looking back and forth between Kate and Harper. Apparently, neither of them wanted to get in the middle. Harper didn't blame them.

"You have to go to college." Kate was using the flat, cold tone of voice that had made Harper slam doors on more than one occasion.

"It's not exactly a choice," she answered flatly.

Becca reached out and touched Harper's hand, which showed Harper just how dire her friends saw the situation. Becca never made physical contact voluntarily.

"Is it the money? Is NYU too expensive for your parents to afford?"

"No, it's not that."

Say the words, Harper ordered herself. *Tell them the rest of it.* She'd been an idiot. She'd been an egomaniac. She hadn't listened when her college counselor told her to apply to safety schools, and now she was shit out of luck.

"So you're *choosing* to be a loser?" Kate asked.

Kate sounded so smug, so maddeningly superior, that Harper wanted to kill her. Not metaphorically. Literally. With her own bare hands. Or maybe with an axe, Lizzie Borden–style, if she'd had one readily available.

"Harper's not a loser," Sophie jumped in. "I'm sure she has a great reason for deciding to . . . follow her dream . . . and stay in Boulder with me." She looked hopefully to Harper. "What is it?"

They were all looking at her, waiting for some reasonable explanation. Except Kate. For her, there *was* no reasonable explanation.

And suddenly Harper knew.

She wasn't going to tell her friends the truth. It was just too humiliating.

She'd felt the same way that day last April, when she'd gotten the dreaded thin white envelope from NYU. The thought of her friends and family looking at her with pity . . . it had been unacceptable. Harper figured she'd wait a few weeks, until the college furor had calmed, then tell the truth. Only a few weeks had turned into a few months, and here she was.

"Look, I've wanted to go to NYU forever," Harper began slowly. "And I'm sure it's great." She was sure it was more than great, but that was irrelevant. "But I also want to express something to the world. Now. Before I get jaded and cynical and decide it makes more sense to become an investment banker."

"You had this revelation in the last fifteen minutes?" Sophie asked, nervously zipping and unzipping her lavender hoodie.

"I've been thinking about it all summer. I just didn't want to

29

talk about it until I was ready." Which was true. "I know it's a cliché, but we only live once. I don't want to look back and wonder what would have happened if I'd had the guts to go for it."

It was the speech Harper had been giving herself all summer. It was the thing that had kept her going.

Kate snorted. Actually *snorted.* "That's the stupidest thing I've ever heard."

"Not everyone thinks going to Harvard with your boyfriend is the ultimate," Harper snapped back at Kate.

"But why didn't you *tell* us?" Sophie demanded. "If I'd *known,* I wouldn't have had to spend the whole summer totally bummed that I was going to be all alone."

Harper smiled. Leave it to Sophie to find a way to be narcissistic at the most inappropriate moment. She was right though. Harper should have told them. She should have told them the day she got that letter. She'd just been so sure she'd get in. . . . She'd talked about going to New York for years. Well, the pride had cometh, and so had the fall.

"You're going to study creative writing at NYU," Becca pointed out, shifting to her knees. "Can't you write a book there?"

Now that Harper had made up her mind to lie, the rest was going to be easy.

"I know how I am," she started to explain, ignoring Kate's still-icy stare. "I'd get to NYU and want to make friends and spend every weekend listening to bad guitar players sing James Taylor songs in Washington Square Park. . . ."

Harper was really warming up now, imagining the details of a life she knew nothing about. It was what she did. It was why she was a writer.

"I'd start crushing on some guy named Dexter across the hall. We'd hook up once. Then again, a couple days later. Pretty soon I'd get obsessed with comic books, 'cause *he's* obsessed with comic books. But it would turn out Dex is a commitment-phobe. And when he

30

eventually broke my heart at a Halloween party, I'd be so paralyzed that I'd spend the next semester lying in bed, watching *American Chopper* and eating Pringles."

Sophie shook her head. "Not a pretty picture."

Harper took a deep breath. "You guys, this is a *good* thing. This is me, taking a chance." She looked pointedly at each of them. "Be happy for me? Please?"

"It makes a weird kind of sense," Becca commented thoughtfully. "I mean, it's insane . . . but not."

"I don't want to let real life get in the way of my passion," Harper declared softly. "I don't want it to get in the way of my Dream."

Sophie and Becca were nodding, and even Kate looked a tiny bit moved. Their kind faces made Harper want to cry. "I'm sorry I'm dropping this on you tonight. I didn't mean to ruin everything."

Kate frowned at her. "We're your best friends," she said, the judgment gone from her voice. "If this is how you were feeling, why didn't you talk to us?"

Harper looked back at Kate. "I was scared."

They were the truest words she'd spoken in the past one hundred and thirty-eight days.

I'm going to follow my Dream, Sophie thought as she pulled a queen-sized slate blue Aerobed from the walk-in closet in Kate's bedroom. Harper's declaration had been reverberating in her head for the last two hours, leaving her both exhilarated and drained.

At first, she had been waiting for Harper to start laughing hysterically and declare the whole thing was a joke. She *wasn't* going to stay home to write a book, she was going to NYU, like she'd talked about forever. But as the minutes ticked by, and the debate over Harper's announcement continued, Sophie had finally realized this was real. Harper was giving up everything to follow her passion.

31

"Sophie, don't you agree?" Kate demanded.

"Huh?" Sophie looked up from the Aerobed, which she was now spreading out on the floor, and realized she'd completely tuned out her friends' chatter.

"I was saying I still don't see why Harper can't go to NYU this year," Kate repeated, punching a pillow to emphasize her point. She'd mellowed over the last couple hours, but hadn't given up on changing Harper's mind. "She can write her book next summer."

"Does anyone care that Becca is *leaving* tomorrow?" Harper was lounging next to Kate on the bed, eating the last of a bag of spicy mustard Kettle Chips. "Are we really going to spend the rest of the night obsessing over this when we should be reminiscing?"

"We can reminisce when I call you from Middlebury." Becca reached up to redo her now frizzed-out ponytail. "Your future is *way* more important."

Sophie looked at Harper, who was now bent over the side of Kate's bed, surreptitiously wiping her hands on the dust ruffle. Was Harper's decision crazy? Definitely. But it was also fucking inspiring. If she were going to be brutally honest with herself — something that didn't happen every day — Sophie would have to admit she was . . . envious.

Harper was willing to go against every convention she'd ever known to make her dreams come true. And here was Sophie, with her own dream of being an actress, doing absolutely nothing to make it happen. Next to Harper, Sophie suddenly felt like a wimp.

No, it was worse than that. Sophie wasn't just a wimp. She was lazy. If she'd worked harder in high school, both on her academics and her acting, maybe she'd be leaving home . . . even going to Juilliard. In any given situation, Sophie used her looks and charm to take the easy way out — from copying homework to cajoling her mom into letting her get away with not making her bed every morning. Now she was paying for it. The rest of her friends were forging ahead with their lives, while Sophie . . . well, *wasn't*.

She plugged the cord of the air mattress into an outlet and turned to Becca and Kate. "I think Harper's pretty damn brave," she declared. "And I'm not just saying that because I'm glad she's staying in town."

Harper grinned. She looked incredibly young in the blue-and-green-striped cotton pj's she'd borrowed from Kate — but she also looked incredibly strong. "Thanks, Sophe."

"Us artist-types have to stick together," Sophie declared.

Not that she was a real artist. A real artist wouldn't let low S.A.T. scores keep her imprisoned in the small world she'd grown up in. A real artist would plunge into the unknown to soak up whatever creative experiences the Universe had to offer.

Becca's and Kate's faces were both still etched with worry. "Have you guys forgotten how to smile, or what?" Sophie asked them over the whirring of the expanding air mattress.

"I'm just . . ." Kate trailed off, at a loss. "I feel like everything's changed."

No one said anything. They didn't need to. Somehow, Harper's decision had altered everything. Yes, they'd all known that after Becca left tomorrow, nothing would ever be truly the same. But as long as they were all marching along their parent-approved paths, it felt safe. Now . . . anything could happen.

"I'm happy for you," Becca said to Harper finally, sounding like she meant it. "Aside from the shock and the fact that you hid, like, a huge secret from us for God knows how long . . . I'm happy for you."

"What about you, Katie?" Sophie asked. "Can you be happy for her?"

Kate sighed. Sophie could see this was killing her. But she knew Kate would come through. She always did, even when she didn't want to.

"I guess I don't have a choice," Kate responded. Then she grinned. "Besides, having a famous writer for a best friend could be cool."

33

Sophie felt a tear working its way through her sinus cavity. She'd already cried once today, but that meeting with Maggie Hendricks at Starbucks seemed like a lifetime ago.

"Thanks, Kate." Harper sounded like she was fighting her own crying jag, and that was saying something.

"I still can't believe you're going to live at home," Becca made a face, unable to keep the dismay out of her voice. Of all of them, she was the one most longing to get away from her family.

"The basement isn't that bad," Harper insisted. "It'll be like having my own place. And Sophie will be around to help me decorate."

"No. I won't."

Oops. She hadn't meant to say that out loud. She hadn't even meant to think it, beyond the realm of normal, everyday fantasy.

"What?" Kate asked, her tone low and dangerous.

"I'm moving to Los Angeles." Sophie's hands were shaking. "I'm going to be an actress."

I'm going to be an actress, she repeated to herself, fighting the urge to giggle. It was everything she'd wanted since she was old enough to stay up and watch the Oscars with her mother. If Harper could follow her Dream, why shouldn't she? It felt right. Terrifying, but right.

"You're *not* funny," Harper informed her.

But Sophie meant it. She wasn't going to be stuck in Boulder for another four years, living in the land of socks and sandals. She was leaving. She was free.

"The old Dream Train's got one more passenger." They were all staring at her a lot like they'd all been staring at Harper a few minutes ago. "Choo . . . choo," she added lamely.

Kate threw up her hands. "I give up. I thought I knew you guys — obviously, I was wrong."

Screw Kate. The girl's idea of throwing caution to the wind was eating a Pop-Tart before dinner. Sophie turned to Harper. She wasn't sure what she'd expected. Maybe a hug . . . or whoop of joy . . . at least a high five. But Harper wasn't even smiling.

"*Choo, choo,*" Sophie repeated, putting her hands on her hips.

Harper shook her head. "You can't do it, Sophe," she said softly. "I mean, I totally appreciate the support . . . but you just can't."

"She's right," Becca agreed emphatically. "You can't."

"Why not?"

"Your parents, for one thing," Kate interjected.

"Frank and Angela will deal," Sophie countered. She'd called her parents by their first names since they got divorced in fourth grade.

At the time, it had been her one act of rebellion.

But this . . . This was a lot more significant than refusing to call them "Mom" and "Dad." It was going to take all of her powers to convince them she hadn't lost her mind. And they still might ground her for life.

"You don't have any money," Becca pointed out, pulling on a pair of well-loved argyle socks. "Even if *most* actresses starve themselves, *you'll* need to eat."

Sophie shrugged, her outward nonchalance hiding the fear that was pumping through her veins. "I'll get a job," she answered defiantly. "Next question?"

Sophie stared at the faces of her three best friends. They could throw any obstacle at her, and she would come back with an answer. Because no matter how scared she was — no matter how much part of her wished that this whole night had never happened, and she could go back to normal — there *was* no going back now.

To hell with Maggie Hendricks and her weird bangs. Sophie Bushell was going after her dream.

PACK for MIDDLEBURY!

hair dryer	razors
backup hair dryer	hair bands
anti-frizz polishing milk	~~CONDOMS~~
hairbrush - 1 round and 1 flat	zit cream
flat iron	Q-tips
shampoo	floss
conditioner - leave-in & rinse-out	
Kiehl's rough-weather face cream	
Kiehl's face cleanser	
whitening toothpaste	
electric toothbrush	
zinc oxide	
chapstick (multiple)	
tinactin	
neosporin	
band-aids	
tampons	
tylenol	
Aleve	
blush (consult with Sophie)	
mascara	
tweezers (steal from mom)	
cotton squares	
hand lotion	
deodorant	
mouthwash	

THREE

It's absurd," Kate's mother said the next morning, as she poured four glasses of orange juice and passed them around the breakfast table.

"They're ruining their lives," her father agreed, shaking his head over the Boulder *Daily Camera*. Habiba sat across from Kate, half-listening, and half-reading a leather-bound book in Amharic. Apparently, Kate thought, when a person had lived through war and famine, not heading right off to college after high school didn't seem like that big a deal.

Restless, Kate's eyes roamed the kitchen. Though it was barely nine AM, the Foster house had already been restored to its pre-party tidiness. The marble countertops were gleaming, plates and glasses were washed and put away in glass-fronted cabinets, furniture was repositioned, and linens were neatly folded in the appropriate drawers.

Everything was exactly as it had been this time yesterday. And the day before. And the day before that. And every day, as far back as Kate could remember.

So why did everything suddenly feel completely different? Why did everything suddenly feel so . . . stifling?

"'Ruining their lives' is a bit of an exaggeration, don't you think?"

Kate replied finally, aware that twelve hours ago she would have agreed with her parents. *Had* agreed, in fact. Vocally. But after listening to Harper and Sophie for most of the night, she wasn't willing to let her friends' intentions be dismissed so summarily. Both Harper and Sophie felt strongly about what they were doing, about the decisions they had made. They couldn't just be *wrong*.

"I mean, I kind of get it," she continued, chopping a fried egg into tiny pieces with the edge of her fork.

And the least her parents could do, as they smeared marmalade on their breakfast toast, was consider the possibility that maybe Harper and Sophie were doing if not exactly the right thing, at least something worthwhile.

"They're following their dreams," she said.

"They're being irresponsible," her mother corrected.

Kate leaned back in her chair. Maybe it was lack of sleep, but she was feeling oddly wired. Maybe even rebellious. She couldn't be sure, since she'd never had exactly this feeling before.

"What would you do," she ventured slowly, "if I did something like that?"

"Disown you," her father answered dryly, folding the paper and reaching for his toast.

"Besides, you don't have any silly dreams," her mother added.

Kate blinked, stung. She didn't have any silly dreams? How could her mother even suggest she didn't have dreams? She had dreams. Big dreams! *Everyone* had dreams. Didn't they? Didn't she?

Then it hit her. With a bolt of clarity, Kate realized her mother was right. She, Kate Foster, did not have dreams.

She only had plans.

And, worse, they weren't even *her* plans. They were her parents' plans for her.

This, she realized, was the thought she'd been trying to push away for the last however many hours since Harper's big announcement. This was what Harper had meant when she'd said it was a done deal that Kate would go to Yale Law because that was what her mother wanted, and what Jared had meant when he'd said she needed to cut the cord.

An ache began to twist its way through Kate's chest.

"You wouldn't really disown her," Habiba asked, the book forgotten on the tabletop, a concerned frown creasing her forehead.

"No, not really," Kate's mother replied. "Though we'd certainly consider it."

Kate would later realize that the next ten seconds were the most pivotal of her life to date. Somewhere within her, she knew that if she didn't say the words now, she would never have another chance. She would wake up in ten years, married to Jared, with a BA from Harvard, and a law degree from Yale, and spend ninety hours a week in a stuffy law firm just to make partner by thirty. Was that really what she wanted?

Maybe.

But she couldn't say for sure. And if it wasn't . . .

"I think we should talk about," Kate began, as the ache expanded into her stomach, "me deferring Harvard for a year."

Kate's mother frowned at her. "What kind of example are you setting for your sister, even talking like this?"

"That's not fair," Kate said stiffly.

Just because her parents had decided to adopt a twelve-year-old girl without consulting her, she was obligated to set some kind of example?

Kate regretted the thought before it was even fully formulated in her head. For the last two years, she'd done her best to set as good an example as she possibly could. She'd helped Habiba master English, taught her the difference between the little hand and the big hand, taken her along on community service projects, driven her to school, and helped with homework. It wasn't Kate's fault that she hadn't completely bonded with Habiba the way she would have liked, or that her relationship with her only sister was her greatest — perhaps only — failure.

Although, she thought wryly, she might have to rethink the rankings any moment now. Either way, it wasn't fair of her parents to use Habiba against her.

Kate's father stood up.

"You're going to Harvard in four days," he instructed in a non-negotiable tone, picking up his plate. "Just like we've planned."

"I'd like to discuss it," Kate replied, realizing that the ache in her chest resembled something like impending liberation.

Habiba's eyes were darting back and forth between Kate and her parents, a piece of toast forgotten halfway to her mouth. Now that disowning was off the table, Kate noted that she actually seemed to be *enjoying* this.

"No," her father answered, turning his back.

And in the time it took for her father to get to the sink, Kate had made the first, real, independent decision of her life.

No matter what her parents said, she, Kate Foster, was not going to Harvard.

Not in four days.

Maybe not ever.

The line between diplomacy and lying was a thin one, and there were moments when Becca was verging on being a liar. Because, as much as she was trying to be supportive — even encouraging — what she really felt, watching her three best friends chatter about their plans for the year, was something closer to betrayal. Harper and Kate, both clad in shorts and belly-baring t-shirts, were sprawled on Becca's narrow bed, while Sophie, in a dramatic batik sarong and beaded leather sandals, lounged on the floor next to them. Every other word of out of all three of their mouths for the last hour had been "dream." What, Becca still didn't quite understand, had happened to *college*?

Half-in and half-out of her closet, Becca tossed a stack of Champion workout bras into an open suitcase. At least Harper, in a rare show of sanity, seemed to think Kate was making a mistake.

"But," she kept repeating, "it's Harvard. *Harvard.*"

So far, Kate wasn't bending. And Sophie, who was thrilled to have been out-crazied by Kate for once, was no help at all.

Becca jammed a pair of red suede Pumas into the inside edge of her suitcase. Her last piece of luggage was almost full. And once it was, she would be ready to leave. Aside from the obvious terrifying implications, these final, few precious inches of suitcase space meant some serious decisions needed to be made. For example, did she want to take the sweatpants she was wearing? The material had long since morphed from white to gray, and the royal-blue stripes on the sides of the legs were chipped and faded. But they were her favorites. She couldn't wear them in public, but maybe she could wear them to bed?

Becca turned to ask her friends.

"I might have to start taking drugs," Kate was fretting. "I don't think I can handle this undrugged."

"Then bail on Paris and head to Amsterdam," Sophie suggested, idly braiding the fringe at the bottom of her skirt.

"Don't encourage her," Harper snapped.

"Please," Kate sighed. "You both know I'd be a miserable failure as a druggie."

"A girl can always . . ." Sophie began, and Kate chimed in for a rousing chorus of "DREAM!!!" Harper covered her face with her hands.

But Becca wasn't exactly sympathetic. The fact that Harper wasn't a hundred percent on board with Sophie's and Kate's plans didn't make her any less responsible. And, well . . . this just wasn't how things were supposed to be.

The feeling of betrayal crept back in.

Of course, Becca knew that her friends were not, in fact, betraying her by pursuing their dreams. It was just that . . . yesterday, they were all four going to college. Yes, they were going to be apart, but they'd be sharing their new experiences together. All dealing with new roommates, new towns (or, in Sophie's case, a new part of the same town), new classes, new friends.

Now Becca was alone.

She was used to feeling alone around her family, epitomized by the fact that she was the only Winsberg in the whole bunch. Her mother, who had gone back to her maiden name after The Divorce, was a Howard. Her stepfather, Martin, was a Markham, as were his kids, Mia and Carter. Her father was a Winsberg-Weldon, having become a modern hyphenated couple when he married the control freak he'd had a two-year affair with, Melissa Weldon.

But until now, she had never once felt alone with her friends. In an hour, she was supposed to be leaving for the airport, and instead of helping her pack and having a tearful goodbye, Harper, Sophie, and Kate were engrossed in a tête-a-tête-a-tête that she just wasn't a part of.

"Kate, you can't," Harper pleaded yet again. "It's *Harvard.*"

Kate dismissed her with an impatient wave. "If they let me in once, they'll let me in again."

"What if they don't?" Becca asked, annoyed. "Colleges don't like being blown off at the last minute."

"I was only going to Harvard because it was what my parents wanted," Kate said. "I have to figure out what *I* want."

"But," Harper insisted again, "it's *Harvard.*"

"Yeah. I get it. I know."

"The Maryannes must've freaked about this whole travel-the-world thing," Sophie interjected.

44

"The Maryannes" were Kate's parents. The girls had initially called them "The Professor and Maryanne" — like from *Gilligan's Island* — until Kate's father had inadvertently heard the nickname and proceeded to deliver a college-level lecture on gender politics. The four of them had agreed that the distinction between the two esteemed professors was sexist, and henceforth, both Professors Foster were simply known as "The Maryannes."

"Yeah," Kate sighed, "they weren't exactly thrilled."

Kate had decided that since she didn't know exactly what she wanted to do, she was going to do everything. Pack a backpack, get a plane ticket . . . and just go anywhere. Sophie thought it was the coolest thing she'd ever heard. Harper seemed on the verge of panic.

"Bec," she urged, "do something. *Say* something."

"What can I do? I can't make her go to Harvard."

And truthfully, there was a rigidity to Kate's life that seemed premature for a girl of eighteen. Maybe it *was* too soon to have everything settled, everything decided. Maybe Kate was doing the right thing.

Maybe, just maybe, they all *should* be thinking about their dreams.

Becca sighed, and zipped her suitcase. Those last remaining inches were going to have to stay empty.

"I guess I'm next," she announced, flopping down on the carpet across from Sophie. "I can't let you guys dream without me."

Kate smiled, probably glad to have the focus on someone other than herself.

"What's your dream, Bec?"

Becca wrapped her arms around her knees. Her dream was simple. "I want to move away from here. Live in peace. Ski for the best coach in the country."

Maybe going to college wasn't as huge, dream-wise, as what her friends had planned. But it was all she wanted. And for her, it was a lot.

Sophie crawled across the carpet and nestled her head against Becca's shoulder.

45

"And that's exactly what you should do," she declared. "Besides, if you don't go to Middlebury, how are the rest of us going to know what we're missing out on?"

Harper nodded. "I *need* you to go to school. Whenever I'm miserable, it's going to be your duty to remind me that I could be studying for a chemistry mid-term."

Kate nodded. "Going to school is your dream. We're not going to let you mess that up."

"Really?" Becca brightened, feeling a burden lift. "You don't think I'm lame?"

In less than a second, she was being gang-hugged by Kate, Sophie, and Harper. They squeezed her tight, and Sophie gave her a big smack on the cheek.

"Totally."

Harper nodded. "Lamer than lame."

Kate, always the worst at keeping a straight face, grinned as she stated solemnly, "We can't be your friends anymore. Sorry, Bec."

Becca laughed. Okay, so she was being ridiculous. Good to be reminded.

Then Kate's face turned serious, and Becca suddenly knew it wasn't going to be that simple.

"Although, I do think your dream needs some work," Kate said.

Sophie and Harper exchanged glances, as Becca frowned at Kate.

"I mean," she continued gently, "maybe you should attach an addendum. Something new, something you weren't going to do already, that we can all help you with."

"Like what?" Becca asked, her green eyes wary.

"I've been thinking a lot about comfort zones the last twelve hours . . . and I just think maybe you should step outside of yours a little."

If Kate was going where Becca thought she was going, she was venturing into dangerous territory.

Harper nodded, catching on. "Growing up with the Manson Family, it makes sense that you're . . . you know, a little guarded."

"But," Sophie added, "maybe you could . . . let the walls down a little."

"We think you should fall in love," Kate explained slowly.

Silence. Harper didn't speak. Sophie didn't speak. Kate didn't speak.

Becca's gut reaction was to feel attacked. Then she took a deep breath, and remembered that of all the people in the world, Kate, Harper, and Sophie always, *always,* had her back. They wouldn't be saying this if they didn't think it was important. The least she could do was give it some thought.

"I can't just *fall in love.*"

Kate exhaled, obviously relieved that Becca wasn't mad.

"I mean, you guys have steps to follow, specific things to do," Becca explained. "Kate has to fly to Paris, Sophie has to go on auditions and make out with letch-y producers —"

"Hey!" Sophie interrupted, adjusting her black bra strap.

"You know what I mean," Becca insisted. "And Harper has to sit down in front of her computer and write. I can't just — *whoosh* — fall in love with someone."

"No," Harper agreed. "But when a cute guy flirts with you at a party, you could smile a little and talk to him long enough to find out for sure if he's a creep, instead of just assuming he is."

"And you could unleash that spectacular cleavage once in a while, let the boys see you as more than just a ski buddy," Sophie added.

Becca wasn't convinced.

"We'll help you," Kate offered. "We won't let you do it alone."

Right, Becca thought. When it came to falling in love, there was no other way to do it than alone. But that didn't mean she couldn't use — wouldn't *need* — her friends' support. She couldn't do the unrequited thing with Jared Burke for the rest of her life. And now that she wasn't going to have to see him all the time, it would be easier to find someone else. Maybe no one as amazing as Jared, but at least someone who wasn't in love with one of her best friends. That would probably be a good place to start.

"Okay." She nodded. "But if it's a disaster, I'm holding you all completely responsible."

As her three best friends dissolved in giggles, Becca said a silent prayer.

Please, she prayed, please, don't let it be a disaster.

"Rebecca!"

Becca exchanged glances with her friends as her mother poked her head in the door. There were tense lines around her small mouth, and her chocolate brown eyes were flat.

"Your father is here. He did not call in advance."

Becca grimaced. "Sorry, Mom."

"It's not your fault."

Her tone implied otherwise. Somehow, everything her father did was Becca's fault.

Becca grimaced at her friends and followed her mother downstairs.

"I didn't know he was coming," she said, then hated herself. She'd been through enough therapy to know that it wasn't her responsibility to alleviate her mother's anger at her father. But old habits were hard to break. Particularly that one, and particularly when her mother was so tense that Becca could see the sinews of her neck below her short brown hair.

"He's on the porch," her mother said coldly. "He was not invited in."

As her mother veered off into the kitchen, Becca swung open the front door and stepped outside.

Her stepfather's house was in a lovely old Boulder neighborhood.

The houses were large, brightly painted Victorians, with front porches hosting wicker table and chair sets and porch swings. They were the kinds of homes in which passersby might imagine quaint game nights and laughing family dinners. None of which happened in Becca's house.

Becca's father was standing on the front porch, a tan suede jacket slung over his arm. It occurred to her that ever since he'd married Melissa, he always looked like he had just stepped out of an upscale men's magazine. Everything about him was Just So, from his tousled blond hair to his unscuffed brown leather loafers. Everything, except the look on his face. He looked about as comfortable standing on her stepfather's porch as a turkey the day before Thanksgiving — which was reasonable, since at least one person in the near vicinity would have been happy to chop his head off.

"Bec." He held his arms for a hug.

"I know you don't want us driving you to the airport," he began, as Becca gave him a quick embrace. "Which is fine. We understand it's important to your mother. But we wanted to give you a little going-away present, so . . ."

He handed her a small, expensive-looking envelope. Becca took it, thinking how annoying it was that her father only spoke in "we's."

"Thanks, Dad." She fake-smiled, knowing not to get her hopes up. Her father was famous for his unfailingly misguided presents. She opened the envelope.

"A year-long membership to the Metropolitan Museum of Art?" she said, confused.

Her dad smiled widely, clearly thinking it was The Best Gift Ever.

"Dad, I'm going to college in Vermont. The Met is in New York." Becca frowned.

"It's the East Coast," her father replied dismissively. "You'll take a train. Trust me, you'll be going to The City all the time."

Becca thought about explaining that no, in fact, she would not be taking a train to The City all the time, because 1) there were no trains in Middlebury, Vermont, so at best she would be catching a bus, and 2) she wouldn't even be catching a bus because she would be training for ski season, and then it would *be* ski season and she would be *skiing,* and the last she heard there weren't slopes in New York City. So, her mental tirade continued, if he felt obliged to get her a present, why hadn't he just gotten her a new ski jacket, or *something* that would at least make it appear like he *sort of* knew who his own daughter was?

Barring that, how 'bout some cold hard cash?

But instead, she gave her father a hug and said she appreciated his thoughtfulness, and would call him in a few days — though she knew she wouldn't. Because Becca also knew that when she didn't call, he wouldn't notice.

"Do you really think she'll fall in love?" Harper wondered aloud now that Becca was safely out of the room.

Kate looked up from a stack of eighth-grade graduation photos. "I don't know . . . maybe . . . If she lets herself."

Harper was lying on Becca's twin bed, totally wiped. She felt like she'd been standing in a wind tunnel the last twenty-four hours, and now all she wanted to do was sleep.

Or go back in time, she thought, looking at her two non-college-bound friends. Harper wished she could turn back the clock and tell her friends the truth — the real truth. If she had, everybody's lives wouldn't be turned upside down.

Not that the situation was *entirely* her fault. If Kate hadn't made the idea of not going to college seem so completely laden with patheticness, Harper would have been able to reveal her secret. She hadn't *planned* to keep lying. She'd been forced to. Only now that two of her friends had actually decided maybe ditching college *wasn't* so bad, the whole rationalization for Harper's continued deceit seemed to have lost some merit.

"Becca deserves it," Kate added, tucking a single out-of-place piece of hair behind her ear. "She deserves someone as awesome as Jared."

"Is he really that great?" Sophie asked as she dug through Becca's ancient Camp Sherwood duffel bag.

"What's that supposed to mean?" Kate sounded pissed.

"Just making conversation." Sophie triumphantly pulled three pairs of pink full-coverage underpants from the duffel.

"Are you saying Jared isn't great?" Kate asked. She wasn't one to simply let things go.

"He's wonderful," Harper assured her. "Handsome, smart, blah, blah, blah. You're the luckiest girl in the world." She paused. "In fact, he's so great maybe you shouldn't let him go off to Harvard by himself where some other girl can appreciate how great he is." She should have thought of playing the boyfriend card earlier.

"Thanks, Harp. Your support is overwhelming." Kate turned her attention back to Sophie and the full-coverage underpants. "What're you doing?"

"Our frizzy-haired friend will get a man a lot faster without these in her drawer," she announced. Sophie was clearly scheming, always a dangerous proposition.

She balled up the offending garments and tossed them in the general direction of the overflowing wicker trash can next to Becca's desk.

"She'll hate you," Kate coolly observed. "Put those back."

But Sophie was already opening her ever-present canvas Gap tote bag. "Not when she sees what I replaced them with."

There was no choice, Harper thought. She had to tell them about getting rejected from NYU. She couldn't let Kate put her entire *life* on hold because she was too much of a coward to be honest. Once they realized her Dream Plan was actually Plan B, they'd come to their senses.

Sophie held up a pair of tiny black thong underwear. "I got her red and leopard print, too."

Kate raised her eyebrows. "I guess if I can travel around the world by myself, Becca can learn to wear lingerie."

Despite the blasé attitude, Kate looked scared. Which made Harper's stomach clench into an even smaller ball.

"You can still go to Harvard," Harper pointed out yet again. "It's not too late to back out."

"Yes. It is." Kate set down the photographs and reached up to pull her long blond ponytail tighter. "After the blowout I had with my parents, I have to follow through."

"Tell them it was a bad case of PMS," Sophie suggested as she zipped Becca's duffel closed. "They'll understand."

Kate gave her a look. Despite her crisp pale yellow polo shirt and knee-length jean skirt, she managed to have the mien of an angry dragon.

"Not that I think you should back out," Sophie added quickly. "Dream Train. Yay."

Kate rolled her eyes. "I have my *pride*." She paused. "Besides, I'm psyched about finding my dream."

Harper and Sophie stared at her, unconvinced.

"Really."

Harper sighed. Kate wasn't going to Harvard. Not now. Not even if Harper came clean. The deed was done.

"What about you, Sophe?" Harper asked. "Are you really sure about moving to Los Angeles . . . ?"

"I was born to be a star," Sophie responded, tossing her black curls over one shoulder. "End of story."

That was that then. The Dream Train was taking off down the tracks, and there was nothing Harper could do about it.

Choo, choo.

US Airways

BOARDING PASS

Foster/Katherine

Flight	Origin	Destination	Boeing 767
407	Denver, CO **DEN**	New York, NY **JFK**	Departs **10:15p** Arrives **6:29a**

SEAT
32A

Passenger Ticket and Baggage Check

***** **GROUP 3** *****

BOARDING PASS

Foster/Katherine

Flight
407

Gate **23**

Boarding Time
9:45

Origin
Denver, CO **DEN**

Destination
New York, NY **JFK**

SEAT
32A

***** **GROUP 3** *****

FOUR

There was something about a seventeen-year-old high school graduate sleeping on *Harry Potter* sheets that lacked dignity. In fact, created a *vacuum* of dignity. Nonetheless, Harper had spent an intimate night with Harry, Ron, and Hermione in the grungy, half-finished basement she now called home. Becca had given her the sheets during yesterday's massive pre-college packing and purge-session, which meant it was Harper's duty as a best friend to actually use them.

Now the digital travel alarm clock on the overturned milk crate next to her mattress read 10:00 AM, which meant that between the teeth-clenching and the stomach churning, Harper had slept for a grand total of three hours. So much for starting her brand-new life as a serious writer at the crack of dawn. Harper rolled over and closed her eyes. I'll start being a serious writer tomorrow, she decided sleepily.

She had just started dreaming about her first guest appearance on *Charlie Rose* when the sound of Sophie's irritatingly cheerful voice forced her to open her eyes. "Hey, Sylvia Plath! Let us in!"

Harper looked around the dim basement, confused. "Hello?"

"Out here," Kate called.

Harper threw off her covers, crumpling Harry's quidditch match, and headed to the window (if a tiny slab of dirty glass with a view of a weed patch could be called a window). Sophie and Kate were crouched in the front yard, peering into the basement.

"Sylvia Plath killed herself," Harper informed Sophie after she'd managed to pry open the window.

"Yeah, but talk about talent. The girl was out of control." Sophie propelled herself through the narrow opening, landing inelegantly on the basement floor. Even sprawled on puke-green linoleum, Sophie looked great in faded cutoff shorts and a tight white tank top that contrasted with her smooth, dark skin.

"Y'know, we do have a front door," Harper pointed out as Kate followed Sophie through the window into the basement.

"We didn't want to risk a run-in with your mom and dad," Kate explained, brushing grass off her perfectly pressed khakis. "Dealing with my own set of disappointed parents is enough."

Harper, Kate, and Sophie had been either on the phone or in each other's presence practically twenty-four seven since the other night, providing each other with minute-to-minute updates on the various parental freak-outs that had occurred in the wake of their decisions to commit the ultimate suburban sin.

"No progress?" Harper asked. Each time she heard how Kate's mom or dad had come at her with another "you're ruining your life" lecture, she died a little inside.

"Does my dad asking for his Harvard sweatshirt back count?" Kate shrugged. "I've decided not to let it bother me. It's their problem, not mine."

Kate looked excited. Like, really, really excited. Which made Harper glad she hadn't done the honorable thing. Sure, it would have been nice to unburden her conscience. But what would it have accomplished, besides creating a vat of doubt for her friends to swim in?

"Habiba gave her a miniature Hello Kitty address book,"

Sophie offered encouragingly, studying the flimsy construction of Harper's desk.

Kate gestured toward Sophie. "More importantly, Frank finally wore down Angela."

Sophie grinned. "My mom decided that 'testing my boundaries and separating from their expectations' was not an entirely bad thing."

"Go, Angie!" Harper exclaimed, hoping the excitement in her voice masked the chasm of guilt inside of her.

It wasn't about not *wanting* to be honest. She *couldn't* be. Not when her friends were on the verge of making their dreams come true.

"Angela gave Sophe an article about mixed-race children needing to have more freedom to explore their identities," Kate added.

Sophie rolled her eyes. "I know *exactly* who I am. That's why I'm doing this."

"But there's a condition," Kate informed Harper, plopping into a green plastic garden chair Harper had pilfered from the backyard.

"I have to live with a friend of my mom's from college," Sophie explained. "Probably some frumpy housewife who lives in the Valley and thinks a trip to the mall is a cultural experience."

None of them had been to Los Angeles. But they knew the Valley was a vast wasteland of bad hair and people who spent their Saturdays at Costco.

"Could be worse," Harper reasoned. "You could be living in your parents' basement."

"Speaking of which . . ." Kate looked around the gloomy room. "This is comfy . . . in a minimalist way."

Sophie nodded. "Yeah . . . kind of like a 'before' room on *Trading Spaces*."

Harper would never admit it, but she had sort of cried when she moved out of her bedroom last night. And not just because the act of taking down her 98 Degrees poster was proof that she'd once *liked* 98 Degrees enough to put it up in the first place.

Her room had been like a retreat, complete with a window seat, a walk-in cedar closet, and an attached bathroom that had one of those old-fashioned bathtubs with the clawed feet. The basement was like a minimum security women's prison cell. All that was missing was a roommate named Bertha and a shank under her pillow.

Her mom and dad had watched wordlessly as Harper carried armload after armload of clothes past the family room, where they'd been pretending to watch a *Law & Order* rerun. The last item to make the trip was her laptop. Holding it gingerly in her arms, Harper had called out goodnight and closed the basement door. Two minutes later, she'd heard her fifteen-year-old sister, Amy, ask their parents if she could have Harper's room. They'd said yes.

"It'll be great when it's done," Harper told Kate and Sophie. "I have a three-month redecorating plan." But for now she could live with the lumpy mattress, milk crate nightstand, and desk she'd constructed at four AM out of an old door and two rusty metal filing cabinets.

Sophie contemplated a pile of Harper's jeans and t-shirts. "Hey, who needs an armoire? This way, you can see all your wardrobe options at once."

Harper looked at Kate. Kate looked at Sophie. Sophie looked at Harper. And then the laughing started. That kind of gut-ripping, soul-filling laughter that happens among friends who have a history of gut-ripping, soul-filling laughter. The last time it had happened was in April after Kate had gotten up to make an announcement in assembly with her mini-skirt tucked into her underwear.

"This place is a shithole," Kate gasped.

"I really am going to kill myself," Harper squeaked between giggles.

Sophie managed a straight face as she pointed at the mattress. "If you do, can I have those sheets?"

The thought of Becca and her sheet-giving made Harper suddenly sad. "I miss Becca." ·

Sophie nodded, the laughter forgotten. "Me, too."

For a moment, they were quiet. The idea that Becca was gone, *really* gone, was still inconceivable.

"I'm leaving tonight," Kate announced in a low voice, breaking the silence. "I got a cheap Expedia ticket to Paris."

"What?" Sophie screeched.

"You can't leave tonight." Harper wasn't ready for Kate to leave. She wasn't ready for any of this.

"There's no point hanging around the house and having my parents glare at me. I might as well leave now."

"But —" But *what?* Kate was right. There was no point hanging around. Not if she was really going through with this.

Upstairs, the basement door opened. "Everything okay?" Mrs. Waddle called.

"Fine!" Harper called back.

She wasn't about to admit that everything *wasn't* fine. That she hated living in the basement, and she hated the fact that one by one her friends were abandoning her.

Harper had presented her Dream Plan to her parents the morning after the Fosters' party. Since she'd neglected to tell Kate, Becca, and Sophie about getting rejected from NYU, there didn't seem a point to telling her parents the truth either. Not after she'd spent an entire summer pretending like she was preparing to be a college freshman.

The conversation had been less noisy than she'd anticipated. Her mom and dad had listened, nodding the whole time she was talking. When she'd finished, her dad calmly let her know he thought she was making the biggest mistake of her life. Much to Harper's surprise, her mom didn't threaten murder. She just sort of sat on the sofa in stunned silence, then asked Harper to at least consider reapplying to NYU — or *anywhere* — next fall.

"Hi, girls," Mrs. Waddle greeted Kate and Sophie as she descended the stairs. "I just wanted to tell Harper it's the first of the month."

Harper exchanged glances with her friends. Her mom sounded cheery — almost *friendly*. Was this some kind of weird parental trap?

"Thanks for the reminder, Mom."

"Always good to know the date, Mrs. W.," Sophie added, flashing her most obsequious smile.

"Kate's leaving for Paris tonight," Harper informed her mother. "Her parents hate her."

"That's too bad," Mrs. Waddle responded. Then she turned to Kate. "Have a wonderful time."

"Thanks," Kate answered warily.

The girls exchanged another look. Clearly, something was up.

"Your rent's due," Mrs. Waddle said casually to Harper.

"My what?"

"I'll need five hundred dollars for September, and another five hundred for a security deposit." She turned to go back up the stairs. "Any time today is fine."

As soon as the basement door clicked shut, Sophie turned to Harper. "I'd try to get her down to four-fifty."

Black spots began to form in front of Harper's eyes. Her parents were going to make her pay. To live in her own house. Correction. To live in the dark, grimy *basement* of her own house.

Five hundred plus five hundred was a thousand. Harper had exactly one thousand, one hundred and forty-two dollars in her bank account. Which meant she was broke. Her brand-new life as a serious writer had officially begun.

"Shit."

The entire Middlebury ski team (twenty-eight in all) was assembled on the athletic field, and Becca's roommate, Isabelle Sutter — a tall, brunette, fellow-freshman skier with curly hair pulled back into a puff-ball ponytail — had been talking to, and cursing at, herself since they hit the ground and started stretching.

Becca, whose forehead was resting on her shin, glanced sideways at Isabelle. She couldn't have agreed more — though she wouldn't have put it quite the same way. After a summer spent watching game show reruns at Sophie's, and rarely exercising more than twice a week, this first "conditioning session" was kicking her ass.

And she loved it.

This was what she was here for. *This* was her dream. Not that there hadn't been moments of sheer horror since her arrival two days ago. The room she shared with Isabelle was the size of Kate's closet. And college life, it turned out, was totally overwhelming. She kept getting lost (a real feat, since she was pretty much only going between her dorm, the athletic field, and the cafeteria), she'd completely screwed up her phone system while trying to set up her voice mail, and she simply couldn't remember the names of the hordes of people she'd met since she arrived.

Thankfully, Isabelle seemed cool. They'd already discovered a mutual love of cheesy romantic comedies. And her friends were always available on the other end of the phone, to talk her through the tough spots. Consequently, she had made it through the first day and a half relatively unscathed.

Now she was surrounded by fellow skiers, all of whom seemed friendly — at least so far — waiting for Coach Maddix to arrive and welcome her to one of the best college ski teams in the country. Becca had wanted to ski for Jackson Maddix since she was eleven years old, when she had seen him on TV coaching an underdog U.S. Olympic Ski Team to a slew of gold medals. He was a God, as far as she was concerned. And she was about to meet him, face to face.

For the moment, anyway, that *other* dream could wait.

Becca stood up, put a hand on her hip, and lifted her opposite arm for a side stretch. Even from the track field, the scenery was amazing. The campus itself was beautiful — regal, gray stone buildings, connected by pathways through manicured lawns dotted with enormous trees — with the Berkshire Mountains surrounding it all, lush and green, and promising a prime skiing season. She could see the now-barren trails from where she was standing, and already she couldn't wait for that first real snow.

"What are you, rubber?" Isabelle asked, as Becca hinged at the waist, bringing her head all the way between and behind her legs.

Becca laughed and stood up. "Yoga in the off season."

"The boys must love you," Isabelle joked, and Becca felt her cheeks turn red.

Isabelle reminded her of Sophie — totally unafraid to speak her mind.

"You're from Colorado. Ever go to Vail?" Isabelle continued. "Best powder in the country."

"It's not bad."

"Please, you probably do that rad black diamond on the Back Bowl just for fun," she said, and cocked her head toward the Berkshires. "These trails are totally slumming for you."

Becca laughed. "Yeah, these trails are definitely slumming —"

"Then feel free to leave."

The blood drained from her face.

The words were spoken quietly, but with deadly seriousness. Becca recognized the New England accent of her skiing idol.

She turned around.

And there, right in front of her, was Coach Jackson Maddix. All six feet, four inches of him.

"No, I didn't mean —" Becca began, desperate to explain that if she had been able to finish her sentence, it would have gone something like, "Yeah, these trails are definitely slumming. They're only the best trails in New England, at one of the best colleges, with one of the best ski programs, and definitely the best coach." There was a *turn* coming in the sentence, there was *irony,* she just hadn't gotten to it yet, and now he thought —

But Coach Maddix looked at her coldly and walked away.

A group of about ten guys — Becca dully observed that they were probably from the football team — had arrived on the field. Along with the other skiers, they had watched this exchange with interest, and now probably thought that she was some stuck-up ski-snob. That was just great. Perfect.

Shit.

As the coach launched into a speech about the upcoming season, Isabelle leaned toward her.

"I'm so sorry," she whispered. "He's an asshole."

Becca nodded.

Right. Asshole. Somehow that didn't make her feel better.

Several rounds of power sprints later, however, Becca was too exhausted to obsess about the fact that Coach Maddix already hated her. She had put her all into the sprints, hoping to say to the coach in action what she couldn't say in words. She would show him — in the intensity of her focus, the pumping of her legs down the track — that she was a hard worker, that she wanted to be here more than anything.

She had done her best and beyond. And, as far as she could tell, he hadn't noticed.

Now she needed to collapse. Which she did, with the rest of the team, on the grassy area beside the track.

"Take five," Coach Maddix instructed, and walked away, deep in conversation with two of his assistants. Becca watched them go into a nearby building, thankful for a few minutes of rest. But as soon as she started to catch her breath, *pang!*

She'd pushed herself too hard, and now her calf muscles were rebelling. Just what she needed. Becca groaned, and stood up. She nudged Isabelle with her toe.

"Wha . . . ?" Isabelle managed.

"I gotta cool down. You want to do a slow lap?"

Isabelle shook her head. "You are a crazy person."

Becca laughed, and forced her long legs into motion. She breathed deeply, concentrating on form.

Heel, toe, heel, toe, and soon the cramping was gone. She could feel her energy coming back. And with it, came her optimism. Okay, so she had gotten off on the wrong foot with Coach Maddix. That happened. He would realize soon enough that he had misjudged her, and it would all work out fine.

It had to.

Then, as if she had conjured him with her thoughts, Coach Maddix emerged from the athletic complex, assistants in tow. Five minutes? More like *two*.

"Alright, let's go!" she heard him yell, as he walked toward the team, who were scrambling to get to their feet.

Without another thought, Becca took off across the grassy interior of the track, making a beeline for the team, who were now assembling into rows for calisthenics.

Becca ran as hard as she could, jumping over anything in her way — a couple hurdles, a bulky piece of metal she assumed was football equipment, a pile of gym bags. It wasn't like she was showing off. She'd run track in high school. The hurdles and the other stuff were in her way. She knew she could jump them, so she did. Simple as that. She didn't notice the guys from the football team watching her. She didn't even notice Coach Maddix watching her.

But he was. And so was the football team.

As Becca ran the last few steps toward her teammates, she heard a collective laugh rise from the nearby group of football players. At the center of the group was a tall, broad-shouldered guy with dark hair and hazel eyes that looked altogether too merry for her taste. He was looking right at her. And laughing.

66

Becca hated him on sight.

Not only was he laughing at her, he had clearly rallied his friends to do the same. What a jerk. Apparently, football players at the college level were no more mature than the football players in high school had been. They were just as shallow, just as obnoxious, just as mean. And her opinion was definitely not influenced by the fact that her high school football team had used her ever-expanding breast size as an ongoing joke for the first three months of her freshman year — until Sophie, Harper, and Kate had festooned the boys' locker room with panty liners and threatened to tell all the players' girlfriends the whole team had genital warts.

Now, four whole years later, this smug, meatheaded jock was laughing at her for no reason. What right did he have to make her feel . . . well, self-conscious? And kind of small.

No right at all, Becca decided. And she was *definitely* not being overly sensitive.

She glared at him, then turned toward Coach Maddix, who was standing in front of the team at the edge of the practice field.

The coach hadn't so much as glanced in her direction since their previous exchange, but apparently he didn't approve of her mad dash across the field, because when she looked at him, his face was red with anger.

"What the hell were you doing?" he growled.

"I-I saw you coming back," Becca stammered. "I was cooling down, and —"

"What did I say earlier?" he demanded.

Becca looked up at him, wracking her brain. What had he said? Lots of things, but she had been so upset —

Coach Maddix turned to Andi Rosenbaum, a junior on the team, who was looking at Becca with sympathy.

"Rosenbaum, since Winsberg, here, doesn't listen . . ."

He gestured for Andi to speak, which she did, haltingly.

67

"He said that . . . um, we're not supposed to do anything that's not . . . safe . . . athletically speaking."

Andi was clearly aiming for a kinder, gentler version of things, which Becca would have appreciated if she hadn't been so confused. What had she done wrong?

"I said your bodies are mine now," Coach Maddix growled. "I said, don't fuck with them. Don't put them in fucking danger. You hurt yourself, you hurt my team."

He looked at Becca.

"You're on probation," he said coldly, and gestured across the field, toward the campus. "Go."

Becca's breath caught in her chest. She wanted to argue, plead with him, explain that he had her all wrong, that she was totally committed to the team, that she wanted to make him proud.

But she couldn't.

Because before she would give him that pleasure, she would go back to Boulder and live in Harper's parents' basement.

So instead, Becca did what she did best. She shut down.

She looked up at Coach Maddix, nodded, and walked numbly away from her dream.

"You're breaking up with me?"

Kate couldn't believe what she was hearing — although it did explain why Jared had pulled his Honda Accord up to the Denver airport's curbside drop-off, instead of taking the exit ramp to airport parking.

Nonetheless, this was not how their goodbye was supposed to go. They were supposed to grope each other in the car in the short-term parking lot until she was almost late for her plane, then whisper intense promises of faithfulness, and confess how much they were going to miss each other. She was supposed to break tradition and cry, and he was supposed to gently brush away her tears, and tell her how much he loved her. He was supposed to promise to meet her in some exotic place with no drinking age for New Year's Eve, where they would sip piña coladas and make mad, passionate love on a beach.

He was definitely *not* supposed to break up with her.

"I'm not breaking up with you," Jared explained, putting the car in park.

"Well, that's what 'taking a break' is," Kate informed him. "Have you not seen *Friends?*"

"It's just . . . you're going to be so far away," Jared said lamely.

Now that was more like it. *That* was why she'd had Jared drive her to the airport instead of dragging Harper out of her depressing mental institution of a basement.

"And you're going to miss me," Kate said softly. "But breaking up isn't going to make you miss me less."

"I know. I just . . . I feel like we shouldn't be tied down right now. What if we . . . meet other people?"

Kate shifted in her seat. *Tied down? Meet other people?*

"I mean," Jared continued, "I'm going to be at Harvard, and —"

"I know," Kate interrupted. "And next year, I will be, too."

"Yeah, but that's a long time," he persisted.

"I don't believe this." She shook her head. "You're mad at me for trying to find my dream, and —"

"What does that even mean?" Jared asked, throwing up his hands. "*What* dream?"

"The one I don't know I have yet!" Kate shouted. "I already explained this to you, and you acted like you got it, and now you want to dump me because I'm going to be gone for one measly year?!"

"I'm not dumping you —"

"Oh, shut up," Kate snapped. She started gathering her carry-on bags — zip-up suede purse, battered duffel, plastic grocery bag with three Fiji water bottles — and got out of the car.

Jared threw open his door, and met her by the trunk.

"Katie, don't be mad —"

"Why would I be mad?" When Jared tried to lift her way-overweight North Face backpack from the trunk, she swatted his hands away and hefted it herself.

As the bag landed at her feet with a thud, she looked up into Jared's blue eyes.

"You know, most guys would like me *more* because I'm doing this," she began. "They would respect that I want to find my own unique path in life, that I'm not afraid to take on the world alone, and —"

Jared was looking at her blankly.

"Oh, forget it," Kate snapped.

She hauled her backpack onto her shoulder, tightened her fists around her carry-ons, and turned to her now ex-boyfriend.

"You suck," she said.

Then she marched into the airport.

Numb, Kate checked her bags, got her boarding pass, and walked to the gate, where she stared out the floor-to-ceiling windows at the passing planes. Jared had actually broken up with her. Or whatever "taking a break" meant. So much for mad, passionate beach love. How could he be so awful? He had always been so . . . steady. Reliable. Perfect. Well, this was a fine time to start letting his flaws show. Breaking up with her was one thing, but his timing, and the whole drop-off lane thing — *that* was pathetic.

Her parents were no better, sending her out into the world with nothing but an international calling card, their one contribution to what they called her "delayed rebellious period" (a ridiculous phrase Kate assumed they'd gotten from Sophie's mother). Like they thought she was going to get to Europe, suddenly see the light, and call home begging for their forgiveness. Ha! Before that would happen, she would —

"Flight 407 to New York will begin boarding in five minutes."

The announcement jerked Kate out of her reverie.

In four hours, she would be in New York. And then Paris. And then . . . anywhere she wanted to go. She had $2,378.42 in her checking account, and $1,068.19 (minus one pack of airport gum) in cash and traveler's checks, which would take her to Istanbul, Athens, Rome. . . .

And when her money ran out, she would work as a waitress at a street café in Nice, or teach English in Japan, or be a street cleaner in Stockholm, she didn't care. She would be in Prague . . . or Tokyo . . . or Santorini . . . Berlin . . . Fiji . . .

A bubbly feeling spread through Kate's chest, part fear, part excitement. For better or worse, the world was her oyster.

And in that scenario, Kate decided with a smile, Jared and her parents were little more than slightly irritating specks of sand.

"I am not in pain," Sophie murmured to herself as she strode through the United terminal at LAX.

Arriving in Los Angeles in the pair of grey alligator Marc Jacobs heels she'd gotten for seventy percent off at the Denver Nordstrom's had seemed like a good idea this morning. But after nearly three hours on the plane, Sophie's feet felt like twice-baked potatoes. And her super-tight, super-low Sevens had cut off the circulation in her legs somewhere over Phoenix.

Not that any of that mattered. She was in LA, and she didn't intend to leave until she was a famous Oscar-winning actress. Or at least until she booked a national commercial that would eventually lead to her becoming a famous Oscar-winning actress.

As she followed the baggage claim signs, Sophie made her first two observations about Los Angeles. The first was that everyone above stroller-age was attached to a cell phone. The second was that the rumors were true. All the women really *did* have fake breasts.

Sophie stepped onto an escalator behind a girl wearing a leopard-print mini and a huge pair of giant Gucci sunglasses.

"Hunter, I'm *telling* you. My agent is *such* a bitch!" the girl screeched into a tiny pink Nokia. "She threatened to *drop* me if I don't start memorizing my lines for auditions." There was a pause as the girl listened to Hunter. "I know! *Nobody* memorizes sides for a guest spot on *Mission Man.* It's not even network!"

This chick was a total idiot. She obviously *wanted* everyone around her to know about her bitchy agent and her *Mission Man* audition. Like anyone cared. Okay, Sophie cared. A little. She wished *she* had an agent, bitchy or otherwise.

I'll have five agents begging to represent me by October, she told herself, determined to be optimistic, no matter how alone she felt in the huge airport. She'd finally gotten off her ass — she was finally *doing* something — and she wasn't going to let a little thing like massive intimidation stop her from envisioning her dream coming true.

As the escalator descended, Sophie scanned the area below for her mom's friend, Mrs. Meyer. In the college photo Angela had shown her, Genevieve Meyer (nee Perry) was large and perky-looking, with a huge head of home-permed brown hair. Sophie hoped she'd tossed her appliquéd PI PHIS DO IT BETTER sweatshirt some time over the last twenty years.

There was no sign of anyone who looked like Genevieve. But Sophie made her third observation about Los Angeles. In the crowd of family, friends, and drivers waiting for travelers to arrive, there was a higher-than-usual per capita of good-looking people.

Her gaze landed on one particular hottie whose just-right shaggy blond hair *alone* would have made him a top ten contender on her Most Drool-Worthy Boy In America list. The fact that he was holding a piece of paper with her name scribbled on it bumped him up to at least number three. If this was Mrs. Meyer's son, she'd totally lucked out.

Sophie tugged her jeans even lower on her hips as she stepped off the escalator. "I think you're looking for me," she announced sexily as she approached the guy with the sign. His features were chiseled, but not in a cheesy, excessive way. Up close, she saw that his eyes were goldish green.

"Sophie Bushell?" he asked, pronouncing her last name *Bush*-ell.

"Bu-*shell*," she corrected.

The goldish-green eyes flicked over her. "Actress, right?"

Excellent. She already looked the part. According to her mom's books on self-actualization, that was half the battle. "Yep. That's me."

He grunted, actually *grunted* in response. "I'm Sam. Baggage claim is this way."

Sam didn't say much as they waited for Sophie's two huge army green L.L.Bean duffel bags. Maybe he was antisocial. Or slow. The Meyers had sent their slow, antisocial son to pick her up. Even taking the hotness into account, this didn't bode well.

Outside the airport, the California sun was shining bright. Sophie breathed deeply as she followed Sam (who'd insisted on carrying both her bags) to his car. Just inhaling the air, she felt different. Freer.

"Palm trees!" she exclaimed. "At the *airport*!"

"Man, you really are new in town," Sam observed, looking over his shoulder.

In the parking lot, they passed a silver Lexus SUV, a black BMW convertible, and a vintage muscle car before Sam stopped at a beat-up gray Honda Civic. "Your chariot," he said, throwing her duffels into the trunk.

"Exactly where do your parents live?" Sophie asked once she'd buckled her seat belt.

Sam gave her a strange look. "New Jersey."

Oh. "You're not the Meyers' son?"

He laughed and started the ignition. "Yeah right."

Sophie felt slightly sick. Angela had been very clear that Mrs.

Meyer was going to pick her up at the airport. But the second Sophie had seen Sam's sign, she'd assumed he was her ride. What if this guy had gotten her name off some kind of flight manifest? What if frumpy Mrs. Meyer was still wandering around baggage claim, while Sophie was headed toward the freeway with a serial killer? She looked around her seat for something sharp.

Sam glanced over. "I'm not planning to murder you, in case you're wondering."

Sophie tried to appear relaxed. "I wasn't."

Stealing a peek at him as he merged into the crawling airport traffic, Sophie was annoyed to see that Sam was smiling. Less than half an hour in LA, and a possible felon was making fun of her.

"So, who are you?" she asked tentatively as the little Honda burst onto the freeway. "Exactly?"

"I work for the Meyers. On most days I'm exactly their pool boy. Today I'm exactly their chauffeur."

None of this data meshed with Sophie's image of a middle-aged suburban housewife. But this was LA. Anything was possible.

"I'm staying with them," Sophie offered, hoping to get Sam talking.

"Good for you." He cranked the radio, and an old R.E.M. tune blasted into the car.

Maybe this guy wasn't slow, but he was definitely antisocial. Sophie rolled down her window, letting in the hot, smoggy air. A few minutes later, when Sam asked her to close it, she pretended not to hear him.

As the city whizzed by at sixty-five miles an hour, Sophie allowed her thoughts to drift to her friends. Kate was probably in a Parisian café right now, practicing her French on some hot beret-wearing poet, wondering what she ever saw in a boring jock like Jared. Becca was, hopefully, shedding her turtle shell and making new friends, maybe even planning to wear one of her new thongs to a keg party tonight. And Harper . . . well, she was the only one Sophie was worried about. Staying home wasn't going to be easy, no matter how committed Harper was to her Dream. Sophie's guess was that right about now Harper was sitting in front of a blank computer screen, wishing she'd gone to NYU.

After what felt like forever, Sam finally exited the freeway. Sophie was dying to know where they were, but she refused to give Sam the satisfaction of asking. Instead, she stared out at block after block of strip malls, and made her fourth observation about the City of Angels. There were more nail salons and massage parlors than there were people on the streets.

Then the neighborhood changed. Mansions and big lawns (complete with armies of gardeners) replaced the dry cleaners and taco stands. Every Mercedes, Range Rover, and Cadillac parked in the vast circular drives looked like it cost more than Sophie's eco-conscious architect dad made in a year.

Eventually, Sam pulled over in front of a terra cotta palace. Or maybe it was a castle. Whichever one required a manmade moat and giant turrets.

"It's a Koi pond," Sam explained. Apparently he'd noticed her staring at the moat. "There's another one out back."

"Oh, right." Sophie had never heard of a Koi pond. "This is the Valley?"

"The Valley?" Sam laughed. He looked good when he laughed, there was no denying it. "You're in Beverly Hills, baby. 90210."

That's when it sank in. She wasn't going to spend the year living in a ranch house in the 'burbs. She was going to live *here*. In a Spanish-style two-story mansion which — turrets aside — was extraordinarily beautiful.

While Sam got out of the car and headed toward the trunk, Sophie just sat there, one hand frozen on her seatbelt buckle. *I will not hum the theme to* The Beverly Hillbillies, Sophie told herself, even as the banjo part started to play in her head.

Jed was shooting up some food by the time Sophie had the presence of mind to flip down the visor above her seat. The tiny mirror told an ugly truth. Spending the last fifty minutes in a wind tunnel had been a bad idea. Her curls had been permanently blown back from her face, giving her a hair halo, and her makeup had melted off. Open purse, she ordered herself. Find lipstick.

But damage control wasn't an option. The giant *palicio* door opened, and a woman who bore only the vaguest resemblance to Genevieve Meyer floated toward the grey Honda.

Sam knocked on her window. "You can get out now."

"Sophie! Sweetie!" Genevieve Meyer cried as soon as she was out of the car. "You look just like your fabulous mother!" She grabbed Sophie's shoulders and air-kissed both her cheeks.

"Hi, Mrs. Meyer. Thanks for having me."

Wow. The formerly plump, frizzy-haired Genevieve was now a bona fide bombshell. Sophie didn't know where to look first. The size zero waist? The expertly highlighted blond-bobbed hair? The pale pink St. John suit she'd seen on Gisele in *Vogue* last week? Sophie was acutely aware of the sheen of sweat that had soaked through her tight red Old Navy t-shirt.

"Can you ever forgive me for not being at the airport? Gifford and I had a charity thing at the Bel Air. And you know how those celebrity auctions drag."

"No problem," Sophie responded breezily. "Sam was a great tour guide."

Genevieve glanced at her diamond encrusted Cartier watch. "I'm dying to sit you down with a bottle of Grgich and hear every last detail about life in the Rockies, but I have to dash. As per usual, Giff forgot to tell me we have dinner plans."

"No prob —"

"Sam will show you to the guesthouse." Genevieve went in for one last air kiss, then darted toward a baby blue Jaguar. "Make yourself at home!"

Sophie stood in stunned silence. Guesthouse. She was going to have her own *house*. Her first instinct was to dig the cell phone out of her decidedly un-Beverly Hills Gap tote bag and call Harper. But what was she supposed to say? *Hi, I'm living in paradise. How's the basement?*

Sam dropped the duffels at Sophie's feet. "Wanna keep gawking, or are you ready to see the new pad?"

No, she thought. She wasn't ready for any of this. "Can't wait," she replied evenly, picking up one of her bags. Then she paused and gave Sam the stare she'd been perfecting since seventh grade. "Are you this friendly to everyone you meet?"

He shrugged. "Stay in this city long enough, you see a lot of people come and go. No point investing time and energy into just anyone."

"I'm not just anyone." She threw back her shoulders and struck her best John Casablanca pose. "And if I can say that with this hair, you know I ain't lying."

His mouth didn't move, but she could tell Sam was trying not to smile. "We'll see."

As Sophie followed him toward her very own guesthouse, she made her fifth and sixth observations about Los Angeles. The fifth was that she was in the nascent stage of what could become a full-blown crush. And the sixth? In Beverly Hills, her feet didn't hurt at all.

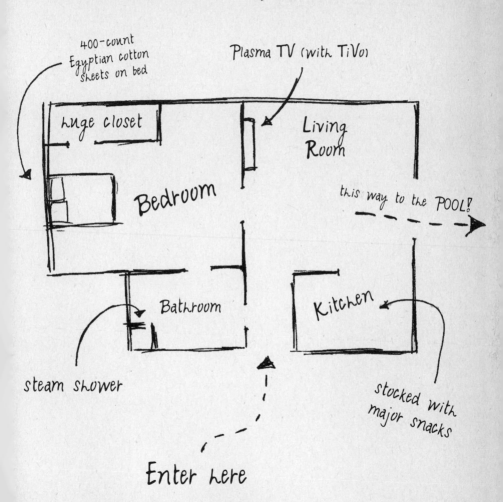

Sophie's Fabulous New Digs
(Note: Do Not View If Suffering From Real Estate Envy)

400-count Egyptian cotton sheets on bed

Plasma TV (with TiVo)

Huge closet

Living Room

Bedroom

this way to the POOL!

Bathroom

Kitchen

steam shower

stocked with major snacks

Enter here

FIVE

Harper hated coffee. She hated scones. She hated perky people who drank coffee and ate scones. The intensity with which she hated these things rivaled what she once felt toward Ms. Finch, her tenth-grade gym teacher, who'd been a big fan of rope climbing.

As it happened, the customers who patronized the Rainy Day Books Café loved coffee and scones, and more than a few tended toward perky. But since October rent loomed, Harper had no choice but to find some small piece of gratitude in her heart for Judd Wright, the former classmate who'd gotten her this ill-forsaken gig.

"Ow!" Harper yanked her elbow away from the espresso maker for the third time since she'd arrived at six o'clock this morning. Did she say gratitude? She meant hatred.

"Happens all the time." Judd appeared behind her, his head of wild black curls blessedly obscuring Harper's view of the ever-growing line in front of the counter. "You'll get used to it."

"Goody. Can't wait." Oh, man. This was her life. It was *really* her life. She'd become one of those annoying hyphenates. Writer-barista. Barista-writer.

It could have been worse. Harper could have been flipping burgers at some McDonald's on Route 36. At least the Rainy Day Books Café didn't have a Frialator. Located in the heart of the Pearl Street Mall, a pedestrian-only, tree-lined part of downtown that housed dozens of boutiques and restaurants, the coffeehouse was a popular hangout for both locals and tourists.

And along with the old-school wooden tables and chairs, there *were* actual books — thousands of them — filling the shelves that lined three of the coffeehouse walls. If she were just a writer, and not a writer-barista, Harper could envision herself plugging in her laptop and spending afternoons sipping hot chocolate and writing great prose here.

Judd handed Harper a triple mocha something or other. "Give this to Tie Guy. Looks like he needs it."

Harper had learned the staff prioritized orders based on who looked most in need of a dose of caffeine. It was a chaos-inducing system. But whatever. She'd do as she was told her for her ten bucks (and that included tips) an hour.

"Have a nice day, sir," Harper chirped with her best fake smile, handing Tie Guy his mocha thingie.

He stared at the coffee drink like it was a bloody, dead rat. "That's supposed to be iced." He glared at her. "Do it right, or don't do it at all."

Do not explode, Harper cautioned herself. She knew nothing about this man. Maybe his wife just left him. Or he recently found out his son had leukemia. *Yeah, maybe.* More likely he'd been born an asshole, seizing any and every opportunity to terrorize innocent writer-baristas.

"Here you go," Judd grinned, once again materializing just over Harper's shoulder, as he handed Tie Guy the correct order. "Little mix-up. It's her first day."

"You blamed me?" Harper demanded, once the guy was gone. "You *told* me to give him *that* drink."

Judd nodded toward a sleepy-looking skater dude in a tie-dyed Grateful Dead t-shirt. "No, him. *Tie-dye* Guy." He patted her shoulder. "You'll learn."

"I quit."

"It's your first day."

"First, last. Who's counting?" Harper untied her stained LOVE ME, LOVE MY LATTE apron. Rent be damned.

"Hey, Mr. Finelli," Judd called out, looking at some point past Harper's aching head.

Mr. Finelli. The name caused Harper's stomach to cramp up in a way that was not entirely unpleasant. She pushed her black, rectangular glasses up on her nose and turned to find her former A.P. English teacher grinning at her.

"Harper Waddle. I heard a rumor you were still in town."

The problem with Mr. Finelli was that he didn't look like a *mister*. In Levi's and a black t-shirt, he looked like a regular guy — a really hot regular guy. Which made it hard to remember he was six years older than she was and completely off-limits.

"I decided to hang around Boulder to write." Did that sound as dumb out loud as it did in her head?

He'd cut his dark brown hair shorter over the summer, which somehow made the aquamarine blue eyes behind his small wire-rimmed glasses seem bigger and more expressive. Harper resisted the urge to reach over the counter and touch the short, soft strands that grazed his temples. *Get a grip,* she thought, reminding herself she wasn't one of those girls who giggled and blushed every time a good-looking guy was in her orbit. She was the antithesis of those girls.

But Mr. Finelli was different. The first day of class her senior year, he'd spent the entire period reading Yeats poems aloud. Sometime during "When You Are Old," Harper had developed a crush. And it wasn't one of those crushes that were light and fun to think about during a boring history lecture. Harper felt like Mr. Finelli was the man she was meant to be with. Emphasis on *man*. Those six years were the one glitch in their not-yet-blossomed relationship.

"What about NYU?" Usually, that question made Harper want to claw out the asker's eyes. But there was no judgment in Mr. Finelli's tone. Just curiosity.

I could tell him, Harper thought. She could admit that NYU had rejected her and that she'd made up this whole Dream Plan and that she'd lied to her friends.

"You only live once, right?" she responded, choosing a stupid cliché over a True Confession. "I want to write a book — so I'm going to."

He didn't say anything for a second, then he nodded. Not like a polite nod of recognition that she'd spoken. A *real* nod, like he agreed with her.

"Harper, I admire your guts," he responded finally. Then he pointed at the pastries. "I'll take a raspberry scone with my coffee."

Harper loved scones. She loved coffee. She loved hot, twenty-three-year-old English teachers who themselves loved scones and coffee. Mr. Finelli admired her. Life was good.

For the next five minutes Harper ignored her customers and talked only to Mr. Finelli. Talked to him about writing and dreams and how he'd started a mystery novel but abandoned it when he couldn't decide which character to make the murderer. It was like they were friends, or colleagues, or anything besides teacher and student. At last she had something to tell Kate, Becca, and Sophie that didn't include several expletives.

"Anyway, try writing in the morning," Mr. Finelli advised as he poured 2 percent milk into his coffee. "Before all the shit that happens during the day messes with your clarity of thought."

"I'm kind of groggy before noon," Harper informed him. "But I'll try."

And then he was snapping the white plastic lid onto the top of his paper cup and leaving. Harper wasn't ready to let him go. She wanted more. "Mr. Finelli?"

He turned. "Yeah?"

"Thanks."

"No problem," he replied warmly, shrugging. "And Harper?"

"Yeah?"

"You can call me Adam." He smiled. "Y'know, now that I'm not your teacher anymore."

Adam. Adam. Adam. It was a beautiful name. Harper found herself wishing she were Eve. Ahhh.

As soon as Mr. Finelli, a.k.a. Adam, was gone, and Harper's heart rate had slowed to somewhere almost approaching normal, she tracked down Judd next to the bagel slicer.

"Has Mr. Finelli been in here before?" she asked, hoping her interest sounded at least vaguely casual.

Judd gave her a look as he pushed a wayward curl away from his forehead. "Yeah. Every day."

Harper processed this information. If Mr. Finelli, a.k.a. Adam, frequented the Rainy Day Books Café, that meant Harper was going to see him. Statistically speaking, it was a certainty. What was also a certainty was that Harper was no longer going to quit this job.

"Usually, he's got Fiona with him," Judd continued. "Don't know where she was today."

"Fiona?" Harper pictured sun-streaked blond hair and one of those really delicate pinky toe rings. She didn't like where this was headed.

"His girlfriend. They're moving in together." Judd went back to slicing a garlic bagel, clearly unaware that he'd just put a major damper on Harper's buzz.

But, hey. Girlfriend, schmirlfriend. Now Harper had a reason to come to work in the morning.

Lying in her youth hostel bed — or more accurately, cot — Kate made a mental list of all the things she could have been doing at that exact moment: buying intimidatingly large books for her new classes, IM'ing with Harper, making out with Jared. . . .

For that matter, she could have been clipping her toenails watching reruns of *Extreme Makeover Home Edition,* which would have been a million times better than being utterly and completely alone in Paris.

Kate cursed to herself and rolled over, searching for a spot of warmth. She was going to kill Harper for getting her into this. If Harper hadn't decided to become a writer *right now* instead of waiting until after college like a normal person, Kate wouldn't be freezing cold under coarse sheets that had probably been used forty million times, starving, and so exhausted her bones ached. It had to be almost noon Paris time, which meant she was about to be kicked out of the dimly lit, aggressively undecorated hostel room that she was sharing with two Australians, a Swede, and a German — all of whom had risen at the crack of dawn and set out to discover the City of Lights. And yet she couldn't force herself to get up, get dressed, get moving.

What was *wrong* with her? She was in Paris for God's sake, and motivation had always been one of her defining characteristics. Even in the midst of her who-am-I crisis, the one thing she would have been able to say about herself with utter certainty was that she, Kate Foster, was a go-getter.

But twelve hours alone in Paris had knocked her on her ass. Yesterday afternoon, she'd stood in line for over an hour to exchange money, only to have some snooty bank teller inform her she could have just used her American bank card at any ATM. Then eight years of studying French had completely failed her when she wandered into a restaurant next door to the hostel, and she'd ended up eating fried eggs and sausage for dinner, because it was the only thing she could remember how to order. Perhaps if she could just get up and brush her teeth, she would feel better. . . .

Knock knock knock.

"Allo?" an older woman's voice said from the hall. *"Il y a quelqu'un dans la chambre?"*

Kate sat up.

"Oui, madame. Je suis la, mais je parte."

"Vite, s'il vous plait," the voice replied.

Quickly. Kate sighed. At least she remembered that much.

Twenty minutes later, she was standing on the street, Paris stretched out before her. And behind her. And to her left and right. It seemed to go on forever. Was she supposed to go the The Louvre, or the L'Arc de Triomphe? Or Montmartre? Or Jardin Luxembourge?

With no one to answer to, no one to bounce her thoughts off of, Kate felt completely at sea. So she pulled out the emergency phone card her parents had given her, found a corner pay phone, and called Harper. Then Becca. Then Sophie. No one was home. Finally, desperate, she called Jared.

"Hello." The familiar sound of his voice made Kate go weak in the knees.

"It's me," she said, wanting to tell him how miserable she was, how she was afraid she had made a terrible mistake, how she wished she was there with him, instead of alone on a bustling street in Paris with nowhere to go and a thousand places to go all at the same time.

But when he said "Oh" in a tone that said instantly he just wasn't that happy to hear from her — part caution, part pretense — Kate knew she would have to lie. Which she did, brilliantly. She said Paris was fabulous, the museums were stunning, she'd met lots of great people already, and had plans to go to dinner with a big group from the hostel.

Then, in the middle of telling Jared how delicious Parisian food was, he interrupted her.

"That's great, Katie. Listen, I gotta go."

"Oh," she replied, totally deflated. But they were broken up, right? What right did she have to keep him on the phone, anyway?

"Yeah, the guys down the hall got a keg, and we're heading over."

"So, you're having fun?"

"Yeah," Jared said. "Harvard rocks."

Then he hung up, and Kate realized she had made the first stop on her road to self-discovery. She had learned she was a really good liar.

"What about the hairs growing out of his nose!" Becca laughed, smearing mustard on her grilled chicken sandwich.

"He's still sexy," Isabelle insisted, and Taymar agreed with an emphatic nod.

Becca, Isabelle, and Taymar, another freshman skier from The D (a.k.a. Detroit), were engaged in a heated debate over whether their Econ professor's hotness outweighed his general hirsuteness. Luke, a stocky dark-haired sophomore skier whom Becca suspected had a crush on Taymar, looked baffled by the whole discussion.

"Okay, so he's pushing sixty, and his ears look like a Brazilian jungle," Taymar said firmly, flipping her long dark braids over her shoulder, "but Dr. Shepard's got it going on." A self-named "goddess of color," Taymar's pretty, round face and soft curves were misleading. It had taken Becca about four seconds to realize that Taymar was anything but gentle. On the contrary, she was loud, intimidatingly smart, and seriously opinionated — in the best possible way.

Luke shook his head and put down his soy burger.

"So all the time I spend working out and clipping nose hairs, you're saying I'd get more girls if I grew a paunch and just let my face sprout?"

Becca smiled to herself as Luke gave a furtive glance in Taymar's direction. There was definite crush action going on there.

"Ask me," Isabelle interjected, "Coach M is still the hottest guy on campus. Even if he does have a serious attitude problem when it comes to our Becca here."

Everyone nodded. Coach Maddix had taken Becca off probation with a curt "hit the track" at the second practice, but he rarely spoke to her directly, and when he did it was always with cold disdain. If it hadn't been for her teammates, Becca was sure she would have given up and quit the team by now. But in a weird way, Coach Maddix's treatment of her sort of had worked to her advantage. The rest of the team seemed to sense that he was being unfair (maybe because Isabelle and Taymar spouted off to them about it every chance they got), and they had rallied around her in a way that actually made Becca blush when she thought about it. Faced with that kind of instant acceptance, she felt like she was coming out of her shell much quicker than she ever had in the past.

"Hey, Bec," Isabelle glanced across the crowded dining hall at the cafeteria line, "it's your boyfriend."

Becca didn't even have to look. But she did. And there, in the line, surrounded (as always) by his burly ball-playing buddies, was Stuart Pendergrass.

The only dark clouds on the horizon of Becca's new life were Coach Maddix and Stuart Pendergrass. Becca had faith that she and Coach Maddix would eventually reach a détente. But Stuart Pendergrass was another matter entirely. Since that first practice, when he had laughed at her on the track, Becca had learned a lot about Stuart. It would have been impossible not to. Everyone seemed to know him, and oddly enough, like him.

For one thing, Stuart was the star running back of the Middlebury football team. Which, even if he hadn't publicly humiliated her, would have been a huge strike against him. It didn't help that every time she saw him he was joking raucously with his friends, or chatting up some blond bimbette. What was he trying to do? Find some ditz to marry so they could populate the world with perfect supermodel freaks?

The worst part was that she had not one but two classes with him, which meant she had to see Stuart five times a week for the whole rest of the semester. Monday, Wednesday, and Friday she sat two rows behind him in chemistry, and Tuesday and Thursday he sat directly across from her in a big circle of desks for an English Romantic poets seminar.

Obviously he was just trying to fulfill his English requirement with a class that didn't meet too early in the morning. Why else would a football player be in a class about Byron, Shelley, and Keats? Whatever the case, the professor, Dr. Stein, adored him. Everything he said — and he talked surprisingly often for a jock — was gold to her. Stuart could have said "Byron is spelled B-Y-R-O-N," and Dr. Stein would have clapped at his ingenuity. Whatever. As far as Becca could tell — not that she'd spent a lot of time thinking about it — Stuart Pendergrass was just another mean, self-centered jock.

At this moment, however, he was a mean, self-centered jock walking toward her table. With a tray. Why was he walking toward her table with a tray? Did he plan to sit with them? Becca's heart started to pound. Was he friends with Luke? Luke, that traitor! Becca picked up her fork and started picking at her salad. He would come over, talk to Luke, and she would be engrossed in her baby greens. She didn't even have to acknowledge him.

"Hey, you're Becca, right?"

Becca studied her plate for just a moment too long before she looked up. She nodded coldly.

"I'm Stuart," Stuart Pendergrass said. "We're in English Romantic Poetry together."

She nodded again. Stuart was trying to be all nice. Clearly he wanted something from her. Yeah, well, he should learn that a guy who laughs at a girl doesn't then get to ask said girl for anything and expect to get it. Stuart seemed to be waiting for more of a response, but he wasn't going to get that either. All the chattering at her table had stopped as her new friends watched the exchange.

"So . . ." he continued, "did you find the Keats book yet?"

"No," Becca replied curtly. "You may have noticed the big sign on the shelf saying the bookstore wouldn't have it for two more weeks."

She wasn't exactly being Ms. Congeniality, but Stuart smiled.

"Guess I missed that." He turned to go. "See you later."

And just like that, her first, official, face-to-face encounter with Stuart Pendergrass was over. He was just as much of a dumb jock as she had expected him to be. Even if he hadn't been mean. This time.

"Ooo, you were cold," Taymar made her voice shiver, rubbing her hands over her arms.

"You may have noticed the big sign . . ." Isabelle mimicked, raising her eyebrows at an imaginary Stuart.

"It's weird he doesn't have that book," Luke pondered. Becca suspected he was struggling to hide a smile. "Mark Williams on the ski team, he took that class last year. Gave all the books to Stu."

Becca felt her cheeks start to get red, though she didn't know exactly why.

"Well, isn't that convenient," Isabelle noted. "Turns out your boyfriend has a crush on you."

Becca's cheeks grew redder, but she forced herself to laugh. "You're the one who started calling him my boyfriend, not me."

As she took a big bite of her chicken sandwich — they couldn't make her talk about Stuart anymore if her mouth was full — she thought about Harper, Sophie, and Kate. She had promised them that she would try to fall in love this year, and it was a promise she intended to keep — even though the whole idea made her feel queasy.

She knew it was important. And she felt like making such amazing new friends would help her take the risk when the time was right.

But she was sure of one thing. The last person in the world she was going to risk anything for was Stuart Pendergrass.

"You're talking like a child," Sam told Sophie, his gaze intense and unwavering. "You don't understand the world you live in."

"No, I don't," she responded. "But now I mean to go into that, too. I must find out which is right — the world or I."

For a long moment, they stared into each other's eyes, each willing the other to back down. The tension was so palpable that Sophie was actually stunned when Sam broke the silence.

"You're ill, Nora — you're feverish. I almost believe you're out of your senses." Sam paused. He seemed to be waiting for Sophie to say something.

Oh, right, she remembered, feeling a familiar tingle travel up and down her spine. They were standing on a small stage, and they were acting. She wasn't Sophie. He wasn't Sam. They were Nora and Torvald Helmer, the unhappy couple at the center of Ibsen's *A Doll's House*. And this was the climactic scene at the end of Act III, when Nora informs Torvald she's leaving him.

Sophie panicked. What if she blanked? What if Sam thought she sucked? What if the whole acting class laughed her out of the tiny theater?

Then she remembered. She never panicked. Never blanked. She could do this, because she was good. Finally, Sophie opened her mouth. She was Nora Helmer and she had something to say.

Half an hour later, Sophie followed Sam onto Hollywood Boulevard to begin the three-block trek to his gray Honda. She still felt shaky, as if it were *she* rather than a fictional character who'd just decided to leave her husband.

"Where'd you go back there?" Sam asked when they finally got to the car.

"Nowhere." Sophie hardly felt that a *slightly* longer than normal pause before a line was a reason to criticize.

"We were in the middle of the scene, and you just, like, disappeared." He snapped his fingers. "What happened? Realize you were missing *Wheel of Fortune?*"

One time Sam had caught her watching a game show. *One time.* And she was branded for life.

"I happen to be a serious actress."

Sam shrugged. "Oh, right. I keep forgetting."

Not for the first time, Sophie felt like hitting him. Since she'd moved into the one bedroom Spanish-style guesthouse on the Meyers' extensive property eight days ago, Sophie had spent most of her time lying by Gifford and Genevieve's huge figure-eight-shaped pool, complete with a hot tub on one end and a waterfall on the other. Sam showed up daily to check chlorine levels and give Sophie a hard time.

So far, she'd learned that he was twenty years old, his last name was Piper, that he usually held at least three jobs, and that he thought anyone who lived west of La Cienega Boulevard couldn't possibly be serious about acting.

Sophie had hoped Sam was thawing toward her when he'd grudgingly agreed to take her to his acting class this afternoon. Clearly, she'd been wrong. Enough was enough.

She stepped away from the Honda. "I'm taking the bus," she announced, heading down the street.

"You can't do that," he called after her.

She turned back. "I'm eighteen. I can do whatever the hell I want."

Sam rolled his eyes. She *hated* it when he rolled his eyes. No matter how beautifully greenish gold they were.

"Do you have any idea how long it'll take to get back to the lap of

93

luxury from here?" He ran one hand through his collar-length shaggy blond hair.

No. Sophie had no idea. And she didn't care. Nothing was going to make her sit next to Sam in a confined space, forced to deal with his tsunami-sized waves of condescension.

"Thank you for taking me to your class." Her voice was cold and distant. "I'll see myself home."

With that, she took off down Hollywood Boulevard in what she hoped was the direction of a bus stop. Sam caught up a few minutes later, inching the car along beside her. But after Sophie ignored him for two blocks, he finally sped up and drove away.

Three buses and a mere one hour and fifty-two minutes later, Sophie stepped out of the steam shower in her pale-blue-tiled guest-house bathroom. Sometime during her second round of Pantene shampoo, she had decided she was going to take up Genevieve on her offer to let Sophie use one of the Meyers' "extra" cars.

I'll never take the bus again, she vowed as she slid into the fraying, short red cotton robe she'd had since sixth grade.

Sophie wandered into the kitchen. Munchies would make her feel better. Munchies or a massage. And she was definitely too broke for a massage. Grabbing a giant bag of Doritos, she heard the knock.

Sophie took her time getting to the door, knowing who would be on the other side.

"What?" she hoped she looked haughty, despite the huge white terry cloth towel that was wrapped around her head.

"You weren't bad tonight," Sam announced. "Laughlin called, said to bring you back to class next week."

Sophie didn't respond. Even in a turban, she knew how to hold her ground. Sam shifted his gaze, suddenly seeming to find the wooden *mezuzah* on the door jamb a fascinating objet d'art.

"I'm sorry I made the crack about the *Wheel*." He offered finally, glancing at her. "Okay?"

94

Bite me, Sophie thought. But she didn't say the words out loud. After all, Sam was the only person under forty she knew in LA. And she *really* wanted to go back to that class.

"Apology accepted." Sophie stepped back and started to close the door.

"If you'll deign to get in my car, I'll drive you to class next week," he offered quickly. "Beats the bus."

"I'll drive myself." Sophie reached up to adjust her towel, which was dangerously close to unraveling and falling limply onto her shoulders.

"Don't be an idiot. Parking's a bitch." Apparently, Sam's contriteness allowed for only so much humility.

She stared at him, trying to think of a snappy comeback. None came to mind.

What's wrong with me? Sophie wondered. Why isn't Sam falling at my feet? In Boulder, all Sophie had to do was *glance* at a cute guy and he was all over her. But Sam seemed different. He was immune to her. A fact that was both infuriating and exhilarating.

"Fine," she agreed finally. "Pick me up at seven." After all, he *had* shown up at her door and done his version of groveling. She'd won this round.

"I'll be here at six-thirty." Sam grinned, then turned and walked away. He was halfway down the flower-lined front path before he called back. "By the way, your robe is open."

Sophie looked down. *Oh God.* Unless Sam was legally blind, he'd been treated to a view of half her left breast during their entire conversation.

Oh well. If she didn't make it as a serious actress, there was always porn queen to consider.

26. Convince someone you're an American soap opera star. SB

27. Find Elvis. BW

28. Stomp grapes. HN

29. Pee in a hole. SB

30. Take a picture of yourself on Foster Street. BW

31. Take the water. HN

32. Talk to the ugly guy. SB

33. Drink ouzo. BW

34. Write us, bitch. HN

35. Touch the Berlin Wall. HF

36. Learn how to say "stop staring at my breasts" in 4 languages. SB

37. Don't call anyone at home for one full week. BW

38. Get a piercing or a tattoo (real, not henna). SB

39. Find out what "bangers" are. Report back. HN

40. Go topless. BW

41. Make up a game, and find someone to play it with you. HF

42. Read Things Fall Apart. HF

43. Read Middlemarch. HN

44. Read Mama Day. BW

45. Read Vogue. In French. SB

SIX

Pride. Envy. Sloth. . . . Harper was running through the seven deadly sins, trying to figure out where lying to one's three best friends fit in.

"I think your novel needs a name," Habiba announced as Harper got to gluttony. "How can you write something that doesn't have a name?"

"Hmm . . . maybe."

Shadows of Summer. The Heretic of Havana. Ripening Agent. Harper switched gears from a list of the seven deadly to a list of possible titles. Too bad each was shittier than the last.

Her shift had ended an hour ago. Rather than go home to her dungeon to stare at a blank computer screen, she'd decided to stay at the café, where she could sit at a corner table and stare at a blank computer screen amid the comfort of strangers.

When Habiba had stopped by on her way home from school, Harper had offered her a free iced mocha latte in exchange for twenty uninterrupted minutes of listening to Harper complain at will. The arrangement was mutually gratifying, if ultimately unproductive.

"I named the moldy bar of soap in my shower Agnes," she confided to Beebs to steer the conversation away from anything having to do with her supposed Great American Novel. "I think of it as a pet."

Habiba had been showing up at the coffee shop more and more often since Kate had left. Harper's relationship with her own sister, Amy, consisted of little more than passing each other in the bathroom, and Amy was clear that was fine with her. But getting to know Beebs on a new level, Harper realized how much Habiba wished she were closer to Kate. How much she wished they were like *real* sisters, instead of polite acquaintances.

Habiba thought for a moment, then nodded solemnly. "Agnes is a good name."

Suddenly, Harper felt lonely. Really lonely.

"I miss Kate," she sighed.

She missed them all, the way an amputee misses an arm or a leg, complete with the ghost sensation that they were still there, ready to walk into the café any second.

"Me, too," Habiba agreed sadly. "I wonder if she misses me . . . I wonder if she even thinks about us."

A shadow passed over Habiba's large, dark eyes, and Harper realized she wasn't just thinking about Kate. Which made Harper consider how petty her own problems were. Or Kate's. Or Sophie's. Or even Becca's.

However messed up any of their relatives were — ranging from the merely annoying to the downright hurtful — at least they all *had* a mom and a dad. Habiba didn't even remember her parents. . . . It was too much to imagine.

But possibly a good subject for a book . . . Harper thought. Then she stopped herself. Had she really sunk this low? So hard up for a plot line that she was willing to dredge up her friend's sister's painful past for story fodder? It was wretched. And selfish. Selfish and wretched.

"Mr. Finelli is staring at you," Habiba announced.

"He is?" Harper forgot all about being wretched and selfish and sat up straighter in her tiny café chair. "No, he's not."

Habiba pointed toward the window. "He's outside, and he's *staring*."

Harper turned. It was true. Mr. Finelli, he of great wit and good hair, was outside the café on Pearl Street, looking in at her. Even from a distance she could see he was wearing her favorite pair of Banana Republic khakis and that faded light blue t-shirt that made his forearms look really good.

He knows, she thought in a panic. The truth had gotten out, and Mr. Finelli knew that Harper lied about getting into NYU. He was so disgusted and disappointed in his former star student that he couldn't tear his eyes away from the wreckage that was her life.

But when she caught his eye, Mr. Finelli smiled. Then he pointed toward her computer and flashed a thumbs up. Harper exhaled. He didn't know. He wasn't disgusted and disappointed. *Thank God.*

As he continued down the street, Habiba poked Harper in the arm. "You like him."

"What? No, I don't." Harper pushed her glasses farther up on her nose and tried not to blush. "He was my *teacher.*"

Habiba shrugged. "I think he likes you, too."

"He's, like, twenty-three," she countered.

Why, oh why, had she not taken a shower this morning? She could have at least hopped in for five minutes to wash her hair and scrub her armpits with the new bar of Ivory she kept next to Agnes.

"Age is meaningless." Habiba stated it with such certainty that Harper could almost believe she was right.

"Don't you have homework to do?" she turned abruptly back to her ever-blank computer screen.

Habiba stood up and grabbed her Hello Kitty backpack. "Get a name," she nodded meaningfully, gesturing to the laptop. "It will all come with the name."

Harper's head was swimming as she watched Habiba stride gracefully out of the coffee shop. Was it possible, even infinitesimally, that Beebs was right?

Could Mr. Finelli *like* her?

The Louvre. Check.

L'Arc de Triomphe. Check.

The Eiffel Tower. Check.

Notre Dame Cathedral, Musée D'Orsay, Luxembourg Gardens. Check. Check. Check.

After two weeks in Paris, Kate's guidebook was full of scribbled directions, notes to herself ("museums are *fermé* on Tuesdays!"), advice from passersby, check marks, cross-outs, and the dark stain of an ill-fated mug of café au lait. Following the guidebook's advice, she had taken a *Bateaux Mouches* down the Seine, walked across all nine major bridges, tried an oddly tasty milk and strawberry syrup drink called a *lait fraise,* and eaten a boatload of baguettes. She had even figured out how to ride the RER to Versailles, where she had eschewed the palace to spend an entire afternoon perusing the legendary gardens.

Indeed, Kate thought to herself as she sipped a *citron presse* at a sidewalk café, in many ways the guidebook had simply replaced her parents. For two weeks, she had been doing everything it told her to do — from getting up early to beat the inevitable crowds at Notre Dame Cathedral, to browsing the used-book stalls along the Seine, to going on more than her fair share of walking tours with an ever-changing band of hostel roommates.

Yesterday morning, at the Rodin Museum, she had stood for a

solid forty-five minutes staring at the exquisite face of a sleeping baby, carved in a perfect piece of white marble. And looking down at the flawless marble, Kate had made the second major realization of her trip.

She was a tourist.

It had happened without her even noticing. One day she was a girl out to find her dream, and the next . . . she was just another American with a guidebook and a bad French accent.

She had called Harper immediately from a pay phone on the busy street outside the museum, expecting sympathy. She hadn't gotten any.

"So," Harper had responded crisply, "what you're telling me is that your dream is to backpack around Europe?"

"That's not what I'm saying." She had called to express her *dissatisfaction* with that turn of events, not to defend it.

"I mean," Harper had continued, "you do intend to leave Paris at some point, I assume."

Well, now Harper was just being cantankerous, Kate had decided.

"I *have* been learning a lot about myself," Kate pointed out, growing increasingly defensive.

For example, Kate had learned that she was an expert map reader. And that she was perfectly capable of spending significant amounts of time alone. Of course she would have preferred to have her friends there with her. At the Louvre, she had imagined Becca getting teary-eyed — and then mortally embarrassed — looking at the Mona Lisa. Climbing the hill to Sacre Coeur, she had imagined Sophie's diatribe at having to climb all those stairs just to see an old church. Strolling along the Seine would have been a lot more romantic if Jared had been there to hold her hand.

But if she had to do these things by herself, she could. She knew that now. And it had been okay.

More than okay, really. Even if it had gotten a little . . . well, less than challenging.

103

But that was about to be rectified. Because this morning, on her way out for the day, the desk clerk at the youth hostel had called her name, then handed her an express letter from Harper.

Kate had immediately recognized the left-slanting scrawl, and known she was in trouble.

She'd known exactly what Harper was going to say: now that she'd gotten over her initial Parisian freakout, now that she was comfortable being on her own, it was time to push herself. If she was going to really figure out what she wanted to do with her life, if she was going to discover her dream . . . she'd better get on with it. No more stalling.

But Harper hadn't just left it at that. She had also enclosed a list, compiled with help from Becca and Sophie — and, interestingly, Habiba. It was a one-hundred-item To Do List — and not your typical "wash the car" kind of thing. Her friends and Habiba had come up with one hundred things for Kate to do in the coming months. Next to each item, Harper had written the initials of the person whose challenge Kate was to complete. SB was written next to entries like "read *Vogue* — in French" and BW was beside "find Elvis." Habiba, for some reason, wanted her to "touch the Berlin Wall."

Kate looked over the list as she sipped her *citron presse*. Then she picked up her guidebook and slowly flipped through its frayed pages. For two weeks, the book had been her security blanket, her crutch. It had given her structure, and a sense of accomplishment each night when she checked off the things she had done and seen.

But no more. Because the first thing on the list, with everyone's initials next to it, was "Toss the guidebook, babe."

From now on, Kate was on her own.

"Is she looking?" Judd asked Harper, nodding his head in the direction of a petite brunette wearing a plastic coconut bra and grass skirt.

"No." Harper took another sip of her lukewarm Bud Light, wondering how long she had to stand here among Hawaiian shirt–clad frat boys before it was polite to leave.

Treatise in Blue. The Gift Giver's Almanac. Unfettered. It was becoming clear that the annual UC Boulder Fiji Island Party was not the ideal place for Harper to come up with a decent book title. Who knew fake palm fronds and sand-filled blow-up baby pools would be so creatively thwarting?

But coming up with a string of bad titles made Harper think of a good one. *Middlemarch.* She'd put the book as a must-read on Kate's list, and she wondered if her friend had gotten the express envelope yet. . . .

"Is she looking now?" Judd poked Harper in the arm, sending a splash of the aforementioned lukewarm beer to spill down her sweatshirt sleeve. Nice.

Harper flicked her eyes toward the brunette. "She's not looking. But the *way* she's not looking is significant. Like she hopes you *notice* she's not looking."

Sophie should be here, Harper thought. If she stared hard enough at one of the baby pools, she could practically *see* Sophie, laughing her head off as she led all the shit-faced guys in a *South Pacific* sing-along.

"I should go over there." Judd ran his fingers through his as-usual completely untamable hair. "I mean, I should. Right?"

Harper regarded Judd. He wasn't unattractive. Some girls probably liked the massive amounts of black curls that covered his head. And his brown eyes were warm and friendly, sort of like a beagle's. At five feet, eight inches, his height was underwhelming. Then again, he had nice hands, even if there were coffee grounds under his fingernails.

If it weren't for Judd's insistence on wearing Phish t-shirts from 1997, Harper might even think he was hot. She doubted, however, that the petite brunette in the coconut bra would be so generous in her assessment.

"Go. Conquer." Harper almost felt bad sending him off to Sorority Girl Hell. But he was really starting to bug her.

Judd took a couple gulps of his beer, apparently steeling himself for the uphill battle with the owner of the coconut bra. Then his eyes locked onto Harper.

"You look stressed," he announced. "You should go home." Judd bee-lined toward the object of his lust before she had a chance to tell him she'd been ready to go since the moment they arrived.

Once he was gone, Harper allowed herself to imagine that she *had* gotten in to NYU. She'd be there now, probably at a party a lot like this one (minus the cheesy island theme). Instead of feeling completely out of place surrounded by college freshmen, she'd actually *be* one.

And she wouldn't be wearing a stretched-out gray hoodie sweatshirt and jeans she hadn't washed for two weeks. She'd be sporting a tight black mini-skirt, her favorite black tank top, and a pair of super-cool black-on-black Pumas. The guys — none of whom would be having chugging contests — would appreciate her sophisticated, urbane style.

Let it go, Harper ordered herself. She had to look at the silver lining. If she were at NYU, she wouldn't have been able to relive two hundred or so times the moment of Mr. Finelli staring at her through the café window.

Not that living in that particular fantasy world was a good thing. But it did help her *not* obsess about all the pages she wasn't writing because she still didn't have that damn title.

Harper picked up the bulky red backpack she carried everywhere she went. If she left now, and turned on her laptop the minute she got home, she could get in three hours of solid writing time before she collapsed. . . .

"I know a good place for that body." The playful voice came from somewhere behind her right shoulder. "Let me take you there."

Harper spun around, expecting to find another Hawaiian shirt–

106

wearing frat boy ogling what there was of her breasts. But this guy's style tended more toward trendy than tropical. He was wearing a gray t-shirt bearing the words J.D.'s HARDWARE, and had thick black glasses a lot like hers. She noticed he had some kind of gel in his hair. But not so much that she couldn't look past it.

The guy pointed at her backpack. "I'm assuming you *do* have a body in there? Or at least parts of one?"

Harper smiled. "It's a laptop. But if I ever need to dispose of evidence, I'll call you."

"I'm Owen." He stuck out his hand. "And I have to warn you, I charge for my services. Burying bodies doesn't come cheap."

Harper realized that Owen reminded her of someone. Holy shit, he was the spitting image of Dexter, the imaginary comic book–loving boyfriend at NYU who broke her heart and caused her to spend a semester eating Pringles in bed.

"Harper Waddle." She shook his hand, noting the calluses. Definitely an acoustic guitar player. "I despise comic books."

"What else does Harper Waddle despise?" He leaned in a little closer, and Harper couldn't help noticing that despite his lean frame, Owen was packing some pretty spectacular biceps.

"Grass skirts . . . red peppers . . . girls who shave off their eyebrows and draw in new ones . . ." Harper paused to take a breath. "Lapsed gym memberships . . . Macs . . . Tom Clancy . . ."

"Is this gonna take a while?" Owen interrupted. "I might need another beer and some microwave popcorn."

"You asked." She was flirting. Engaging in actual flirtation that might lead to an actual date.

Harper hadn't partaken in this kind of behavior since the rejection letter. Having her future blow up in her face had definitely screwed with her sexy quotient.

"Let me guess. English major? Emphasis on creative writing?" Owen grinned. "My ex-girlfriend was a poet. I recognize the type."

This was good. This was healthy. Flirting with Owen was far superior to daydreaming about Mr. Finelli and their supposed moment.

Harper smiled back. "Yes, I'm a writer. No, I'm not an English major." She shrugged. "I'm not going to school right now. I came to the party with a friend from high school."

"So . . . you're from Boulder?"

"Born and raised. I still live in my parents' basement a couple miles from here."

"That's cool," Owen responded, only his tone suggested he thought it was anything *but* cool.

"Why waste my time taking Rocks for Jocks when I could be following my dream, right?" Harper noticed that Owen was staring at some vague spot over her head, and her defenses went up. "I'm writing a novel. It's going to kick ass."

He nodded. "Anyway . . . I really do need that beer."

That's when Harper realized that guys like Owen-slash-Dexter didn't want to date quirky local girls who lived in their parents' basements and trolled fraternity parties for business major boyfriends. They wanted to make out in dorm rooms and hold hands on the way to the cafeteria.

Watching Owen walk out of her life as quickly as he walked in, Harper was suddenly overwhelmed with the need to make an impression. She didn't want to be forgotten, even if it was for all the wrong reasons.

"I lied to my three best friends!" Harper shouted after him. "I'm a raging, psychotic bitch!"

He acknowledged her crazy rant with a tiny nod, but didn't bother to turn around. She didn't care. It felt good to be honest.

And now that she'd cleared her conscience, Harper was free to go back to fantasizing about Mr. Finelli and thinking of a title for her book. She was through engaging in the real world.

The real world sucked.

Kate was lost. And not a pleasant, meandering kind of lost. This particular lost was disorienting, verging on panicky. It had occurred to her too late that although she excelled at map reading, without the map in the guidebook her innate sense of direction was abysmal. North, south, east, and west were one and the same. If someone had told her the way back to her hostel was up, at this point she would have just nodded and tried to jump.

So when she spotted a relatively clean-looking bar with a pay phone sign on a back street somewhere in the Latin Quarter (she thought), it seemed like a good opportunity to accomplish two very important goals.

One. Call Harper and tell her how much her list completely sucked.

Two. Call a taxi. Enough was enough.

But first, she decided, as she made her way through the smoky bar, she would take advantage of France's drinking laws and order a big glass of anti-oxidizing red wine. It was the healthy thing to do.

"You are American?" a guy beside her asked as Kate took her first sip of Merlot. His accent was neither French nor American. She glanced at him coldly over the rim of her glass. Was that the best pick-up line he could come up with?

He was tall and gangly, with a square face and a long, sharp nose. His eyes were wide-set, and dark. Kate stifled a grin.

Talk to the ugly guy, the list had said.

Might as well get it over with.

Two hours later, Kate was halfway through her life story and Magnus (Ugly Guy's name) was listening intently. Kate had never told her life story before, and she was chagrined to find out how staggeringly boring it was. Apparently, her whole existence up to this point consisted of hanging with her friends, going on dates with Jared, and studying. Magnus had been intrigued to hear she had a younger sister from Ethiopia, but the last thing Kate had wanted to dwell on was her failure to connect to Habiba. So she'd changed the subject and given him a brief rundown of her community service activities — though she'd quickly realized that talking about getting homeless people's dogs neutered and vaccinated didn't exactly make her sound like Ms. Exciting.

And for some reason, she really wanted Magnus to think she was one of those girls who took chances, who wasn't afraid.

"So now, you are trying to change your life, jump off a . . . big rock," Magnus made a jumping gesture with his hands.

"Cliff," Kate corrected. Then hated herself. "Or rock. Right. I'm trying to shake things up a little."

"You should come to my friend Chantal's," Magnus offered. He was looking at her in a way that would have made her uncomfortable, except she found herself wanting him to look at her that way.

"She's having a party," he continued. "Dinner. I'm late, but she doesn't care. She likes new people."

"Oh," Kate said. "Your girlfriend?"

Magnus laughed. "Chantal is . . . how do you say, she like girls?"

"Oh." Kate admitted she felt the tiniest bit of relief to hear Magnus didn't have a girlfriend. Or, at least, if he did she wasn't a lesbian named Chantal.

"She wouldn't want you to just show up with someone," Kate continued, hoping he would disagree, and he did.

"Nah, she'll like you," he said. "Just like I do."

Kate tried not to smile. She really gave it a valiant effort. She even tried to come up with some reason why she shouldn't go to a strange Parisian apartment with a random Swedish guy she'd just met, who until moments ago she'd thought was ugly (looking at him again, she could see that he was just interesting-looking, but was in no way ugly).

But, for whatever reason, she felt safe with Magnus.

Which was a good thing, because she absolutely did not feel safe with Chantal. Chantal was one of the littlest people Kate had ever seen who wasn't actually a little person, and though she was barely five feet, and dainty in build, she was overpoweringly dynamic. Her white-blond hair was short and choppy, and bare feet peeked from beneath the fringe at the bottom of her long, narrow black skirt. A gray cashmere shawl was wrapped haphazardly — and yet impeccably — around her shoulders.

Chantal and Magnus had struck up a friendship when he audited a class she taught at the Sorbonne on Jean-Paul Sartre and Simone de Beauvoir, and a framed photograph of the literary duo hung from the wall of the entry foyer. As Chantal dramatically chided Magnus for his late arrival, Kate surveyed the apartment. It was nearly midnight, she realized, and all of the other guests had gone home. Several empty wineglasses dotted the contemporary coffee table that sat in front of a fragile, antique sofa, loaded with crumpled throw pillows. Chantal's whole apartment seemed to be a study in contrasts. Much of the furniture — and there was a *lot* of it, crammed into every nook and cranny — was from two centuries ago. Several pieces, however — like the dining room table, which sat under what appeared to be the building's original paned windows — looked like they had just come straight from IKEA. Somehow, it all worked. Perhaps because the apartment had a single unifying theme: books. They were everywhere. In stacks, on shelves, under lamps, several propped open, others with little sheets of paper sticking from the edges of the closed pages.

Chantal, it seemed, took her job quite seriously. Or, like many of the academics in Kate's experience, she had chosen her career be-cause the subject itself fascinated her. That was the thing about academics — and Kate had quite a bit of experience with professo-rial types. They could never seem to get enough of their particular area of expertise. She'd sat through hundreds of dinner parties where the discussion revolved around feminist film theory, or post-modern political thought. She never saw her parents happier than when they were engaged in a lively academic discussion about op-posing theories of world history. Kate, however, usually found such discussions more tedious than golf.

But when Chantal spoke about Sartre and Simone de Beauvoir, she was talking about two people who were ruled by their passions — passionate love, passionate politics, passionate work. And all that was fine, fascinating even, until Chantal turned the spotlight on Kate.

"You, Katherine, what brings you passion?" she asked, her pierc-ing blue eyes locking on Kate's.

Kate froze. For the first time in her life, she couldn't even babble something she knew was bullshit but sounded good enough to ap-pease. Magnus was kind enough to jump in.

"Kate is now on a journey to find her passion," he said.

He filled in Chantal about Kate's friends, and her search for her dream — all the things she had told him at the bar. Only, coming from Magnus, it sounded really brave and cool. Even important. It wasn't just some impulsive choice she had made and was then forced to live up to. It was a life-altering Quest, and she was a trail-blazing modern goddess, out to discover the most important thing of all: herself. Jared, of course, had seen nothing of the sort. But Magnus got it. He got *her*. Which was weird, considering they'd just met.

Even weirder, Kate had the odd sense that she got him, too.

She got that he enjoyed everything he did, that she could trust him, that he didn't like to be told what to do, but that he would do anything he could for anyone without needing to be asked. She got that he had a close family, and that he had been hurt by someone, and that maybe he was running away a little bit. And she got that he was smart, and funny. Best of all, she got that he seemed into her. And not just the surface of her.

Magnus had taken Kate's hand on the walk to Chantal's, and though she had felt a thread of lava make its way through her body at his touch, she had also felt perfectly comfortable. It hadn't felt too soon, it had just felt like how things were supposed to be.

And she didn't even know his last name.

"Show me this list," Chantal demanded when Magnus got to the part about how he and Kate had met. (Kate hadn't told him he was the Ugly Guy — she'd said he was number 67, "Tell a stranger your story.")

Kate took the list from her backpack and handed it to Chantal, who scanned it critically. Then she raised her eyebrows, and blew an approving puff of smoke. It really was true, Kate thought, that all Parisians smoke.

"Your friends are like your guides," Chantal mused. "From far away, they show you what you must do."

Kate nodded. That was the idea.

"But they also don't," Chantal continued. "Some of these things, they are just . . . for fun. But the others, they are . . . *from the soul of you*. They must come from within. 'Take the water,' *par example*. What does this mean?"

"I . . . don't know," Kate answered, suddenly realizing that the list was far more challenging than she had given it credit for.

"These are the things that will define you. They will tell you who you really are."

Kate turned to look at Magnus. He had one arm thrown casually across the back of the sofa behind her. His fingers, resting against the curve of her neck, sent a steady trickle of electricity down her back. His eyes, which she had earlier thought to be too wide-set, were totally focused on her. They were warm, unguarded. They made her want to forget everything else.

So when Chantal announced she was tired and casually offered them her guest room for the night, Kate ignored her pounding heart, met Magnus's questioning gaze, and nodded. She wasn't ready for the night to be over. She wasn't ready to lose the feeling she had when she looked at him — as if, maybe, he held the key to who she really was.

More than held the key. As if he already knew.

Ten minutes later, before the guest room door was even closed behind them, Kate was in his arms.

"This is crazy, how I feel," he said quietly. He ran a hand through the length of her hair, sending a shiver all the way down Kate's back.

For a long moment, they simply looked at each other. And then he kissed her, and the frenzy began. Kate couldn't get close enough to him. She couldn't get his shirt off fast enough, or touch enough of his smooth, tanned skin. As Magnus gripped the back of her neck, Kate realized vaguely that she had never been kissed properly before.

"You haven't told me I'm beautiful," she whispered, as they landed, entwined, on Chantal's lumpy guest bed. Every guy she'd ever kissed — not that there had been *that* many, but still — had told her she was beautiful. Kate hated it. It made her feel like she was a mannequin, or a trophy. Jared told her she was beautiful all the time.

"Why would I say this?" Magnus grinned, settling on top of her. He ran his hand through her hair, and kissed her temple gently.

Kate felt her breath grow shallow as she explored the lean muscles of his shoulders. Her black t-shirt was crumpled on the floor across the room. She hadn't even noticed it coming off — and now that she was lying beneath him in a pink bra and khaki shorts, she didn't feel shy.

Suddenly, Kate wanted to tell him everything. How she was a sucky sister, how she wasn't sure she was ever going to find her dream, how jealous she was of Becca for being at college, and of Harper and Sophie for having dreams in the first place. . . .

Then Magnus kissed her again, and Kate — for once in her life — stopped thinking.

But when she woke up the next morning with her head against Magnus's chest, cradled in his arms with her leg sandwiched warmly between his, she slid away from him quietly as he slept. And she left him behind.

Because she knew.

If she stayed with him, she'd be in love by the end of the week. She was practically in love with him after one night. And, just like she hadn't dropped her whole life to be a tourist, she hadn't dropped her whole life just to come to Paris and fall in love. Even with the most amazing guy she had ever met.

If Magnus opened his brown eyes she knew she would throw the list in the trash and spend the next year just being with him. And at the end of that year, she would go to Harvard without ever finding out what "take the water" meant. If she did that, her friends would kill her. And she would never forgive herself.

She wrote a note, telling Magnus she was sorry and giving him her address in Boulder. Maybe he wouldn't hate her, she thought as she set the note on the scuffed oak desk beside the bed, and he would somehow track her down someday. Kate closed her eyes and said the first prayer she'd uttered in the five years since her parents had "strongly encouraged" her to get confirmed in the Catholic church.

Please God. Please don't let this be over. Please let him find me again.

Then she slipped on her clothes, took one long last look at Magnus, and slipped out the door.

She could now cross two things off her list. "Talk to the ugly guy." And "Break someone's heart." Unfortunately, she thought as the door closed behind her, the ugly guy was beautiful, and she had broken her own heart as well.

Spider Solitaire   ▭ ✕

🔍 Search   object of the game

How to Play Spider Solitaire

The object of Spider Solitaire is to remove all of the cards from the ten stacks at the top of the screen in the fewest number of moves.

To play: Move cards from one column to another and until you line up a suit of cards in order from king to ace. Once a complete suit is lined up, those cards will be removed.

When all the cards are removed, you have won the game. Which means you have successfully procrastinated long enough, and must now go back to your writing.

SEVEN

I hate lawyers," Gifford Meyer announced, slamming his Treo down on the table at Mojito, the hip outdoor restaurant at the even hipper W Hotel in West Hollywood. "Never get involved with lawyers."

"Got it," Sophie responded calmly. "No lawyers." Pointing out that Gifford himself was one of the hottest entertainment lawyers in Los Angeles didn't seem like a good idea.

Instead, Sophie smiled politely and hid her hand under the tiny table. She didn't want Gifford, in his four-thousand-dollar suit and Gucci loafers, to see that she'd scraped off half of her perfectly applied nail polish in the twenty-five minutes she'd spent waiting for him to arrive. Not after Genevieve had been nice enough to set up this informational meeting.

As Gifford picked up his phone to make another call, Sophie forced herself to take a deep, calming breath. This was stupid. Sophie Bushell didn't get nervous. She made other people nervous. If she so chose. It was her gift, along with great looks and a natural ability to slip into other people's skin.

Sophie sighed. Four weeks ago, her biggest challenge had been dealing with gingham curtains and a roommate who cataloged the pros and cons of drilling for oil in Alaska for fun. Four weeks ago, she had been the most beautiful, talented, confident girl in her small pond.

But this wasn't four weeks ago. This was now. Los Angeles was an ocean, and she was barely the size of a guppy.

"I brought those pictures," Sophie ventured once Gifford again slammed his Treo on the table. "My friend Kate took them before I left Boulder."

She pulled prints of the dozen digital photos Kate had taken — all of Sophie in different outfits, striking different poses — out of her really-needed-to-be-replaced Gap tote and placed them in front of him. Gifford eyeballed the photos for about point-oh-one-seconds, then looked up and gestured for the mongo-breasted waitress who'd been hovering nearby since he sat down.

"Cobb salad. Iced tea. Same for her," he told the waitress, then turned back to Sophie. "You're a pretty girl."

Well. *Yeah*. "Thank you."

"But these pictures are a joke." Gifford pushed the prints across the table. "You look like a homecoming queen."

"I *was* the homecoming queen," Sophie informed him. "And the prom queen." Not that she was bragging. Okay, maybe a little.

"Great. Good. Nobody in the Business gives a shit about that." Gifford's phone began to vibrate, but for once, he ignored it. "You need a decent head shot, and you need a plan." He paused as Mongo Breasts set down their iced teas. "What's your plan?"

Sophie scratched at the nail polish on her left pinky finger. It wasn't that she didn't *want* to have a plan. She did. But dreaming about becoming a famous actress and actually *becoming* one were two very different things. The truth was, she didn't have a clue.

"I guess I don't exactly have one," she admitted finally.

So much for being a guppy. She was the *embryo* of a guppy, if guppies had embryos. Thank goodness she was wearing her favorite pink-and-red-striped BCBG sundress. It was the only thing keeping her from melting into a puddle of humiliation right here at the table.

Gifford pulled a business card from the inside pocket of his suit jacket and handed it to her. "See Armando. He's the best photographer in the business."

Sophie stared at the expensive-looking, cream-colored card. Armando (no last name) probably charged thousands of dollars for one session. Unless she planned to track down Heidi Fleiss for prostitution tips, there was no way she could pay this guy. She was doomed.

"By the way, I got you a job," he mentioned casually. "You'll be a hostess here." He waved his hand around the restaurant. "I'll front you the money for the pictures until you can pay me back. Once you have the head shots, I'll talk to an agent about getting you into some auditions."

Gifford's phone vibrated again. He glanced at the caller ID and picked it up. "Hey, Larry. Why'd you screw me on that deal this morning?"

Sophie didn't know what to say or feel or think. She wasn't exactly sure she was breathing.

"Why are you helping me?" The question popped out before she had a chance to censor herself.

"You're my wife's friend's kid," Gifford explained as he pulled the Treo away from his ear. "And even though right now you're nothing, you might be the next big thing." He shrugged. "If that's the case, you'll hire me as your lawyer, and give me five percent of everything you make until you die." He stuck out his hand. "Agreed?"

"Agreed." Sophie shook his hand, trying to register exactly what had happened during the last ten minutes.

After a month in Los Angeles, she had the name of an awesome photographer, the money to pay him, and a powerful lawyer who seemed willing to help her. She even had a job. So why did she feel like she'd just been eaten by a shark?

Snow. From her dorm room bed, Becca could smell it before she even opened her eyes. She'd left the window open a crack the night before — much to Isabelle's irritation — and the air in the room was sharp, light, slightly atmospheric, as if a part of the sky had descended for a brief sojourn. Grinning, Becca made the bed with a quick toss and fluff of her red flowered comforter. Then she grabbed her toiletries caddy from the floor of her closet, slid Isabelle's iPod into the Bose speaker dock on top of her dresser, twirled the selector to Coldplay, pumped up the volume, and headed for the shower down the hall. Isabelle groaned grumpily. But there was no way Becca was letting her sleep in. Not today.

Because, today, they were going skiing.

After more than a month of intense (though unofficial) preseason training, finally she would show Coach Maddix she was worth her salt. She wasn't sure exactly what that meant, but Maddix seemed to think salt was a very precise measure indeed. After a sprint around the track, he would pat someone on the back and say, "Parker's worth his salt today." Or, the inverse, "No salt there, Parker." Having salt was the highest compliment one could receive. And having no salt was a worse offense than bad form, lack of effort, or showing up hungover.

Not that Becca had ever shown up hungover. Although, if she had, it wouldn't have mattered. As far as Maddix was concerned, Becca hadn't even joined the ranks of the salted and unsalted. She was the anti-salt.

Well, today she was going to show him how much salt she had, and if he didn't see it. . . .

Then screw him.

Unfortunately, the attitude she had managed to cultivate from the coziness of her bed in no way resembled how she actually felt two hours later, when she was on top of the mountain. The snow was perfect — powder, with ice beneath. Becca's breath haloed around her as she took her position. The upperclassmen had completed their runs first, then the sophomores, and now it was the newbies' turn. Isabelle was the first one down the mountain, coming in just over her all-time record. Then Taymar, then a fellow Coloradan named Scott. Now it was Becca's turn.

She adjusted her gloves, firmed her grip on her poles . . . and took off.

This mountain was hers. In the first fifty yards, she shook off the rustiness of the off-season. Then it was all instinct. And the closest thing to love that Becca had ever felt. She trusted herself here. She knew how her body was supposed to work, how the skis were supposed to feel, how to make the snow bend to her will. And there was something new inside as well. She had something to prove, which gave her a singular focus. Coach Maddix was at the bottom of this hill. And he wasn't going to ignore her anymore.

As Becca reached the bottom of the run, she knew she'd beat her best time. She didn't even need to look at the clock.

"Yeah, Bec!" she heard Isabelle scream, from where the rest of the team was cheering, several yards away.

"That was nasty!" Taymar shouted.

But her friends' words barely registered as Becca walked up to Coach Maddix.

He glanced up from his clipboard.

"Not bad," he commented.

Not bad?

"Oh, come on!" The words came out before she could stop them. Coach Maddix raised his right eyebrow. His ice blue eyes locked with hers.

In those three simple words, Becca's voice revealed all the

123

frustration she had been feeling the last two months. All the unfairness she felt she'd been subject to at his hands. And the absolute certainty that she deserved better.

Coach Maddix looked at her for a long moment. Then he gave the tiniest little glimmer of a smile.

"May have some salt there after all."

Becca's heart pounded in her chest.

"Thank you, sir," she said.

And then she turned and walked away. Only this time, when she walked away from Maddix, she was walking toward her new friends. As they slapped her on the back and congratulated her on her great first run, Becca thought of Harper, Kate, and Sophie.

Tonight she would call them all to share her victory. Except . . .

She tried to push the niggling doubts to the back of her mind, but still they lingered.

Harper was writing her book and getting into some weird cerebral relationship with Mr. Finelli. Kate was God only knew where. And Sophie was living the high life in LA. They all had their grand plans, while Becca was doing the same stuff she'd always done. Going to school, skiing. Maybe they would be bored with that.

Maybe, with all the time and distance between them, they wouldn't understand how important it was to be worth something as simple as salt.

Harper clicked on a nine of diamonds and dragged it to a ten of spades. She only needed to move three more cards to have a chance to win the ninety-sixth straight game of Spider Solitaire she'd played since she sat down at her computer one hundred and eighty-two minutes ago.

Self-loathing was a feeling familiar to Harper. She'd experienced it for the first time in Toys "Я" Us, when she'd thrown a temper tantrum until her mom finally caved and bought her the high chair she wanted for her favorite doll, Pumpkin. Then there was the time Eddy Fierro had been so drunk he'd thrown up on her during her first-ever makeout session at Elise Devon's fifteenth birthday party. And when her first article came out in the high school newspaper, and she realized she'd misspelled the word "curriculum."

But not since she had received her rejection letter from NYU had Harper spiraled so deep into a pit of self-hatred that she actually had to avoid going into the bathroom to pee because she was scared of looking at herself in the mirror.

It was almost November. And the most creative thing she had done since proclaiming her dream of being a "real" writer was name the new green tea smoothie at the Rainy Day Books Café. And, really, who *couldn't* have dubbed the drink the Green-Eyed Monster?

Harper took a deep breath. She shouldn't hate herself. She should love herself. That's what Oprah and Dr. Phil and anyone else with a daytime talk show always said.

Okay, so she didn't have a title for her book yet. Big whoop. She *had* started. That was significant. Writing twelve pages of *anything* was way more creative than naming a beverage. So what if the chapter she'd completed was rambling, nonsensical, and clichéd? She should be proud.

Feeling almost hopeful, Harper forced herself to close her game of solitaire and open the document she'd starkly labeled "Novel."

Melinda so slowly slid open the cherry drawer of her mother's tea-stained bureau and held her breath one, two, three seconds as she anticipated the feline steps of her youngest cousin on the stairs outside the rarefied room. Four, five, six. None came, which meant that for now solitude belonged to Melinda. For that, and for the not yet dried corsage that lay in her own room, she was thankful to whoever had a watchful eye on her life thus far. . . .

Harper had just started to gag on the drivel that was supposed to be her book when she became vaguely aware of voices coming from upstairs.

Correction. Voice. It belonged to her dad, and he sounded . . . well, jovial. Harper leaned in so that her chair was approximately four inches closer to the door at the top of the basement stairs.

"Margo, I'm so happy," Mr. Waddle said, presumably to someone named Margo he was talking to on the phone. "I can't even tell you."

There was a long pause, and then he laughed. Or giggled. It was hard to tell the difference with a flight of stairs and a plywood door between them.

"Just try to stop me," he continued. "I'll chase you down to the ends of the earth."

Harper realized she was no longer sitting. She'd apparently gotten out of her chair and climbed halfway up the steps. Not that she was eavesdropping. She simply needed a little movement to get the artistic juices flowing.

"I should go," Mr. Waddle said finally. "Cindy's waiting for me upstairs."

Harper heard her dad hang up, and then his footsteps as he climbed toward the bedroom he shared with her mom, the aforementioned waiting Cindy. It wasn't possible. It couldn't be.

There was no way that Harper's stable, loving, boring dad had been talking to a woman besides her mother like she was his girlfriend. She'd misheard the laugh/giggle. Maybe Margo was a stand-up comic. Or maybe her dad had needed to cough, and it came out sounding more like a guffaw.

Joe Waddle was the ultimate family man. Harper couldn't imagine him telling her mom he was at work, while he was really off trysting with some floozy. He would never lie. But if that was the case, why did she feel like she'd been punched in the stomach?

Harper descended the stairs and picked up her cell phone from its place of honor on the milk crate nightstand. She might as well see if Judd wanted to break into the café and gorge on Green-Eyed Monsters.

There was no way she was going to write the next Great American Novel tonight.

From: beccawinsberg@middlebury.edu
To: waddlewords@aol.com
Subject: me rambling

Harper Lee--

It snowed early in New England this year! Nineteen whole beautiful inches!
That's got to be a good sign right? Not sure what it's a good sign about,
exactly, but still. Good sign. Maybe it means your book is going to win a
Nobel Prize. Or whatever books win. Pulitzers?

That dumb jock guy (who will hereafter be known as semi-smart jock)
keeps trying to talk to me about English Romantic Poetry. What's up with
that? I know you think I snap-misjudged him or something, but he was such
a jerk, and I wasn't being overly sensitive. Or maybe I was. Whatever.

Okay, I'm stopping before I start to rant.

Chemistry test tomorrow. Consider that your official reminder that certain
things about college suck.

Love ya, babe.
B.

Delete   Reply   Reply to All   Forward   Save   Print

EIGHT

"You're lying," Sophie accused Harper thirty-five minutes into their phone conversation. "I don't believe you've written anything in the last week."

Harper rolled over in bed and glanced at her desk, where her laptop was currently draped with a Harry Potter pillowcase. She'd covered her computer in an insomnia-induced fog around four o'clock in the morning, convinced its mocking visage was the reason for her tossing and turning.

"I'm on the third draft of my Pulitzer Prize acceptance speech," she informed Sophie. "Does that count?"

Sophie sighed dramatically, which made Harper feel a pang of the dreaded loneliness. She wished her friends were *here,* to sigh dramatically in person.

"Writing is your Dream. So quit feeling like shit about yourself and *do it.*"

"I'm trying," Harper moaned. "It's not like I can turn on a switch." She didn't think it prudent to add that she'd deleted the first twelve pages of her manuscript last week and not written a word since.

For a few moments, Sophie didn't say anything. Harper could picture her on the other end of the line, twirling one of her curls around her finger and thinking hard.

"Something's going on with you, and whatever it is, it's keeping you from being able to write. I can feel it."

"You're wrong," Harper insisted. "Nothing's going on."

"Harp, this is *me,*" Sophie reminded her quietly. "You know you can tell me anything."

For one dizzying second, Harper considered doing just that. She'd tell Sophie everything, starting with the rejection letter from NYU. *And then what?* Sophie would call Kate and Becca and tell them Harper had screwed with all of their lives because of her ego. Everyone would hate her, and she'd still be stuck living in a basement, working at the Rainy Day Books Café.

"What?" Sophie demanded, when she didn't say anything. *"What?"*

"I — I think my dad's having an affair," Harper blurted out. She didn't realize how much her suspicion had been bothering her until now.

"Oh God," Sophie exclaimed. "You poor thing. No wonder you're a mess."

Sophie's always dramatic, Harper thought when she finally clicked off her cell phone after a half hour analysis of every word Harper had heard from her dad's end of the phone call. *Of course she thinks I'm right.* But still . . . the longer she had talked to Sophie, the more convinced she'd become.

So . . . what? Harper was hardly going to march up to her father and demand to know the details of his sex life (what a horrifying thought). She'd keep doing what she was doing. Waiting for more information.

But in the meantime, it was noon, and she had until her shift at the café started at five PM to write. If Sophie could get fabulous new head shots, drive herself through LA traffic to auditions, *and* get invited to a hip Hollywood party by Sam the cute-but-cranky Pool Boy, the least Harper could do was de-sheet her computer. After all, she was the one who'd *started* this whole Dream thing. It was her duty to see it through.

Harper turned on her laptop and opened a fresh Word document. She centered her cursor and typed "Chapter One" at the top of the page. What she needed was a plot. The twelve pages she'd thrown out had been aimless stream-of-consciousness that was going nowhere. If she could write just one new sentence, maybe a story would unfold in her imagination. Okay, probably not. But it was worth a try.

Write, she ordered herself. *Write.*

She was waiting for inspiration to strike when the basement door opened.

"Honey, are you busy down there?" Mrs. Waddle called down the stairs. "I need a favor."

Harper glanced back at the two whole words on her screen and thought about her conversation with Sophie.

"No," she called back. "I'm not busy."

Her long-suffering mom needed her. It was definitely time for a break.

Harper had never wanted to be one of those nostalgia hounds who haunted the corridors of their former high school, reliving the glory days of Friday night football games and Latin Club bake sales. But here she was. Haunting.

Not by choice, she reminded herself. She was darkening the linoleum-lined hallways of Fairview High with a purpose. Amy had forgotten to bring her American History essay to school, and the teacher, Ms. Mazarra, was notoriously unforgiving about late assignments.

"Harper, hey!" A big-nosed guy with too-long hair and worn Birkenstocks waved at her from the vending machine.

"Hey . . . !" she called back, hoping it wasn't obvious she couldn't remember his name. By the time she reached senior year, learning the names of underclassmen had seemed like a waste of time.

It was weird to look around and know that she wasn't going to see Kate, Becca, or Sophie coming around one of the corners. Sure, people were smiling and saying hi. But she had no doubt that as soon as she was out of earshot, there were whispers about Harper Waddle, the girl who — gasp — didn't go to college.

Bucking middle-class tradition on such a major scale was not without scandal. Of course, if her fellow Dream Trainers had been here they'd be feeling the same way. There was some comfort in that.

Harper knew exactly where to find her sister. She'd be spending her lunch hour in the newspaper office, just like Harper had done for four years. But unlike Harper, Amy wasn't interested in writing. She just liked hanging out with her boyfriend, Taylor, who edited the sports section. Harper automatically followed the path to room 134. She could have found her way in her sleep — probably had.

"Special delivery," she announced to Amy when she walked into the familiar office. "Mom says next time she's going to make you take the F."

Amy hopped up from her perch on Taylor's lap. The girl was only a sophomore, but she acted like she literally owned Fairview High. Harper envied her sister's confidence, as well as her shiny dark hair and perfectly straight white teeth. It would be awesome to go for more than two minutes without getting caught up in crippling neurotic thoughts that required hours of analysis over a late night bowl of Shredded Wheat and salsa.

"Thanks, Harp." Amy took the history paper. "How's it feel to be back?"

Harper looked around the room. Her Papa Hemingway poster had been replaced with an electronic dartboard, but otherwise the place looked pretty much the same. Even the energy was familiar. Like she could have been gone five minutes instead of over four months.

"Great," she lied.

After leaving Amy, Harper intended to head straight back to the red vintage ten-speed bike she'd left in one of the visitor's spaces directly in front of the main entrance. But somewhere between the cafeteria and the library, she found herself veering toward the stairs that led to the English teachers' offices on the second floor.

It's habit, she told herself. She'd spent how many free periods in Mr. Finelli's office, discussing the theme of solitude in *Mrs. Dalloway* or whatever, while he graded papers? Plus, now that she saw him at the café nearly every day, they had an extremely intimate barista-customer relationship. One could even make the argument that it would be rude if she didn't at least poke her head in to say hello. That's what visitors did. They visited.

And her desire to make contact had nothing to do with the fact that since he'd flashed her the thumbs up from outside the café window, their conversations had been limited to give-me-a-scone-with-my-coffee. Nothing.

Harper knocked on the door to Mr. Finelli's office. For a millisecond, there was silence. Oh well. He wasn't there. She turned away from the door, so relieved she didn't even care that she'd changed into her cleavage-baring brown cashmere Max Studio sweater for nothing.

"Come in." His familiar voice made her heart do something funky.

Harper opened the door and did the head-poking-in thing. "Hey, Mr. Finelli."

He looked up from what appeared to be a stack of English essays. Ah, memories. Her last one had been on *Bastard Out of Carolina,* and Mr. Finelli had written "searing and incisive" in the margins.

"Harper!" He sounded genuinely pleased to see her, and if she wasn't so positive he could never, ever lust after her, she would have thought his eyes flicked over the aforementioned cleavage.

"I was just bringing Amy a paper . . ." Harper trailed off as she noticed that Mr. Finelli's face was adorably scruffy, like maybe he'd woken up late and hadn't had time to shave.

"Come on in." He stood up and swept a stack of newspapers off the chair reserved for students. "Save me from beach-book-musings hell."

Shit. Now that she was here, Harper had less than no idea what she was actually going to say. She wished she were home, in front of her computer. Or at the dentist. Or anywhere but here.

"How's it feel to be back?" he asked as she sat down.

He asked the question like he wanted to know the answer. The real answer. "Like I'm home, and like I never really belonged here." She shrugged. "Does that sound totally insane?"

He shook his head. "I felt the same way when I wandered around the University of Chicago last summer. I'd spent four years at the place, but suddenly it was like I was an intruder."

Phew. She wasn't a freak. That was something. Harper looked around his office. Was it possible she'd never noticed he didn't have a window before?

Mr. Finelli gave her a look. "What?"

"Did your office used to be bigger?" she asked, regretting the question as soon as it popped out.

He laughed. "That impressive, huh?"

"I didn't mean . . . never mind." Harper wracked her brain for something innocuous to say.

Sadly, something along the lines of a request to jump his bones was the only thing that came to mind. And that seemed inappropriate.

"How's the book going?" He was looking at her, *really* looking at her. The office suddenly didn't just feel small, it felt coffin-sized.

"It's going . . ." God, she hated that question. "Really, really badly."

He nodded. "Writer's block?"

"Major."

Mr. Finelli leaned back in his chair, his penetrating stare making her feel naked, body and soul. She found herself wishing his glasses didn't have that anti-reflective coating stuff. She'd rather be looking at the glare of the fluorescent light over their heads than straight into his eyes. "You know what I think you need?"

A corkscrew to the heart. A knitting needle to the eye. A clue. "What?"

He grinned. It wasn't fair or right that a man in the teaching profession should have such full, red, distracting lips. "A pep talk."

"I was thinking of something in the area of a bullet to the head," she responded. "But I guess a pep talk couldn't hurt."

He gave her a half-smile, an indication that she'd said something slightly funny but also completely ridiculous. "Call me later this week, and we'll get together, talk about your artistic angst." He indicated the stack of papers on his desk. "After I've had a chance to wade through the latest crop of not-so-searing-and-incisive essays."

Searing and incisive. Mr. Finelli obviously remembered writing that on her paper . . . What did that *mean*?

"Great," she managed to squeak out. "I'd love that."

Harper walked out of the office a different girl than she'd been when she entered. Mr. Finelli wanted to meet with her outside of school, outside of the café. They were going to have an adult conversation about writer's block and artistic integrity. They were going to *relate*.

It felt . . . and this was completely crazy in every way . . . almost like a date. Harper shook her head. Too many games of Spider Solitaire had rotted her brain. A date with Mr. Finelli . . . ? Never.

Still . . . she wished she hadn't used up her best sweater. Now she was going to have to spend the rest of the day shopping for something that was sexy and understated and, most importantly, cost less than fifteen dollars.

Art would have to wait. Harper had a pep talk to prepare for.

Becca stared into her French onion soup and tried to remember a time when she'd been more embarrassed. Maybe in seventh grade, when her mother had tried to make her dad feel like he was out of touch with his daughter's life by announcing — in front of Becca's whole class — that she'd had her period for over a year. Or, possibly, the Corvette Episode, when her father had been so furious that her mother wouldn't allow him to buy her a used car for her sixteenth birthday (which he'd only wanted to do to make her mother look bad) that he'd rented a ridiculously expensive bright red Corvette for a week and demanded Becca drive it to school.

Or there was always her personal favorite — the night last year when her mother had gotten drunk and announced to Becca, Harper, Sophie, and Kate that Becca's dad was the love of her life, and she'd still be married to him if Becca hadn't been born. Her father, it seemed, had never wanted kids, and the introduction of a baby into their relationship had been the beginning of the end. That knowledge had been less embarrassing than outright awful. And more than a little hurtful. Although the pain scale for this evening was quickly reaching the same agonizing heights.

"I'm sure your father would never cheat on your mother, dear," Becca's mom was saying, leaning close to Isabelle. She was on her third glass of wine.

Isabelle kept her face carefully expressionless as Becca's father leaned in from the other side and added, "I'm sure your mother would never drive him to it." He was on his third scotch.

Her stepmom, Melissa, tried to hide a smile as Becca's mom threw her napkin down and left the table. Her stepdad, Martin, maintained his usual blank mien, as Isabelle slowly turned to look at Becca.

"The croutons on this salad are exceptional," she commented brightly. "Very crunchy."

Oh God, Becca thought, *we aren't even on the main course yet.*

In the moments when she wasn't joining her parents in wishing she'd never been born, she deeply regretted the decision to ask Isabelle to join her for this family dinner. She'd been hesitant about subjecting Isabelle to her parents, but she'd needed a buffer, a neutral party, and Isabelle had agreed to act as her Switzerland. Unfortunately, Switzerland was no match for the war her parents were waging.

And they weren't even supposed to *be* here. Even before school had started, she'd discussed Parents' Weekend with them, and they'd both made excuses for why they couldn't come. Her dad and Melissa had planned a Caribbean cruise, and her mother and Martin had said they didn't want to leave Mia and Carter alone. Not having to deal with her parents until Christmas was like a dream come true, a prayer answered, a pot of gold at the end of a very long, screwed-up rainbow. Which meant of course that her parents were going to find that pot and piss in it.

Melissa had decided at the last minute that cruise-related stomach ailments were too big a risk to her carefully regulated diet, leaving the Dad-Side free for the weekend. And on the Mom-Side, the stepsiblings had both been shipped off to some kind of therapy camp for two weeks. Suddenly, her parents had been engaged in a game of passive-aggressive chicken, with Becca about to get crunched in the middle. She'd tried to make each side veer off the road, tried to convince one or the other that one of them could come for Parents' Weekend next year, but neither side would flinch.

So here she was, in her favorite Lucky Brand denim skirt, sitting at the nicest French restaurant in Middlebury, Vermont, having what easily qualified as the most miserable evening of her life. In front of Isabelle. Becca had warned her it might get ugly, but this was even worse than she had imagined.

Sighing, Becca brushed a sprinkle of bread crumbs from the linen tablecloth. It looked flammable. Maybe she could grab the candelabra from the heavy mahogany sideboard behind her and . . . No, that would be too dramatic. Drama was Sophie's department. Becca just sucked it up and kept her mouth shut. And waited for it to be over.

Only, it was never over. There was always some new way for her parents to show how much they hated each other.

Her mother proved that point as she returned to the table and slid into her upholstered seat.

"Becca, tell your father you know all about what he did to me," she suggested with a sickening smile.

The white-tuxedoed waiter, oblivious, arrived and started serving their entrées.

Becca stared at her sea bass. Of course she knew. She'd been hearing about it for years. That didn't mean she wanted to *talk* about it.

But Melissa did.

"Becca only knows what you've told her, and we all know the truth isn't exactly your strong suit." Then she reached across the table and put a chilly hand on Becca's arm. Becca wanted to throw up.

"Right, Jakey?" Melissa said, looking at him.

Her dad had the grace to look embarrassed.

"Bec," he began, "you know we love you."

Then he turned to her mom.

"But, Sandra, you're turning her into some kind of cipher for your crazy ideas. . . ."

Becca tuned out.

Why did they always do this? Why did they always act like she didn't exist, except as some tool to use to batter each other around? Like she had no feelings, like she was just supposed to sit there and take it, and be embarrassed in front of her friend, just because they all hated each other. Well, what about her? The whole idea of Parents' Weekend was to come and see what your kid's life was like now. Parents came because they missed their kids. But Becca hadn't even figured into her parents' reasons for coming. The whole point of the weekend, for her parents, was to win.

And the worst part, she admitted to herself with a sharp pang of shame, was that she had . . . well, sort of hoped, maybe, things would be better. She had allowed herself to think, just for a moment, that maybe, just maybe, it meant something that her parents had wanted to come see her. That maybe they did miss her. That maybe she was, after all, more important to them than their hatred for each other.

She should have known better. And after nearly two months of freedom from it all, Becca couldn't take it anymore. She had sucked up all she could, and now it was time to spew.

"Stop it!" She shoved her chair back and stood up.

She didn't realize until later that the whole restaurant must have been watching. To Becca, her parents were the only people in the room. All four of them were to blame. They had made her life a living hell for years, they had ignored her, treated her like she wasn't supposed to have feelings or opinions about what was going on in her own life, made her feel to blame for everyone else's problems, used her as a weapon against each other, then bandied her around like a pet or a piece of furniture.

"You hate each other!" she yelled. "We all get it! You've made your point."

She looked at her father.

"You're a cheater. You cheat and you lie and then you just expect everyone to love you. You don't even *try* to know anything real about me."

Then at her stepmom.

"You are a self-centered bitch. And I hate J.Crew."

Then at her stepdad.

"You have no fucking spine, and your kids are spoiled, self-centered little shits."

Then she looked at her mother.

"And you . . ." she said, her eyes welling with tears.

Her mother's face was bright red.

"If you want to hate me because you hate my dad, or because you think it was my fault he left you — yeah, you were pretty clear about that — go ahead. Because, trust me, I hate you, too."

Becca was halfway out the restaurant door when Isabelle caught up with her.

"Wow." Isabelle's eyes were wide. "You cursed like a pro. So . . . you okay?"

"I'm really sorry." Becca swiped a tear from her cheek with the back of her hand. She was *not* going to cry. She had finally told her parents how she felt. She should feel proud — even if she didn't, exactly.

"Don't apologize to me," Isabelle insisted. "In New York, people just get drunk and hide their feelings. That was refreshing."

Isabelle fell in step with Becca. Campus was only a fifteen-minute walk away. And when she got there . . .

Becca turned to Isabelle. The awful words she'd said to her parents were reverberating through her brain, fighting for space with the image of her mother's bright red cheeks, her father's open mouth, her stepmom's Botoxed lack of expression, and her stepdad's confused pucker. It was all more than Becca could take.

"Screw training," she said. "I need a drink."

There were at least three kegs on campus that she knew of. And one of them had her name written all over it.

Becca's head felt wobbly. Or maybe just her eyes. She considered it, and concluded that wobbliness was definitely happening in the upper part of her body. Exact details were unimportant.

The important thing was that she, Becca Winsberg, was now having the best night of her life. Parents be damned. So what if they never spoke to her again? The purple punch was fan-tastic, and she felt grrrrreat! Oh yeah.

Aside from the wobbliness. Which was nothing, when you really thought about it. And Stuart Pendergrass. What a big lunky dope, she thought, heading for the dance floor. Oh yeah, she knew he was watching her. Well, she'd give him a show, the big, stupid lunky . . . asshole. Yeah, he was an asshole. Even if he did look semi-cute in those Levi's and that Giant Robot t-shirt that hugged his muscular chest. Who did he think he was, watching her like that? Like she wasn't supposed to have fun. Like she wasn't supposed to let go once in a while.

She was just going to dance. When had she become such a great dancer? Damn, she was on fi-ya! Let it go, baby!

Becca closed her eyes and moved her hips to the music. She let her arms rise over her head. She imagined that she looked like Sophie, all confidence and sexy moves. Nothing else mattered but the music and her body —

Until her body slammed into another body. A big body. She opened her eyes.

Some guy named . . . something . . . whom she vaguely knew

from somewhere — she briefly tried to figure out where, but it was far too much effort — was leering down at her, his hand on her arm.

"Watch where you're going." He grinned. "You almost made me spill my beer."

Becca laughed. He was funny, this what's-his-name. She'd never known that before. And he was cute, too. Over his shoulder, she noticed, Stuart Pendergrass was watching her. Well, she'd give him something to look at, then.

"Let's dance," Becca heard herself saying as she took his beer and set/splashed it down on a nearby table.

And then she was dancing again, this time with cutie what's-his-name.

Maybe cutie what's-his-name was The One. She was supposed to fall in love this year, right? Well, she had to start somewhere. Might as well be with him. The world was a beautiful place, Becca thought as she threw her arms around his neck.

If this was what being drunk was all about, she should have explored this whole lush thing sooner.

I will not kill a pedestrian, Sophie told herself as she inched the silver 2001 BMW the Meyers' had "loaned" her onto the entrance ramp of the 101 freeway. Her hostess shift at Mojito had started fifteen minutes ago, and the way traffic was going, it looked like Sophie would barely make it in time for the lunch rush. So much for the The Dream. Today felt more like The Nightmare.

On the verge of a major pouting session, Sophie cranked up Aimee Mann on the deluxe car stereo and completed a mental rundown of her morning. . . .

6:00 AM: Dragged self out of antique sleigh bed and into steam shower.

6:30 AM: Began forty-five minutes of intense Paul Mitchell hair-styling.

7:15 AM: Slipped into black Donna Karan pants and white Theory button-down.

7:22 AM: Poured Seattle's Best medium roast coffee into Starbucks travel mug, ran to car.

Then she'd sped as fast as rush hour traffic (and the act of applying mascara while driving) would allow to Paco & Blackjack Productions in Burbank, where she'd joined eighteen other girls waiting for the privilege of auditioning for Maura the Hostess in a B movie about cheerleaders gone bad.

Forget how insulting it was to have to audition to play a part that she was already *living*. There was, at least, something to be said for method acting. Forget that she'd circled the studio for thirty minutes looking for a parking space. That was to be *expected*.

The tragedy was that after sitting in an uncomfortable chair for over two hours, during which time her butt had actually *melded* to the plastic seat, the casting director informed her that the producers had decided that for the integrity of the hostess character, the role needed to be filled by a dwarf.

Of course, any idiot knew that casting directors didn't appreciate surly young wannabes. Any idiot knew that ninety percent of all auditions were a bust, and that the important thing was to make a good impression on the people who might call her in for something else. Any idiot knew a lot of things.

But not Sophie. Oh no. She was a *particular* brand of idiot.

She told the casting director to screw herself, then slammed the door of Paco & Blackjack Productions so hard that a security guard had shown up to escort her off the studio lot. Oops.

By the time Sophie finally walked into Mojito, forty-two minutes late, she'd calmed down enough to realize that all she needed was an evening devoted entirely to decompressing. Tonight she'd chill out in the guesthouse, spill the details of her miserable day to one of her friends on the phone, and write affirmations about how awesome she was in her journal.

Except — damn — that party was tonight. The one she was going to with Sam, where there would most likely be famous, successful people who could discover her and give her the big break she needed. The one she'd spent all of last night trying on different outfits for.

"I'm not going," Sophie announced to Celeste, her thirty-something pink-haired manager, three hours later when the lunch rush finally died down.

"You're going." Celeste tended to manage her employees' lives as well as their jobs, which was usually a quality that Sophie found endearing. Today, she didn't.

"Becca sent me a home spa kit," she explained. "Why would I exchange meaningless banter with strangers when I could be lathering my face in oatmeal and avocado?"

Celeste expertly folded a napkin into the shape of a fan — a skill Sophie still hadn't mastered after a month at her hostess job. "Because exchanging meaningless banter with strangers is fun." She raised a perfectly plucked eyebrow. "It's also a crucial part of the LA equation."

Celeste's "LA equation" was a nebulous formula that included any and all "x" and "y" factors that might contribute to one's future success as an actor, writer, or director. Sophie sighed, resigned.

"I just want to *act*," she moaned. "Why won't anyone let me *act*?"

Celeste gave her a long look. "Tell you what. My boyfriend is an A.D. on *Bringing Down Jones*. I'll see if he'll hire you as an extra."

Sophie perked up. "Like, I'll actually get to walk in front of the camera?"

"Don't get excited," Celeste warned. "Being an extra consists mostly of sitting in a cold, damp warehouse, waiting for lunch."

Sophie didn't care. If Celeste's assistant director boyfriend came through, she was going to be in a movie. Suddenly, she felt like partying.

Introductions at a Party,

from *The Amy Vanderbilt Complete Book of Etiquette*

*I*f you are a guest who suddenly finds herself in the awkward position of standing alone with no one to talk to, it's easier to approach a number of people talking together than two people engrossed in conversation. Putting self-consciousness aside for the moment, go over to the group and when there's a pause in the conversation or someone acknowledges your presence speak up, "Hello [or Hi], I'm Sally White. I was Martha's roommate at Carlton College." Admittedly, it takes a certain amount of courage to break into a group, particularly when everyone knows everyone else, but it's a lot less painful than standing alone with no one to talk to. Also, by handling the situation yourself, you're not burdening your host or hostess with further introductions.

If, despite your best efforts, everyone ignores you because you don't even have an agent yet, proceed to the corner and call one of your best friends on your cell phone. They will most likely make you feel okay about being a party pariah.

NINE

Sophie was proud of her butt, and it looked particularly good tonight. As she and Sam made their way through the crowded party, she caught at least three guys — one of the three being Sam — eyeing her curves. Thank the Lord for tight jeans and strappy silver sandals.

"Pretty crazy, huh?" he asked as they walked into the kitchen, which was a sea of ultra-modern polished cement and stainless steel appliances.

The place looked like something out of a magazine. In fact, if Sophie wasn't mistaken, it *had* been in a magazine.

"I could get used to it," she responded casually. She hated being in awe of wealth — it made her feel like a total hick. Surprisingly, Sam appeared totally at home in the foreign environment. In casually ripped Diesel jeans and a plain black t-shirt that set off his tan, he could have easily been mistaken for the star of some testosterone-heavy WB show.

"Yeah. Not like you're living in a shack." Sam never missed an opportunity to needle her about the fortunate circumstances surrounding her struggling-actress hood.

"Who lives here?" Sophie asked to change the subject.

"Marcy Roth. Up and coming talent agent to the next generation of stars."

Next generation of stars. Sophie loved how that sounded. But she didn't say so to Sam. His view was that striving to be famous undermined the integrity of the art of acting. Maybe. But Sophie wanted it all — integrity *and* the infinity pool she'd spotted through the French doors that led to the backyard.

Sam handed her a Heineken from the industrial-sized fridge. "So . . . you wanna split up . . . attack the party solo?"

Split up? He had brought her to a party where she knew no one, and now he planned to abandon her? So much for the power of her extremely nice ass.

"Absolutely," Sophie responded, as if she hadn't assumed they'd attack the party together. As if she weren't the least bit intimidated by the group of over-coiffed, under-dressed twenty-something party-goers.

Sam was already looking over her shoulder. "I see my friends over there. Have fun."

As he took off toward the cavernous living room, Sophie reminded herself that she was the most socially capable girl she knew. Parties were her forte. Even parties like this one.

She took a last look at Sam, who seemed to have already forgotten she existed, and turned to head outside. If nothing else, she could get a good look at that infinity pool.

"Oomph!" Her face plowed into the very hard chest of a very tall guy. Apparently, being distracted by stealing a glance at one's wayward party companion wasn't the best way to exit a room.

Sophie looked up at the face that was attached to the chest. And nearly dropped her beer. She hadn't crashed into just any chest. This one belonged to Trey Benson. Sophie stared at her favorite indie actor, praying her lipstick hadn't smeared in the collision.

"Sorry! I didn't see you . . . I mean, I wasn't looking . . . and then you were *there* . . . Sorry."

"No worries." Trey Benson didn't move. He was just *looking* at her. She felt mesmerized by his dark brown eyes. Who knew a guy's lashes could be that long?

"Anyway . . ." *Say something funny and cute,* Sophie ordered herself. But nothing funny or cute came to mind.

"I'm Trey." He held out his hand for her to shake. His hair — such a deep, rich brown it was almost black — contrasted beautifully with his olive skin.

Sophie took his hand, her fingers numb. "I'm . . ." What was her name again? "I'm Sophie."

"You must be an actor," Trey Benson—*Trey*—commented, his eyes traveling every inch of her.

"Why?" Sophie forced herself to inhale. Breathing was good.

"Isn't everyone?" He sort of half-smiled, exactly the way he had in the final scene of *Marigold,* last summer's surprise sleeper hit that had turned Trey Benson into a semi-household name — at least in those households that contained girls between the ages of fourteen and twenty-five.

Sophie nodded, but no actual words would come out. She hadn't been this tongue-tied since Mike Mancowitz had asked if he could feel her up next to the chocolate-covered strawberry tree at his bar mitzvah.

Trey smiled again, obviously used to girls going mute in his presence. "Have you been in anything . . . or are you still doing the waitress thing?"

Sophie wasn't about to announce that not only had she landed exactly zero roles, but that she also hadn't even climbed the restaurant food chain from hostess to waitress. She had her *pride* after all.

"I'm going to be in a movie that starts shooting next week," Sophie informed Trey. "It's called *Bringing Down Jones.*"

"Really?" Trey sounded amused. "I don't remember seeing a Sophie on the cast list."

She had a very bad feeling. "Cast list?"

Trey took a sip of his Pacifico. "I'm starring in it."

"Oh." Sophie glanced at Sam, who was currently deeply engrossed in chalking his pool cue.

This conversation could only go one way — down. But her ego forced her to hold her head high.

"I'm gonna be an extra," she explained, oozing fake confidence. "It's a favor for a friend on the crew."

The statement was half true. Her gig as an extra *was* a favor. To Sophie — or, more accurately — to Celeste. But whatever.

Trey raised his beer to her. "Maybe I'll see you on the set."

Thankfully, a six-foot-tall blond model chose that moment to drape herself over Trey. Sophie breathed a sigh of relief and melted back into the general party throng.

"Looks like you fit right in."

Sophie turned to find Sam staring at her, a weird look on his face. "I always do," she replied quickly.

No need to add that she'd made a total jerk of herself in front of Trey Benson. Let Sam think what he wanted. He always did.

I'm going to forget I ever met Trey Benson. She'd forget she met him, and in that state of forgetfulness, the shame of pretending she had a real part in his movie would wash away to nothing. Well, first she'd tell Harper, Kate, and Becca all about the encounter. *Then* she'd forget.

"We're here," Sam's voice broke into her interior monologue. "Unless maybe you're waiting for me to carry you to your door?"

Sophie looked out of the window of Sam's Honda. Whoops. She'd been so busy obsessing about Trey that she hadn't even noticed they'd finally made it from Mulholland Drive to Beverly Hills.

"Thank you so much for the ride to the party." She'd been treating Sam with what she hoped was maddening formality since he suggested they split up at the party.

He sighed. "Look, I'm sorry."

"For what?" She adopted her most innocent expression. Yes, it was incredibly passive-aggressive. Yes, he deserved it.

"I'm getting the sense that I pissed you off." The look on his face was so painfully awkward that Sophie was tempted to feel sorry for him.

"It's been my past experience that when one asks another one to accompany the aforementioned one to an event, *that* one usually doesn't leave the other one to fend for herself."

Sam looked confused. Even she wasn't exactly sure what she'd just said. "You blew me off," she clarified. "Get it?"

"I figured . . ." His voice trailed off. Apparently, he wasn't sure *what* he'd figured.

"What?"

"Maybe you should just go," Sam responded dismissively. "There's no point to this conversation."

But Sophie wasn't going to let him off that easy tonight. She wasn't going to storm out of the car, or end this with some scathing one liner.

Sam was the closest thing she had to a friend in Los Angeles, and despite his constant criticism, she still had just the tiniest bit of a crush on him. If nothing else, she deserved to know why he'd invited her to a party, then pretended like she didn't exist.

"You didn't have to tell me about the party tonight," Sophie said calmly. "So why did you?"

He shrugged. "I was trying to be nice?"

Sophie laughed. She couldn't help it. The concept of "nice" was totally antithetical to Sam's overall vibe of superiority.

"You've treated me like some shallow, poser wannabe since I

walked off the plane. But I'm no different from you. I'm just trying to make my dreams come true."

He turned off the car ignition. "Look, I really wanted you to come to the party. But you're so into making it . . . and you've got the whole Beverly Hills thing going on . . . I figured you wouldn't want to be seen slumming it with a pool boy."

It was both the nicest and the meanest thing he had yet said to her. For once in her life, Sophie wasn't sure how to proceed with an argument. Was it possible . . . did he feel *vulnerable*?

"You're a lot more than a pool boy," Sophie said quietly. "You're an amazing actor."

The street light coming in through the windshield illuminated Sam's face in such a way that he almost appeared to be glowing as he turned to look at her. "Really?"

Sophie just nodded. Sometimes words made things less profound, and this was definitely one of those times.

"Thanks," he replied softly. "As many hours as I've logged checking chlorine levels and trimming bougainvillea . . . I guess I needed to hear that."

"So you don't hate me?"

He smiled. "I don't hate you."

And then she started to get That Feeling. The one she'd first experienced during a rousing game of girls-chase-boys in second grade. It was an odd sensation (not always good) in the pit of her stomach that indicated a guy was about to kiss her.

Usually, she would have calmly shut her eyes and let the kiss happen. But Sam wasn't usual in any way. She didn't want to kiss him unless they were going to be completely honest with each other. It was confession time.

"I wasn't fitting in at the party," she admitted. "I made a total fool of myself in front of Trey Benson." She giggled nervously. "I tried to pretend I had a part in his movie."

Sam's eyes jerked back to the steering wheel. "I wouldn't worry about it," he said coldly. "The guy obviously liked you."

Just like that, The Feeling was gone. Sophie yanked on the car door handle, suddenly desperate to get back to the guesthouse, away from this guy who turned on and off like a faucet.

"I'll see you in class," she stepped out and slung her purse around her shoulder, her voice equally cold.

As Sophie walked across the Meyers' enormous lawn, listening to Sam's car screech off into the night, she decided she didn't give a shit about his split personality.

After all, she didn't come to LA to meet guys. She came to follow her Dream. And from now on, that's the only thing that mattered.

Something smelled.

Like vomit.

Becca tried to roll over, away from the smell, but her body felt like molasses, thick and heavy. Her head hurt. Why did her head hurt? For that matter, why did *everything* hurt?

She should open her eyes. That would be the thing to do. Just open . . . her eyes. Or . . . oh God she was gonna . . .

The remaining contents of Becca's stomach landed in a well-placed trash can beside her bed.

Only now that her eyes were finally open, she realized it wasn't her bed. It wasn't even her room. *Where was she?*

With mounting horror, Becca realized she was in the Middlebury Health Center. Please, let her die.

"Hey," Isabelle said from the next bed over.

At least Becca wasn't the only one who'd gotten too drunk.

"You're here, too?" She moaned, wiping her mouth with the back of her hand. The other two beds in the room were empty — at least no one else was there to bear witness.

"No, they just let me stay with you," Isabelle said, clearly totally un-hungover.

Of course.

A pain throbbed in Becca's left ankle. She decided to ignore it. She was going to take this one thing at a time. And maybe, by the time the pieces of the night came together, her ankle would feel better.

"What happened?" she asked.

"Well . . ." Isabelle began. "It was a rough night."

She could say that again.

"Sorry about my parents," Becca said sincerely.

Isabelle shook her head. "It's okay. It was actually interesting. And it definitely made me appreciate my parents more."

Becca noticed that her denim skirt and green shirt were across the room, and she was wearing a cotton-white hospital gown. As if this situation could get any more humiliating.

"What do you remember?" Isabelle asked as she climbed out of her bed and took the vomity trash can to the far side of the room. Then she came to sit on Becca's bed.

Becca searched the recesses of her bleary memory.

She remembered the purple punch. She remembered . . . dancing with some very tall guy. Had he kissed her? She had a vague recollection of drunken slobbering. She remembered Isabelle yelling at someone. . . .

"Did you yell at some guy?" she asked.

"Yeah, that asshole you were making out with on the dance floor tried to leave with you."

"I was making out with someone . . . on the dance floor?"

Becca was sure she was going to die.

"Did everyone see?" she ventured carefully.

"Oh yeah," Isabelle said, not one to couch things in more pleasant terms. "*Everyone.* And when I finally pulled him off you, you kept yelling "*I'm on fi-ya! I'm on fi-ya!*""

"Oh God," Becca groaned.

"From now on, you're the 'I'm on fire' girl." Isabelle grinned.

Becca, who had never been known for anything — other than maybe skiing and her three best friends — was now going to be known for an extremely drunken make-out session in front of two hundred people and a moronic phrase she used to motivate herself (*only to herself*) as she slalomed down a mountain.

Oy, everything hurt. Especially her ankle. But she wasn't ready to think about that yet.

Becca had a sudden sickening thought. Stuart Pendergrass had been there. More than that, she semi-remembered that he had . . . done something.

"When did Stuart Pendergrass get involved?" she asked, dreading the answer.

"Around the time I was explaining to Jason Winkowski why he couldn't take you home with him. It took more muscle than just me to get that point across."

"I made out with *Jason Winkowski?*"

Becca buried her head in her hands. He wasn't even *remotely* cute.

"What do you mean it took more than just you? Was there, like, a rescue posse or something?"

"No," her roommate responded quickly, to Becca's relief. Then she added, "Just Stuart. He punched him."

"He *punched* him?"

Isabelle nodded, clearly enjoying revealing the pieces of Becca's night to her, one juicy detail at a time.

"And by then, you'd wandered down the stairs and landed flat on your face —"

"I . . . on my face?"

Isabelle nodded again.

Suddenly the throbbing ankle made sense. Filled with dread, Becca pulled back the covers. Her ankle was a mottled mixture of black, blue, and some disgusting yellowish green color. It was also triple its usual size.

"Sorry," Isabelle said. "I tried to stop you, but I was too busy cheering for Stuart."

Becca's heart fell to her stomach.

"Is it broken?"

Isabelle shook her head. "You'll get an X-ray later, but they think it's just a sprain."

"Either way, I'm going to miss the beginning of the season." Becca was feeling sick now for an entirely different reason. There was no way Coach Maddix wasn't going to hear about this.

Isabelle nodded.

"So . . . I obviously didn't get here on my own," she said slowly.

"Stuart carried you," Isabelle said. "It was very *Officer and a Gentleman*. Until you threw up on his chest."

No, no, no, no! Becca screamed in her head. This was an infirmary, they must have something here she could overdose on.

"So," Isabelle continued casually, "not to change the subject, but who's Jared?"

Becca felt her blood run cold. She'd been talking about Jared? While Stuart was carrying her?

"My best friend Kate's boyfriend," she answered carefully. "Why? What did I say?"

Isabelle tried to contain her smile, knowing Becca's humiliation had already reached Herculean proportions.

"You were . . . mostly babbling about fate. And destiny. Stuff like that. How you thought once that Jared was your destiny, but clearly he wasn't."

Becca nodded. Well, that was true enough.

"Then you said some very flattering things about Stuart's chin," Isabelle added.

"His chin?"

160

Isabelle nodded. "Apparently you're quite fond of it."

"Of his chin?"

"Yes, and his eyes. You like them, too."

"I do not!"

Isabelle shrugged. "That's not what you said last night," she teased.

"Well, I was clearly impaired."

"That's for sure."

"You don't think he thinks . . ."

"You like him? He might, after that."

"That's ridiculous!"

"He did save you from Jason Winkowski's lips."

"I'll thank him the next time I see him," Becca replied haughtily.

"Oh, you also said he's not some stupid meathead after all."

Isabelle couldn't stop herself from grinning.

Well, Becca thought, Isabelle better enjoy this while it lasted. Because she was never, ever going to be in this situation again. She was never going to drink or dance or say she was "on fi-ya" or . . . any of it.

She was going to do everything she could to get her ankle better, and get back out on the ski slopes to show Coach Maddix what she could do.

Most importantly, she was never, ever, ever going to allow herself to be anywhere around Stuart Pendergrass again for as long as she lived.

And at the moment, she hoped that was only about five more minutes.

Kate had never felt as uncool in her life as she did in Berlin. Everyone and everything seemed consummately hip — from the aggressively grim apartment buildings to the severe hairstyles to the nightclubs that didn't even open until after two AM. Every single person on the streets, from children to the elderly, seemed to know exactly where they were going, and the faster the better.

All of it together made Kate feel unsettled, like she couldn't quite hold her own. Which was perhaps why the city so moved her — as if, in some way, her own sense of being off-kilter helped her see beyond the surface of Berlin's living, breathing present into the vast, weighty presence of history.

Kate had been barely four when the Berlin Wall fell, and her father had sat her on his knee to watch the breaking news on CNN. In child-friendly terms, he'd explained how, in the wake of World War II, the city had ultimately been divided into two sections — with communism on one side and democracy on the other. As the wall came down, Kate half-remembered a high cement barrier, enveloped by celebrating crowds on streets that looked like they could've been just blocks from her own house. Except, her father had explained, the streets on TV were thousands of miles away, and the people were celebrating the demise of "the last relic of the Cold War." At four years old, Kate had imagined everyone within the boundaries of the wall suddenly being released from an endless winter.

Fourteen years later, she was now facing one of the last remaining sections of that high gray wall. In this part of Berlin, the wall was little more than a well-weathered urban art gallery, a monument to its own past. And yet hundreds, some said thousands, of people had died trying to get over it. Women had thrown babies from high-rise windows into waiting nets on the other side, desperate to have their children grow up in freedom.

"Touch the Berlin Wall" was one of Habiba's additions to the list Harper had sent her. So Kate put her hands to the cold concrete, spread her palms wide, and tried to figure out why. What was Habiba trying to tell her? What was Habiba hoping she would learn?

Maybe it had something to do with war. Habiba, after all, had lived through more than one. The first twelve years of her life had been spent fleeing it, starving from it, suffering its losses. War had taken her father, and ultimately her mother, as well as her home and education.

It had destroyed the entire landscape of her life, stolen her history. Habiba didn't even know her birth father's name. Maybe that was what the wall meant to her — a war-torn separation between a hidden past and a transparent present, between the known and unknown.

Or maybe, she thought, Habiba simply wanted her to feel grateful for all of the things that Kate herself regularly took for granted — from the basics like food and water to education and friendship to parents who supported and encouraged her. At least, until recently.

And maybe *that* was what Habiba wanted her to think about. Her parents. About the wall that had suddenly come up between them. Kate had depended on their counsel for her entire life. Suddenly, she found herself alone on one side of a metaphorical wall, with her parents on the other side. Maybe, then, the message of the cold cement beneath her palm was one of hope — that walls come down. Eventually. Maybe that was what Habiba had wanted her to figure out.

Or maybe it wasn't about Kate at all. Maybe Habiba was just trying to express what it was like for her. Maybe she was trying to tell Kate that, like the path of the wall, the scars of her past were still there. The city of Berlin had become one city, just as Habiba's old life had blended into her new one. But unlike the former East Berliners, who could now cross back and forth every day if they wanted, who spoke the same language and had a common history with the people on the other side of the wall, Habiba couldn't go back. She had lost everything but the pain. And gained everything, too, Kate supposed.

But at what price?

Kate pulled her hand away from the wall.

She could keep theorizing or she could call her sister and ask her herself. She and Habiba could have a real conversation for once, get beyond the surface of things, talk about something real.

Like sisters.

Yes. She would do that. Definitely.

Just . . . not today.

Dear Sophie —

I am enclosing the enclosed napkin, because I have to stop looking at it. If I don't stop looking at it, I will never write the next Great American Novel. If I don't write the next Great American Novel, I will hate myself forever. I'm sure you understand.

Please do not destroy this napkin or use it for its intended purpose. I would like it returned to me upon the completion of the aforementioned next Great American Novel.

Thank you,
Harper Waddle

P.S. Can you believe I'm going to Mr. Finelli's!?

MR. FINELLI
11025 EAST ROSE DRIVE
555-9127

Rainy Day Café

TEN

Harper didn't feel good. She felt very, very bad. One of two things was about to happen. Either she was going to throw up, or she was going to pass out. The prudent thing to do in this situation would be to sit down, put her head between her knees, and aim past her black leather boots should anything find its way from her stomach through her mouth.

But seeing as she was standing in front of the door to Mr. Finelli's duplex, and she didn't want to put him in the position of having to call an ambulance, she held her stomach and prayed. God — at least tonight — was on her side. Because by the time Mr. Finelli opened the door, she had neither lost consciousness nor tossed the Green-Eyed Monster she'd slurped down for dinner.

"Have you been out here a long time?" he asked. "I didn't hear a knock."

Because Harper had forgotten to knock. Because she was a drooling numbskull. Even the bordering-on-sexy almost-tight black shirt she'd bought for the occasion couldn't change that fact.

"I just got here," she told him breezily. "Good timing."

Harper followed Mr. Finelli inside and looked around the

apartment, feeling awkward. She loved the hardwood floors, the enormous fireplace, and what looked like original crown molding around the edge of the cream-colored ceiling. It was exactly the kind of place — classic movie posters, throw pillows, and messy, overflowing bookcases included — that Harper had always fantasized about moving into.

"Is Fiona here?" At least part of her was holding out hope that he'd kicked his girlfriend out for the evening.

Mr. Finelli shook his head. She noticed his hair was getting longer again. Finger-running-through longer. "Nope, it's just us."

"Too bad. I was looking forward to seeing her," Harper lied. She'd exchanged small talk with Mr. Finelli's delicate-boned, strawberry-blond girlfriend on several occasions at the coffeehouse. It was never a pleasant experience.

"Maybe you noticed . . . She hasn't been coming into the café with me lately," he said as he led Harper into the retro kitchen at the back of the apartment.

"Oh . . . no . . . I hadn't noticed." Another lie. Harper practically jumped for joy every time Mr. Finelli showed up for his morning coffee minus Fiona.

"We broke up, actually." He took an old-fashioned silver percolator from his stove and began to fill it with water. "She was going to move in . . . she moved on instead."

Broke up, broke up, broke up. They were beautiful, glorious words. Not that Harper even had a chance with Mr. Finelli. She didn't. But still. It was more fun to lie in bed at night and think about a guy who *didn't* have a girlfriend. And Harper certainly lay in bed thinking about Mr. Finelli . . . a lot.

"I'm sorry." She stifled the enormous grin that was threatening to spread across her face.

He bit his lip, his gaze moving to somewhere over her head. "I guess Fiona was looking for a corporate type . . . and I was looking for an artist. Or something." He shrugged. "Anyway . . . love is weird."

"Yeah . . ." Harper wasn't sure how to respond to the fact that her hot former English teacher had just opened up to her about his personal life.

If she were Sophie, or even Kate, she'd probably know just what to say. But Harper's romantic encounters were limited to several awkward make-out sessions with guys who'd been too inexperienced even to know they should take her glasses off before they kissed her. The closest thing she'd felt to love — real love — was with Mr. Finelli. And talking about *that* would have completely shattered the Appropriate Meter.

Mr. Finelli seemed to sense her verbal paralysis. "It's okay, Harper. Really."

"I never liked Fiona," she blurted out. "Whenever she came into the café without you, she didn't tip."

He laughed. "I like your honesty — even if the truth hurts."

What else do you like? Harper wanted to ask. *Dishwater blondes with thick black glasses, perhaps?* Instead, she sat down at the kitchen table and took out the green spiral notebook she'd brought from her backpack.

"Tell me about the novel," Mr. Finelli said as he poured Harper a cup of rich black coffee.

She didn't think she could put her feelings about her book into actual sentences. But over two hours and three cups of coffee, she told Mr. Finelli more about her writing process and the world she was trying to create with words than she had anyone else. Including her best friends.

She gave him vivid descriptions of her main characters, four generations of women who'd grown up, lived, and died in the same old Victorian house. She explained that she wanted her book to be epic, full of births, marriages, deaths, and all the gory moments of life that came between. She even confessed that she *wanted* to write all of that, beautifully, but that the story was stuck in her head, unwilling to come out, no matter how hard she tried to pry it from her brain. . . .

"Maybe I'm not meant to write a book," she finished sadly.

There. She'd said it out loud. There was a chance that Harper Waddle had not, in fact, been born to write. There was a chance that she was just a regular person who had nothing interesting to say and no interesting way to say it.

Mr. Finelli pushed a stray lock of dark hair from his forehead. "You want to know what I think?"

"What?" She hoped desperately he wasn't going to agree with her.

"I think you're not writing from the heart." He took a sip of coffee and let the thought sink in. "It sounds to me like you're approaching this from an intellectual standpoint, as opposed to an artistic one."

Harper nodded. What he said made total sense. Whenever she'd written short stories in high school, she'd simply sat down at her computer and let the words flow. This time, she couldn't type the letter A without questioning whether or not she was making a huge mistake.

"It's not the heart I need to write from," she realized, staring at her still blank notebook page. "It's the gut."

Mr. Finelli put down his mug and leaned forward. "And that epiphany, Harper Waddle, is why you're going to write a great book."

They were sitting next to each other at the kitchen table, and with Mr. Finelli's weight shifted forward, their knees were almost touching. Harper stared into his pale blue eyes. She wasn't sure exactly what was happening, but it felt like her brain had left her body and

170

traveled back to her parents' basement. All that was left here, in Mr. Finelli's kitchen, was blood, guts, heart, soul . . . and desire.

"It's weird. You don't feel like my teacher anymore," she commented softly.

He raised his eyebrows. "Then how come you still call me Mr. Finelli?"

Harper had tried to call him Adam. She really had. But it felt alien rolling off her tongue. Like she was playing dress-up with names.

"Bad habit?" she offered.

"Bad habits are meant to be kicked," Mr. Finelli responded.

"Okay — Adam." Her breath was coming in short, hot bursts. "Better?"

"Much." He was still. So still that he could have been a sculpture rather than a man.

Harper wasn't even aware that her body was moving. But somehow her face was getting closer to Mr. Finelli's; she could have stopped, but she didn't.

And then her lips touched his.

For a brief second, Harper forgot about her book, and lying to her friends, and being rejected from college. The only thing that existed was this kiss, which was doing things to her nether regions that usually only happened when she was alone in bed with her fantasies. . . .

Suddenly, his lips were gone. Harper opened her eyes — which she hadn't even realized she'd closed — and blinked. Mr. Finelli was staring back at her. In her haze, she noticed that his cheeks were beginning to turn red.

"That shouldn't . . . it shouldn't have happened." He stood up quickly and took their cups to the sink. "I'm sorry, Harper. I don't know what I was — I'm sorry."

"But —" She didn't know what to say. Every object in the kitchen looked brighter and clearer than before, but seemed somehow far away. Her notebook on the table might as well have been in Montana.

"Maybe you should go now," he suggested softly. It was barely a whisper, but the words hit her like a punch in the face.

Humiliation. Shame. Embarrassment. How else could she describe the feeling of complete and total mortification she was experiencing right now? She had *kissed* Mr. Finelli. He probably thought she was some sex-crazed teenager, or worse, some forlorn little girl looking for some kind of twisted father-figure thing.

This was exactly why Harper always kept a running stream of self-commentary going in her head. She'd let down her guard for one moment, acted before she thought, and consequently ruined everything.

"I'm . . . I'm sorry," she stuttered, getting out of her wooden chair so fast that it fell backward and crashed to the floor. "I didn't mean . . . I didn't . . ."

Where was the door? There was a door, and she needed to find it. *Pick up backpack, run to door.* Harper stumbled through the kitchen, unaware that Mr. Finelli was following.

As she grabbed the front doorknob, she felt his hand on her left shoulder. "It's okay, Harper. You were caught up in the moment. So was I. That's all."

She nodded blindly and rushed out onto the street. She could not believe that a mere few hours ago she was worried about passing out or throwing up.

Compared to the spectacle she'd just made of herself, a little bile on the street was nothing.

Becca found Coach Maddix in his small, spare office on the second floor of the athletic complex. She knocked quietly on his open door as a photo of his gold medal–winning Olympic team taunted her from the wall behind his desk. The blood drained from her face as Coach Maddix glanced up, then slowly took in her crutches. When his eyes stopped for a long moment on her bandaged ankle and his lips formed a grim, narrow line, Becca was even more ashamed than she had been two days ago in the infirmary.

"It's just a sprain," she said, knowing he hated her. Knowing he had every right.

Coach Maddix's jaw got tight. He nodded. *Keep going.*

Becca took a deep breath and almost choked on her own self-loathing.

"I was . . . being stupid. I think. I don't actually remember . . ."

Why was she telling him this?

A vein in the coach's left temple began to pound.

"The doctor said I'm not out for the season," she continued quickly, trying to sound positive. "Just maybe the first couple races, and obviously I can't practice exactly, but I'll still be there, and I have a physical therapy schedule all worked out. I can . . . I don't know, clean skis for the rest of the team, or carry stuff — okay, I probably can't do that — but I'll be useful, still, somehow. . . ."

Becca ran out of breath. Coach Maddix stood up and turned to his office window, his back to her.

"Get out," he said. He didn't even raise his voice.

More than anything, Becca wished she were capable of running. Because all she wanted to do was burst into tears, and she still had to navigate her way out of the gym, across campus, and back to her dorm room before she could let the dam burst. On crutches, it seemed like a million miles.

She'd made it down the hall, down a flight of stairs (she was too stubborn to use the elevator), and halfway to the gym door when she saw Stuart Pendergrass. He was coming out of the guy's locker room, wearing gray athletic shorts and a blue Middlebury t-shirt, a gym bag slung over his shoulder. And he was heading straight toward her.

"Hey," he said. "You need some help?"

Did she need some *help*?

What was *wrong* with this guy, Becca thought, furious. She had blatantly refused to look him in the eye during class today — or she had been utterly unable to do so, what with all the humiliation. Either way, it should have been obvious she didn't exactly want to chat with the person who'd carried her halfway across campus while she babbled about the aesthetic acceptability of his chin.

Yet here he was, being so . . . *nice,* when he should have been shunning her like she had a scarlet DL for "Disgusting Lush" across her chest.

And what was up with him always being everywhere? At *all* the worst times? Couldn't she live through one humiliating moment without having Stuart Pendergrass there to see it? Becca's frustration boiled over.

"Leave me alone!" she yelled, struggling to hold back the waterworks even more now.

Then she turned and pushed her way through the glass doors into the cold Vermont air. As she hobbled as fast as she could down the cement path to the gray stone building that was her dorm, the remorse flooded in. She hadn't meant to yell. She hadn't even meant to tell him to leave her alone. But it had felt cruel that he was standing there, that he had the gall to smile at her. And in some twisted way, Becca thought, all of this was Stuart's fault anyway. If he hadn't been at that party, if he hadn't been looking at her. . . .

Okay, she probably would have been drunk and stupid regardless, after the miserable dinner she'd spent with her parents — whom

174

she still hadn't heard from, though she assumed they were all back in Boulder by now. But she wouldn't have been *as* drunk or *as* stupid. That was Stuart's fault.

And now he would hate her, she realized. If he had any sense, he'd already hated her. She was a bad drunk, for one thing. And grumpy, and overly emotional. . . .

Choking back tears, Becca realized that every single goal she'd had when she arrived at Middlebury — being the best freshman skier on the team, falling in love, and not making an utter ass of herself in front of the whole campus — had been destroyed in one night. If this was what happened when she let go of her emotions, Becca decided, she was simply never going to let go again.

From now on, she was going to be an ice queen.

On crutches.

Sophie's nipples were hard. They were hard because she was cold. Very, very cold. Celeste was right. Being an extra on a movie was all about shivering for hours in a frigid warehouse and waiting for the assistant director to announce lunch.

But, hey, at least she'd been smart and worn her four-inch high Jimmy Choo knock-offs with her red BCBG cocktail dress. She'd have feeling in maybe one toe by the end of the thirteen-hour day.

"There's coffee over at craft services." A pale, mousy-looking extra, wearing a full-length navy cowlneck blue dress that had seen better days, pointed toward a meager-looking food cart by the door. "You can use it to warm your hands."

"Thanks." Sophie already knew all about the hand-warming tip. She'd been cradling tiny Styrofoam cups of coffee since six o'clock this morning. "Are you an extra a lot?"

The thirtyish woman nodded. "Beats waitressing, right?"

"I guess." Sophie wasn't sure she agreed, but far be it for her to judge. After all, she wouldn't even be here if Celeste's boyfriend, Leo, hadn't taken mercy on her. "I'm Sophie, by the way."

"I'm Tess." She leaned forward a bit to emphasize what she was about to say. "Don't worry, Sophie. You'll get the hang of it. Just takes time."

But Sophie didn't *want* to get the hang of being an extra. She wanted to lounge in a heated state-of-the-art trailer, engaged in intense discussions with a major director about the emotional arc of her character.

For now, though, she headed toward a row of metal chairs, where several other extras were camped out with books, blankets, and iPods. Everyone looked miserable, and Sophie made a mental note to pay more attention to the "background artists" next time she went to a movie.

Torn between a desire to make conversation with her fellow actors and a desire to close her eyes and pretend she was in Hawaii, she propped herself across two metal chairs and tried to get comfortable. Fifteen minutes later, she was half-asleep, sipping a Mai Tai beachside at the Four Seasons Maui while a large man named Bernardo fanned her with palm fronds.

The fantasy ended abruptly when the huge warehouse door slid open, allowing bright sunshine to pour in. Sophie opened her eyes to find Leo striding in her direction, his heavily tattooed arms swinging purposefully.

"Thanks for coming, everyone," he yelled out. "We need you on Stage Nine five minutes ago, so let's get moving."

"Damn, that means lunch ain't until after the party scene," the balding, fifty-something white guy sitting next to Sophie grumbled as he slid his feet into what looked to be decade-old penny loafers.

The Nextel attached to Leo's hip squawked, and he pushed a button. "They're in transit," he barked.

Sophie followed Leo and the herd of extras out of the warehouse and across the lot to what she presumed to be Stage Nine. With every step she took, the boredom of the morning seeped away. She was in Hollywood (okay, Burbank, but close enough), and she was being *paid* to act. Sure, it was only eighty dollars . . . but still. A start was a start.

"Let the magic begin." Tess had appeared next to Sophie, and her eyes were shining as they filed in. "I love this part."

Sophie could see why. Unlike what she'd come to think of as the "extras holding cell," this particular warehouse had been completely transformed. *Bringing Down Jones* was about a young British diplomat who was on a mission to avenge his father's death. One of the big scenes took place at some kind of gala, and the movie crew had built the ballroom of a nineteenth century mansion right here on stage, complete with crystal chandeliers, Monet reproductions, and a parquet floor. The whole effect was, well, magic.

Her heart leapt as she looked across the ballroom, where Trey Benson was being powdered by a makeup artist. Even at a distance, with a pound of pancake makeup on his face, he looked gorgeous.

Trey glanced toward the crowd of extras. Then he turned to a harried-looking nearby production assistant. There was no way he'd remember her from the party. Girls probably humiliated themselves in front of Trey on a nightly basis. She'd just fade into the background . . . like she was being paid to do . . . and it would be as if the whole incident had never happened.

"Leo's waving you over there." Tess pointed in his direction.

Sophie had been keeping her eyes averted from Trey. But now she snuck a peek. Tess hadn't been lying. Leo and Trey were both staring at her, and when Sophie caught Leo's eye, he gestured for her to cross the ballroom.

Don't trip, she prayed as she sauntered across the stage, aware of a hundred pairs of eyes watching her every move. She felt sweat stains forming at the underarms of her cocktail dress, and she wished she had an Altoid. Trey Benson wanted to talk to her. Voluntarily. She just hoped he wasn't so offended by her false bragging the other night that he intended to have her kicked off the set immediately.

"Hey, again," Trey greeted as soon as she approached. "Sophie, right?"

She nodded. "Trey, right?"

He grinned. "How'd you like to get your big break today, Sophie?"

Her big break? Of course she wanted it. She glanced over at Leo for an explanation.

"Trey's going to get you bumped up," Leo told her nonchalantly. "You're getting a line."

A line? She, Sophie Bushell, was going to say an actual line in an actual movie? To merely say 'thank you' seemed insufficient. "Okay . . ."

"Come with me," Leo instructed. "I'll take you to hair and makeup."

Sophie waved to Trey, following Leo back across the stage, past the extras she'd been hanging with just minutes ago. She couldn't help but get a rush of pleasure from the envy on their faces.

"Leo, this is incredible," she gushed as her heart continued to pound. "Celeste is going to freak when I tell her."

Leo shrugged. "Trey does this all the time."

"He does?" Sophie felt just the tiniest bit less special.

"You want my advice?" Leo asked.

She gave him a look. "Depends on what it is."

"Stay away from Trey." Leo didn't expand on *why* Sophie should stay away from the star of *Bringing Down Jones*. And she wasn't about to ask him to.

She was on a high. And she intended to ride that high straight up the Hollywood ladder. This was her big break. And she wasn't going to screw it up.

"Take the water," the list said. Harper wanted her to take the water. Okay, but *what* water? And take it where?

In Paris, Kate had taken a boat down the Seine, which could qualify as taking the water. In Berlin, she'd run out of euros and had taken a bottle of water from a cute Spanish guy staying in the same hostel. But she'd repaid him the next day, so that water had actually been borrowed. Both times, when she'd taken out the list, it hadn't felt right to cross off number 42.

Kate pulled her long pale blond hair back into a ponytail as she walked along a quiet Athens street toward the hill that led to the Acropolis. She'd left the hostel without a map, but even with her lousy sense of direction and the thick layer of smog that covered the city, the Acropolis was hard to miss. Her plan was simple: walk toward the big hill. Other than that, she was free to explore and discover. So far, that freedom had led her past three ancient ruins, six fountains, and at least one Laundromat. And in the process she had reached the conclusion that, while the ruins were very cool, her dream had nothing to do with archeology or ancient civilizations.

Kate ran her hands through a knot in her hair as a group of Greek teenagers leered at her from a nearby wall. She rolled her eyes and kept walking. Yes, she was blond. Yes, she was beautiful. Get over it already.

Maybe "take the water" meant she was supposed to do some kind of reality show challenge, like taking ten gallons of water over a narrow bridge, barefoot, while balancing a bucket of chickens on her head. Kate grinned to herself. Okay, that probably wasn't what Harper had in mind. She felt a rivulet of sweat drip down her back. Her day pack was getting heavy. Maybe, she thought, she should take out her water bottle, drink up, and call number 42 done.

As she started to shift her pack, Kate sensed rather than saw a presence behind her. Suddenly, her head jerked back. Someone was holding her ponytail. She tried to twist around, but she couldn't move, and now there were more of them. The three teenage guys she'd seen before. Only now they were doing more than staring. They were dragging her off the street into an alley —

Frantic, Kate screamed, aware through her terror that she could not allow these assholes to take her off the street. She kicked her legs at the shortest of the three attackers, but he caught them and held on. She screamed louder, desperate — someone had to be nearby, someone had to *hear* her! But even in her panic, she knew that there had been no one else on the street. She'd been walking alone in a strange city without a map. And this was the price she was going to pay for her stupidity. Goddamnit, not if she had anything to say about it —

Kate torqued her entire body, slamming her head backward into the face of the bastard holding her. He grunted, letting her go, and she landed hard on the ground. She tried to scramble away, but the second asshole was still holding her ankles. The third guy — the tallest of the three — picked her up in one quick motion and slammed her against the alley wall. Her feet slammed back to the pavement, but she couldn't find any purchase. She started to scream again, but the tall one's hand clasped over her mouth, blocking her breath.

I am *not* going to die, Kate thought. I am *not* going to let these assholes rape me or rob me or whatever fucking thing they think they're going to do. She bit hard at the hand over her mouth, and tasted salty blood. The hand jerked back, and the tall one cursed loudly in Greek. For the briefest moment, Kate was free. She took

180

off toward the street — but the other two were ready for her. They grabbed her arms and threw her backwards. She skidded hard against the pebbly ground. Almost in slow motion, she watched the tall one rise above her and raise his clenched fist. . . .

Kate gave one final explosive scream.

And then everything went black.

Sophe—
You said you wanted to see what you-know-who
looks like. Got this out of the Middlebury newspaper:

FYI— My dad called yesterday. He left this weird,
like almost apologetic message. I mean, he didn't
actually apologize for anything, but he sounded...sort
of hat-in-hand, if you know what I mean. Should I
call him back? What do you think I should say?
Should I just pretend it never happened? That
worked with my mom—we finally talked last week.
Sort of—all we talked about was the weather.

What's going on with you and the movie star? I
sort of thought something was going to happen with
you and Sam.

CALL me and stop being so mysterious about everything.
It's not like I'm going to sell your story to the tabloids.

XO, B.

✦ ✦ ✦

ELEVEN

Kate stared at her reflection in the train window. So much for being beautiful, she thought bitterly. Her jaw was purple and black; seven stitches bisected her left eyebrow. Her hands were scraped and bandaged, her knees bruised.

After she'd been released from the hospital in Athens, she'd borrowed scissors from the hostel desk clerk and cut her own hair in front of one of the cheap, wavy mirrors in the communal bathroom. It barely reached her shoulders now, too short for a ponytail.

Beyond her reflection, vineyards passed by in the darkness. She was going back to Paris. Harper had convinced her that she shouldn't be alone.

"I'll be alone in Paris, too," Kate had argued.

"No," Harper countered. "You met that Chantal woman. She sounds just nutty enough to take in a homeless waif like you."

Then she had paused for a long moment.

"Or you could come home."

Kate had heard a slight note of hope in Harper's voice.

"I can't come home."

How could she go home? She hadn't even called her parents since she'd arrived on European soil. Letting them see her like this, letting them know what had happened to her, would be an admission that she had made a mistake. That she should never have gone off on her own. That she was helpless and useless in the wide, wide world.

And maybe all of those things were true. But that didn't mean she was going to admit it. To anyone. She hadn't even told Harper the truth about being attacked. She'd just said three guys had ganged up on her and taken her money and passport. Which wasn't a lie. It just wasn't the whole truth.

When she'd woken up at the hospital, a middle-aged woman in a coarse brown wool dress was holding her hand. The woman's face was heavily lined with age and worry.

"Girl is fine," she'd said warmly, struggling with her English, and patting Kate's hand.

The doctor later explained that the woman and her husband had heard Kate scream from their apartment. While the woman called the police, the husband had come to her rescue. He'd landed a good solid whack on the head to one of her attackers, who'd been treated and taken into police custody. The other two had run off with her day pack.

Kate remembered nothing past the pain.

A nurse had come in and given her a shot, and Kate had gone back to sleep. But her sleep had been full of hands grabbing, tangling in her hair, pulling her backwards. She'd awoken sweaty and panicked, her jaw throbbing with pain.

The woman who rescued her had returned her clothes laundered and mended. Kate had examined the clothes like clues.

There were three new buttons on the shirt. One arm had been artfully reattached. Her jeans had new patches on the knees — a light pink heart and a Greek flag. It was sweet, grandmotherly, but Kate knew as soon as she got back to the youth hostel she would throw the clothes away.

"You okay," the woman had reassured her, handing over the folded clothes. "You okay, no bad happen."

Yeah, Kate thought bitterly, no bad.

The woman had looked her in the eye, clearly not having the right words to express what she wanted to say.

"We come." She pointed at Kate's clothes. "On," she said firmly. "Okay?"

Kate nodded okay.

Good to know.

She was permanently disfigured and would never go to a Greek restaurant again, much less the actual country, but at least she hadn't been raped.

That was a good thing.

She tried to remember that as she got a new passport, took the remainder of her money out of the hostel safe, called Chantal, and boarded the train. So what did it matter that every guy who looked at her now seemed menacing? What did it matter that she now knew if anyone ever attacked her again, she would just pass out like an annoying heroine in one of Becca's stupid favorite movies?

All that mattered, she told herself, was that Chantal had offered to let her stay in her spare room. And that Magnus was no longer in Paris. The last thing she wanted was for him to see her like this.

And maybe, someday, when she was barricaded in Chantal's spare room, with a bureau across the door and a weapon at her side . . . Maybe, then, she would sleep again.

"Tomatoes are the secret ingredient," Harper informed Judd, brandishing her butcher knife as if she were competing in *Iron Chef*.

They were in the Waddles' kitchen, which, thanks to her mom's love of gourmet cooking, was the nicest room in the house. Whereas the rest of the Waddles' abode sported worn-out carpet and peeling wallpaper that her dad, in his euphemistic contractor's language called "charming," the kitchen had almost-new black granite countertops and shiny almost-new appliances. In case of natural disaster, the cabinets were stocked with enough homemade strawberry jam and industrial-sized boxes of Wheaties to last a decade.

Judd looked skeptical. "Harper, it's a BLT. How do *tomatoes* count as a secret ingredient?"

Guys were so simple. So linear in their thinking. "It's all in the way you slice them," she explained. "A tomato can taste completely different based on the thickness of the slice."

"Are you okay?" The concern on Judd's face was in absurd contrast to the giant yellow smiley face emblazoned on his white t-shirt.

"Me? I'm fine." Harper waved her knife. "What about me doesn't seem totally and completely fine?"

"Uh . . . everything." Judd had a way of distilling the truth that made Harper want to hit him.

"Tell me about Amber or Tiffany or whoever you're dating this week," she suggested. "Tell me about her breasts."

In Harper's limited experience, men could talk about breasts for at least twenty minutes at a time. It was part of being simple. But Judd just looked offended.

"Being a frustrated novelist has turned you into a real bitch. FYI." He took two yellow ceramic plates from the cabinet and set them on the granite counter with more force than was absolutely necessary. "Maybe I should just go."

Harper had invited Judd over for lunch so she wouldn't have to think about what she wasn't accomplishing. Or about Mr. Finelli and her pathetic attempt to shove her tongue down his throat. Or about the Other Thing that had kept her from sleeping last night. BLT sandwiches were a great neutralizer of anxiety. Something about the crunchiness of iceberg lettuce pushed everything else to the back of her brain.

"Fine. I'll go." Judd headed toward the kitchen table and grabbed his graffiti-covered purple backpack.

Uh-oh. It was decision time. Harper could either send him away with a nasty comment, or she could tell him about the latest thing that was bothering her. Two months ago, she wouldn't have been in this position. She would have been telling her sorrows to Becca, Sophie, or Kate. But they weren't here. Judd was.

"I'm sorry." Harper cleared her throat, summoning the humble place inside. "The thing is . . . I need a favor."

"A favor." He wasn't amused. He didn't appear even remotely on the way to being amused.

"It's important."

Around dawn, Harper had devised a plan. It was a devious plan, born out of desperation, and it required the use of a vehicle.

Why had she devised this? Because yesterday she had been, as usual, sitting in front of her computer, expanding her computer game repertoire to include Canfield Solitaire. And in this state of pseudo-activity, she'd heard her dad on the phone again. This time she was absolutely, positively sure he'd been talking to a woman in a manner not appropriate for a married man. She could no longer ignore the possibility that her father was having an extramarital affair. She had to act.

"Are you going to be nice?" Judd asked warily, staying as far away from the butcher knife as was possible in the Waddles' nice-but-none-too-large kitchen.

"I can't promise anything . . . but I'll try." It was the best she could do under present circumstances. Harper set down the butcher knife and stuffed her hands in the pockets of her gray hoodie to show she was sincere.

"Do I at least get a sandwich before I have to do this favor?" Clearly, he wasn't quite ready to forgive and forget.

Harper nodded. "You're going to love what I do with a piece of bacon."

Sophie held a photo of herself wearing faded jeans and a simple white button-down shirt up to one of the faux Tiffany desk lamps that were scattered around the guesthouse. If she squinted her eyes the tiniest bit, she was pretty sure she looked better than Halle Berry. Not bad. Not bad at all.

Between the new head shots (finally sent via messenger this afternoon by Armando) and her actual line in an actual movie, it was only a matter of time before Genevieve's husband, Gifford, followed up on his promise to get her into *real* auditions. Auditions where the casting directors were looking for something besides a dwarf with hostessing skills. She was on her way.

So if she was so awesome, why hadn't Trey called? Not that she had been checking her cell phone for missed calls every five minutes. She'd never be that girl.

But she couldn't deny she'd eaten more than her fair share of Ben & Jerry's Cherry Garcia while analyzing every moment they'd spent together on the set of *Bringing Down Jones,* including the ten minutes they'd been alone in Trey's deluxe Starwagon trailer, where he'd purposefully brushed against her as he'd passed by to show her the widescreen Plasma TV.

Rat tat tat tat. By now, Sophie recognized Sam's knock at her door. She also recognized the fact that he'd been a total asshole since their showdown after the party two weeks ago. She had two options. Go forth and tell him to his face that she didn't appreciate the way he'd weaseled out of being her scene partner at acting class last night. Or lie down on the Mexican tile floor and pretend she wasn't home.

"I have a peace offering," he called through the door. "I know you're in there."

Option one it is, she thought. If nothing else, she could make Sam drool with jealousy over her superior head shots. She looked down to check her white short shorts and light green tank for random food stains, then went to open the door.

"What kind of peace offering?" Sophie made a mental note that asshole or not, Sam *did* know how to wear a pair of Levi's.

"We have an audition," he announced as they walked into the airy living room. "I mean, *I* have an audition and *you* have an audition. This afternoon."

The very word sent a rush of adrenaline pumping through her circulatory system. But she wasn't ready to accept the olive branch. Yet.

The constant up and down nature of their . . . whatever it was . . . was getting old. Much as Sophie loved to spar, Sam had a way of getting under her skin that bordered on distracting. And she didn't need any more distractions.

"What's the audition for?" she asked casually as Sam followed her into the living room.

"The Larchmont Playhouse is putting up *The Cherry Orchard,*" Sam announced. "I know the director . . . mentioned your name. He wants you to audition for Anya."

Sophie fought back a small wave of disappointment. She'd assumed the audition was for a movie or new TV show. The Larchmont Playhouse wasn't exactly Broadway. Then again, *The Cherry Orchard* was one of her favorite plays, and who knew what big shot might see her performance and realize she was destined for stardom?

Sam eyed the Halle Berry look-alike photo she'd intentionally left on the middle of the coffee table, then flopped onto the rattan sofa. Apparently, he was done talking until she came up with a response.

"Why are you being nice?" She knelt on one of the thousand or so chenille floor pillows that populated her little casa.

For several seconds, Sam didn't respond. He just sort of looked at her like she was a science experiment he didn't understand.

"You really bug me," he responded finally. "And I don't know why."

Not the answer she was expecting. Not an answer at all. "Okay . . ."

"I think maybe I'm jealous," Sam admitted. "You've got the kind of confidence I wish I had —"

"You're confident!" Sophie interjected. "You're so confident you're obnoxious."

"On the outside . . . yeah. On the inside, not so much. Like I told you before, being the pool boy doesn't exactly build self-esteem."

One of the little muscles next to Sam's left eye was twitching. This admission was killing him — a fact that warmed Sophie's heart to such a degree that she actually felt generously toward him.

"I could torture you by making you go into deep psychoanalysis on yourself," she smiled. "You know, my mom's a shrink."

Sam winced. "Please, don't."

"You need to spend a night with my friends. We all have our issues . . . but when we're together, it seems like anything's possible."

"The Fearsome Foursome rule the world?" She'd told him about Becca, Kate, and Harper during one of their poolside chats, and he'd immediately given the friends the nickname.

"Make fun all you want. We're unstoppable."

At least, that's what Sophie told *herself* in those dark moments in the middle of the night when she woke up wondering if coming to LA had been a huge mistake. Usually, if she thought back to the night on Kate's roof, and remembered Harper's inspiring speech, she could concentrate hard and talk herself back into believing.

Sam was looking pointedly at her. "Why do I always confess my deepest neuroses to you?" he asked. "I'm not even sure I *like* you."

"It's the shrink gene." She grinned. "Thanks for getting me the audition."

"Friends?"

"Friends." Sophie breathed an internal sigh of relief. She needed Sam, no matter how annoying he could be.

She reached for her cell. "I'll call Celeste and beg her to get someone to cover my shift."

"Use tears if she tries to say no," Sam suggested. "Crying is the ultimate weapon in a girl's arsenal."

Sophie giggled. She couldn't deny that Sam was funny, in addition to being cute. If he ever stopped having a chip on his shoulder, maybe he'd open his eyes and ask her on an actual date. Not that she'd say yes right away. She'd make him wait for a week or so to prove a point.

Just as she opened her Motorola to dial, it began to vibrate. Probably Harper or Becca, calling to see whether or not she'd heard from Trey yet.

"I'm busy," she announced into the phone. She wanted to be clear right up front she didn't have time to chat.

"Too bad. I was hoping to take you to the beach."

Oh God. Oh God. Oh God. It wasn't Harper or Becca. "Hi, Trey," she managed to spit out. "What's up?"

"I had fun hanging out on the set the other day."

"Me, too." Sophie hoped that if she fainted, Sam would make sure she didn't hit her head on anything sharp. "And I'm not *that* busy."

"I haven't been to Zuma in ages," Trey continued. "The snack bar there has the best corn dogs on the West coast."

"I like corn dogs."

Oh God, she sounded like a complete fucking moron. Where was the Sophie Bushell she knew and loved? The one who always knew just what to say?

"Great. I'll pick you up in an hour." The line went dead before she could remember to tell him she had an audition and wasn't available in an hour.

Sam looked up from a stack of headshots as she stuffed her cell phone into her back jeans pocket. "You're not going to the audition," he stated flatly.

"Trey Benson wants to take me to Malibu." She bit her lip, awaiting one of Sam's typical rants about how she lacked seriousness as an actor.

But he just nodded. "Trey's the It Boy. Hanging with him could be the best thing for your career." He stood up and headed for the door. "Just remember the little people when you're discovered, huh?"

Sophie would definitely remember the little people if she ever made it. But right now her career wasn't uppermost in her mind. And neither was worrying about Sam Piper's fragile male ego. She was thinking about Trey Benson's lips — and wondering how they'd feel against hers.

This is not my life. Sophie wasn't sure whose life it *was* — maybe Mischa Barton's — but it definitely didn't belong to her. Sophie Bushell didn't cruise the Pacific Coast Highway in a silver Mercedes convertible in the middle of the week. Sophie Bushell didn't stop to have her picture taken by a photographer from *People* magazine. Sophie Bushell didn't dine with up-and-coming movie stars who made Tom Cruise look like "the ugly guy" on the list they'd made for Kate.

Maybe her afternoon with Trey Benson wasn't happening at all. Maybe she'd had a horrible accident on the 101, and she was lying in some hospital bed in a deep coma. She could almost hear Angela at her side, begging her only daughter to return to consciousness. Even Trey's outfit, light gray slim-cut pants and a semi-fitted plain white t-shirt, was probably a figment of her imagination.

"What's your name?" At first, she thought Trey was talking to her. Then she realized a freckled giggling tweener had approached their table, paper napkin and pen in hand, to ask for an autograph.

Sophie snapped out of her reverie, hoping that Trey hadn't noticed she'd disappeared. If he had, she'd blame it on the dolphins she'd seen out the window. *Everyone* took a moment to enjoy a frolicking dolphin.

"I'm Olivia," the giggler squeaked, glancing over at her mother to make sure she was getting a digital photo of the exchange.

Halfway to Malibu, Trey had decided it was too windy for corn dogs on the beach. Instead, he'd taken Sophie to Gladstone's for smoked salmon bruschetta and crab cakes. Large and airy, with comfortable booths and a view of the Pacific, Gladstone's was — according to Trey — a must-visit for anyone new to LA. The restaurant was also, apparently, a tourist destination. Since they'd sat down half an hour ago, overexcited pale-faced eaters who had probably traveled hours to do the Universal Studios tour had been staring at Trey and whispering.

The giggler, now identified as Olivia, turned shyly to Sophie after Trey had handed back her freshly signed Gladstone's napkin. "Can I have yours, too?" she asked eagerly, her blue eyes big with hope.

Sophie was grateful her caramel skin camouflaged the blush she knew was rising to her cheeks. "I'm not famous. Sorry."

But Trey's brown eyes had a mischievous glint. "Don't be modest, Sophie. Give the girl an autograph."

Sophie stared at him. He grinned back, nodding toward the girl. She felt her blush deepen as she realized that Trey wanted her to pretend to be a Somebody as opposed to a Nobody.

"Please?" Olivia was sort of hopping up and down. Sophie had the sense that this was the most exciting thing that had happened in her short suburban life.

For a few seconds, she was frozen in the booth, torn between

195

wanting to please Trey Benson and wanting to slip under the table to hide among crab cake scraps and lobster shells. Then again . . . Sophie *was* an actress. And she *looked* like she could be famous in her skintight Diesel jeans and the pale pink Valentino jacket she'd gotten for twenty percent off its retail price at Loehmann's in the Beverly Center.

A tingle of excitement in her fingertips, Sophie reached for the pen. "To Olivia," she recited, writing it down as the girl practically trembled with excitement. "Never give up your Dreams." Then she signed her name, making the *S* and the *B* so big they barely fit on the napkin.

God, this felt good. This was what she was meant to do. Sign autographs and have leisurely lunches with movie stars. This *was* her life. And she absolutely adored it.

"What can I see you in?" Olivia asked, bursting Sophie's fantasy bubble. "I'm going to tell all my friends."

"Uh . . ." You're an actress, she chided herself. *Make something up!*

"She's got a pivotal role in *Bringing Down Jones,*" Trey said, coming to her rescue. "Look for her in the ballroom scene."

Once Olivia was gone, she raised her eyebrows at Trey. "You're Satan."

"He had all the fun, right?" Trey teased. His elbows were on the table, and he was leaning in close to her. Sophie could smell his sandalwood soap and see the tiny birthmark at the edge of his right temple. She was longing to reach out and touch his deeply tanned forearms.

"You're dangerous." She was flirting, but it was also a fact.

He slid forward in the booth so that their faces were almost touching. "I guess you'll find out." Then he picked up his crab cake sandwich and took a bite.

Sophie felt a wave of disappointment. Trey wasn't going to kiss her. At least, not right now. *He's waiting for the perfect moment. He doesn't want our first kiss to be in front of a bunch of nosy tourists.*

But three hours later, after a romantic walk on the beach and a long drive home, the perfect moment still hadn't come. Trey didn't so much as hold her hand or accidentally-on-purpose brush her knee as he shifted the gears of his Mercedes. Apparently, he didn't want to.

"We'll do this again," Trey smiled when he finally pulled up to the Meyers' mansion. "I had fun."

"Me, too," she responded, as if she didn't expect him to kiss her. As if it weren't the only thing she'd been thinking about since he picked her up.

She got out of the car and headed toward her guesthouse, deflating like Kate's Aerobed when its plug was pulled. Being a Somebody for the afternoon had been pure bliss. But it had also been a mirage.

In LA, Sophie was a Nobody.

As far as Becca could tell, football consisted of nothing more than a bunch of big, oaf-y guys in padded suits crashing into each other over and over, and trying to get a ball that looked like a meatloaf from one end of a field to another. Seriously, what was the point?

She'd been expressing exactly that sentiment from the moment she climbed into the stands of the Middlebury-Williams game with Isabelle and Taymar.

"Then why are you here?" Isabelle asked, starting to get annoyed.

"School spirit," Becca muttered.

Why *was* she there? The temperature had to be below zero, and Becca's red fleece gloves and hat weren't cutting it. Her ears and fingers felt like they were about to snap off, and she was sure her nose had succumbed to frostbite at least twenty minutes ago. No one else seemed to mind — there were at least a thousand other people in the stands, students and alumni, parents and professors, all dressed in Middlebury blue, all cheering and screaming Stuart Pendergrass's name. She wasn't sure why. Middlebury was winning, but it didn't seem to Becca that Stuart was doing such a spectacular job. Despite the fact that she didn't like the guy, she still didn't enjoy seeing him get flattened over and over again by a bunch of Williams thugs.

Wasn't he a running back? Weren't running backs supposed to *run,* not get clobbered every three seconds? He had managed to score two touchdowns, which was impressive by any standard. But every time the ball came toward him, Becca found herself gripping her crutches with one hand and covering her face with the other.

How could people stand to watch this? How could people call this a game? There was nothing enjoyable about watching someone you . . . had any kind of feelings for, even negative feelings, get smacked around.

The halftime buzzer sounded, and Becca breathed a sigh of relief. Fifteen whole minutes without further battering.

Then the weirdest thing happened. As the team ran past the stands on the way off the field, she would have sworn . . .

She had to be wrong.

But she could have sworn that Stuart smiled up at her. And winked.

Even weirder, Becca realized, as she tried to quell an unwelcome, fluttering feeling in her stomach . . . she didn't hate him for it.

"I am *not* insane," Harper repeated for a third time as she popped open another can of Diet Coke. "Define insane."

Judd munched on a sour cream and onion Pringle. "Harper, you're stalking your *father.*"

She rolled her eyes. If Judd couldn't understand why she found it necessary to park his 1994 Saturn outside her dad's office building for three hours in an attempt to catch her father cheating on her mom, that was *his* problem. She wasn't about to be thwarted in her mission because Judd's butt was getting sore.

"I'm trying to protect my mother from further pain and humiliation," Harper informed him. "It's called being a good daughter."

"It's called procrastination," Judd countered. "You're making up this whole twisted fantasy about your dad having an affair so that you don't have to sit in front of your computer and write."

"Can we just sit *here* and stare, please?"

"Fine by me."

Harper dug into a jumbo bag of Skittles. Judd was wrong. She wasn't procrastinating. If she wanted to procrastinate, she'd lie on her mattress and relive those humiliating moments with Mr. Finelli again and again. Staking out her dad was productive, even necessary.

So far, there hadn't been much action on the street. Two people had sped by on mountain bikes. One dred-locked guy had approached to ask if they wanted to sign one of the wildlife petitions that were constantly circulating in Boulder. And several birds had successfully aimed their droppings on Judd's windshield. But Harper was willing to wait for as long as it took. Even if it meant giving up a whole night of writing.

Suddenly, Judd jabbed her in the side with his elbow. "That's him, right?"

Harper forced her thoughts away from the horrified look on Mr. Finelli's face when she'd kissed him and looked in the direction Judd was pointing. Six feet, two inches. Salt-and-pepper hair. Plaid work shirt. There he was. Her dad.

Walking with a woman who wasn't her mother. Who in no way *resembled* her mother. The woman had bright red poufy hair and legs that went on forever. In tight black pants and a maroon sweater set, she looked exactly like the kind of person a perfectly happy middle-aged man would abandon his family over. Sort of like Becca's stepmom.

"Oh God . . ." Harper felt like she couldn't breathe. Until this moment, she hadn't realized how desperately she'd hoped her spying would be in vain.

"She's probably a colleague," Judd surmised. "Or someone who works in the same building."

"My dad's a contractor," she snapped. "Does she look like a contractor?"

"Harper — you're spinning." Judd pulled at his already-mussed dark hair in frustration.

The woman veered off toward a lime green VW bug. Harper felt a wave of relief until her dad also veered, then folded his tall frame into the tiny, too-cute car.

"Follow them!" She pushed her glasses higher on her nose and leaned forward to try to get a better look at her dad and Red-Headed Tramp.

"I will *not*."

"Judd, I'm begging you. This is me, begging."

The VW headed out of the parking lot and turned left. Judd gave Harper a look that communicated both pity and disdain, then reluctantly started his engine.

"Go! Go! Go!" she screeched.

Judd cut through two lanes of traffic, successfully navigating the teal-blue Saturn into position behind the Bug. They were going east on Canyon Boulevard, away from downtown. Probably toward some seedy motel on U.S. 36, Harper conjectured. As they cruised through the streets, she crouched down in her seat, praying her dad wouldn't turn around and see a familiar pair of black glasses peering over the dashboard.

"She's got an I BREAK FOR DOLPHINS bumper sticker," Harper ranted. "There *are* no dolphins in Colorado."

"Maybe she's from California," Judd suggested. "Or Miami."

Harper stared him down. "Can you be a decent person and *hate* her? Please?"

200

About a minute later, Judd glanced over at her. "As your friend, I have to advise that we turn around now. This is not healthy behavior."

"Turn right!" Harper yelled as, in front of them, the VW took a sharp turn. "RIGHT!"

Judd jerked the steering wheel. . . .

WHAM!

The Saturn plowed into the curb with a sickening crunch. The VW sped off in the distance, gone.

"Jesus Christ!" he shouted, sounding just a tad infuriated. His hair looked like it was going to leap off his head.

"I didn't mean to turn exactly that second," Harper offered lamely. "Whoops?"

Judd threw open the driver's side door and stomped toward the car's front bumper. Harper trailed him, trying to think of why he shouldn't punch her in the face. Unfortunately, no reason came to mind.

The bumper was half-ripped off, and there was a dent the size of her fist in the right front panel, where the Saturn had hit an ill-placed fire hydrant.

"You're paying for that," Judd stated flatly.

And she knew she would. In more ways than one.

"Is he still there?" Becca whispered to Isabelle, who glanced casually over Becca's shoulder.

"Five feet behind you," she informed her quietly.

The after-game party in the student union was a huge, crowded mass of sweaty people; loud, throbbing music; and raucous drinking games. But somehow Stuart Pendergrass had been five feet away from her all night.

"Doesn't he have better things to do than hover?" Becca muttered.

"He's into you," Taymar grinned. "I saw that wink today."

Isabelle raised an eyebrow at Becca.

"Wink? Clearly I am out of the loop."

"It was nothing," Becca said, taking a sip of her Diet Sprite. Her alcoholic days were over and then some.

Isabelle nodded knowingly. "Mmm-hmm."

"What?"

Isabelle shrugged. "Suddenly it makes sense why you wanted to come to this party tonight, that's all. And why you're wearing the sexy black pants."

Becca went into defensive mode.

"I came because . . . I wanted to hang out with my friends . . . and there's free soda," she finished lamely.

Taymar and Isabelle exchanged an amused glance. It was more than Becca could take.

"Fine, me and my sexy black pants are going home."

Isabelle laughed. "Someone can't take the heat."

Becca rolled her eyes. She'd hobbled halfway across campus on crutches, withstood several humiliating "on fi-ya" jokes, and managed to stay upright in the crushing crowd. All to be accused of having feelings for Stuart Pendergrass.

"Enough," she said with a grin, and headed for the exit.

Getting through the crowd on crutches was an obstacle course worthy of *Survivor*. By the time she'd made it to fresh air, the back of her neck was sweaty and her arms ached. Just a half mile more, she said to herself, starting down the path toward her dorm.

"Hey, Becca," a male voice called behind her. "Wait up."

A herd of butterflies sprang to life in her stomach.

She turned around. Stuart Pendergrass was squeezing through the crowd at the double-doors.

Becca wanted to shrink into the ground. All those people had heard him call her name. Now they were watching as he came jogging up the path toward her. She recognized Luke at the door, and Andi, and a couple other people from the ski team.

When Stuart got to her, he seemed almost nervous. Becca thought vaguely that he couldn't have been warm enough in his Middlebury striped sweats and black puffy jacket.

"You want a ride?" He switched his weight from one foot to the other, then back again.

Becca blinked. After all the horrible things she'd said and done, he wanted to know if she wanted a ride?

"You have a car?" she asked, flustered.

"Nope," Stuart replied. Then he turned around and presented his back.

"Hop on."

Becca laughed. She hadn't meant to, but the laugh just bubbled up before she could stop it.

Stuart looked over his shoulder. He had the nicest smile, she decided, and she didn't even add "for a dumb jock."

Becca glanced back at the crowd at the door. No one seemed to be watching them anymore.

"You scared?" he said, daring her.

Becca Winsberg had never turned down a dare in her life. She handed him her crutches. He bent down. And she jumped.

Immediately, she wished she hadn't.

For one thing, Andi yelled, "Go, Bec!" and the crowd at the door started cheering. Actually cheering. While Becca blushed furiously, Stuart gave them a little wave, and started off toward her dorm.

"Am I too heavy?" she asked, genuinely concerned.

"Light as a feather," he said.

Becca resisted the urge to say "stiff as a board." She didn't want to use any words that had any kind of sexual connotation. Not when his back was so . . . wide. And breathtakingly strong.

With her legs wrapped around his waist, her hands had nowhere to go but his shoulders. They were hard and muscular . . . and perfect.

She closed her eyes. One of her hands had somehow landed partway under his jacket collar, and the warmth of his skin burned into her palm. She found herself wanting to lean into him, rest her head against the back of his neck . . .

Becca gave herself a mental shake.

Stuart was just being nice. He was, she had to admit, a nice guy. Not at all like she'd imagined him. But that didn't change the fact that he had seen her at her absolute worst. That he was carrying her home just showed he felt sorry for her. It was nothing more than that.

Becca cleared her throat. There was something she had to say.

"Um, I should thank you. And, uh, apologize about the other night and about what I said at the gym —"

"Not a problem," Stuart replied.

As he hiked her up higher on his back, Becca's cheek brushed against his hair. She closed her eyes. It was not soft, she told herself. It did not smell like fresh-baked cookies. Above all, she did not — absolutely did not — want to run her fingers through it.

"That purple punch," he said, "sneaks up on you. Last year, I woke up in my underwear in the middle of the quad once."

"No, you didn't," Becca laughed, hardly able to believe he had managed to make her laugh about the most humiliating moment of her life.

"No," he admitted. Becca could tell he was grinning. "But I easily could have."

Then, as he took a shortcut across the lawn that led to her dorm, he forced her — under threat of "accidentally" dropping her in a snowbank — to reveal every single college she had applied to (Harvard, Williams, Amherst, Bowdoin, Bates, Brown, Michigan, Penn, and Chapel Hill), every college that had rejected her (Harvard,

Williams, Amherst, Penn, and Chapel Hill), and the reason why she had chosen Middlebury.

"Coach Maddix," Becca answered, her laughter fading. "I've always wanted to ski for him. All the other schools were back-ups."

"Don't tell Harvard." Stuart smiled, pushing open the door to her dormitory. "Where to?"

"Up," Becca instructed. "But I can walk —"

But Stuart was already halfway up the stairs to the second floor.

When he put her down at her door, and they were once again face to face, the idle conversation frittered to awkward silence.

"So . . ." he broke the pause, handing her her crutches.

Becca looked at the floor.

"Thanks for the ride," she mumbled.

And when Stuart said "Anytime," there was a shift in his voice that forced her to look up.

I'm going to have a heart attack. The pounding in her chest could mean nothing else.

Stuart took a step toward her.

"Becca —"

Becca panicked.

"I have to go," she said quickly.

Two seconds later, she was inside her room.

By the time she got to her bed, rivulets of tears covered her cheeks.

No one had ever looked at her the way Stuart looked at her. It made her feel warm and wanted and beautiful.

Most of all, it scared her to death.

WARNER BROTHERS STUDIOS
VISITOR'S PASS

Time: 13:45
Date: November 3
Expires: 21:00

Sophie Bushell

Destination:
Stage 12

Contact:
Trey Benson

Security (323) 871-5446

TWELVE

Qu'est ce que c'est?" Kate asked as Chantal slid a blank piece of paper across the dining table toward her.

"C'est papier," Chantal responded briskly, getting up to whisk away the dinner plates. As had been their custom for the last three weeks, Kate had picked up groceries after work at the nearby café where Chantal had found her a job, then Chantal had spent an hour working magic in the kitchen, as if she thought a healthy French meal could cure all of Kate's ills. This morning, the list she'd handed Kate had been a little more elaborate than usual, and at dinner she'd insisted Kate join her in a glass of red wine.

"Je sais que c'est papier," Kate said cautiously, as Chantal returned from the kitchen, *"mais pourquoi?"*

"La liste," Chantal said simply.

Harper's list.

A tight panic began to thread its way through the space between Kate's breasts. She'd grown accustomed to the feeling lately — every time she rounded a blind corner, every time a teenager with a certain shade of brown hair passed the café, every time anyone looked at her just a little too closely. And anytime Chantal tried to get her to talk about Athens.

"The list is gone," Kate explained, switching to English. "They took it."

"*Oui,*" Chantal said, as her tiny figure settled determinedly in the chair across from Kate. "But you remember it, *non?*"

Kate hesitated. If she tried she probably could, but the list — combined with her own stupidity — was what had gotten her in trouble in the first place. She wasn't ready to put those pieces back together. Not yet.

Slowly, Kate had grown comfortable in Paris. She loved Chantal's spare room, which was cluttered with antiques and books, and her French was improving daily. Every night she fell asleep in the lumpy iron bed she had slept in with Magnus. If she tried, she could imagine his smell still lingering on the pillow. And every morning she got up, walked three blocks to Café Bazin, and served coffees and sandwiches until six. Then she hit the corner market, and ate a delicious dinner with Chantal.

On the nights Chantal went out to *le cinema* or to lectures at the Sorbonne, or when she had guests over — students from Chantal's classes were a constant presence, as was a lively group of academics and artists — Kate retired to her room early and read American westerns, the only English books that were readily available at the book stalls along the Seine. She wasn't trying to be antisocial. She just didn't feel up to answering the inevitable questions. How did she know Chantal? What was she doing in Paris? What was up with the huge, hideous scar on her forehead?

Chantal seemed to understand, for the most part, that she was in hibernation mode — resting in seclusion, recovering quietly. Only, Kate wondered, was she really recovering? She still had nightmares every night of grabbing hands in thick, tarry blackness. And every day, she struggled against an encroaching unease. She'd started this journey to find herself, to learn to trust herself the way she had always trusted her parents and her friends. Instead, she had found that

210

she couldn't trust herself at all. More than fear, more than anything, that awareness was paralyzing.

And now, Chantal was staring at her from across the table, trying to force her back into motion.

"I only remember a few things from the list," she lied, twisting the ends of her now-chin-length hair.

"*Cherie,* your hair!" Chantal had exclaimed, horrified, when Kate arrived at her doorstep three and a half weeks ago. "No, no, no, it will not do."

Chantal had barely given her time to put down her backpack before she'd called in Marcielle, a downstairs neighbor.

"Marcielle is *genius,*" Chantal had explained as she spread a frayed purple towel beneath a chair in the kitchen and made Kate sit. Kate hadn't cared about her hair either way, so she sat quietly while Marcielle and Chantal consulted in fast-paced French, and then Marcielle had gone to work. The results were good, though Kate hadn't spent much time looking in the mirror lately. Just enough to know that, with her stitches now out, an ugly pink scar bisected her right eyebrow.

On the surface, at least, everything else was pretty much healed.

"Katherine," Chantal said now, gently, "you must let me help you."

Kate forced a smile. "You've helped me so much already," she said sincerely. And then, standing up, she added, "I'm fine. Really."

She touched a hand to Chantal's shoulder as she walked into the kitchen. The dishes had to be done, and now seemed like a good time to make an escape.

But Chantal followed her, leaving the piece of paper on the table. Standing in the kitchen doorway, she said, "You know, *cherie,* to be safe always . . . is the same as to be dead."

Kate turned on the faucet over the sink. She didn't want to talk about this, even more than she didn't want to be rude.

Chantal stood there for several moments, then lifted her hands in a gesture of regret and acceptance.

211

"*D'accord,*" she said, turning back to the living room.

The next morning, Kate noticed on her way out the door, the piece of paper was gone.

"Of course he wants to kiss you," Sophie informed Becca, half-hoping that her cell phone battery would die mid-pep talk. "The piggy back ride was a non-threatening way to let you know he's ready to boink."

They had been having the same conversation ever since Becca almost-kissed Stuart. Usually, Sophie loved the ongoing analysis of her friend's burgeoning romantic life. But today she was distracted with a capital T-R-E-Y.

On the other end of the phone, Becca sighed. Sophie could picture her in Nike track pants and an oversized Middlebury t-shirt, probably lying on the floor of her dorm room. "I don't know if I even want him to kiss me . . . it's all too weird."

"That's just nerves," Sophie told her, checking out her outfit in the reflection of the glass-fronted refrigerator in the catering truck on the set of Trey Benson's new movie, *Gradual Healing*. "Trust me. You want it."

"Then how come the thought of anything having to do with Stuart and me and the possibility of tongues touching makes me want to run?" Becca asked.

Sophie adjusted one of her gold dangly earrings as Ga, the head of catering, headed toward her with the triple espresso she'd requested. "I gotta go, Bec. Trey's coffee is ready."

"Doesn't he have some blue-eyed bimbo assistant for that kind of stuff?" Becca wondered aloud, clearly not wanting to get off the phone. "Aren't you supposed to be his guest?"

"I *offered* to get him coffee," Sophie replied haughtily. "Go practice kissing on a pillow or something. I'll talk to you later."

She snapped her cell shut and smiled at Ga, who'd no doubt heard her end of that last exchange. Well, the caterer could think what he wanted. And so could Becca. Sophie knew she was a lot more to Trey than a coffee mule — she just wasn't sure what "more" was yet.

Until this morning, Sophie hadn't heard from Trey since their day at the beach. She had played the whole thing off to Sam and her best friends like she didn't care. Who wanted to be at the beck and call of a pretty-boy actor, anyway?

They'd all gone along with her, saying it was probably for the best. She needed to focus on her career, blah, blah, blah. Even Sam, who'd gotten the part of Peter Trophimof in *The Cherry Orchard,* had only rubbed her nose *slightly* in the fact that she'd blown off that audition.

And then this morning, Trey had called full of apologies for not getting in touch sooner and invited her to the set of his new movie. Sophie Bushell of Boulder, Colorado, would have hung up on him without bothering to hear an explanation. *That* Sophie rarely gave guys a second chance. She didn't need to. In Boulder, Sophie dictated her own terms and was always at the center of the action.

But Sophie Bushell of Beverly Hills, California, hadn't been able to resist the chance to see Trey again. *That* Sophie was more than a little starstruck. She was also aware that to be in The Business, she had to be *around* The Business. And spending the day on a movie set definitely qualified. She had already learned she wasn't the same person here as she was at home. So why fight it now, when she had the chance to get to know Trey better?

Sure, maybe her friends would say that scrapping her plans for the day just to be close to a fairly famous actor was superficial, even weak. But they weren't going through this. They didn't know what she'd learned. To make it as an actress, she had to be trying — in whatever form that took — every hour of the day, every day of the week. It was all part of Celeste's LA equation. And she really *liked*

Trey. It wasn't like she wanted to be with him just because it might be good for her career.

So here she was. Only Trey had been so focused on work he'd barely talked to her in the past two hours. And instead of acting in front of the camera, she'd been stuck in the quaintly designed kitchen of the Middle-American suburban house the movie crew had built on Stage 12 of the studio lot, sitting behind the director's monitor, watching the action like the hanger-on she, in fact, was.

Not that she'd been hoping Trey would get her another line. That kind of hope would be selfish. But still.

Sophie took the espresso and headed back to the set, where Trey was running lines for his next scene.

"Triple espresso," she announced, handing the coffee to Trey, who was sitting in a chair emblazoned with his name.

Gradual Healing was about a dysfunctional family in crisis. Sophie had read only Trey's pages of the screenplay, but as far as she could tell, his character had refused to speak to anyone in the family since they boycotted his wedding to a young stripper. Now the stripper had died in a car accident, and the family was slowly realizing they'd been total assholes. It was a big role, and Sophie knew Trey had a lot riding on it. If the movie was a hit, he would go from a sort-of-household name to a total-household name, and his career would reach a whole new level.

According to the script, the next scene took place after the stripper's funeral. Trey had changed into a black suit for the scene, but wardrobe had rumpled his shirt and set his blue-and-green-striped tie askew to convey his character's inner turmoil.

He smiled at her. "Thanks, babe. You're the best."

Babe? Did Trey even remember her name? Maybe it was the way Becca had questioned Sophie getting Trey's espresso, or maybe it was her frustration over not having her own chair with her own name on it. But as he went back to his lines, Sophie felt an inner rebellion brewing. She didn't care who Trey Benson was. He didn't have the right to pretend like she wasn't there. After all, *he* had called *her*.

"I don't think we're at 'babe' level yet."

"What?"

Sophie tried to keep her hands from shaking. "You just referred to me as 'babe.' I'd appreciate it if you used my name." She raised an eyebrow, glad she'd spent the time to do the "smoky eyes" she'd read about in *Elle* this month. "It's Sophie, in case you forgot."

"Sorry, it's a Hollywood thing." Trey grinned. "Forgive me?"

She was dying to say yes, but pride stood in her way. "Anyway, now that you've got your espresso, I'm gonna go. See you around."

She turned to leave, but he caught her elbow and pulled her close.

"I'm an asshole," Trey said. "I invited you down here, and then I got caught up in working."

Sophie hesitated. If she were all about dignity, she'd do what she said she was going to, and walk. He could call and beg for forgiveness later. But . . . who was she to walk out on Trey Benson? Really, if she thought about it, she was being a baby. The guy was in the middle of making a major motion picture, and she wanted . . . What? For him to blow off memorizing his lines so they could banter?

"No biggie," she responded. *I love being your coffee mule,* she added silently.

"No, it is a biggie." He frowned. "Being an actor is a head trip. Sometimes you forget to be a decent human being."

Sophie shrugged. "I don't think I'd ever be like that, but whatever." After all, he could have at least called her by her *name* in between memorizing lines. That wasn't too much to ask.

For a moment, Trey didn't say anything. As he stared off in the distance, musing about his lack of decency, she wondered what it was about Los Angeles that produced so many egomaniacal jerks. So many good-looking egomaniacal jerks.

"The director can shoot my side of this scene tomorrow," he responded finally, hopping off his chair. "My stand-in can fill in while he gets coverage on the other actors."

Sophie just looked at him. All this lingo was new to her, but she didn't want to admit she had no idea what Trey was talking about.

"Which means we can get the hell out of here," he clarified. "Let me take you someplace special. Show you I'm still a real person."

"Fine. Just no babe-ing me."

As he threw an arm around her shoulders to lead her off the set, she felt a wave of pleasure. Telling off Trey had been almost as much fun as telling off Sam. And twice as worthy of an internal pat on the back.

No doubt about it. Sophie Bushell was a force to be reckoned with, and she wasn't going to let anyone — especially herself — forget it.

"'This Living Hand,'" Becca whispered. "Keats or Donne?"

"Keats," Stuart answered. "Thou wouldst wish thine own heart dry of blood, so in my veins red life might strain again . . ."

He kept his voice low as he spoke, which was only proper, considering they were in the middle of the main room of the library, with a hundred people studying all around them. He wasn't *trying* to make her insides all gushy with the sexy voice. It was hardly Stuart's fault that studying for mid-terms involved reciting lines of the most romantic poetry ever written in the English language.

Becca almost groaned. Instead, she murmured, "Mmm-hmm," and flipped to the next page of her *Norton Anthology*.

For the last twelve days, she and Stuart Pendergrass had been Friends. The day after she had fled from the almost-kiss, he'd casually taken the seat beside her in English Romantic Poetry. After class, he'd walked with her to the dining hall. They'd chatted amicably —

or rather, *he* had chatted, and she had given herself a mental lecture about not being nervous. Stuart had kept the conversation going through the food line, where Becca had managed to ignore the elderly food server's raised eyebrows, and then walked with her to her regular table, where Isabelle, Taymar, and Andrew tried to hide their grins. Stuart had smiled, said hey to everyone, looked at Becca and said, "I'll see you later."

Her stomach had done flips.

And when he'd headed off to join the football team, leaving Becca to reams of teasing, she'd found that she was somehow disappointed.

Later that night he'd called to ask a question about chemistry, their other mutual class, and when Becca hung up she realized she'd been on the phone for forty-five minutes. Amazingly, after the first twenty, she hadn't been nervous at all. It had actually been . . . sort of enjoyable.

And so it had gone for the next eleven days. They sat next to each other in class, walked to the dining hall together, and talked on the phone almost every night. A couple times she'd caught him maybe looking at her in a more-than-friend way, but for the most part it just seemed like they were . . . pals.

And with every passing day, being a pal sucked more and more. For one thing, it turned out Stuart Pendergass was *smart*. And not just smart-for-a-football-player. He was in the smart-for-an-astrophysicist range. He was also really nice. Not annoyingly so — he didn't find homes for stray kittens on Saturdays, or say "holy cow" instead of "damn." But he did tolerate his roommate's penchant for three-thousand-decibel Mötley Crüe with a wry "It's his room, too." And he always carried her backpack whenever they walked anywhere together, which was seriously nice, since it was her own stupid fault she was on crutches, anyway.

And then there was the matter of him carrying *her*. Twice.

Now, with mid-terms fast approaching, it had seemed only natural that they would study together. Being such good pals, and all.

And it only made sense that they would be sitting so close together, heads almost touching, as they pored through the *Norton Anthology* and Blake's *Songs of Innocence*.

Becca froze as an electrical jolt shot up her spine.

Stuart was leaning down to get something out of his backpack, and as he moved his whole thigh had suddenly pressed against hers.

Oh God. Oh God oh God oh God.

Stuart straightened and put his chem book on the table. But his thigh stayed where it was.

Should she move? If she didn't move, would he think she *wanted* his leg pressed against her? *Did* she? Maybe she did . . .

Stuart gently knocked his knee against hers.

"You ready to switch gears?" he asked, opening his chemistry textbook.

So clearly he was *aware* of the touching. Did that mean it was I'm-so-not-attracted-to-you-it-doesn't-matter-if-we-touch touching? Or was it . . . something else?

Becca nodded stiffly.

Stuart looked at her, and seemed to sense that she was uncomfortable.

"Sorry," he said, pulling his leg away.

Becca almost moaned in dismay. She had to do *something*. So she gathered up her nerve, and twisted toward him slightly until her leg once again rested gently against his.

He looked at her, surprised.

"Listen," she whispered. "I'm kind of an idiot. And I know I've been horrible to you —"

"You haven't —"

"Please, I have. I mean, not lately. I just . . . I'm really sorry."

Stuart smiled. "Okay."

He had a really nice smile.

Becca plowed on, before she lost her nerve.

"It's just that, the first day . . . you know, on the track?"

"When you pissed off Maddix?"

She nodded.

"Yeah . . . You whispered something about me to your friends and . . ." Becca faltered. "I guess it kind of . . . made me feel bad, and I just decided you were a jerk, and I have this thing about football players, usually, about how I don't usually like them, which is probably stupid, so . . ."

She took a deep breath.

"Anyway," she continued. "I'm really really, sorry. I don't think you're a jerk. At all."

Stuart had stopped smiling. Why wasn't he smiling? Was he mad? Why did he look so serious? Oh god, she was going to throw up.

And then Stuart Pendergrass pushed the chemistry textbook aside, and took her hand. Right there on the table in the crowded library. Becca's heart skipped at least two beats.

"Just so you know," he whispered, "I don't think you're a jerk, either."

"Oh," she managed. God, his voice was sexy.

"And I think what I said was that I'd never seen anyone so beautiful jump hurdles like that."

Becca's mouth opened. Beautiful?

Stuart half-smiled. "Actually," he admitted, "I may have said 'hot.'"

"Hot?" she squeaked. Hot was even better than beautiful.

Stuart nodded. He was looking at her lips. Leaning toward her.

"If I try to kiss you, will you run?" he whispered.

Becca stared into his totally unjerky, deep brown eyes, and forgot she was in the middle of the library.

"No," she whispered back.

He leaned closer.

"Good."

Then he kissed her.

And when she curled into sleep that night, smiling, she was no longer Becca Winsberg, the girl who got wasted and yelled "I'm on fi-ya!" Instead, she was Becca Winsberg, the girl who made out with Stuart Pendergrass for twenty minutes in the middle of the library . . . and who had her first real date in exactly forty-three hours and nineteen minutes.

Not that she was counting.

"What're you going to do with your first big acting paycheck?" Trey asked Sophie as they sped up the 101 Freeway in his silver Mercedes convertible.

"You mean, if I ever get one?"

They'd been driving for forty-five minutes, during which time Trey had kept up a stream of conversation in order to evade her questions about their destination. He'd changed out of his suit and into an old pair of Levi's and a faded orange t-shirt. He looked so . . . normal . . . that Sophie could almost forget who he was.

"You'll get one," he assured her. "It's just a matter of time."

"Easy for you to say," she retorted. "You probably don't even remember what cattle call auditions are like."

He glanced at her as he guided the Mercedes toward the exit ramp. "Uh-oh."

"Uh-oh, what?"

"You've got The Look." He shook his head sadly.

"What look?"

"Defeat." Trey shook his head again. "You've been here less than three months, and you're already giving up."

"Bullshit!" Sophie exclaimed, flattered that Trey had remembered exactly how long she'd been in town. But there was a teeny tiny part of her that doubted she'd ever really have a career in Hollywood that didn't include showing people to their tables.

"If you say so." He slowed the car to turn onto a tree-lined side street. "But let me show you something, just in case."

Sophie looked around the neighborhood, confused. She wasn't sure where she'd expected Trey to take her. A romantic restaurant overlooking the ocean . . . a hot nightclub so exclusive it didn't have a name . . . his three-bedroom apartment with a view of the Hollywood sign . . . There was no way any of those places were on this modest street in what as far as she could tell amounted to suburbia.

Trey observed the look on her face. "Welcome to Whittier," he announced, pulling up in front of a small, stucco house. "Home of Miguel Estoban the Third."

"Who's that?" Sophie asked, more confused than ever.

"Me." He pointed to the house. "That's where I grew up. Long way from Beverly Hills, huh?" He grinned. "Thirty-four miles, to be exact."

"Your name isn't Trey Benson?"

"It is now."

She stared at the house. It was a beige, one-story ranch, with a brick chimney, and a tiny driveway that led to what looked like a one-car garage. The front yard was well-kept, with a big palm tree and a plastic jungle gym. She tried to picture a young Trey, toddling down the front path or riding his Big Wheel in the driveway. The house looked warm and welcoming, even if it lacked the elegant columns and huge circle drives of a Beverly Hills mansion.

"Why'd you change your name?" Sophie couldn't imagine throwing away something that she so identified with the essence of her being.

"Easy explanation is there's not always a lot of work for young Mexican kids from Whittier." Trey shrugged. "Truth is, I guess I wanted to fit in."

She nodded, understanding. She knew being a person of color could be tough. How many times had kids in grammar school called her an Oreo? It made her ashamed to think about it, but there was a

221

period when she'd wished she had a magic wand to wave to make herself one hundred percent Caucasian.

"Do your parents still live here?" She wondered automatically how many girls he'd taken home to meet them.

"Never did." He smiled wryly. "My so-called mom and dad couldn't handle having kids. They sent me and my sister, Gabriella, to live here, with my godparents, when I was four."

"Wow. That's harsh." Sophie couldn't imagine how scary that must have been. Angela and Frank gave her so much attention, sometimes she wondered where they stopped and she started.

He nodded. "For a long time, I felt like nobody except Gabriella would ever love me. Like I didn't deserve to be loved."

"Abandonment issues," she said in a quiet voice, thinking of Becca. "They can really mess you up."

Trey glanced at the house, then back at her. "Point is, if I can move to Hollywood and make it as an actor, anyone can." He paused. "As long as they've got the talent."

"But how do you know you've got talent? I mean, *I* think I do. But I've been known to have an overblown opinion of myself."

Trey stared — really stared — into her eyes. "You've got It," he answered quietly. "I can tell."

Sophie was fairly sure she was still attached to the tan leather passenger seat of the Mercedes. But it was possible her body had spontaneously levitated to some higher plane. *You've got It.* The words wiped away three months of doubt and fear. They made her feel invincible.

"Why didn't you kiss me that day at the beach?" she asked softly. The question had been burning a hole in her brain — despite all protestations to the contrary — since their date.

He laughed, breaking the seriousness of the moment. "Were you offended?"

"Surprised," she retorted. "I may not be famous, but I have my fair share of guys who want to get personal with these lips."

"And what beautiful lips they are." He reached out and traced her mouth lightly with his thumb, sending a shiver down Sophie's spine.

"That's not an answer," she breathed. She was starting to get The Feeling, and this time she didn't think it would be interrupted by a cold front coming from the guy in the driver's seat.

"My character in *Gradual Healing* denies himself pleasure after his wife dies," Trey explained. "I was trying to get in touch with that feeling before I started shooting."

"So it wasn't because I didn't buy my breasts at a doctor's office?"

"Is that what you thought?"

"No." She felt herself blushing. "Maybe."

He leaned in closer, whispering as his dark hair brushed lightly against her right temple. "If I kiss you now, will I dispel your crazy ideas?"

"No," she whispered back. Melting. And oozing. Her body was doing both things, simultaneously. "Maybe."

And then Trey kissed Sophie, his lips touching hers gently but firmly. As a thousand sensations coursed through her body, she turned into honey, fine, golden honey.

When she finally opened her eyes, Sophie smiled at him, realizing that for the first time she was really *seeing* Trey. Not the actor, not the guy whose picture was in *Us* and *People*. But the boy named Miguel, who'd had a dream, just like she did.

Ninety-eight-year-old Violet Strong lay on her death bed, surrounded by her daughters, Beatrice, Phillipa, and Lucille. In the corner, Reverend Simon, now frail from a heart condition, dozed in a rocking chair, the Bible loose in his grasp. Wearing a flowing white nightgown from younger days, Violet had insisted that Phillipa apply her lipstick and her rouge, determined to look like a lady to the end. As the three daughters leaned in close to their mother to hear her final words, Harper held her breath.

And kept holding it. Seconds passed. Harper exhaled, willing Violet's thoughts at this moment of greatest transition to flow into the creative landscape of her mind. But rather than a lush forest of dialogue and description, Harper's brain was an arid desert, where only three-letter words could grow. She had no idea what the oldest character in her novel was thinking. And, therefore, she had nothing to write.

Violet Strong was the cornerstone of her novel. She was the matriarch who produced four generations of women, each stronger than the last. Her death began the book, but Harper planned to see Violet's life unfold in flashbacks, paralleling her experiences to those of the women who followed.

On her optimistic days (as rare as they were), she hoped the book would be a statement about society and culture as well as an examination of the changing role of estrogen in society. On her pessimistic days, she hoped she would be hit by a falling piano and never have to write another word.

Harper sighed as she reached for the box of Hostess mini powdered-sugar donuts she'd stolen from the kitchen. How was she supposed to know how a ninety-eight-year-old woman felt lying on her death bed? She was seventeen, she had a sugar headache, and all she really wanted to do was crawl under her Harry Potter sheets and will away the world.

But she couldn't. Kate was out there diligently checking off the items on the list she, Becca, Sophie, and Habiba had written. Sophie was auditioning and cozying up to a guy who could make her acting career. And, awkward moments with Stuart Pendergrass, or whatever his name was, aside, even Becca was moving closer to her dream of falling in love. Harper had started as the engine of the Dream Train, but now she was officially the caboose. If she didn't start writing, *really* writing, she wouldn't be able to look her friends in the faces when they showed up for Christmas. Which was only six weeks away.

She swallowed her last bite of donut and poised her hands above the keyboard of her computer. One. Two. And then she started to write.

"I love you all," Violet whispered. "I'll miss you, but I'll always be in your hearts."

Harper read the words over, then pressed down on her favorite key — Delete. Violet's speech sounded like a Hallmark card from 1955. Death was ugly and messy and, yes, maybe even beautiful. But it wasn't trite.

Closing her eyes, she tried to mentally shed the walls of irony, cynicism, and free-floating anxiety that protected her from her deepest emotions. She wanted to dig deep.

Almost immediately, she was awash in fear, guilt, embarrassment, and shame. This was good. This was what she needed. Mr. Finelli had told her to write from the heart, before The Incident. And Harper had promised to write from the gut . . .

Out of nowhere, she heard a high-pitched chirp. And then again. Was it her unconsciousness, rising up to deliver her from writer's block? No . . . It was her cell phone. She resisted the temptation to hurl the offending object at her wall and instead glanced at the caller ID.

Judd. Calling, no doubt, to remind her she'd promised to give him two hundred dollars toward the repair of his Saturn by the end of the day. As an image of her lying, cheating father and Red-Headed Tramp flashed through her mind, Harper ignored the chirping and turned back to her keyboard.

Violet looked at each of her daughters in turn, her pale blue eyes still as sharp and steely as they'd been when she was seventeen and thought she could beat whatever life threw her way.

"Your father wasn't faithful to me." Violet's announcement reached the ears of Reverend Simon, whose glasses slid down his nose as he awoke with a jerk.

"Mother, that's not true," Beatrice pleaded. "The medication is confusing you."

Violet shook her head. "I spared you from this knowledge all these years because I thought it would protect you. But it's important for you to know, to teach your daughters . . ."

"What?" Lucille asked, clasping her mother's hand and leaning close.

"Never trust a —" And with those last words, Violet's eyes drifted shut. She was gone.

For a moment, the sisters stared at one another. The death had been inevitable, but the revelation was a shock. Their beloved, trusted father a rogue, a philanderer? It seemed impossible.

"Never trust a man," Phillipa said, finishing her mother's statement. "I learned that lesson when I was still in high school."

Beatrice shrugged. "Never trust anyone. Even your best friend will lie to your face."

Harper hit Save and reached for another donut. As it turned out, she hadn't had to dig too deep. Death wasn't the only thing that was messy. Life was, too.

University of Colorado at Boulder

ucb.edu

From: hablba@ucb.edu

To: katherinef@ucb.edu

Subject: Hi

Hi Kate,

Harper said I should e-mail you. So here I am, e-mailing. I hope you're
having a good trip. Mom and Dad are doing fine, but I think they miss you.
I'm doing good. It's weird having the bathroom to myself. I hope you don't
mind, but I used some of that facial scrub stuff.

Your sister,
Habiba

Compose   Inbox   Sent Mail   Drafts   Trash

THIRTEEN

You disappeared for an hour with that pretentious freak!" the lanky, black-clad young man at the corner table was saying to his girlfriend in rapid-fire French.

Kate set down a citron presse for him, and a café au lait for the girlfriend, then lingered at the nearby register. She wasn't eavesdropping, exactly. She was *learning*. She'd picked up more French in a month of listening to other people's conversations than she had in four years of high school — and she had been an excellent student.

The couple at the corner table, *par example,* had been together six months, and the girlfriend apparently had a tendency to hang all over her ex whenever they ran into him at a party. The burly man at table three, who was plodding through a messy pile of paperwork, had received four cell phone calls in the last twenty minutes, all from his nine-year-old daughter, who was home from school with the flu. The two women at table eleven were regulars who spent an hour every afternoon planning some kind of humanitarian aid trip to Africa. And the elderly couple at table nine had recently returned from Majorca, where they'd honeymooned thirty-six years ago.

Kate envied them all their sense of purpose, whether grand or small. The boyfriend wanted his girlfriend to love him, the man wanted to finish his paperwork and get home to his daughter, the two women wanted to save the world, and the older couple . . . they just seemed happy.

In the corner of her eye, Kate saw a customer enter the café, and she turned toward the door with a practiced smile.

"*Bonjour* —" she started to say, but the end of the word was lost in a sharp intake of breath.

The customer was tall, with shaggy dark hair and brown wide-set eyes. He grinned at her.

Magnus. Magnus was *here*.

"Hi."

"Hi," Kate breathed.

He walked toward her, smiling.

Kate's stomach clenched. He should hate her. Why didn't he hate her?

But he opened his arms, wrapped them around her shoulders, and enveloped her against his chest.

"I heard you need a friend."

Chantal, Kate thought, staring up at him. Chantal had called him. And he came.

After everything, he still came.

"Cappuccino's are all about the foam," Harper informed Habiba, expertly flicking her wrist to get a lather going. "Customer doesn't see foam, they're not going to be a happy camper."

"Got it," Habiba answered, concentrating intently on the task at hand.

It was an excruciatingly slow night at the Rainy Day Books Café, and Harper was killing time training Beebs in the Tao of Barista. Of course, she could have done something productive, like rearrange the thousands of books that were spilling out of the overflowing black cherry shelves that lined the walls. Or wipe down the long maple counter. But, really, wasn't filling in as Habiba's surrogate big sister more important?

"How come you're so good at this?" Harper asked as Beebs managed to produce a perfect decaf nonfat cappuccino in thirty seconds flat.

"Ethiopia exports coffee. The stuff's in my blood." She paused. "Like writing's in your blood."

"Give it a rest. I'll write when I'm ready."

Since Violet's death bed scene, Harper hadn't gone near her computer. Writing required thinking. And thinking led to thoughts. Horrible thoughts that ranged from humiliating to horrifying to pathetic.

"You keep saying I should e-mail Kate." Beebs set down her cappuccino. "I think I'm gonna go home and do that."

"But I haven't taught you how to make a Red-Eye yet."

This information was not enough to sway Habiba. She grabbed her Hello Kitty backpack. "Whatever's going on in *here,*" she indicated her head, "will be made better if you write from *here,*" putting a hand over her heart.

"Yeah, yeah, write from the heart. I know."

Once Beebs was gone, Harper filled a to-go cup with a fresh Colombian brew and approached her one remaining customer. His name was Steve. He wore only fatigue pants and black t-shirts, and his thin blond hair was always in perpetual need of a good shampoo. Steve spent every evening sketching other Rainy Day Café patrons on his Mac, but he rarely ordered more than two small beverages.

"On the house," she stated, setting down the coffee. "For the road."

Steve glanced at the clock on his computer. "You're not closing for another forty-five minutes."

Harper gave him a look. "Pretend otherwise."

Habiba was right. She needed to sit down in front of her computer and write. No matter what obsessive, neurotic thoughts tried to get in her way. As Steve began a painstakingly slow process of unplugging and packing up his laptop, Harper walked over to the front door and sighed loudly.

Finally, he sauntered past her and out the door. She watched him walk down Pearl Street, clearly oblivious to the fact that some people didn't *want* to spend their entire lives behind a coffee counter while he nursed an espresso for three hours.

We need a no loitering policy, Harper thought as she locked the door and headed to the cash register to close up.

She was counting singles when she heard the knock. "We're closed!" she yelled, not bothering to look up. *Thirty-one, thirty-two . . .* Or was it thirty-three?

The knocking continued, and Harper finally glanced toward the door. Where she saw none other than Mr. Finelli staring inside, smiling at her. Harper dropped the bills into the cash register, and race-walked toward him.

"Mr. Finelli . . . hi," she stuttered once she'd managed to fumble open the locked door. He was wearing olive green cargo pants, a soft brown suede jacket, and new pair of black-rimmed eyeglasses that were almost identical to hers. The statue of David in Florence was not so beautiful.

"You closed early."

"No . . . I mean, yeah." She gestured around the café, avoiding his eyes. "It was dead, so you know . . ."

"I'm glad I caught you alone." He stepped inside and closed the door behind him. "I wanted to talk to you about —"

"I wasn't stalking you!" she blurted out. "I swear!" Harper paused. "Okay, maybe I biked by your apartment, like, twice. But that's it."

She'd had a few weak moments, during which no amount of giving herself stern lectures could keep her from wheeling her ten-speed past Mr. Finelli's to see if Fiona had reappeared on the scene. She was a masochist, plain and simple.

"Harper —"

"It wasn't even on purpose," she continued, weeks of shame spilling out. "I just happened to be going that direction —"

"Harper?" he interrupted.

She swallowed. "What?" His hair had grown out even more, giving him the look of a nineteenth-century poet. Only hot.

Mr. Finelli grasped her hand. She stumbled as he gently pulled her toward him. "Shut up."

"Why —"

But she didn't get to finish the question.

Because Mr. Finelli kissed her.

Not a nice-to-see-you kiss. Not an I-feel-sorry-for-this-lonely-girl kiss. A real kiss, complete with lips moving and tongues touching. When he finally pulled away, Harper made a mental note that her legs were numb.

"Did I die?" she asked. It was the first explanation that came to mind.

He smiled shyly. "I've wanted to do that ever since that night in my apartment."

"You . . . you have?" She had to stop with the stuttering.

"I was feeling everything you were . . . I had the same impulse . . ." He trailed off, apparently at a loss as how to further discuss said impulse.

"But you said —"

"I know what I said. . . ." He took her hand again and lightly traced the lines of her palm with his thumb. "And this is probably a really a bad idea . . . But you're eighteen, and I'm not *that* much older. . . ."

"You like me?" Harper asked. She was seventeen, but who was counting?

"I don't want to — but yes." He stuck his hands in the pockets of his cargo pants and rocked back. "I shouldn't have kissed you, right?"

233

She couldn't stop staring at Mr. Finelli. Adam. Whatever. None of this made sense. "No. I mean yes." *Damn.* Why couldn't she get her yeses and nos straight? "It's just . . . I'm such a —" She wanted to say loser, but she didn't. "I'm such a dork."

He shook his head. "You're not a dork. You're funny and brilliant and . . . adorable."

"I am?" She saw herself as the opposite of funny and brilliant and adorable. Okay, maybe she was funny. But that was it.

"You are."

If this were a short story, Harper would have ended it here, letting her heroine walk off into the night with the man she loved. Instead, she gazed at the spot just over Mr. Finelli's head and tried to think of something else to say.

"I'm sorry." He dropped her hand. "You probably think I'm some lecherous old guy who should be put in jail."

Harper couldn't believe it. This was everything she'd hoped for, dreamed of. Well, not everything. The real Dream was her book, which so far existed only in her head.

"I'm not going to kiss you again." Was that her? Had she said that?

"Okay, sure." Mr. Finelli took a step away from her. "I get the message."

Harper lunged forward, grabbing the lapels of his jacket. "No!"

"No?"

"I mean, I *am* going to kiss you again," she clarified. "Just not right now."

Mr. Finelli raised an eyebrow. God, he was cute when he raised an eyebrow. "I'm not following."

"I said I was going to spend this year writing a book. Well, it's been almost three months, and I haven't accomplished shit."

"And that relates to kissing me . . . how?" He looked utterly confused, and utterly kissable.

"If I don't write my novel, I'll never forgive myself. And you're going to be my incentive."

"Sorry . . . still not following." He looked like he was beginning to regret that he'd ever stepped foot in the café tonight.

"I will not kiss you again until I have completed the first fifty pages of what I hope becomes the next Great American Novel," Harper announced.

She prayed Mr. Finelli agreed to this plan. If he didn't, she would crumble. Willpower wasn't exactly her forte.

He nodded, his face thoughtful. After what felt like a lifetime, Mr. Finelli smiled. "Do what you need to do. I'll wait."

"Really?"

"Really." He pushed her glasses a little higher on her nose. "I want you to fulfill your dreams, Harper. If you want to use me as a . . . tool for that, I'm okay with it."

As she stood staring into his eyes, she felt a warm glow spreading through her. It wasn't just that Mr. Finelli, a.k.a. Adam, liked her, actually *liked* her. The glow came from knowing that she'd finally put her Dream first. That whatever else was going on in her life, her book had to take priority.

Obsessive, neurotic thoughts aside, Harper Waddle was ready to write.

So *this* was why Becca liked to cry, Kate realized, as she sobbed against Magnus's shirt. It felt *good*. And awful, and wrenching, and embarrassing. But, overall . . . good. It helped. Magnus didn't even seem to care that she'd gotten snot all over him, or that her face was so red and blotchy it looked like her cheeks had diaper rash.

"You're okay," he kept saying soothingly. One reluctant cell at a time, her mind had started to accept that he might be right.

Kate took a big, gasping breath, and realized her butt was cold. She lifted her head, and wiped her nose with the back of her hand. "Sorry," she snuffled.

She was practically on Magnus's lap in the middle of the stone staircase leading up to Chantal's third floor apartment. She'd tried to keep it together until they at least got inside, but Magnus had been so *nice,* telling her he didn't hate her, that it wasn't her fault she got attacked, asking if she had been scared ... slowly but surely, chipping away at the rock wall she'd built around her pain. And then, finally, the wall had crumbled, and Kate had fallen to pieces with it.

"It's good I packed extra shirts," Magnus smiled.

"It's your fault," she said, eyeing his soggy shirt front. "You made me talk about it."

"It's good to talk about it."

"Speak for yourself," Kate said.

"I'm speaking for you," he replied, not quite understanding the English phrase.

"Well, tell yourself I'm sorry I left like that last time we were in Paris."

"I know when," Magnus said. Kate thought she caught a flash of pain behind his eyes.

Then he took her hand, and pulled her up.

"How about some tea?"

What was it about Europeans and tea?

Back in Chantal's apartment, Magnus settled her on the couch, and went to work in the kitchen. Kate watched him. She watched the sinews of his neck as he bent down to open a low drawer. She watched the long, angular curve of his jaw as he popped a sugar cube into his mouth. How had she ever thought he was ugly?

"So why *did* you leave?" he inquired finally, handing her a cup of tea. He sat beside her on the couch — close, but not touching.

She shrugged, unsure.

"I just . . . kinda freaked out. I mean, I barely knew you, but I thought . . ."

She trailed off, embarrassed.

"You know me well enough," Magnus said.

"But that's what was weird," Kate tried to explain. "I felt like if I waited for you to wake up, I *wouldn't* leave."

Magnus reached out and ran a finger over the scar above her eye.

"And why was that so bad?" he asked.

Kate felt herself getting defensive. "I only have a year, and I have to figure out all this stuff. What I want to do, who I want to be —"

"And yet you're still in Paris," Magnus pointed out, and Kate realized he'd set a trap for her and she had fallen right into it. If it had been anyone else, she would have been furious.

"It's different now," she said.

"No different." He shook his head.

"Of course it is. For one thing, they took most of my money —"

"You've been working at the café almost a month. With no costs."

"I tried to pay rent," Kate countered quickly, "Chantal wouldn't let me."

"I know." Magnus nodded. "She likes having you here, and she knows you need your money. But your dream is not in Paris."

Kate frowned at him, suddenly angry.

"Then where is it? *What* is it? I don't even know *that.*"

Magnus smiled softly, totally unruffled by her anger. He kissed the top of her head.

"I have two weeks," he began. "Then I must go back home. My brother is getting married."

"You're staying here?" Kate's anger dissipated. Two whole weeks with Magnus was more than she would ever have hoped.

"No," he said.

"Why?"

"Because you won't be here."

She frowned at him.

"You'll be looking for your dream, whatever it is. I'll go wherever you want to go."

The familiar fear crept in.

"But I can't leave my job —" Kate began.

"What would your friends say if they hear you talking like this?"

"That's not fair."

Magnus shrugged. "I think it's fair. I'll stay with you until you're not afraid."

"That's going to take longer than two weeks."

"It won't." Then he cupped her chin and kissed her.

And Kate fell apart again, only this time in a good way. She slid her tea cup onto the sideboard, and threw her leg over his lap, wrapping her arms around his neck, and kissing him back ferociously. Now that they were finally together again, she never wanted to let him go —

"Oh," Chantal said, coming through the door. "Bonsoir, Magnus."

Kate leaped off Magnus's lap. He pulled her back down.

Chantal stood grinning at them both.

"I'll be going out tonight. You'll have the apartment to yourselves."

As Chantal swept into her bedroom, Kate turned to Magnus. They had the whole night to themselves, so why did he look so serious?

"What is it?" she half-whispered.

"That morning," he replied, seriously. "I would have told you to leave."

After the night they had spent together, after the connection that they had both so clearly felt, he would have told her to leave?

"Really?" Kate was hurt.

Magnus nodded, then smiled. "Well, I may have given it a couple days first. But this . . . quest, whatever you want to call it, is important to you. And you are important to me."

Kate brushed her hand over the rough surface of his cheek. "You're important to me, too."

He grinned. "So when I wake up in the morning, you won't be disappeared into thin air?"

Kate curled into his side and nestled her head in the curve of his shoulder.

"I promise."

Now all she had to do was find a way to keep the promises she'd made to herself.

Beatrice had known Mr. Hadley since she was fifteen, known him since before she met Jonathan, since before Eva and Patrick were born. His kindness showed itself in lemon drops, a piece at a time, and always with a little tartness. He was so old now that his skin reminded her of the faded drapes in the sitting room, and she wondered how she must seem to him.

"I'm selling the house," Beatrice proclaimed, raising her voice as she was accustomed to doing with those of a certain age, the age she herself would soon reach.

"It was a good one," he responded, a bit forlorn. "Aside from those creaks in the floorboards."

Yes, the creaks. The creaks she knew like she knew her own children, better than she knew them now that they'd left home and started families of their own. She would miss them. But then, that's what she did these days. She missed what once was.

"Without Jon, it's so big," she added quietly, and suddenly felt like she might cry. Two years, and she still felt the same longing when she mentioned his name.

Mr. Hadley nodded, averting his eyes from her pain. "Get a good price," he instructed, as if she wouldn't, as if she'd offer the house for a pittance. But

FOURTEEN

Harper had a shooting pain in her left wrist. Her head ached, and her eyes felt like they'd been pinned open with shards of glass. She'd been like this for three days, and it was nothing short of a miracle.

Because she was writing. Really writing. Actual sentences that didn't suck. Twelve pages worth.

I should turn on a light. The vague thought infiltrated her altered state, along with the notion that sometime in the past two hours, it had become dark outside.

As Harper leaned back in her chair, she heard the *pop, pop, pop* of her spine cracking. How long had she been sitting in the exact same position, staring at the computer screen? It could have been an hour or a day. Time had ceased to have its usual delineating markers.

But she was supposed to be doing something. Something that had seemed important a few seconds ago. . . . Oh, right. The light. Turning on the light. She stood up and walked toward the switch at the base of the stairs.

On the way, she glanced toward the tiny basement window. And screamed. "Aaaaaaaah!"

A face was pressed against the dirty glass, its features wild and distorted in the moonlight. Stranger abduction, Harper thought, feeling a swell of panic.

"I have a gun!" she shouted. "I'll kill you!"

The window opened, and Judd thrust his head inside. "Harper, it's me."

A combination of relief and anger flooded through her. Relief that she wasn't going to be abducted. Anger that Judd had freaked her out like that.

"Why didn't you *knock*?"

"I didn't want to startle you," he said, wriggling through the window and into the basement. He was wearing her least favorite Phish shirt, the acid purple one from a 1994 concert in Toronto he'd bought on eBay.

"Good job on that." She turned on the light, feeling like an idiot. "Ever heard of ringing a door bell?"

"No one answered upstairs," Judd explained, at which point Harper remembered that she *had* heard the bell ring a few minutes ago. "It smells like something died in here." He wrinkled his nose. "Something large."

Harper looked around her subterranean sublet, noticing for the first time the mess that had accumulated during her self-imposed exile from society. The floor was littered with Diet Coke cans, bags of crushed potato chips, and half-eaten Snickers bars. There were also several empty Chinese takeout cartons, which she suspected accounted for the odor of rotting flesh.

"It's all part of being in Writer's Heaven," she informed Judd, totally unapologetic.

"Or Writer's Hell, depending on your point of view," he countered, eyeing an empty pizza box. "But I guess it's better than stalking your dad."

"Are we going somewhere with this visit?" Harper inquired. She was suddenly aware that she'd been wearing the same pair of pink and lime-green argyle socks for the past seventy-two hours.

"I was wondering if you plan to show up for one of your shifts anytime soon."

"My shifts?" she asked innocently, pushing up her really-needed-to-be-cleaned glasses.

"At the café?" Judd reminded her. "The job you have so you can support the genius that takes place in this little slice of Writer's Heaven?"

"Oh right. Those shifts." Harper had been hoping that maybe nobody at the Rainy Day Books Café would notice she hadn't been coming to work. This was the kind of insane wishful thinking that often accompanied one of her creative comas. "I'll be there in the morning," she promised.

"You might want to take a shower first," he suggested. "Just a thought."

She lifted her arm and took a sniff. Yikes. It wasn't the old Chinese food that smelled. Judd started back through the window, then stopped halfway and turned to her.

"By the way, Mr. Finelli says hi."

As he continued through the window, Harper stood paralyzed with shock at a realization. It was kissing Mr. Finelli that had sent her into this writing frenzy. But in the three days she'd been holed up with her computer, she hadn't thought about him once.

"I have a love-hate relationship with my *hair*," Sophie murmured to herself. "I have a love-*hate* relationship with my hair . . . I have a *love*-hate relationship with *my* hair."

"Sophie Bushell?" A curly blond casting director called out her name from the sign-in sheet attached to her clipboard.

"Right here," Sophie called. She stood up and grabbed her still-not-replaced black Gap tote bag.

One line. Her entire audition would consist of that one line. But it was the most important line in the national shampoo ad Sophie was up for, and she wanted to nail it. She wanted to *own* her love-hate relationship with her hair. She wanted to *be* it.

As Sophie headed toward the casting director, she glanced around at the competition. There were about twelve other girls, all at least part African-American, and unfortunately none of them looked like they had any real-life hair problems. They were gorgeous.

But they don't have Trey Benson telling them they've got It, she reminded herself. All she had to do was harness Trey's positive energy, and there'd be no stopping her.

She had dressed down for the audition in a simple winter-white skirt and a chocolate Bebe V-neck sweater. Her hair was supposed to be the star, and she didn't want her outfit to upstage it.

"Good luck," said one of the girls as Sophie passed. No doubt she was secretly hoping that Sophie would break out in hives somewhere between the waiting room and the audition.

Gifford had called to tell her he'd pulled strings to get her into this producer session at the last minute. Luckily, she'd been getting ready to meet Trey, so she'd already spent at least an hour on her hair and makeup. And she'd had the whole drive over to rehearse her line.

The casting director led her to a small room, where three thirty-something looking guys wearing baseball caps and jeans were drinking Diet Cokes and munching on low-fat pretzels. Looking at their bored faces, Sophie wished she'd been able to talk to Trey, instead of his new assistant, before the audition.

She stood in front of a video camera, and the casting director pressed play. "Whenever you're ready," she announced.

"Sophie Bushell," Sophie stated for the record.

Then she paused. And thought about her hair. *Really* thought about it. All the mornings before school when she'd woken up with major cases of bed head. All the nights she'd spent in front of the mirror, spritzing and spraying, trying to get her unruly curls just right. Her hair had been her best friend, and the bane of her existence. That was real. That was true.

Sophie raised her eyebrows at the baseball-capped producers and gave them a wry half-smile. "I have a love-hate relationship with my hair."

It was nothing short of a confession. She had let the words roll off her tongue as if she were talking to Becca, Kate, and Harper out on Kate's roof. She was just a girl, talking about girl stuff, and wishing there were a solution to her problem.

The brown-haired guy in the middle, who was wearing a Yankees cap, laughed. "You know what?" he said. "I believe you."

She sailed out of the audition as if gravity were no longer a factor in her life. She whispered good luck to the other actresses, almost feeling sorry that none of them had a chance in hell of getting the part.

It was hers. She felt it in her bones.

As soon as she was back out in the bright LA sun, floating toward "her" BMW, Sophie pulled out her cell phone and turned it back on. She couldn't wait to call Trey with the news. This deserved a celebration.

She smiled as she saw that Trey had already left her a message. He'd probably wanted to say good luck after his assistant passed on the news that she had to push back their date. Sophie dialed her voice mail and inhaled deeply. God, she loved smog.

"Hey, Sophe." Trey's voice caused butterflies to dance in her stomach. "Yeah, so Eli just told me you canceled for some shampoo audition." He sounded . . . sorta pissed. "A little notice would've been nice, considering I rearranged a wardrobe fitting so I could spend

247

the afternoon with you. But, hey, whatever. You've got more important stuff."

That was it. No good luck wishes. No break a leg. Sophie's butterflies balled into a massive hard knot.

She barely noticed as her voice mail moved to the next message. "Hey, Bushell. It's Sam."

Maybe Trey's having a really bad day, she thought. Or maybe he'd been too distracted to realize that his tone of voice had been a tad asshole-y.

"I just ran into Gifford by the pool . . ." Sam's message continued. "Don't ask me what he was doing there. Maybe a nooner with Mrs. M. Who knows?" He laughed. "Anyway, he told me about the audition. I just wanted to say good luck. I know you're gonna do great. 'Cuz you rock." There was a pause. "Okay, then. Bye."

Sophie grinned to herself as she saved the message so she could listen to it again later. Leave it to Sam to go and be a nice guy when she wasn't looking. Without thinking, she started to dial his cell phone number.

And then she stopped.

There was plenty of time to call Sam later. Right now, she needed to get in touch with Trey. So what if he'd been a jackass? There was probably a perfectly reasonable explanation. Such as the fact that he was crazy about her and wanted to spend every free minute in her presence. It wasn't like she could fault him for that.

She dialed Trey's number. He'd apologize. And then they'd celebrate her first real acting job.

Sitting across a candlelit table from Stuart, Becca tried desperately to remember the advice her friends had been giving her all day.

Isabelle: "Just remember, he's lucky to be going out with you."

Harper: "Don't tell him he's your Dream Guy–slash–Love Guinea Pig. That might freak him out."

Taymar: "I'd brush up on football if I were you."

Sophie: "Wear a thong, you'll be fine. It's not like it's your first real date or . . . oh. Just wear a thong."

Kate (via e-mail): "The way you describe this guy, it sounds like he might actually be worthy of you. Just have fun."

Well, Becca had worn a thong. And it wasn't helping. Even in her sleeveless black Ann Taylor dress, she didn't feel sexy or confident or anything remotely approaching worthy. She'd tried to do everything her friends had suggested — she'd even looked up football stats online — but this date was an unmitigated disaster.

On the surface, everything was ideal. Stuart had picked her up at her dorm and they'd driven in his roommate's Saab to Killington, where they could have dinner with a view of the mountains. The restaurant, an old ski lodge with cathedral ceilings and a giant stone fireplace, was intimidatingly romantic. The food — not that she'd tasted a bite — seemed excellent. Stuart looked unbelievably hot in a gray cabled fisherman's sweater, jeans, and Timberlands. And Becca's ankle was actually healed enough for her to venture out sans crutches.

The problem was everything going on below the surface. Her surface, specifically. Maybe the three exams she'd taken in the last two days had turned her brains to mush. Or maybe she was actually the most boring person on the face of the earth, and she'd just never realized it before. Face to face with Stuart, on a *date* . . . it was like her whole personality had switched to "off," and she couldn't figure out how to turn it back on again.

"What'd you tell your parents about your ankle?" Stuart asked, taking the last bite of his penne. He'd been doing an admirable job of keeping up the conversation for the last hour. His patience seemed infinite. Yet another reason there was no way he would be interested in her once he realized the whole most-boring-person-on-earth thing.

"Nothing," Becca replied, concentrating on her chicken cordon bleu as if it were her last meal.

She could have told him that she hadn't actually talked to her parents about her ankle at all — that, in fact, she'd barely talked to either of them since Parents' Weekend. She could have told him that when she did talk to her mother, they both made an effort to limit the content of their conversations to exciting subjects like the weather and Oprah's most recent hairstyle. She could have told him that, after years of inconsistent contact at best, her father had suddenly started calling every Sunday afternoon. And that after much consultation with her friends she had decided, against their advice, not to call him back. Ever. She could have told him that when she'd called to say she was going to New York for Thanksgiving with Isabelle instead of going home, she'd left the message on her mom's work voice mail.

But Becca simply couldn't talk to Stuart about her family. Not when his family was apparently so blissfully nuclear. Stuart had started the evening with a story about his older brother, a lawyer in Manhattan, who'd called as Stuart was on his way out the door. The warmth in his voice when he talked about his brother was something she had never experienced in non-televised families before. Harper and Amy weren't bonded that way. Sophie was an Only. And Kate and Habiba . . . It was just a different kind of relationship.

"It sounds like your family's really close." Becca tried to keep a note of longing from her voice. Stuart had given her the Cliff's Notes version. His mother and father were high school sweethearts. They'd married right after college at the University of Missouri, moved to the big city (which, in Western Missouri, meant Kansas City), and had three boys, all three years apart. His dad was a lawyer, his mom was a homemaker. His grandmother had lived with them since his grandpa died when Stuart was eleven.

Then he'd asked about her family. Becca had avoided the question with a graceless "They're, you know . . . not that interesting," and she'd been practically mute ever since.

What the hell was her problem? She wanted to be witty and fun, and tell winsome stories about her childhood. She wanted to make him laugh, and look at her longingly and with admiration. For the first time in a long time, Becca wished she were Kate. Kate could talk to anyone.

As Stuart paid the check, she stared out the window at the mountains and listed all the reasons she hated herself. One, she hadn't made him laugh once tonight. Two, she'd spent an hour straightening her hair, which was so pathetic and desperate. Three, she couldn't stop being afraid.

They drove back to her dorm in near silence.

As they pulled up to the redbrick building, Becca reached for the door handle almost before the car was fully stopped. Fleeing seemed de rigeur.

"Thanks for dinner," she said quickly, preparing for her escape.

"Bec," Stuart said. She looked at him. He was going to break up with her already, and they weren't even officially going out. How completely humiliating.

He held out his hand.

Uh-oh. In the near dark of the car, she put her hand in his. It was warm, calloused. Perfect. It really sucked to be broken up with by a guy with such amazing hands.

"What's going on?" he asked.

Becca wanted to crawl under the car seat.

"I suck at this," she whispered, willing herself not to cry.

"*I* suck at this," Stuart said. "I'm supposed to make you comfortable, and I just kept asking stupid questions. . . ."

251

"They weren't stupid." Becca shook her head. She almost felt a giggle welling up, somewhere deep inside. He wasn't breaking up with her. At least, not yet.

"I asked if you'd ever been snorkeling," he said pointedly.

She sighed. "I don't know why you wanted to go out with me. This must have been the worst night of your life."

"Hardly. And I wanted to go out with you because you're funny and smart and gorgeous, and you're a hellion on the track and on the slopes, and —"

"Stop," Becca laughed.

Stuart was quiet a moment.

"Maybe," he said, "we should just forget about tonight, pretend it never happened."

Becca's heart sank. He *was* breaking up with her.

"We can start over after Thanksgiving break," he continued. Her heart soared.

"Seriously?"

"Yeah." Stuart smiled. "And no big, high-pressure dates. We'll just hang out."

"Definitely no more big dates," Becca agreed. "I clearly can't handle it."

"I don't think we should give up on the big dates *permanently,*" Stuart said. "But we'll give it a few months."

Becca nodded. A few months was assuming a lot — all of it good.

"Tonight was like a practice game —" he began.

She knew where he was going. "Where everyone's nervous, and they make all these mistakes. So then, in the big game . . ."

"The kinks are all worked out," Stuart finished. "Exactly."

For the first time all night, Becca felt herself relax.

"You want to know why you were nervous?" There was a smile in his voice.

"Why?" she asked cautiously. This should be interesting.

"Because you like me," he said, grinning mischievously.

"I do not," Becca countered automatically.

"Do too."

"Do not," she answered, smiling.

"Do too," he whispered, leaning toward her.

He kissed her once, softly.

"Okay," she sighed, "maybe I do."

"What d'you think about *Buck Naked Soul*?" Harper asked Tie-Dyed Guy as she handed him his obviously much-needed espresso shot.

He squinted. "Who's in it?"

"Never mind." She headed to the cappuccino machine, where she was three orders behind.

But even the morning rush couldn't ruin her good mood. Having sprung herself, at least temporarily, from the Waddle Detention Center for Wayward Writers, Harper felt like a new woman. Being out in the world, even the tiny world of the Rainy Day Books Café, was a new adventure. This was how Helen Keller must have felt at the water pump when she uttered her first word to Annie Sullivan. Reborn.

Plus, there was always a chance Mr. Finelli would stop in for coffee and a raspberry scone. She'd worn her one pair of clean Levi's, just in case.

"Would you read a book called *Women in Relief*?" she asked Judd cheerily as she frothed the foam on a decaf cap. "Or how 'bout *Wandering Suburbia*?"

"Don't think," he ordered her. "Brew."

She reached out and patted his tangled curls. "You're cute, you know that?" The title needed to sound epic and evocative. Or at least clever. Later, she'd dig a thesaurus out of one of the bookshelves and look up cool words.

Judd shook his head. "I miss the procrastinating bitch. This is just weird."

As she strode back to the crowd of coffee-deprived customers, Harper kept one eye on the door. She and Mr. Finelli had established they wouldn't *kiss* until she'd finished the first fifty pages of her book, but they hadn't set any ground rules on *seeing* each other. She knew with every fiber of her born-again being that he would show up. It was that kind of glorious day.

"Enjoy your day," she chirped to a fanny-pack clad tourist as she handed him his drink. "And look for my book, *Just Desserts,* in stores sometime next year."

"Congratulations!" the man responded jovially, tipping his cappuccino to her.

"Thanks!" So what if publication wasn't exactly official? She had no doubt that her book would make it to the shelves, *whatever* the title ended up being.

As Fanny Pack made his way toward the half-and-half, Harper focused on the café entrance. Mr. Finelli will walk through that door in three seconds, she told herself.

The door opened, but it wasn't Mr. Finelli who walked in. It was some woman wearing a bright pink suit that clashed with her red hair. Harper was concentrating so hard on the vision of Mr. Finelli's face that it wasn't until the woman neared the counter that she recognized her.

Red-Headed Tramp.

Harper crashed back to the real world. Everything wasn't good and right and beautiful. It was horrible. Evil wore bright coral lipstick, and she was staring it in the face.

Suddenly, Judd was at her side. "I'll take this order."

"No." Harper couldn't take her eyes off the woman's lipstick, which was slightly smeared at the corner of her mouth.

"Harper." Judd's tone was a warning of sorts. Leave the counter, or suffer at the hand of the super sharp bagel slicer.

"Good morning," she greeted Red-Headed Tramp, ignoring Judd's tacit threat. "What can I get you?"

"Black coffee," she answered casually, as if she didn't have a care. As if she weren't a home wrecker.

"Right away." Harper shot a look at Judd and took off for the coffee machine.

The cup was shaking in her hand as she held it under a stream of hot breakfast blend. "No spitting," Judd hissed in her ear.

She slapped a lid on the cup and returned to the counter, where Red-Headed Tramp was dropping her business card into the "Win Free Coffee for a Week" jar next to the register.

"Thanks, hon." She took the cup, handing her two singles. "Keep the change."

And then Red-Headed Tramp was walking away and out the door. Harper stood there, watching her, unable to believe that she hadn't said a word. No snide comments. No pithy accusations. She'd just handed over the coffee like a good little barista girl. Weak.

Judd breathed a sigh of relief and turned to the next customer in line. But Harper wasn't ready to take a mochaccino order. She plunged her hand in the jar of business cards and pulled out Red-Headed Tramp's, which was resting on the top of the pile.

Margo Rosen. Her name was Margo Rosen, and she was a real estate agent. She even had one of those cheesy pictures next to her name, along with the address of her home business. Interesting.

"What are you doing with that?" Judd asked slowly, using that tone again.

"Will you quit *lurking*?" Harper snapped. "I'm just looking."

"You were doing so good. Now you're gonna get all crazy and stop writing again."

He tried to pull the business card out of her hand, but she held on tight. "Stay out of my family business," she said coldly. "I mean that."

Harper ignored the hurt look on Judd's face and slid the card into her pocket. Margo Rosen and her lipstick weren't going to get away with anything.

SAM'S EVERY-TIME-A-WINNER POKER CHEAT SHEET

High CARD

ONE PAIR

TWO PAIR

THREE OF A KIND

STRAIGHT (FIVE CARDS OF ANY SUIT IN A ROW)

FLUSH (ANY FIVE CARDS OF THE SAME SUIT)

FULL HOUSE (ONE PAIR PLUS THREE OF A KIND)

FOUR OF A KIND (NOT GONNA HAPPEN)

STRAIGHT FLUSH (REALLY NOT GONNA HAPPEN)

ROYAL FLUSH (NOT A CHANCE IN HELL)

NOTE: IT MIGHT BE EASIER JUST TO HAND ME YOUR MONEY.

FIFTEEN

The winery in the hills of Umbria appeared and disappeared so quickly that Kate almost thought she had imagined it. But the barest whisper of vine-laden trellises through the Italian fog was enough.

She tapped Magnus on the shoulder.

"Stop here!" she yelled into the wind.

Magnus nodded and steered his motorcycle to the side of the narrow road. Staring into the fog, Kate could make out the edge of a vineyard — rows and rows of dark, leafy green dividing spans of rich, brown dirt. Getting off the bike, she thought — not for the first time — that her parents would kill her if they knew she'd been riding a motorcycle through France, Switzerland, and Italy for the last week. When she had first climbed on the back of Magnus's bike and settled her knees tightly around his hips, she was pretty sure they wouldn't *have* to kill her — she'd be dead momentarily anyway, especially in Paris traffic. But Magnus was an experienced and conscientious driver, and it had taken her about ten seconds to feel comfortable. It had taken about ten seconds more to fall in love with the feel of the wind in her face, and the exhilaration of speed.

She unsnapped her helmet.

"There's a winery up there." She pointed toward a nearby hill that rose from the surrounding fog. A large, medieval-looking structure with stern, square lines and arched stone doorways nestled into a curve of the hill.

"Are you turning into a lush on me," Magnus's lips curled up in amusement, "like your friend Becca?"

Kate laughed. "She's not a lush. That was a one-night thing."

She'd told him all about Becca's night in the infirmary.

"I remembered something from the list," she continued. "Number twenty-something. Stomp grapes. I think it was one of Harper's."

It took several minutes to find the entrance to the vineyard in the thick fog, and several more to maneuver the bike up the long, winding gravel drive that led to the winery's ancient, stone main building. Inside, at a long counter set at the far end of the wide, oak-floored entryway, a red-vested elderly clerk stared at her blankly when she explained that she would like to stomp some grapes, please.

"But, we don't do that," he explained in heavily accented English. "We have machines."

Kate deflated.

"Really?" she said.

The clerk nodded.

She looked at Magnus. He shrugged. No help there, which Kate knew was intentional. He'd told her in the beginning he was just along for the ride. But his presence was enough to spur her on. She turned back to the clerk.

"You must have some grapes, somewhere."

"Yes, but . . ." The clerk looked confused. "The harvest is done. What we have is only for . . . decoration —"

"I'll take them."

"We don't sell grapes," the clerk continued, growing ever more nonplussed.

Kate leaned her elbows on the counter and smiled. "Let me explain. I have to stomp on some grapes. Today. It's very important. Any grapes will do."

The clerk opened and closed his mouth, unsure how to proceed. Then he held his finger up, seeming to have an idea. He searched behind the counter, found a calendar, flipped through it quickly. Revelation spread across his face.

"This is . . . American Thanksgiving tradition?"

Kate blinked. Thanksgiving? *Holy shit,* today was Thanksgiving. She'd completely forgotten. Four months ago, she'd planned to spend this day with Harper, Becca, and Sophie in New York. They were going to hole up at NYU, have pizza and Diet Coke for Thanksgiving dinner, and dish on everything they'd done in the months since they'd been apart. Instead, she was motorcycling through the Italian countryside with Magnus, and hitting up a very confused Italian winery clerk for Sagrantino grapes. And she couldn't imagine anywhere else she'd rather be.

"Yes." Kate grinned, giving her hand a vague wave. "It's something to do with the Pilgrims."

The clerk nodded, satisfied.

"One moment."

As he disappeared into a back room, Kate turned to Magnus.

"He's getting me some grapes," she said proudly.

"You were very . . . assertive, is the word?"

"Yep." She *had* been assertive. And unafraid. Not like wimpy clerks and grapes were really anything to be afraid of, but still. . . . Today was Thanksgiving, and she was going to be thankful. Especially since she'd been anything but assertive a week ago when she had said a tearful goodbye to Chantal and climbed on the back of Magnus's bike.

"Which way?" he'd asked her, hands poised on the chrome handlebars.

"I don't know," Kate had answered, flummoxed. They hadn't discussed a plan, so how was she supposed to know which way?

"Up to you," Magnus had responded, waiting to start the ignition. Kate had wanted to hit him. Or scream. Or both.

Then she'd remembered Sophie's nonsensical number 82 on The List: "Turn your eyes to the east." What the hell, she figured, why not?

"Go east," she said, and within seconds they were zooming through Paris traffic, heading east.

East, as it turned out, was a lovely direction — though not without challenges, as she'd discovered two days later on a three-hour hike up Mount Pilatus in Switzerland.

"Please," she'd gasped, lungs screaming, legs like quivering jelly. "Let's turn around."

It wasn't like the Alps weren't beautiful. To someone, somewhere, the chain of snow-capped peaks undoubtedly would have been inspiring. But Kate hadn't felt up to trudging over snowy dirt trails, ducking wayward evergreen limbs, and stumbling over rocks. She'd just wanted to rest. For two days, she'd been doing her best to be the leader, to make decisions, to be in charge. But climbing a mountain was beyond her — even if the list told her to (number forty-something, if she remembered correctly), even if she wanted to. She was so *tired*. . . .

But Magnus had taken her hand. He had rubbed her back. And he had waited until, somewhere within herself, she'd found the will to keep climbing. Had it been worth it? Not for the view — which she later informed Magnus was just as good halfway down the mountain as it had been at the top — but definitely for the sense of accomplishment. She had taken success for granted so many times in her life, that she'd never stopped to consider the circumstances under which she could fail, and whether she would have the ability to get back on her feet again.

So even if climbing a mountain wasn't exactly the world's greatest hurdle, and reaching the top wasn't the world's greatest accomplishment, she was still proud of taking baby steps. As baby steps went, she'd decided, this one was stable and well-balanced, and didn't end in an embarrassing stumble.

In fact, it ended with her not even caring that this poor winery clerk, who walked toward her now with two huge clumps of slightly-past-their-prime red grapes, thought she was just another crazy American.

"You will stomp outside, no?" he requested, handing them to her warily.

"Certainly." Kate nodded.

Outside the main building, she steered Magnus toward a grassy knoll that led toward the vineyard. The fog had lifted slightly, revealing rolling hills and a tiny village in the valley below.

Kate set the grapes on the grass, then slipped off her socks and hiking boots.

"You, too," she gestured to Magnus, who was watching with a disbelieving grin on his face.

"It's your list," he said.

"It didn't say 'stomp grapes *alone,*'" she replied.

Magnus shook his head, sighed dramatically, and slipped off his tennis shoes and socks.

"Ready, set, go!" she yelled, and planted her foot squarely in the center of the cluster of grapes. The grapes squished between her toes, and the vine nudged stiffly into the soles of her feet. She squealed as Magnus jumped — literally jumped about two feet in the air — and landed solidly in the center of what quickly became a mass of juicy red pulp.

Kate stomped and stomped, and squished and splatted, until the grapes were nothing but mush and they were both doubled over laughing.

"My toes are purple," she giggled, still squishing her toes in grape remains.

Magnus was laughing too hard to answer.

She loved his laugh, absolutely adored it. Like him, it held nothing back, even as it faded into a series of harrumphs and snorts.

"You're crazy," he said, finally, grinning as he stepped into the cold, clean grass.

"I know!" she shouted. She *felt* crazy. Bubbly, almost — and she was not the bubbly type. At least, she'd never considered herself to be. Perhaps it was time to reconsider. There were benefits to bubbliness. Purple toes being one of them.

"I think you're ready," Magnus declared as they wiped their soggy feet on towels retrieved from the back compartment of his motorcycle.

"For what?" It occurred to her that only a week ago the question would have been asked with trepidation. Now, she was simply curious.

Magnus tossed her the keys to his bike.

"No, no, no," she insisted. Stomping grapes was one thing. Suicide was another.

"Yes, yes, yes," he replied.

"But, I don't know how."

Magnus gestured at the virtually empty parking lot, and the long, winding drive.

"Your classroom," he said.

Kate considered arguing more forcibly, but the bubbly feeling had yet to recede, and she gave in to it. What the hell, she thought, I've already been in one European hospital.

She paid close attention as Magnus talked her through the mechanics of operating the motorcycle. Clutch on the left handlebar. Gear shift by her left foot. Front brake on the right handlebar. Back break on the right pedal. Bike in neutral, turn key, clutch in, shift to first, release clutch . . . and go.

Conceptually, she got it.

But her heart was still pounding as Magnus climbed on the bike behind her.

"Whenever you're ready," he said.

Slowly, Kate released the clutch. The bike jerked forward, and she slammed on the brakes.

Oh, so that's what abject terror feels like.

Behind her, she could feel Magnus's chest constrict as he tried not to laugh.

"Just you wait," she promised, and released the clutch again. This time she was ready for the jerky start. She steered the bike around the parking lot, slow and wobbly at first, then steadily and with more speed. Magnus reached around her to point toward the long driveway.

Kate turned the bike toward the driveway entrance, held in the clutch, lifted the gear shift, released the clutch. She was a natural!

She steered up the drive, then turned around and headed back to the winery. She was breathless as she brought the bike to a halt.

"That was amazing!" she said as Magnus climbed off the back.

"You're done?" he asked. "There's a whole road out there. I can wait here."

Kate hesitated, but if she were being honest with herself, she would admit she really *wanted* to take a spin alone.

Magnus smacked the side of the bike.

"Off you go," he said.

Kate grinned at him. Then released the clutch. Off she went.

At first, she was terrified, certain that she would forget to shift, or would turn too fast or brake too sharply. But by the time she reached the road, her knuckles had relaxed from white to their usual pinkish shade, and the pounding of her heart was all excitement, no fear.

Kate turned the bike toward the village below. Left hand clutch, left foot shift.

As the vineyard zipped by to her right, and the hills curled in to her left, she felt, for just a moment, as if she could go anywhere. Do anything. The feeling was fleeting, there and gone in the time it took to whiz past a signpost on the side of the road. But it left her with the certainty that as long as she kept moving, it was okay to be afraid. Because at the other end of the fear . . .

She wasn't sure, yet, exactly what was at the other end of the fear. But she was finally starting to believe that whatever it was would be worth it.

"Angela, I'm *fine,*" Sophie insisted to her mother as she studied the Lean Cuisine vegetable lasagna that was spinning forlornly in the microwave oven. "I'm going to some friends' for dinner."

Dinner with friends; her friends being the TV and a low-fat frozen dinner. Her mom didn't need to know the extent of her aloneness.

"I should have sent you a plane ticket," Angela responded on the other end of the phone. "I just can't believe Genevieve left you alone for Thanksgiving."

There was a pause.

"She *is* keeping an eye on you, right?"

"Of course," Sophie answered.

The Meyers had, in fact, invited Sophie to join their last-minute skiing trip to Mammouth with a hotshot from Gifford's law firm. But the thought of listening to Gifford, unabated, for three days, was unbearable. And that was as far as keeping an eye on her went.

"I'm an adult, remember?" The microwave beeped, and she popped open the door. "I can take care of myself."

"You're redefining your boundaries. I get that."

Sophie rolled her eyes. Once her mom got going with the shrink-speak, who knew how long this conversation could last? "I have to go, Angie. I'll call you tomorrow."

She clicked off the phone before her mother had a chance to launch into a speech about id versus ego. Okay, so it sucked that after three months in LA she had nowhere good to go for Thanksgiving dinner. But it wasn't like she was a loser. If Trey hadn't had to go to Europe for a press junket, they'd be sharing turkey and apple-pecan stuffing at the Regent Beverly Wilshire right now.

Besides, having a two-acre Beverly Hills estate all to herself for three days wasn't exactly a hardship. Between now and Saturday, Sophie planned to avail herself of the Meyers' state-of-the-art screening room, lounge by the pool, and use Genevieve's power blender to make herself a month's worth of smoothies. Or she'd hang out in the guesthouse in her pj's. Whichever.

She took the lasagna out of the microwave. It looked sort of mealy. And dry. Who cares? she thought, grabbing a fork.

She'd eat dry mealy lasagna every day for the next year if it meant she'd get to shoot another national commercial or a TV show or a movie. A small case of holiday blues was nothing compared to her elation over her first paycheck.

"I have a love-hate relationship with my hair," she informed the piece of lasagna as she crossed into the living room. She'd taken to repeating the line like a mantra a few hundred times a day since she shot the Remédé shampoo commercial a few weeks ago.

Still . . . It'd be nice to have someone to talk to. Sophie set down her Thanksgiving feast and grabbed her cell phone. So. One problem. Who could she call?

Becca was in New York with her roommate. Harper was probably elbow deep in her infamous mashed potatoes. And Kate . . . God only knew what Kate was doing. She thought for a moment. She *could* call —

BAM! BAM! BAM! Someone was pounding on the door to the guesthouse. "Sophie, are you in there?"

She ran to the door, her heart pounding. "What's wrong?"

Sam grinned. "Nothing, I just wanted to make sure you actually answered the door for once."

Seeing Sam always set her slightly off-balance. Her feelings for him teetered between exasperation and affection, and always, always she felt the same buzz of attraction that had been there when he picked her up at LAX on her very first day in Los Angeles. Lately, though, they'd barely crossed paths. Sam's rehearsals for *The Cherry Orchard* conflicted with their acting class, and Sophie usually wasn't home when he cleaned the Meyers' pool.

"You're contemptible." She noticed he was wearing his nicest pair of jeans and a tan linen sportcoat that she couldn't believe he actually owned.

He laughed. "Maybe. But I'm also inviting you to come to my friend Roz's house in Silver Lake for a potluck Thanksgiving dinner." He glanced over her shoulder at the Lean Cuisine lasagna. "Unless you've got something better to do?"

"I thought you were going to Redondo Beach to meet Michelle's parents tonight."

Sam had started dating one of the actresses in his play, a piece of news he'd managed to share when they'd passed each other in the Meyers' driveway last week.

He shrugged. "Change of plans."

Sophie thought about her agenda for the night, most of which involved walking back and forth to the kitchen for more munchies while she watched an *Inside the Actors Studio* marathon on Bravo. She smiled at Sam.

"Do you think your friend will mind if all I have to contribute to the pot luck dinner is a lukewarm piece of lasagna?" she asked, glad she was already wearing her favorite pair of Sevens and a cozy-yet-sexy black cashmere sweater set.

He grinned. "I'll do you a favor. Put your name on my yams."

As Sophie went to grab her Gap tote bag, she found herself surprised both by the fact that Sam knew how to make yams and by the unexpected feeling of warmth that was spreading through her.

It was nice to see him. Even if he was contemptible.

"It is impossible to make mashed potatoes on a hot plate," Harper announced to her mother as she entered the Waddles' kitchen Thursday evening. "I give up."

Mrs. Waddle looked up from the ten-pound turkey she was basting. "You know, you're allowed to use the kitchen."

Harper heaved her huge metal pot of peeled potatoes onto the stovetop and sighed. "I was trying to be independent."

Mrs. Waddle stuck the turkey back in the oven. "You can be independent tomorrow. Thanksgiving won't be complete without your infamous mashed potatoes."

"*Famous,*" she corrected her mother. "Not *infamous.*"

As Harper turned up the heat on the stove, she listened to her dad and Amy yelling at the TV set in the other room. Every year they worked themselves into a nearly psychotic state over some football team playing some other football team. It was something she could count on, like Sophie's practice acceptance speeches on Oscar night or Kate's perfect hair.

Watching her mom take the cranberries out of the freezer, like she did at exactly this time every Thanksgiving, she realized that for all that *hadn't* changed, the last twelve months might as well not have happened. If it weren't for Red-Headed Tramp's business card hidden behind a box of Bioré strips in her medicine cabinet, she'd have almost felt normal.

"How's the book going?" Mrs. Waddle asked, handing Harper a bag of Pepperidge Farm rolls to butter.

"You really want to know?" Harper asked. So far the extent of her mom's interest in her novel had been to request that any names that reflected real-life persons be changed to protect the innocent.

"Of course, honey." Mrs. Waddle looked hurt as she wiped her hands on the light blue Williams-Sonoma apron Harper had gotten her for Mother's Day last year.

"I think . . . I think it's going to be really good." Admitting that out loud was scary, and she immediately wished she'd deflected the question with a joke.

Mrs. Waddle smiled as she crushed the cranberries. "I'm really proud of you."

Standing beside her mother at the counter, Harper narrowly missed jabbing herself with the butter knife. "You — are?"

"When I was eighteen, I dreamed of being a chef," Mrs. Waddle confided. "I even applied to the Cordon Bleu in Paris."

"What?" Her mom was a full-time homemaker with a part-time catering business. Harper never pictured her wearing a white poofy hat and ordering around prep cooks.

She gave Harper a look. "You're buttering your hand."

Harper looked down. Oops. "Why didn't you go?" she asked, wiping her hand on a dish towel.

"I didn't get in." Her mom shrugged. "I was so devastated it didn't occur to me I could reapply." She smiled. "Then I met Dad and had you and your sister. . . . My dream became something else."

Harper stared at her, shocked. She'd never bothered to imagine what her mom was like pre-herself. She'd just assumed her parents had sprung up fully developed sometime around the time of Harper's birth.

The idea that her mom was somehow . . . *less than* . . . that she'd given up her dreams for her and Amy . . . it made Harper feel sick to her stomach. But if all this was true — it meant her mother was the one person who could really understand. . . .

"I didn't get in, either," Harper heard herself say. "NYU rejected me."

As she spoke the words, it was as if she'd gotten the letter from Dean of Admissions Phoebe Pettler five minutes, instead of eight months, ago. It was like watching her future go down the carrot peel–filled garbage disposal all over again.

"Harper . . ." Her mom took a step closer to her, and she half-wondered if she was about to be slapped. If she were, the physical pain would be a welcome distraction from what was happening inside.

"I didn't want to tell you," Harper said, her voice thick with tears. "I didn't want you to be disappointed." There. She'd said it. The whole, horrible, ugly truth.

Mrs. Waddle reached out and squeezed her shoulder. "I know." She must have looked baffled, because her mom gave her another squeeze. "I know you got rejected."

"You *know?*" Harper instinctively jerked away from her mom, feeling a sudden need to protect herself, feeling naked.

"NYU never sent us a request for money, or housing information, or anything else that happens when you're admitted to a college," Mrs. Waddle explained. "Between that and the haunted look on your face all summer, I figured it out."

"But you didn't *say* anything." She didn't even try to stop the tears that were running down her face. "Were you just going to let me fly off to Manhattan in September to live on the street?"

"I assumed you'd tell us when you were ready, or deal with it yourself." Mrs. Waddle smiled. "I was right."

Harper felt certain she was experiencing her first migraine headache. Her vision was fuzzy, and there was a throbbing behind her eyes that felt like a miniature monkey was playing the bongos in her brain. In the living room, Amy threw something at the TV.

"I didn't apply anywhere else." Her voice was barely more than a

271

whisper. "I was so sure NYU would want me I decided filling out forms anywhere else was a waste of time."

"I figured that out, too," Mrs. Waddle smiled as she calmly removed the now-boiled potatoes from the stove. "We better get mashing."

"That's all you have to say?" Harper demanded. "We better get mashing?"

"You were stupid, and you're paying for it." Her mother handed her a kitchen tool that looked like some kind of medieval torture device. "What am I supposed to do? Ground you?"

Harper started to pound the potatoes, the rhythm matching the pounding of her own heart. She had to ask.

"Do you think I'm a loser?" The label was her worst fear. It's what had driven her to lie to family and friends.

Mrs. Waddle set down her masher and looked Harper in the eyes. "You took a bad situation and turned it into something wonderful. Into an opportunity to fulfill your dream." She ran a finger down Harper's cheek. "Would a loser do that?"

And then she reached out and wrapped her arms around Harper, hugging her close. Harper buried her face in her mother's hair, inhaling the mom-scent she'd known for as long as she could remember. It was the thing she'd been longing for since this whole nightmare began. Comfort. And she couldn't get enough.

She also couldn't help wondering if she'd misjudged Kate, Becca, and Sophie as much as she'd misjudged her mom. Was it possible they would've responded the same way? By giving her a hug and telling her it was all going to be okay?

"You're an amazing girl," her mom told her, rubbing her back like she used to do when she was little. "And you're going to be an even more amazing woman."

"Thanks, Mom." Harper wasn't sure her mother had heard her,

but it didn't matter. She was going to make sure she said thank you more often in the future. Her mom deserved it.

She swallowed hard, forcing herself to pull away. The tears portion of this mother-daughter confab definitely pushed it into the made-for-*Lifetime* TV category. "Does Dad know?"

"Of course he knows," Mrs. Waddle responded. "We share everything."

Harper's warm fuzzies suddenly dissolved. Her mother was wrong. They didn't share everything. They didn't share Margo Rosen.

And now that she was seeing her mom in this new light, she was more determined than ever to protect her. Cindy Waddle, world-famous-chef-that-never-was, deserved to know the truth.

And Harper intended to find it.

Sophie was slightly tipsy. Correction. Sophie was slightly drunk, which was the difference, in her estimation, between glass number two and glass number three of delicious California Pinot Grigio.

Sam waved his hand in front of her face. "Your turn, Bushell."

She blinked. Maybe she should switch to water . . . after finishing this glass. Usually, she never drank more than one beer. Maintaining control of her faculties at all times was a priority. But tonight was so relaxed, so different from the couple of other LA parties she'd been to, that Sophie was actually enjoying letting go.

"I'm in for fifty cents," she announced confidently, throwing two poker chips into the pot at the center of the massive-but-unstable garage sale–type table at which she'd eaten Thanksgiving dinner.

They were in an area of Los Angeles called Silverlake, and although it was a lot fewer miles away from Beverly Hills than Trey's childhood home in Whittier, the neighborhood felt like it was a world apart. Windy streets climbed into the hills above a manmade reservoir, and the houses — everything from ultra-modern to 1920s Spanish-style bungalows — were scrunched together so close that Sophie imagined the artists and writers who populated the trendy area could hear their neighbors at the dinner table.

"You're bluffing." The accusation came from their hostess, Roz O'Connor, who was a self-admitted online poker junkie. "You don't have shit."

Roz was an auburn-haired, exceedingly loud friend of Sam's from New Jersey. They'd met doing summer community theater in Princeton two years ago and had been friends ever since. Every Thanksgiving she opened the craftsman house she rented to anyone and everyone who had nowhere better to go. She'd dubbed the event her Annual LA Orphan Ultra Thanksgiving Dinner Potluck Extravaganza, and she was the current chip leader in their haphazard Texas Hold 'Em game. Sophie had liked her right away.

"If you consider two aces nothing," Sophie lied, relying on her acting technique to maintain a poker face.

As the bets circled the table, she noticed that one of the guys was staring at her. His name was Mario, and he had a pierced right eyebrow and a tribal tattoo that covered his entire forearm. He worked on movie sets as a grip (Sophie still wasn't sure what that meant) and claimed to believe that "the only path to world peace was through anarchy." Next to Mario, Sophie felt outright matronly in her cashmere sweater set. Luckily, no one at the orphan dinner seemed to care what anyone else was wearing.

"I know where I've seen you!" Mario finally shouted at her from across the table. "It's been bugging me all night."

"Where?" Sophie asked, glancing at the poker cheat sheet Sam had made her. If she didn't win a hand soon she was going to have to retire to the porch with the serious wine drinkers. And that was *not* a good idea.

"You're the girl with the love-hate relationship with her hair."

Mario imitated her rinsing shampoo out of her curls. "Great wrist action in that spot, by the way."

A chill went down Sophie's spine. She'd officially been *recognized*. She was famous.

"Thanks, I still can't believe I got it." Apparently, in LA, even anarchists paid attention to who was doing what in The Business.

An Asian guy named Hank, who was wearing blue-mirrored sunglasses and a t-shirt that read I HATE JESSICA SIMPSON, flashed her a thumbs-up. "First national commercial is a biggie. Once you get one, they just start coming."

"Hank's the guy who makes all the disgusting noises when he eats a burger in those ads," Jasmine, a tiny aspiring oboist, explained. "He bought his condo off the residuals."

"I also played Hamlet at the Williamstown Theater Festival," Hank pointed out. "The ad stuff is just to pay the bills."

"He says that now," Sam joked as he folded his cards. "Wait 'til he gets a sitcom pilot."

"Sellout!" Roz yelled, throwing a poker chip at Sam.

Sophie laughed. She'd never seen Sam act so . . . goofy. It was refreshing, if somewhat unnerving.

Being here, stuffing her face, sipping wine, and playing cards, she felt like she'd been holding her breath since Labor Day, and finally she could exhale. She was also remembering why she was in LA in the first place. Not to be seen at parties or to pray that some magazine took a photo of her with Trey. She was here for her acting. For her . . . dare she think it . . . *art*.

"Sophie won't be doing commercials much longer," Sam informed the group. "She's dating Trey Benson." He raised his eyebrows. "She's big time hooked up."

As everyone oohed and ahhed, Sophie shot a glance at Sam. She didn't want to brag about her thing with Trey. At least, not to anyone besides Kate, Harper, and Becca, to whom she'd been writing extremely long and involved e-mails documenting every moment of her interaction with the actor.

"We've gone out a few times," she explained to the table. "We're pretty much just friends." Friends who spend a lot of time kissing, she added silently.

"Is he as good in bed as he looks like he would be?" Roz asked bluntly. It was the kind of thing Harper would say.

Sophie felt Sam's eyes boring two holes in her head. Death. He deserved death for bringing up this whole topic. She was an extrovert, sure. That didn't mean she had a desire to discuss what there was of her sex life with a bunch of people who happened not to have anywhere better to go for Thanksgiving.

"Um . . . I wouldn't know," she responded finally, standing up. "I think I'll clear the table."

"Does that mean you're folding?" Mario inquired, looking like a Cheshire cat.

Sophie threw her cards — a crappy seven and deuce — onto the table. It wasn't like she was a *prude,* Sophie fumed as she carried the turkey platter into the kitchen. She'd had sex tons of times. Well, three times. His name was Barton, and she had convinced herself she was in love with him when they'd costarred in their Fairview High production of David Mamet's *Oleanna.*

For months, Sophie had given Barton under-the-shirt access only. Then she had decided that if she were ever going to be a serious actress, she needed to gain some "real-life experiences" beyond hanging out every Friday night on Kate's roof. First on her list? The seminal Losing of the Virginity.

She and Barton had engaged in their real-life experience in his parents' wall-to-wall carpeted finished basement. Afterward, Sophie had felt let down and more than a little hollow. She hadn't felt connected to Barton, despite the fact that they were, literally, connected. And when he'd tried to cuddle, she just wanted to get away. She

276

gave sex with Barton two more tries before she broke down and confessed all to Kate, Harper, and Becca, who'd patted her on the back and told her about born-again virgins. Sophie ended it with Barton and vowed not to give herself to anyone until making love was going to be a lot more than an experiment to improve her acting technique.

Not that she hadn't thought about having sex with Trey. Eventually. She *wanted* to. But there was no way she was going to do it before the time was absolutely right. Before she knew she was in love.

Besides, being a born-again virgin was nice and uncomplicated. She wasn't going to venture into the world of condoms and STD tests lightly.

"Sorry if I offended you," Roz apologized as she entered the kitchen behind Sophie. "There are those who say I don't know how to keep my mouth shut."

Sophie shrugged it off. "You should meet my friend Harper. She'll say anything."

"Sounds like we'd get along."

"My friends are the best. Kate, Becca, Harper . . . they're totally real. Not like a lot of people out here."

Roz looked thoughtful. "Sam's real."

"*Too* real," she commented with a laugh. "I could do with a little of the fake polite from him."

Roz dumped a stack of plates into the sink. "You know he's in love with you."

Sophie snorted. "Sam and I are friends. Sometimes. That's it."

"Whatever you say," she responded with a smile, handing her a dish towel. "I'll wash, you dry."

As Roz started the water, Sophie peeked into the living room and stared at Sam. After a moment, he caught her eye and smiled. She quickly turned away, catching Roz staring at *her* staring at *Sam*.

"You make a cute couple," Roz observed. "But that's just one person's opinion."

Sophie grabbed a dish and started to dry. Roz was wrong. Sam had had his chance with her when she first moved into the Meyers' guesthouse. And he'd blown it, time and time again. She wasn't going to start getting confused just because an online poker junkie said something was the case that clearly wasn't.

Sam had his life. Sophie had hers. Nice and uncomplicated, just the way she wanted it.

From: beccawinsberg@middlebury.edu
To: waddlewords@aol.com, katherinef@ucb.edu, herDivaness@aol.com
Subject: Thanksgiving

So here's the update: Horrible date (my fault) followed by much amazing
kissing. Some hands-on-boobage, but we were in a car. I know that
doesn't stop some people, but I swear I don't get how that works.

I am in serious like. Not love. But definite like. Which means
this is bound for disaster. He is a football player, after all.
Though not at ALL what you would expect.

I don't know, I just really like him. He could be the Dream guy.
I wish you guys were all here so I wouldn't have to write about it in
some stupid e-mail, where it all sounds sordid and dumb.

How weird is it that I'm in New York for Thanksgiving? Remember how we
were all going to meet up at NYU, and sleep on the floor in Harper's
dorm room? Well, instead, I've got the guest bedroom in Isabelle's
parents' "classic fourteen." That's what they call their apartment, but
I think it's a joke. I don't get it. All I know is it's on Park Avenue,
and the view is insane.

Also, they have a DOORMAN, which apparently isn't that big a deal in
New York. I am such a rube.

Miss you guys beyond. After Thanksgiving dinner we all shared what we were
thankful for, and it totally wasn't cheesy. I said I was thankful for you.
I miss you a lot. I know I said that already, but I really, really do.

XO, Bec

Delete   Reply   Reply to All   Forward   Save   Print

SIXTEEN

Becca stared down at the soles of her feet. How was it possible that they could be so soft? So pink, and flawless, and . . . tender?

She took a sip of ice cold cucumber water and closed her eyes as Trina, the pedicurist at Melan, New York's chicest salon, went to work painting her now-perfect toenails.

This was heaven.

For the last two days, Becca had felt like she'd been dropped into a blissful alternate universe. Yesterday's Thanksgiving dinner in the Sutters' formal dining room had actually been *pleasant,* even enjoyable — unlike any holiday in her recent memory. Walter and Joan (they had insisted) wanted to hear all about the girls' classes, and had asked knowledgeable questions about Coach Maddix and the ski team's hopes for the upcoming season. When Isabelle's thirteen-year-old brother, Henry, had pulled out his PSP in the middle of the meal, they had simply laughed and reminded him to use his ear-phones. There had been no explosions or freak-outs. Then Stuart called after dinner and they'd talked for almost an hour. When she hung up the phone her face had hurt from smiling. And today . . .

Today was like a dream. Better.

She'd slept in late, nestled under the ridiculously soft down comforter in the Sutters' guest room. After a quick shower, she and Isabelle had walked to a corner diner for Becca's first ever real New York bagels and lox. Then they had gone shopping. Serious shopping, the kind of shopping that simply didn't exist in Boulder. Or anywhere in Colorado, for that matter. Isabelle had convinced her to try on short clingy skirts, and even clingier tops, then purchased said items with her father's platinum American Express card.

"No, you can't," Becca had argued desperately, as Isabelle handed the card to the clerk.

"Trust me," Isabelle had assured her, running a hand through her shoulder-length spiral curls. "I can. My dad wants us to have fun. Besides, we're going to a party tonight."

"A party?" Becca asked. The thought of going to a party with all of Isabelle's rich New York friends made her slightly queasy.

Isabelle nodded. "Abe is having people over."

"Ah," she replied, knowingly. Abe was Isabelle's unrequited high school crush. Suddenly the shopping made sense.

"It's nothing big," Isabelle continued. "But this is New York. And we, my friend, are going to look hot."

Becca had wanted to argue. But the clothes were unlike anything she'd ever owned, and unlike anything she was ever likely to own if she didn't concede. Isabelle's parents could definitely afford it. Her dad did something in venture capital, and her mom was a literary agent at an agency with initials even Becca had heard of.

So she'd smiled, and accepted graciously, knowing that when she got back to Middlebury she was going to have to write the longest, most effusive thank-you note she'd ever written in her life.

And now she was being pampered beyond belief at Melan. The manicurist had done the best she could with Becca's short, square fingernails. The pedicurist had worked magic on her feet. And the combination of New York water, expensive cherry-almond conditioner, and a professional blow dry had literally transformed her hair, which drifted in graceful waves around her shoulders.

The only way it could be more perfect, Becca thought, was if Stuart were there to see her.

Three hours later, the two girls were ensconced in Isabelle's mother's bathroom, which was bigger, brighter, and better stocked than the Bobbi Brown counter at Bloomingdale's. Isabelle had decided they would do their own make-up for the night. "Professionals go too heavy on the foundation," she'd explained, obviously the voice of experience.

Becca closed her eyes as her roommate meticulously applied a thin line of black liner to her eyelids, then launched back into the story she'd been setting up for the last five minutes — ever since Isabelle had asked her to tell yet another story about Harper, Sophie, and Kate. From the moment Becca had told her about their Year of Dreams, Isabelle had considered herself if not an active participant, then an exceptionally interested observer. She was determined to facilitate Becca's dream in whatever way she could (thus all the prodding about Stuart), and she also wanted to know, in detail, the progress the other three girls were making. Consequently, she had developed an interest in their past misadventures as well.

"So the car's totally dead, in the middle of this intersection," Becca continued, "everyone's honking, right, and we're about to start pushing when this Adonis-looking guy pulls over. . . ."

"Open," Isabelle instructed, listening. Becca opened her eyes.

"But Harper's wearing her A WOMAN NEEDS A MAN LIKE A FISH NEEDS A BICYCLE t-shirt."

"Don't tell me," Isabelle grinned, "Adonis got offended."

Becca nodded. "His face turns red, and he gets all huffy, and he goes off about how if she's this radical lesbian feminist she doesn't need *his* help getting the car off the road —"

Isabelle leaned her head back and laughed.

"So Sophie goes up to Harper," Becca continued, "and plants this huge wet kiss right on her lips."

"Just like Sophie."

"And then Kate starts in on this lecture about the historic persecution of women. . . ."

"Go, Kate," Isabelle cheered. "How's she doing?"

Isabelle knew all about the mugging.

Becca shrugged, worry clouding her eyes. "Last I heard, she's still staying with that Chantal woman. She says everything's fine."

"Stranded in Paris. Could be worse." Isabelle had finished with Becca's eyes and was now artistically applying three different shades of blush to her cheeks.

In her last e-mail, Kate had insisted she was fully recovered, but something hadn't felt right. If she were perfectly fine, why was she still in Paris? Worried, Becca had e-mailed back, but Kate hadn't yet responded.

Isabelle dabbed powder over Becca's lips and reached for a lip liner.

"I don't look like a circus freak, do I?" Becca asked. Makeup for her usually meant a quick stroke of mascara, a couple swipes with the blush brush, and tinted SPF lip gloss.

"You look like a sophisticated New Yorker, out for a night on the town," Isabelle declared, brushing a layer of pale pink over Becca's lips.

Then she sat back and examined Becca's face.

"Check you out, hot mama," she said finally, with an approving nod.

Becca turned toward the mirror.

And gasped.

She *was* hot.

"Wow," she breathed.

"It's just you *plus,*" Isabelle said. "Didn't take much really, just working with what's already there."

That was the best part, Becca thought. She looked *natural,* just like herself. Only better.

"So, what did you do while Harper was being a radical lesbian feminist, and Sophie was kissing, and Kate was lecturing?" Isabelle asked, starting to work magic on her own face.

"Oh. I . . . watched, I guess. I get uncomfortable in the middle of . . . you know, drama."

Isabelle grinned.

"Then you better watch yourself tonight. Because looking like that, drama's gonna find you."

Becca took in her reflection in the mirror and smiled. If drama *did* find her, the girl looking back at her could handle it just fine.

1931 Normandie Avenue. Harper checked the address again of the small one-story white house with royal blue shutters against the information on Margo Rosen's business card. Yep. Still matched.

I am a truth-seeker. I am a ninja warrior princess, whatever that is. I am . . . not to be fucked with.

Harper had been parked across the street from Red-Headed Tramp's abode for almost forty-five minutes now, but she hadn't been able to make herself get out of the car. It turned out *imagining* confronting one's father's mistress was easier than actually doing it.

"We share everything." Harper whispered it aloud, each word coming out with a little puff of frost.

Was it possible that Judd was right, and that this was all in her head? Maybe Margo Rosen *was* a colleague. Or maybe Harper really hadn't heard her dad laughing on the phone like he was relishing some big secret. Maybe this entire suspicion was born out of her need to not work on her book. To have something else to fill up the space so she wouldn't have to stare her computer in its face.

Except that Harper *had* been writing. She was up to page thirty and going strong. And she hadn't even been obsessing (too much) about Mr. Finelli.

No. This was real. Unfortunately, so was her love for her dad. Sitting across the dinner table from him last night, she'd studied his every movement. Tried to read every facial expression like it was the key to unlocking the key to his secret universe.

And he'd caught her. "What? Do I have turkey skin in my teeth?"

"Don't lie to me," she'd responded bitterly, jabbing her fork into perfectly smooth mashed potatoes her mom had helped her whip until they were the Platonic ideal of mashed potatoes. "I know what you're doing."

Everyone had looked at her like she was insane. Her dad had even reached out and put his hand on her forehead to check for fever. But she'd pulled away, citing sudden inspiration for her novel as the source of the outburst.

"That's what my character's dialogue should be," Harper had informed her confused family. "During . . . uh . . . one of the climactic scenes."

She'd then excused herself early from Thanksgiving dinner under the pretext of putting inspiration to paper. She'd been awake all night, and finally slipped out of the house early this morning. So here she was at seven-thirty AM in decade-old sweatpants and a too-tight 98 Degrees t-shirt. Sitting and waiting — for something. She wasn't sure what. Maybe another kind of inspiration.

Just do it, Harper commanded herself. *Three . . . two . . .* She bolted out of her mom's car and ran to the front door of 1931 Normandie before she could think herself out of it.

She rang the doorbell twice in quick succession to let Margo Rosen know she meant business. A few seconds later, she heard footsteps, and then the door opened.

"Hello." It was Red-Headed Tramp herself, clad in a lavender terry-cloth robe and large fuzzy pink slippers. "Can I help you?"

"I'm Harper Waddle." Pounding heart. Check. Sweaty palms. Check.

Red-Headed Tramp studied her for a moment. "Joe Waddle's daughter?"

Harper pushed her glasses higher on her nose. "Bingo."

Bingo? She wasn't the type of person who said things like "bingo." Then again, she wasn't the type of person who stood at the door of her father's lover's house, ready to cause a scene of major proportions, either. Causing a scene was Sophie's territory.

"Is everything okay?" Margo Rosen looked bewilderedly over her shoulder, like she expected to see her dad waiting in the car.

"No, it's not." Harper was no longer herself. She was some character out of a Greek tragedy. Medea, maybe. "If you don't stay away from my family, I'll hunt you down and make your life a living hell."

"Excuse me?" Red-Headed Tramp took a step backward, but she seemed totally unruffled, like she didn't feel the least bit guilty. *Bitch!*

"I know what you're doing with my dad. I *saw* you." Harper was much louder now, only her voice sounded like it was coming from a million miles away. "You can't just walk into a man's life and screw up everything. It's not right!"

There were more footsteps, and a tall man with sandy blond hair, wearing striped flannel pajamas, appeared in the doorway. "Margo, what's going on?"

"This is Joe Waddle's daughter." Red-Headed Tramp motioned to Harper. "We just need a few minutes."

"Should I call the police?" he asked, looking at Harper like she was a person in the midst of a psychotic episode. Which, in a way, she was.

Red-Headed Tramp smiled. "Everything's under control."

As Flannel Pajamas left, Harper geared up for another rant. "You think you're so hot in your pink suits, but you're really —"

"Engaged," she interrupted. "That was Glen, my fiancé."

"Your — what?" Harper glanced at Red-Headed Tramp's left

287

hand, where she noted there was a large pear-shaped diamond on her ring finger.

"I work with your dad sometimes," she continued. "If I have a client who can't find the home they're looking for, I send them your dad's way to do the contracting if they want to build a new one."

Huh.

"As a thank you, Joe agreed to help with the contracting for the house Glen and I are building."

"But I heard them on the phone. . . . He was talking about going away for the weekend. . . ." She didn't realize she'd said the words aloud until Margo responded.

"Honeymoon suggestions. Your dad's a great believer in marriage." She smiled again. "I guess because he loves your mom so much."

"Oh." Relief washed over Harper. Relief and more than a little humiliation. This had been an Enron-sized mistake. This was the Chernobyl of mistakes.

Margo (no longer Red-Headed Tramp) looked at her with green eyes that were, she now realized, unequivocally kind. "Can I go back to my fiancé now?"

Harper stepped away from the door. "I'm sorry — I didn't . . . I mean . . ." Her stammering trailed off as a horrible thought entered her head.

"It's okay," Margo replied. "But next time you have a question about your dad, maybe you should just ask him." Margo started to close the door, but Harper stopped her.

"Could you not tell him about this?" she asked meekly, her mortification complete. "He might not see the humor in it."

"It's our secret," Margo promised.

As Margo Rosen closed the door in her face, Harper realized she'd been wrong on a massive scale. Her dad was the same boring, stable guy she'd always thought he was. Honest and true and good.

There was only one liar in the Waddle family. And that was her.

Becca had long wondered at the ease with which, it seemed to her, most people floated through unfamiliar social situations without screaming, fleeing, or gouging out their eyes. Over the last three months, however, she'd become more social than ever before — with some notable humiliations and failures to show for it — and in the process had come into her own as, if not a social butterfly, at least a social caterpillar.

Tonight, she felt as if she had skipped right over the awkward co-coon phase and suddenly sprouted wings. She wasn't even phased by Abe's parents' spacious Upper East Side penthouse, with its rich oil paintings and dark leather furniture. And when Isabelle abandoned her to cozy up on the couch with Abe, she'd laughingly held her own with a group of Isabelle's high school friends, when in the past she would have retreated into a corner with a book. Without even a sip of alcohol, she had shared her opinions on college food, Hillary Rodham Clinton, the top brands of skis, and whether, in the realm of comedy greats, *Wedding Crashers* was in fact a better movie than *Old School*.

Then Jared Burke walked through the door.

Suddenly Becca was no longer a butterfly. She wasn't even a caterpillar.

She was larva. Quivering, unformed, pupae.

What is *he* doing *here,* she thought, stunned. It had been weeks since she had even *thought* about Jared, weeks since she had thought about his smoldering blue eyes, his dimples, the timbre of his laugh . . . which was longer than she'd once imagined she would ever go with-out thinking about him.

Standing just inside the door, Jared absently brushed a hand through his short blond hair as he laughed at someone's joke. How many times had she seen him do that? How many times had she imagined what his hair would feel like, soft and thick in her hands?

And now he was no longer Kate's boyfriend.

The thought had barely registered in Becca's mind when Jared saw her from across the room. At first, it seemed as if he didn't quite recognize her. Then he looked confused. Then he smiled, and she thought her knees would fail her.

"Holy shit." He grinned, coming toward her. "You look awesome, Bec."

He wrapped his arms around her and hugged her, then looked down into her eyes.

"Seriously, I almost didn't recognize you."

"Thanks," she responded, not quite complimented. "What are you doing here?"

"My friend Quint from Harvard knows Abe. I didn't want go all the way back to Boulder for a four-day break, so I figured I'd party in New York instead."

Becca smiled. Jared liked spending time with his family about as much as she did — something Kate had never really understood about him.

"What about you?" he asked.

"Same, sort of," she answered. "Only my friend's name is Isabelle."

Jared smiled, an assessing gleam in his eye.

"You look different."

Becca stared at him. God, she'd been in love with him for so long.

"Have you talked to Kate?" she asked.

"Not in a while. You know, we broke up."

He was standing so close Becca could smell the fresh, clean scent of him.

"I know." Then she couldn't stop herself from adding, "She's dating some Swedish guy now. They met in Paris. Apparently she's totally in love with him."

The words came out in a rush, and she regretted them immediately.

"Really?" Jared looked around the room, obviously pretending not to care. And failing.

Why had she told him that?

"That's cool," he continued finally. "It was time for both of us to move on."

Becca nodded, wishing she could take it back. After all, she couldn't be in love with Jared anymore. She was with Stuart now. Sort of. It wasn't like they'd made any *commitments* or anything. Still, she did like Stuart. A lot. And Jared was just an old friend. Nothing more.

"You want a drink?" he asked.

"No, thanks," Becca shook her head.

"C'mon." He slid a hand up her arm. "I haven't seen you in months. We should . . . celebrate."

He put the other hand on the small of her back and guided her toward a bar lined with half-empty liquor bottles. He poured two tumblers of vodka, handed one to her, and raised his glass.

"To the prettiest girl in the room," he toasted, and slammed back his shot.

Becca looked at the glass in her hand.

Then she looked into Jared's blue eyes. His smile urged her on.

Why not? she thought.

What harm could one shot do?

I am one with the steering wheel. I am one with the road. Sophie eased the BMW onto the 405 freeway, imagining herself on an open stretch of highway, driving toward a gorgeous mountain, music swelling as her hair blew in the wind.

I'm also going to be twenty minutes late for my audition, she worried, glancing at the digital clock on the dashboard. Damn. If only

Celeste hadn't kept her at work late for yet another "conquering LA" strategy session, she would be at the production office by now.

Oh well. At least she had on her lucky outfit — the winter-white skirt and chocolate brown V-neck sweater she'd been wearing when she got the Rémedé shampoo ad. If she got this car commercial, she could consider giving up her hostess gig at Mojito. More time for auditions. More time to rehearse brilliant monologues to have ready in case a casting director ever wanted to hear one. More time for Sam.

Sam?

Trey. More time for Trey.

I am one with the steering wheel, she repeated, forcing herself to focus on being prepared to wow the Chevrolet executives. *I am one with the road. . . .*

There had been that night she and Sam almost kissed after the party. But that didn't mean anything. People almost-kissed all the time. It was a natural hazard of being young, beautiful, and unattached. But as for being an actual couple? They wouldn't last five minutes. Jeez, she'd barely gotten to the point where she didn't hide when he knocked on her door.

I am *a car,* her mind went deeper. *I can* sell *a car. . . .*

She was only even obsessing the tiniest bit about Roz's claim last night that Sam was in love with her because she hadn't seen Trey for so long. He'd be back from his press junket by tonight, and they'd have a quiet romantic dinner . . . Tonight could even be The Night. If it felt right. If Trey had missed her enough. If she decided upon seeing him that she was truly in love.

Sophie was in the middle of imagining herself in a sexy lace negligée, standing in front of Trey in all her glory, when her cell phone started to chime the opening bars of Norah Jones's "Sunrise."

Trey.

"Are you back?" she asked as the second bar started.

"And dying to see you," Trey answered. "I missed my girl."

She grinned. Just hearing his voice made her realize how stupid this whole Sam situation was. She was dating — like, really dating — *Trey Benson*. Sam was a pool boy. A cute, talented, pool boy. . . . But he wasn't Trey.

"Like there weren't a million girls screaming your name everywhere you went for the last few weeks."

He laughed. "Yeah, but none of them call me on my shit like you do."

After Trey had left her that less-than-encouraging message during her Rémedé audition, she'd told him in no uncertain terms that that kind of behavior was unacceptable. She didn't care *how* many movies he'd made. Rude was rude. He had responded by issuing a *mea culpa* and behaving the total gentleman ever since.

"Meet me at the Chateau Marmont. I'm having a welcome home party in one of the bungalows."

"I can be there in a couple hours depending on traffic," she told him. "I've got a commercial audition."

The Chateau Marmont on Sunset Boulevard was one of those classic Hollywood hotels Sophie had read about in magazines like *Us* and *In Style* when she lived in Boulder. The idea of going to a party there gave her butterflies, Silverlake be damned.

Trey groaned. "I have to wait to see you?"

She felt all melty inside. He was probably wearing her favorite faded orange t-shirt. "Just for a little while."

"Is the audition that important? More important than seeing me?"

"Trey . . ."

"It's just that you're too good to be hassling with this pissant stuff. I wanna talk to Marcy about representing you, putting you up for *real* roles."

Sophie's heart skipped a beat. Was he serious about recommending her to his agent? Or did he just want her to blow off the car commercial?

Remember it's about the process, she reminded herself. After Sam dropped her off last night, she had spent an hour writing in her journal about the importance of the journey over the destination. But she wasn't *insane*. Any one of Roz's friends would've *killed* to get a meeting with Marcy Roth.

"That'd be great . . ." Sophie responded nonchalantly, not wanting to sound too excited. "But right now I want to take any chance I can get."

"I know. I know." He sighed. "Can I help it if I'm impatient?"

Sophie glanced at the clock. At this point, she was going to be at least twenty-five minutes late. They'd only hold her spot so long, and then she'd lose it. And she'd have wasted all this time on the freeway when she could have been kissing Trey. She eased the BMW into the right-hand lane.

"I'm getting off at the next exit. I'll be there in half an hour."

"I knew you cared." Trey's voice was warm and gravelly. "I'll meet you there."

Thirty-one minutes later, Sophie used twelve of the last twenty dollars in her pocket to valet her car at the Chateau Marmont. Entering the dimly lit gothic-style lobby, she waited a few seconds for her eyes to adjust, then scanned the adjacent Tiki bar. She loved what she saw — art deco furniture, including a retro lamp for every table — but there was no Trey.

After fifteen minutes, she had managed to persuade the coiffured snobby front desk clerk that *yes* she was really a friend of Trey Benson's and *yes* he had really invited her to meet him here. At which point Snobby informed her in a dismissive voice that neither Trey nor any of his friends had checked into the bungalow yet.

I'll soak in the history, she decided as she sat down at the bar to wait. Every star since the 1920s had hung out here — it was practically a prerequisite for being famous. In a way, it was better that she'd gotten here first. When Trey arrived, he'd see her looking cool and glamorous and oh so classic Hollywood. It would be a beautiful reunion, straight out of one of Trey's romantic comedies.

Besides, he hadn't *asked* her to skip the audition. She'd made the decision herself. There were, like, a million car commercials being produced every day. She'd get the next one. Or the one after that.

Four bottles of Perrier later, Trey finally arrived with four of his look-alike buddies in tow. When he saw her, his face lit up.

"Sorry about the audition, babe." He hugged her close. "I guess you had time to go after all."

One hour and fifteen minutes of staring at the wallpaper, *and* Trey was still calling her babe. Sophie forced herself to ignore his extreme hotness as she pulled out of his embrace and stared him down.

"I'll make it up to you," he promised when he realized she hadn't hugged him back. "Whatever you want."

"Can you turn back the clock so I can make it to my audition?"

Trey put his arm around her shoulders and led her away from his friends. "Listen, I put in a call to Marcy. Don't worry about the commercial."

"You can't just pick up the phone and make everything okay. There's a little thing called respect."

Trey looked intensely into her eyes. "I didn't know my meeting with my publicist would take so long, or I would have been here ages ago." He touched his nose to hers. "Please . . . don't stay mad."

Sophie felt herself soften. Trey was busy. She couldn't expect him to be everywhere he said he would be at exactly the moment he said he'd be there. Plus, he had a lot on his mind. Like helping her pursue her dream.

What were seventy-five minutes alone at the Chateau Marmont compared to that?

Becca wanted to say stop. More than anything, she wanted to open her mouth and tell Jared to stop kissing her.

But he was Jared Burke. And she had been in love with him ... forever. A thousand times, she'd dreamed of being in his arms, imagined the taste of his skin, the sound of his voice in her ear.

And now that it was finally happening ...

How could she stop it? Maybe it was destiny after all.

Jared had been so utterly charming all night, so focused on her. He'd hardly even asked about Kate. She couldn't possibly have said no when he'd whispered, "Let's get out of here" and steered her into Abe's parents' bedroom. Isabelle had disappeared long ago with Abe, and the party had dwindled to only a few stragglers passed out on the living room couches. Where else were they going to go? And it was so romantic — the view of New York City from twenty-eight stories high was like a living painting beyond the bedroom window.

So she'd let Jared take her hand and lead her to the bed.

She had just wanted to kiss him, feel her fingers in his hair, touch him, finally, after all this time. . . .

But things had gone frighteningly out of her control.

All she would have to do, she kept thinking, as Jared snaked a hand under her bra and groped at her breast, was say no. If she could just say that one simple word, everything would be fine. But everything was happening so fast, and when she imagined Jared's face, full of contempt and disappointment, she knew she couldn't speak.

Anyway, wasn't this *really* what she had always wanted? And even if it wasn't, he couldn't be blamed for making the assumption, could he? She tried to kiss Jared back as he pulled awkwardly at her panties. He kept murmuring how much he wanted her. His breath smelled like gin.

Becca fleetingly wished she'd had more to drink. If this was going to happen, she wanted to enjoy it — or be able to forget it — instead of being stuck in her head, nervous, uptight, afraid. And constantly thinking about Stuart, which was the worst part of all.

And it was going to happen. Jared reached for his discarded khakis and pulled a condom from the wallet in his pocket. Becca looked at the ceiling over his shoulder as he put the condom on.

Then he kissed her again, this time harder, and she thought wildly that Stuart was a much better kisser —

And then she just felt pain. Followed immediately by sharp regret.

"That was great," Jared said several minutes later as he was pulling on his khakis.

Then he said, "You're not gonna tell Kate, right?"

Becca felt sick. She shook her head, got up, and found her new silk panties and matching black bra in the folds of the bed sheets. She slipped them on. Then she picked up her black skirt and silvery tank top from the bedroom floor, and went to the window. She pressed her cheek against the glass. It was ice cold, punishing. The people on the streets below were the size of ants.

As Jared casually buttoned his shirt behind her, she felt smaller, even, than that.

Greetings Earthling!

To Whom It May Concern:

The friend formerly known as Harper Waddle has been taken by aliens and replaced by a humanoid writing machine. Which is why she hasn't returned any of your e-mails for the past five days. She will be returned to Earth after she has accomplished the mission set forth to her.

She hopes you're having fun in Plastic Surgeryland.

Sincerely,
Xighaghei
Minister of Communication
Planet Fargone

Sophie Bushell
11583 Rexford Dr.
Beverly Hills, CA 90210

DENVER, CO
AM

SEVENTEEN

Of course it doesn't sound crazy," Becca consoled Harper, whose mortification over confronting her father's "mistress" was painfully evident, even over the phone.

"Really?" Harper wanted to believe.

"You had good reasons for thinking what you did. You heard them on the phone, you saw them together, the laughing thing is very suspicious —"

"But it was nothing, and I — I can't even say it. You should have seen me. If I believed in hell, I would definitely be going there."

Becca, who did believe in hell, would be glad for the company. Nothing Harper had done was remotely as hell-worthy as losing her virginity to her best friend's ex when she was supposedly dating someone else. Someone wonderful.

"Hello?" Harper beckoned into the silence. "Do not make me say 'yoo hoo.'"

"Sorry," she apologized quickly. "I was just . . . you know, thinking about . . . your dad." But Harper was onto her.

"Don't lie to me. I can't take it in my fragile mental state. What's going on? Is it Stuart?"

"Sort of," Becca admitted.

"You've been back a week, things should be hot and heavy by now."

Isabelle, who was studying on her bed, had picked up on the direction of the conversation.

"*Tell her,*" she mouthed. "She'll make you feel better."

Becca put her hand over the receiver. "No, she'll tell me I'm an idiot, which I already know."

Isabelle raised an eyebrow and shrugged. Her position wasn't going to change.

"I feel a 'yoo hoo' coming on," Harper was saying.

"I'm here."

"So," Harper continued, "what's up with studly man? Don't change the subject."

"I haven't really seen him. Just in class."

"Who's avoiding who?"

"Um . . . that would be me doing the avoiding."

There was a long silence on the other end of the phone. Then Harper started in.

"Becca, you finally have a great guy who sees all the amazing things in you that we've seen forever. From the first moment he saw you, *literally,* he's been into you. He *likes* you. And I know that's scary, and whatever, but you have to let yourself trust him."

Every word she said was like a knife to the massive ball of guilt that had taken residence in Becca's chest. Stuart wasn't the one who couldn't be trusted.

"I had sex with Jared," she mumbled, barely audibly. But Harper'd heard her clearly enough.

"*What?*" she gasped. "You . . . had *sex?* With . . . *what?*"

There was a long pause. Isabelle was listening intently while pretending to be engrossed in her anthropology book.

"Oh my God. How did that happen? Are you okay?"

"No," Becca sighed. She was *so* not okay.

She gave Harper an abbreviated version of what had happened in New York — how Jared had shown up at the party, how she had told him about Kate and Magnus, how Jared had seemed to be so into her until *after,* when it was clear he was just retaliating against Kate in some way.

"Bec." Harper's voice was full of compassion. "I don't know what to say."

"Well, I had sex for the first time with someone who couldn't care less about me, and ruined my chances of ever being happy with a guy who actually really likes me," Becca summarized, her voice oddly high pitched. "Just say I'm an idiot and get it over with."

"Not . . . exactly." Obviously Harper could tell Becca was too upset for her usual candor.

"God, I just realized," Harper mused, "that means I'm the last virgin. That's so sad."

"It's not sad. Anyway, maybe you and Mr. Finelli will get it on when the book's done."

"Not funny."

"Nothing's funny." Becca sighed. "I can't even look at Stuart when I see him in class. He keeps calling, and I make Isabelle tell him I'm not here. I'm so stupid."

"You were confused. And Jared's an asshole. I mean, we've known that for years."

"We have?" How had she missed that?

"Well he's also incredibly charming, when he wants to be," Harper said. "You don't have to tell Stuart, you know. It's not like he and Jared are going to run into each other at the bookstore. You can just pretend it never happened."

"Yeah." She'd been trying to pretend exactly that, but Becca knew now that she didn't deserve Stuart. Everything he thought about her was a big, huge, fat lie. Just like everything she had thought about Jared was a big, huge fat lie. A horrible misjudgment. A delusion she had created to . . . what? Keep her safe? Ouch, she thought wryly. The irony.

"So . . ." Harper ventured slowly, "there's someone else we seem to not be mentioning."

Becca groaned. "I can't even think about Kate, it's too awful."

"So you're not going to tell her."

"I don't know. You know how she is when she's mad."

"The temperature drops several degrees all around the world," Harper agreed.

"I'm a horrible person," Becca said. "And Dreams suck. They just set you up to fail. Or at *least* be miserable."

"That's not true," Harper countered, without much force.

"I could have fallen in love with him," Becca said sadly.

"You still can," Harper said, encouragingly.

"If I don't tell him — and if I don't tell Kate — that's essentially lying," Becca said. "It's too big a thing to lie about."

"I don't know." There was a strange tone in Harper's voice. "Sometimes . . . maybe it's best not to tell the whole truth."

"I don't think so," Becca disagreed.

Harper was silent again.

"It'll work out," she said finally.

Becca wanted to believe that, with all her heart. But this was *her* life they were talking about, not Kate's or Sophie's. For Kate and Sophie, even for Harper, everything always worked out in the end.

But for her . . .

Things always got screwed up. And this time, she'd brought it entirely on herself.

"You can come with me to the wedding," Magnus offered quietly.

His hand gripped hers on the rail of the Copenhagen-Malmö ferry.

Kate leaned her head against Magnus's shoulder, and stared off the bow across the Baltic Sea toward Sweden. She was taking him home. A sliver of land had appeared in the distance. Which meant that she and Magnus were almost . . .

Not *over,* but —

She gripped Magnus's arm. Over, she concluded. Just deal with it. They were over. At least for now.

"I can't," she said. "I have to jump off the big rock again."

In silence, they watched as the coastline came inexorably closer.

When the ferry docked, Magnus would go north on his motorcycle. After his brother's wedding, he would move into a friend's apartment near Kungsträdgården (he'd told her about it in such detail that she could imagine the creaky windows and the worn wooden floors), in central Stockholm. In January, he would begin his first semester at Stockholms Universitetet.

January. Kate had no idea where she would be by then. Magnus had given her an envelope the night before and made her promise that she would make the "very special place" he'd written down on the paper inside the next stop on her travels. After that, she didn't know.

She only knew that she would miss Magnus. Probably desperately. Yet, in the last few days, she had felt a building anticipation of being on her own again. She would do things differently this time around — she was smarter, safer, stronger. And she owed that to herself as much as to Magnus. He'd been there to give her the initial shove, but ultimately, the forward momentum had to come from her. And it had.

The night after her first solo motorcycle ride, sprawled out on the bed at a roadside inn, they had reconstructed Harper's list. She'd remembered 76 of the 100 items on the list — 77, actually, but she'd left out "talk to the ugly guy." Magnus had remembered several more — his favorite was "take a picture of yourself on Foster Street."

Then, starting the next morning, she had embraced the bubbly feeling she'd discovered with grape innards between her toes.

Everything on the list that she had resisted before — either because she didn't want to look stupid, or she didn't get the point — she tackled first. She'd learned to say "Stop staring at my breasts" in French, Swedish, Italian, and Danish. (Magnus had agreed to teach her the Swedish version only if he was exempt from the directive.) She'd shouted her name in the middle of the crowded *Grand Place* in Brussels. In Copenhagen, she'd eaten a whole slice of blood sausage without throwing up.

With every single stupid thing, she'd felt herself moving toward something. What it was, she hadn't yet figured out. But every day she awoke feeling slightly different than the day before — lighter and deeper and fuller, all at the same time. She hadn't had a nightmare in over a week.

The ferry boat pulled into the dock at the Malmö station with a clang.

Wordlessly, Kate turned into Magnus's arms. He held her as the ferry emptied. Finally a porter approached, and they broke apart to retrieve Magnus's motorcycle from the hold. Heart aching, Kate climbed on the bike behind Magnus for the last time, and together they rode over the gangway and onto land.

"You're home," Kate said.

"Mmm," he responded. Kate was absurdly pleased to hear he didn't sound happy about it.

She climbed off the bike. This was as far as she went. Magnus handed her her backpack, but kept a tight hold on her hand.

Kate laughed as tears sprang to her eyes.

"I only cry around you," she said.

"I'm too manly to cry." He smiled.

"Liar," she laughed. "You'll cry all the way to Stockholm."

"Like a baby," he said. "The second you're out of sight."

They grew silent. Kate drew in a ragged breath, then leaned in to kiss him. She wanted to remember everything about him — the

306

curve of his lips, the slight cedar-ish scent of his smell, the way his eyes wrinkled when he smiled down at her. She pulled away to kiss the tiny scar she had found one night on the back of his left hand.

"Thank you," she smiled.

"You're welcome." He kissed the scar over her eyebrow.

Then he gripped the clutch and put the motorcycle in gear.

"Jag älskar dej."

He'd never said it before, but Kate knew exactly what the words meant.

Before she could respond, he was gone.

"You're making me nervous." Habiba glanced up at Harper, who was pacing nervously back and forth across the garbage-strewn basement.

Harper stopped. "I won't move," she promised. "You won't know I'm here." She gestured toward the fifty-one pages in Habiba's hands. "Keep reading."

Habiba dutifully went back to the pages, and Harper remained still, determined not to flinch until Beebs had finished reading the twelve thousand five hundred and forty-two words that existed of her as-yet untitled novel.

"I can hear you breathing," Habiba commented, looking up again. "It's kind of loud."

Yes, hyperventilating tended toward the noisy, Harper thought. She hadn't even realized she was doing it. "I'll just — wait in the bathroom," she offered.

Habiba nodded, her brown eyes unreadable. "Good idea."

Harper tiptoed into her bathroom and shut the door behind her. Sitting down on the cracked pink toilet seat cover, she tried not to focus on the hugeness of this occasion. Habiba was the first person to whom she'd given her partial manuscript. The first person who had the ability to crush her dream or convince her she was a genius. It was an ugly job, but someone had to do it. Luckily, Beebs had volunteered.

Harper took off her glasses and actually cleaned them with the special solution she'd gotten from her optometrist for the first time in three weeks. She flossed her teeth. She examined her face for a new outbreak of blackheads. Then she glanced at her black digital watch. Five minutes had passed.

Ten minutes after that, as she studied a line of ants that were crawling from a small hole at the back of the toilet up the side of the sink, Harper concluded that between mental and physical torture, she would definitely go with the physical. Nothing could be worse than sitting in a confined space, awaiting her hour of judgment.

Unable to stand her own anguish, she dumped her toothbrush out of the crusty glass on her bathroom sink. Putting the glass to her ear, she leaned against the wall, trying to hear any reaction from Habiba. A laugh. A snort of derision. *Anything.*

But there was only silence. She forced herself to count to one thousand, then opened the door and peered into the basement. Uh-oh. Habiba was holding the last page she had written, and tears glistened against her dark skin as they streamed down her face.

"Was it that bad?" Harper asked quietly, shoving an opened box of Entenmann's coconut donuts aside with her foot as she crossed the room.

Habiba shook her head. "It's beautiful."

Rainbows. Butterflies. Harper had been transported to the Happy Place from one of those cheesy yoga mediations. All that had been wrong with her world was now right. She could breathe.

"Really?" she asked, as doubt immediately crept back in. "You're not just saying that?"

Habiba sniffed, but the tears were still coming. "I love it. You're a wonderful writer."

Harper plopped onto her Harry Potter–sheeted mattress and re-garded her. "Why am I getting the sense that my gorgeous prose isn't the source of those tears?"

"My father wrote poems," Habiba explained, wiping her eyes. "My mother left some of them with me when she took me to the or-phanage. . . . They're the only things I have from either of them." She looked down.

"I'm so sorry, Beebs. I didn't know."

Harper felt like absolute shit. She was constantly going on and on about herself to Kate's little sister. But did she ever stop to ask Habiba one thing about herself? With her friends gone, she had used Beebs as a fill in to ease her loneliness. But she'd given her noth-ing in return.

"No, it's okay," Habiba replied, wiping her nose with her sleeve. "It's just reading this made me think of them. . . ." She smiled. "That's a good thing."

Harper wanted to reach out to Habiba and ask her a million questions about her life. And she would. But first she had to ask one more time.

"So you really liked it?"

Habiba rolled her eyes and laughed. "Yes!" She handed her the fifty-one pages. "And so will Adam."

Harper flipped through the pages, feeling like she was going to puke. Having a fourteen-year-old girl with a soft heart and a pen-chant for Hello Kitty products read her book was one thing. Mr. Finelli was another.

And Harper wasn't sure she was ready to go there.

University of Colorado at Boulder

ucb.edu

From: katherinef@ucb.edu

To: herDivaness@aol.com

Subject: Betrayal

Hi, Sophe—

Okay, you can stop freaking out. It's better that I know, right?
I mean, this is information I should have.

You didn't exactly TELL me, anyway. If anything, you tried NOT to tell me—
but you know me, I don't exactly let up when I sense weirdness. So no guilt.
If I never speak to Becca again, it's totally not your fault.

K.

Compose   Inbox   Sent Mail   Drafts   Trash

EIGHTEEN

Sometimes a person had to re-evaluate everything they had ever thought about everything and everyone they had ever counted on.

Unfortunately, Kate thought, now was one of those times. First, Becca had slept with Jared. Then, as if that hadn't been enough of a knife between the shoulder blades, Magnus had turned on her too. With seven little words, he had sent her spiraling back into the depths of the fear and mistrust she had felt so strongly in the weeks after her attack.

The betrayal was even more acute because she'd been so excited to open the envelope he'd given her on their last day together. Surely, she'd imagined, he was going to send her someplace wonderful, someplace exciting and meaningful. Like, maybe, to a romantic park in Norway, where she could think and dream about the next time they were going to see each other. Or, even better, a Buddhist monastery in Tibet, where she could reflect on the deeper meaning of life in peace and mindful meditation.

No such luck.

After Magnus had ridden away on his motorcycle and Kate had dried her eyes, she'd made her way to the Malmö shoreline and ripped open the crumpled white envelope, full of excitement and anticipation.

But the seven words scrawled in blue ink on the paper inside were the last she had ever expected to see.

"Go where you don't want to go."

The breath caught in her throat. She knew what that meant. Magnus wanted her to go back to Athens. And he wanted her to go alone.

What. A. Bastard.

She had railed at him mentally for the entire multiple-train ride south from Copenhagen to Greece. But she'd promised him she would go wherever he sent her, and she wasn't going to let him down — because, deep down, she knew that her anger was rooted not in betrayal but in fear. And that Magnus had known she would have to face those fears if she ever truly wanted to move on. As much as she dreaded it, she wanted that for herself, too.

So she had gotten a bed at the same grungy hostel in Athens where she'd stayed the last ill-fated time she'd been in the city. After a sleepless night spent listening to three other girls snore and toss on their creaky bunks, she'd gotten up, thrown on a pair of jeans and her trusty Harvard sweatshirt, and followed the same circuitous path she'd taken on the day of her attack.

And what she'd discovered was that she hadn't been so stupid that day after all. It wasn't like she'd wandered blindly into an obvious gang hangout or terrorist den. The neighborhood wasn't seedy. The people weren't threatening or antagonistic. The neighborhood was just a neighborhood. And the people were just people. Kate had simply had the misfortune to run into the *wrong* people at the wrong time.

She'd also been extraordinarily lucky, she realized, gazing into the darkness of the alley where she'd been dragged that day. She'd been lucky that the gray-haired woman and her unseen husband had heard her cries and come to her rescue. Far from being helpless she had in fact been courageous. She'd fought hard and savagely. She'd been determined that someone would hear her, and someone had. That was what had saved her.

She, Kate Foster, was a fighter after all. Even in the most terrifying moment of her life.

Staring down the deep, dark alley, Kate knew that there was one other place she had been afraid to go.

A telephone booth.

It was time, finally, for her to call home.

Over the last several months, she had sent postcards letting her parents and Habiba know where she'd traveled and the things she'd seen and done. But talking to them had seemed daunting and overwhelming — she still didn't have the answers to the questions they were sure to ask. When was she coming home? What was her elusive dream?

Nonetheless, her parents at least had the right to ask. And, truth be told, she missed them. Plus, she still had a question to ask Habiba.

So she went back to the hostel and waited in line for an hour to get into the tiny dank phone booth off the ground-floor lobby. Settling herself on the corner stool, she dialed her phone number in Boulder.

"Hello?"

Kate closed her eyes. She had almost forgotten the prim, quiet lilt of her mother's voice.

"Hi, Mom," she began nervously.

There was a long moment of silence. "Kate?" her mom asked quickly, her voice rising an octave. "Is that you?"

"It's me. Are you okay?"

"Where are you? Is everything alright? Why haven't you called? Andrew, it's Kate!"

Kate laughed. For the next ten minutes she answered a barrage of questions as her mother and father and Habiba each picked up a phone at various locations in the house, all talking at once. She was surprised to find that it was *nice* to talk to them. They didn't seem angry anymore — just happy to hear from her.

And then her father asked the question she had been dreading most.

"When are you coming home?"

Kate took a deep breath. "Not for a while. Probably not until May. Or June."

Kate heard her mother sigh.

"Well, alright," she said. "I suppose."

"We'll miss you," her father added. He sounded genuinely sad.

Kate drew a ragged breath. "I miss you guys a lot, too," she said, then she added, "So, could I talk to Habiba, please?"

"She's been on the line the whole time," her mother said, confused.

"I know. We had that whole exchange about falafel stands in Paris, remember? I meant, alone."

"Oh," her father said. He sounded pleased.

"Of course," her mother agreed. "We love you, sweetie. Call again soon."

"Anytime, day or night," her father added.

"I will." She smiled.

"I think you should start calling once a week," her mother said firmly.

Kate laughed. "Fine, Mom. I'll call next week."

"Alright. I love you," her mom said. And then it was only her and Habiba on the line.

"So . . . what's up?" Habiba asked, sounding slightly wary.

Kate hesitated, then plowed ahead. "I've been wanting to ask you something for a while. About the Berlin Wall."

"Oh. Okay."

"I went there, you know, because you put it on the list. And it made me think about a lot of things. Like . . . your life before Mom and Dad came to Ethiopia."

Kate still wasn't sure if that was what Habiba had intended, but it seemed important to discuss either way. If nothing else, she needed

316

to reach out . . . *really* reach out, beyond her usual "Hey, you can borrow my sweater."

On the other end of the phone, Habiba made a sound somewhere between acknowledgment and bafflement.

"Just, you know, you've lost so much," Kate continued awkwardly, almost as a confession, "and I never . . . I could've been more compassionate."

"You've been okay," Habiba responded. She was doing her best to reassure Kate, but couldn't quite hide that she was lying.

"No, I haven't," Kate replied. "And I'm really sorry."

She *was* really sorry.

At the other end of the phone, Habiba sniffled. Then she gave a little cough. "So . . . thanks. But I totally didn't send you to the wall for that."

"You didn't?" Now Kate felt silly.

"No."

"Was it because of Mom and Dad?"

"Sort of," Habiba answered. "I mean, I wanted to remind you that walls come down. Mom and Dad aren't even really mad anymore. They just worry about you."

"I'm fine," Kate assured her. "Will you be sure they know that?"

"Yeah. But," Habiba continued, "the wall thing? I was sort of thinking about *your* wall."

"My wall?" Now Kate was the baffled one.

There was a pause. "Yeah."

"What wall?"

"Well . . ." Habiba said slowly. "You know how you never cry?"

"I'm kind of over that," Kate said.

"That's good," Habiba sounded surprised. "That probably means the wall's coming down."

"Again . . . what wall?"

Was Habiba trying to say she had a wall . . . around her heart?

317

Maybe she didn't want to have this conversation after all. But her sister was already talking again.

"At the place I grew up," Habiba said, referring to the 180-child orphanage in Addis Ababa where she had spent nine years of her life, "there were kids who didn't cry. No matter what."

"But, that was because they'd been traumatized or something. I mean, those kids saw things —" Kate stopped. Habiba knew exactly what those kids had seen.

"Walls are built of all different materials," Habiba continued gently. "Some are stone, some are cement, some are wood. Some walls grow from bad things, others are more . . ."

"What?" Kate asked. Habiba couldn't stop now. Kate had a feeling her sister was onto something she had been grasping at for a long time, but had been unable to reach.

"I would never say anything bad about Mom and Dad. But you know what they're like. All about the noggin."

Kate grinned. The one thing her sister had never quite mastered was slang. Use of the word 'noggin' aside, what Habiba had said was true. Everything, for their parents, could be thought through and assessed based on evidence and historical records. And because they reasoned everything out, they believed strongly in the conclusions they reached. They had trained Kate to be the same way.

Her three best friends must have known about the wall, even if they wouldn't have put it the same way. So had Magnus.

"I understand what you're saying," Kate said. She braced herself. "And you're right."

Habiba released a breath on the other end of the line. "I thought you were going to hate me."

"Nope. I don't hate you."

In the two years since Habiba had joined her family, there were three words that Kate had never said to her. Not because she was trying to be mean, but because, until now, she hadn't been entirely sure they were true. But if she had learned anything in the last four months it was this: knowledge was great, feelings were even better . . . but neither meant anything without action.

Kate took a deep breath.

"I love you," she said.

And was surprised to find that she meant it.

"You're doing GS today," Coach Maddix informed her as Becca snapped on her skis.

She looked at him, surprised. She was a slalom skier, always had been. She liked the speed and focus the slalom required, and he wanted her to switch to giant slalom *now,* her first practice back on skis since the ankle debacle? Not to mention that GS skiers were widely acknowledged to be the best.

"It's not a compliment," he continued. "With that ankle, slalom turn radius is gonna be tough." He looked at her a moment, then added, "We'll see how you do."

He obviously wasn't expecting much.

At the top of the mountain, he shot out a few terse words of advice. Don't push too much too soon, remember your knees, stay close to the gates.

Becca gripped her poles and waited for the buzzer. The gates were farther apart than she was used to, so she went through the course in her head, one gate at a time. Isabelle had already taken her first run and reported back that the snow was a little soft, but good. She could do this.

The buzzer sounded, and Becca surged forward, snapping the wand with her knees. The clock had started. Now she just had to get through the whole course and make it to the light beam at the end without making a fool of herself. She'd done enough of that lately, and she really didn't want it to happen here on the mountain, the one place she felt in control.

For the first thirty meters, she was the tiniest bit off-balance, over-compensating for her ankle, but she tested it on the turns, and it seemed sound. The pain was minor enough to ignore. She really *could* do this. She let herself go. And for the next two minutes, Becca was aware of nothing but the mountain, the snow, and the satisfying *thwap* of the gates as she swooshed by.

Then she crossed the light beam, and the run was done.

She checked her time as she took off her skis. Not bad. Better than a couple of the regular GS women, worse than most. But not bad.

The assistant coach at the bottom of the mountain approached, cell phone in hand.

"Coach," he said, handing it to her.

"Hey, Coach," she began, cautiously.

"Welcome back," Coach Maddix said. "You're GS from now on. Start working on your endurance."

Before Becca could even say thanks, he'd disconnected.

Later that afternoon, she was going over the pros and cons of her semi-promotion with Isabelle as they walked down the hall toward their dorm room, when —

"Becca."

Becca turned as Stuart came out of the common room.

Her heart started to pound.

"Hey," she smiled nervously.

Isabelle waved at Stuart, then went down the hall to their room.

"You want to walk?" he asked. His hands were jammed nervously into his coat pockets. Becca's heart went out to him. The last thing she wanted was to make him nervous or tense or any bad feeling whatsoever. Which was exactly why she'd been avoiding him the last week and a half. She couldn't stand the pain — his if she told him about Jared, her own if she didn't.

When they were outside, Stuart led her to a private bench on the edge of an empty courtyard.

He looked at her a moment, then said, "I just want to know if you want me to stop calling."

"No," Becca said. As awful as it was, she knew that she wanted him to call her every day, every hour, every minute. "It's not that," she added.

"What is it?"

Becca tried to find a way to explain, but everything was jumbled in her head — Jared, Kate, her family, the Dream, the nightmare it had become.

Stuart tried to make a joke. "What, you got together with some other guy?"

The answer must have been plainly written across her face, because Stuart stood up.

"I'll stop calling," he said.

Then he turned and walked away.

December in Boulder was *not* the time to wear a mini-skirt. Especially when the only pair of black tights a person owned happened to have a huge hole in the left calf. Nonetheless, Harper and her goose bump–covered legs were standing at the door of Mr. Finelli's apartment, waiting in exalted anticipation to hear what he had to say about her fifty-one pages of blood, sweat, and tears.

The door opened, and Mr. Finelli smiled. "You knocked this time."

"I've been taking lessons," Harper joked lamely. She wasn't interested in small talk. Not when they could be discussing her book.

As she followed him inside, Harper managed to step out of her nervous box long enough to appreciate the way Mr. Finelli's faded blue jeans molded perfectly to his well-toned butt. The well-toned butt that she theoretically had access to now that her fifty pages were done.

He stepped behind her and tugged at the sleeves of her puffy red jacket, easing it down her arms as if he were unwrapping china. She could feel his warm breath on her neck. More goose bumps. This time, not from the cold.

We kissed. Harper shivered inside. Even now, standing so close to him, the idea was surreal. Like it had happened to someone else.

"You look great," he smiled, draping her puffy coat over a chair. "I haven't seen you in so long . . . I forgot."

After telling Judd to say hello, Mr. Finelli (she *still* couldn't think of him as Adam) had studiously avoided the Rainy Day Books Café since Harper had put the kibosh on their makeout session. He'd called to say that in the interest in one thing not leading to another, it was best if he stayed away.

She had finally stopped by the high school with her book this afternoon. And in the interest of not looking like a wimp, she hadn't mentioned that she'd been sitting on the manuscript for over a week while she built up the guts to give it to him.

"I don't look great," she responded automatically. "I never look great. Cute, maybe."

He shook his head. "You have no idea what you've got, do you?"

Harper wasn't cold anymore. She was excruciatingly hot. Partly because of the way Mr. Finelli was looking at her. But mostly because she wanted to know if he'd spent the afternoon reading about the lives of Violet and Beatrice and Lucille and all the other dozens of characters she'd packed into the beginning of her novel.

They could talk about "them," whatever "them" was, later. Right now, all Harper wanted was validation. She wanted to know she wasn't a fraud. She glanced around the apartment, looking for evidence of her fifty-one pages or the crisp manila envelope she'd put them in. But all she saw were stacks of *The New Yorker*, ungraded papers, and coffee cups.

Mr. Finelli grinned, his blue eyes gleaming at her from behind the lenses of his rectangular glasses. "You probably want to hear what I thought about your book."

"Uh . . . *yeah.*"

He stood up and retrieved the manila envelope from the top of his dark wooden bookcase. "*The Moments in Between.* I like the title."

"Thanks." But Harper already knew it was a good title. One night, she'd woken up at two in the morning and scrawled the words on one of the four notebooks she kept by her bed. Afterward, she'd slept like a rock for nine hours, knowing that at last her book had a name.

"Great job," he pronounced, handing her the envelope. "It's a really nice first draft."

Her heart sank. Great job? He sounded like he was praising her for acing a pop quiz.

"So it's not searing and incisive?" she asked, avoiding his eyes.

Mr. Finelli put his hand at the small of her back and guided her toward the couch. "Harper, writing fifty pages of anything is an amazing achievement."

"Fifty-one," she corrected him.

He sat down next to her and leaned in close. "I think it's going to be wonderful when you're done."

"So . . . what?" she demanded. "It has potential, but at the moment it sucks?"

"There's a lot of good stuff in there." He reached out and stroked her hair. "You've worked hard. Let yourself relax a little."

For over a year, Harper had fantasized about this moment with Mr. Finelli. She wasn't his student, and he wasn't her teacher. They could do whatever they wanted, and no one — not even the school board — could say a damn thing about it. But when she looked at his lips, all she saw where the words "great job" coming out of them.

Harper stood up and started to pace. "Tell me the truth," she begged. "Just tell me it sucks."

He sighed. "Harper, it doesn't suck. It's good." He paused. "But if you want me to be brutally honest, I'd say, yes, it needs work." He shrugged apologetically. "A lot of work."

Weeks of hand cramps. No sleep. Eyes that felt like they'd been carved out with an X-Acto knife. And she had nothing to show for it. She was a college reject, doomed to work at a coffeehouse for the rest of her life. No, worse. She'd lose her barista job and be forced into a career in the fast food industry.

Unless . . . Unless Mr. Finelli was jealous. He always said he'd wanted to be a writer. *Those who can't do, teach,* she thought. Maybe he was threatened by her talent.

"I'm leaving," Harper announced. "This was a bad idea."

She went to grab her puffy jacket, but Mr. Finelli got there first. He held it away from her so that she couldn't leave.

"Harper, you're a talented writer." He bent down so he could look at her eye to eye. "Your short stories are original and funny and poignant." His free hand reached out and rested against her cheek. "With more work, this will be, too."

"Only, according to you, right now it sucks," she snapped back, jerking away from him. She tore the jacket from his hand and strode toward the door.

"Harper, don't be like this," he said quietly. "Please."

She faced him. "You were right the first time. You and me and that kiss? It shouldn't have happened."

He studied her a moment, then nodded. "I guess you're right."

She threw open the front door to his apartment. Then she turned back to him. "I'd like my manuscript back, unless you were planning to use it for kindling."

"Being a writer . . . it takes a thick skin," Mr. Finelli said, handing her the envelope. "Let's talk about it."

324

Harper didn't want to talk about it. Mr. Finelli had just dropped her metaphorical baby on its head, and all she felt was a maternal instinct to protect.

Holding her manuscript close to her chest, she stormed outside, slamming the door behind her. It wasn't until she was safely inside her mom's Camry, halfway home with the radio blasting some awful Kelly Clarkson song, that she allowed herself to cry.

Kate in Greece:
Dial 011 + country code +
city code + phone #

Greece: 30
Athens: 1
phone: 226 438

7 hours later there!

NINETEEN

H e's not going to call," Sophie informed Celeste, who was standing at the hostess desk, going over that night's reservation list.

Celeste, who'd recently dyed her hair purple, shook her head.
"Nope."

It was four o'clock, and the Mojito patio was still packed with
beautiful people who apparently had nothing better to do three days
before Christmas than sit at tiny tables in the sun, pushing very expensive lettuce leaves around on their plates. Every minute that
passed was a minute Sophie wouldn't have to spend at the Beverly
Center doing her Christmas shopping (which emphatically did not
include buying those really cute size 10 forest-green Pumas that
would have looked great on a certain actor she knew).

"He's not going to ask his agent to represent me," she continued.
The more she said it out loud, the easier it was to stomach. Supposedly.

"Nope." Celeste handed Sophie two menus as an Armani-clad
fifty-something man headed toward the hostess stand with his *much*
younger, much-skimpier dressed, supermodel-looking girlfriend.

Since Trey's welcome home party at the Chateau Marmont two

weeks ago, Sophie had talked to him exactly once. And that was because she'd broken down and called his cell phone. She still shuddered when she thought about it.

Now all she wanted was to go home for Christmas, hang with her friends, and forget that Trey Benson ever existed. Maybe she'd even get in touch with Barton when she was in Boulder. Being fawned over — even by the wrong person — sounded like a nice change.

She forced herself to smile brightly as the Armani/model couple approached. "Table for two?" she asked, the grin practically cracking her face.

Just keep smiling, she thought as she led the couple to a quiet table at the edge of the restaurant patio.

"Enjoy your lunch!" Sophie oozed as Armani planted himself in his seat and immediately pulled out his cell phone. "Let me know if I can be of any assistance."

She couldn't believe she'd been stupid enough to think she'd actually be able to quit her gig at Mojito. One commercial, and she'd imagined herself with an infinity pool and a personal chef. Then again, if she'd actually gone to that Chevrolet audition . . . but she couldn't dwell on that. Not when she needed to be perky.

"I should have listened to Leo," Sophie told Celeste when she got back to her post at the hostess stand.

Celeste looked up from the reservation book. "Yep." She nodded toward the inside of the hotel. "Hey, isn't that your pool boy?"

Sophie followed Celeste's gaze. Sam was walking toward them, a small gift-wrapped package in his hands. "He's not *my* pool boy," she pointed out.

Celeste shrugged. "Whatever. I'm going back to the kitchen." She started to head off, then turned back to her. "He's a lot hotter than Trey Benson, if you want my opinion."

"I don't."

Sophie pasted a smile on her face. "Welcome to Mojito!" she chirped to Sam as he neared. "Table for one?"

He studied her for a moment before responding. Despite the fact that Christmas was a week away, he was wearing blue surfer shorts and flip-flops. There were some things in LA she'd never get used to. "You need to work on your fake smile."

"Always a critic." But Sam's judgments were comfortingly predictable. "Is that for me?" she asked, indicating the package.

"It's nothing." He thrust the gift in her face. "Just a mix CD I burned when I was bored."

"Gee, I'm overwhelmed." She took the present. "It so happens I have a nothing gift for you, too."

As Sam recovered from his apparent shock that he'd been on her Christmas list, she went and informed Celeste that she was taking a break.

"It's not wrapped yet," Sophie told him a few minutes later, as she opened the trunk of the BMW and took out his gift.

"Holy shit," Sam breathed, staring at the cover of the playbill from his production of *The Cherry Orchard,* which Sophie had had professionally framed. "This is . . . amazing."

She shrugged. "I was having some other stuff framed, anyway. No big deal."

"Right. No big deal." He finally looked up from the memorialized playbill cover. "Thanks, Sophie. This means a lot."

"Is that sincerity I detect?" she asked, suddenly feeling very self-conscious.

"You know it is."

Sophie slammed the trunk of the car shut. Part of her wanted to walk away from him and go back to work like it was any other afternoon. But the other part of her wanted to *know*. Had to know.

331

"Are you in love with me?" The question came out more bluntly than she'd intended.

"Excuse me?"

"Roz thinks you're in love with me."

Sophie held her breath, waiting for his response. What did she even want it to be? Her friendship with Sam had been a roller-coaster. . . . But a roller-coaster she could count on. If he said he was in love with her. . . . What would she do with that?

He looked at his feet, then back up at her. "Roz thinks a lot of things, most of which are complete bullshit."

"Oh."

"Maybe I had thing for you when you first got here. But that's so in the past it's barely a memory."

"Good." Sophie wasn't disappointed. She was *relieved*. "Because, you know, I think we make pretty decent friends."

Sam shrugged. Was that hurt she detected on his face, or was he just anxious to get to the beach? "Yeah. Some days."

For a long moment, they stared into each other's eyes. Sophie knew there was a dare there, but she wasn't sure who was daring whom. Or to what end.

"Are you really gonna come back from Boulder?" he asked finally. "Or are you one of those people that came and went?"

"I'll be back," Sophie assured him. "I haven't won that Oscar yet, remember?"

As she watched Sam walk away, Sophie couldn't help wondering what would have happened the night of that party if she hadn't met Trey. Because however casual she acted, however many rationalizations and reasons she had for *not* wanting to get involved with Sam, he still got to her.

Sam had answered her question. But she hadn't answered her own. If Trey Benson didn't exist . . . could she have fallen in love with him?

"Are you going to call her, or are you going to stare at the phone for another hour?" Isabelle asked, carefully placing a pair of black leather ankle-boots in her suitcase.

Cross-legged on her bed, Becca gave the question some consideration. Staring at the phone for another hour seemed appealing. At the same time, since she'd decided she had to call Kate, she might as well get it over with.

"Are you even sure she knows?" Isabelle wrapped the cord around her hair dryer. It was Christmas break already. Two whole weeks without even seeing Stuart from afar, which was the only way she'd seen him lately.

Becca nodded. "Her e-mail yesterday was weird. Like . . . formal. She said she hoped I enjoyed my time at home."

"That is freaky. You think Harper told her? That's seriously uncool. Not at all Harper-like."

Isabelle fancied herself an expert on Becca's friends. And she sort of was.

"My guess is Harper told Sophie, and Sophie accidentally let something slip," Becca guessed.

"That, I get." Isabelle zipped up her suitcase. "Okay. I'm gone. Call me and let me know how it goes."

Becca got up and gave her a hug.

"Have a great Christmas." She squeezed hard. "And thanks for . . . everything."

Isabelle had found her on the bench after her conversation with Stuart and brought her inside. She'd made her a hot cup of mint tea, and passed her Kleenex after Kleenex while she cried.

"You know, you could come home with me," Isabelle said, hesitating in the doorway. "You don't have to go back to Boulder."

Becca shook her head. "I have to deal with my family some time. And Harper's there."

Her roommate nodded. "Okay. Good luck." She gave a supportive grin, then wheeled her suitcase out the door and was gone.

Becca looked across the empty room at the phone on her desk. Whatever Kate was going to say to her honestly couldn't be worse than all the things she'd been saying to herself.

She picked up her notes on international dialing — Harper had given her a quick tutorial the night before when she'd given her Kate's number at the hostel in Greece. She pressed 011. Then 30. Then 1. Then six numbers instead of seven, which was sort of bizarre. There was an odd ringing sound on the other end of the line.

Finally, a woman picked up the phone and said something foreign that didn't sound remotely like hello.

"Um, hi. Is Kate Foster there?"

The woman on the other end of the line inhaled sharply — what was that about? — and said something else indecipherable. Did that mean Kate was there?

Becca's chest was tight, her stomach in knots. And it only got worse when Kate picked up the phone.

"Hey," Becca began, trying to sound confident.

"Oh," Kate said, her voice turning to ice. "Hey."

Everything Becca had planned to say flew out of her head. There was nothing she hated more than conflict, and conflict with one of her best friends was almost unbearable.

The silence stretched until Kate finally broke it. "Are you in Boulder?"

"Not yet," Becca answered. "I'm leaving in a couple hours. How's Greece?" she stalled.

"Great."

There was a pause.

"How's Magnus?" Becca asked.

"Good, but he's in Stockholm now." Kate's voice thawed a little.

Should she just plow forward, Becca wondered, make a full confession? Or was there some subtler approach that didn't actually involve using the words "I slept with Jared"?

"How were finals?" Kate asked, back to being chilly.

"Hard," she replied. "But I think I did well."

"That's nice."

That's *nice?*

Suddenly Becca found herself getting irritated. If Kate knew, as she obviously did, *she* could say something, too. She didn't have to put her through some meaningless Stepford Wives-esque exchange. Becca had *lost her virginity,* after all, in a way that she would likely regret for the rest of her life, *and* in one fell swoop lost the only guy she'd ever actually cared about — other than Jared, which she now knew had never been real. Had Kate even *thought* about that? Why did she, who was flitting all over Europe with her new Swedish boyfriend, have any right to judge her?

"Well," Becca said, changing her mind about apologizing. "I guess that's it. Merry Christmas."

She was about to hang up when she heard Kate, her voice ripe with disbelief, say "What?"

"I'm hanging up."

"You called to *apologize.*"

"I've thought better of it," Becca answered. She was emphatically *not* going to apologize. What happened happened; she was the one who'd suffered, Kate and Jared had been broken up for months, and now that she thought about it, it was none of Kate's business.

"You. Had sex. With my boyfriend," Kate said.

"*Ex*-boyfriend," Becca corrected.

"We're taking a break!"

"Please, we all know that means you're broken up, which means you have no right to be mad."

She knew that wasn't quite true, but it sounded good.

"Sophie says you've had a thing for him for, like, ever." Kate's voice raised.

Becca paused. Now that was a turn she hadn't expected.

"Is that true?" Kate pressed.

Becca started to deny it, but she couldn't flat-out lie. How had Sophie known? She had done everything, *everything,* within her power to keep her feelings to herself for five whole years, and Sophie *knew?* How many conversations about this had gone on behind her back?

"Okay, yes," she snapped, "it's true. Do I have any other secrets you'd like to unveil, while we're at it?"

"How could you have a thing for *my boyfriend* for years, and not tell me?"

"You can't be serious." She was almost enjoying standing up for herself. "You're mad at me for not foisting my problems on you? For wanting you to be happy with Jared instead of worrying about my feelings all the time? You're mad at me for *that?*"

There was a long silence.

"I don't know," Kate answered wearily. "It's just so weird. I feel like I've been hurting you, and I didn't even know it, and . . . I hate that."

"I know. And I wouldn't have wanted you to ever find out, but . . . The whole thing was a huge mistake. I'm a complete asshole."

"No, you're not," Kate sighed. "I think I am. I've been such a bitch."

"Me, too," Becca admitted. "Anyway, it's not like it was even remotely a pleasant experience."

"It hurt, didn't it?"

"It was awful," Becca said, blushing at the memory.

Kate lowered her voice. "Jared's not exactly . . . skilled. If you know what I mean."

Becca nearly belly-laughed. "That's good to know, actually, because it was . . . I mean, even other than the pain . . . 'yucky' is a good description."

"Well, he's a terrible kisser."

"It's like he has *lockjaw*."

"And then it's like he forgets you're there," Kate went on. "I never once had an orgasm with him."

Becca, who'd never once had a conversation where the word "orgasm" was used, felt she was getting in over her head. Kate seemed to sense she was uncomfortable.

"Europeans are much more open about these things. If you decide to have sex with Stuart, it'll be much better. I promise."

"Stuart isn't even speaking to me."

"Yeah," Kate said slowly. "We think you need to talk to him."

"We?" So there *had* been conversations going on behind her back.

"When we started this whole Dream thing, we promised we would help you."

Well, that was true.

"But we've all been so caught up in our own stuff," Kate admitted. "Anyway, we all think it's not too late with Stuart."

"Trust me, it's too late." It hurt Becca more than she could express, but she was sure she was right.

"If he really cares about you, it's not. I left Magnus in Paris, just walked out without a word after the most amazing, intense night of my life, and when I got mugged, he came back. He was upset, but . . . he understands me."

"This is much worse," Becca said quietly. "And Stuart doesn't understand me like that."

"He will if you let him. But you have to let him. You can still save this. And even if you can't . . . it's worth the risk, Bec."

Mr. Finelli had once read a short poem by DH Lawrence aloud in class.

There is nothing to save, now all is lost
but a tiny core of stillness in the heart
like the eye of a violet.

Later, when Becca hung up the phone, she thought about Kate's parting words ("I hope you get what you want for Christmas.") . . . about the core of stillness. . . .

. . . About the tiny bloom of hope in the eye of a violet.

Maybe, just maybe, she *should* try to talk to Stuart. He couldn't hate her *more* than he already did, and the possibility that he might hate her less, even just a little bit less . . .

That might be worth the risk, after all.

"This music blows," Harper announced, pulling her black wool cap lower over her ears to drown out the sound of Christmas carols. If she had to hear one more verse of Judy Garland dreaming about a goddamn white Christmas, she might do something violent.

"How 'bout that one?" Judd asked, ignoring her as he pointed to a puny tree that looked about a day away from dropping its needles.

She shot him a look. "I said I wanted a Christmas *tree,* not a bush."

In a moment of what she could now only consider depravity, Harper had decided that the scent of a Colorado blue spruce would get her into the holiday spirit. But the moment she and Judd walked onto Dan's Big Lot, she knew she'd made a big mistake.

All over Boulder, houses sported twinkly lights and life-sized reindeer, and it seemed like every shop on Pearl Street had tinsel in its window. Unfortunately, Dan's Big Lot was no less oppressive. Happy families frolicked among the rows of fir and spruce trees, humming along to cheesy carols blasting from speakers and throwing handfuls of fake snow at each other. Harper wanted to kill them all.

"Just a suggestion," Judd said. "No need to lash out at the guy who's helping you get the thing home."

Harper had been hurling insults at anyone who would listen since the debacle at Mr. Finelli's the other night. Being rude didn't make her feel better, but it was satisfying, nonetheless.

"Sorry," she apologized quickly. "I'm having rage issues."

"No kidding." Judd moved off toward another row of trees, walking fast enough that Harper had to trot to catch up with him.

"I said I'm sorry," she repeated. "Are you going to be mad all day?"

Judd kept walking. "Probably."

She grabbed his elbow and pulled him to a stop next to an abnormally tall balsam fir. "Okay, we'll go with the bush," she conceded. "Happy now?"

"Ecstatic." Judd stomped off just as Judy Garland swelled to a crescendo.

Merry Christmas. Fa la la. Maybe instead of decorating her bush, she would chop it up and use the wood to make a funeral pyre. At least burning herself to death would get her out of participating in Secret Santa at the café.

Aside from a snide comment about how she still hadn't had the front end of his Saturn repaired, Judd barely said a word as he attached the mini tree to the roof of his car and drove her home. Harper expected him to shove her onto the street the second they pulled up to the Waddles', but instead he turned off the engine and crossed his arms in front of his chest.

"You need to consider the possibility that Mr. Finelli is right about your book needing work," he informed her. "The whole jealousy thing doesn't feel right."

Harper's jaw clenched. She'd told Judd the gory details of her encounter with their former English teacher (minus the kissing). Clearly, that was a mistake.

"Now you're an expert on Mr. Finelli?" she asked, digging her hands deeper in the pockets of her puffy jacket.

He raised his eyebrows. "No. That's your department."

Harper wasn't going to touch that. The last thing she wanted was to have an in-depth discussion with Judd about her aborted relationship with Mr. Finelli. Let him think what he wanted.

"There's nothing wrong with having an imperfect first draft," he reminded her. "You should be proud of what you've accomplished so far."

"But you read the fifty-one pages," she pointed out. "You said they were awesome."

"I was too scared to say anything else. I didn't want to deal with your wrath."

Harper felt like she'd been slapped in the face. Judd was part of her cheerleading team. He wasn't supposed to cut her down, even if he *was* mad. So much for friendship.

"Maybe you're jealous, too," she accused him. "I would be, if my only claim to fame involved making pretentious coffee drinks."

Judd shook his head, his black curls matted to his head from the striped ski cap he'd been wearing at Dan's Big Lot. "You know what, Harper? You're not worth it."

"What's that supposed to mean?" She'd gone too far, and she knew it. But she wasn't about to beg for forgiveness.

"Figure it out for yourself." He started the car. "Now get your tree, and from now on leave me out of Harper World. I don't want to live there anymore."

She jerked open the car door handle and stepped out into the night. On the way home from Dan's Big Lot, it had started to snow. Usually, she would have taken a moment to stick out her tongue and catch a flake, letting it melt on her tongue.

Instead, she yanked her measly Christmas bush from the bungee cords Judd had wrapped around it and trudged toward the house.

Judd's tires squealed as he sped away, turning up his car stereo so that booming percussion blasted through the quiet street.

Screw him, Harper muttered to herself. Sophie and Becca would be home soon, and they were all she needed.

"I've come a long way. I've come a long way and never even left LA. . . ." Sophie was singing along at top volume to the Michelle Shocked tune Sam had put on her CD mix.

Her bedroom in the guesthouse looked like it had been ransacked by a S.W.A.T. team. Bikinis, short-shorts, and tank tops had been tossed into piles on the floor while she looked for something — anything — warm enough to bring home for winter in Boulder.

"Aha!" she exclaimed, pulling out a red fleece Patagonia she'd bought on sale at Nordstrom's in case she ever ended up in the freezing extras holding cell again.

She threw the fleece into her huge L.L.Bean duffel bag, along with three pairs of sneakers from Sporty LA and a stack of her new headshots. She planned to pass them out to anyone who asked, autographed upon request.

The Michelle Shocked song ended, and she waited for track five, the Red Hot Chili Peppers' *City of Angels,* to start playing. She'd listened to the CD, like, a thousand times since Sam had given it to her. Every song he'd chosen had an LA theme, and being able to relate to the lyrics made her realize how much she'd learned about the city.

Sophie glanced at the digital clock next to her bed. Yikes. Her taxi to LAX would be here in ten minutes, and she wasn't even *close* to being done packing. Nonetheless, she allowed herself ten seconds to pick up Sam's CD case and look at the inscription again. "For Sophie, who's not just anyone."

What did that *mean?* She thought back to almost four months ago, when she'd struck her John Casablanca pose, wild hair and all,

341

and informed Sam, "I'm not just anyone." Did he actually *remember* that? Or was the message a coincidence?

A loud knock on the door brought her out of her reverie. *Shit.* The cabbie was early.

"Come in!" Sophie called, running to the bathroom for her hair dryer. "You can wait in the hall!"

As she emerged from the bathroom, she heard footsteps. "I'd rather wait in here." The voice came from just outside her room.

Her stomach — along with her eyeballs, her brain, and various other organs — dropped into her toes. "Trey?"

He was grinning widely as he appeared in the doorway. "I prefer Santa, but it's your call."

Sophie gripped the hair dryer. It was a semi-heavy object that could probably do a good amount of damage if she threw it right. Even more if she used it to beat him at close range.

"Get out," she instructed coldly, dropping the hair dryer into her duffel. "I don't want to see you."

On the surface, she hoped she appeared calm, cool, and collected. Because underneath, she was a quivering mess of . . . well, mess. A girl could be as firm in her stance against a guy as she wanted to be. In her mind. But actually seeing those dark smoldering eyes and shiny dark hair . . . that olive skin . . . It was seriously screwing with her sense of self-righteousness.

"You have every right to hate me." He wasn't getting out. He was coming closer. "You *should* hate me."

"I do." Sophie zipped up her bag. Anything she'd forgotten would simply have to be begged, borrowed, or stolen from Harper or Becca. They'd understand.

"Sophie, I'm so sorry," Trey pleaded. "Will you let me explain?"

"Uh . . . no." Be strong, she ordered herself. She picked up her bag and started past him, but he stepped sideways to block her path.

"I *wanted* to call." He told her. She'd forgotten how red his lips were. "I promise."

"Unless you're gonna say you've been tied up by Iraqi insurgents with a bag over your head, I don't want to hear it."

"I was in seclusion." He was wearing light green linen pants, she noted. Most guys couldn't pull off light green linen pants. Trey was the exception.

"With who? That Swedish girl you were all over at Chateau Marmont?"

"I was training for my next film." Trey ran his fingers through his perfectly coiffed hair and sighed. "I'm playing a samurai, and the director wants it to be as real as possible."

"They don't have phones at samurai training camp?" Her voice dripped with sarcasm.

She wanted to believe him. God, friends, and country forgive her, she wanted to believe him.

"He didn't want anyone to know I was there!" he insisted. "I didn't even tell my sister."

"You're lying." *He's lying, he's lying, he's lying.* She repeated the words to herself like a mantra. It was the only way to get out of this with her integrity intact.

Trey shook his head. "Gabriella was supposed to spend Christmas in Aspen with me. But she's so mad she booked a cruise instead."

Sophie processed this information. It *was* true that Trey's picture hadn't shown up in any magazines or newspapers lately. And she knew from the day he didn't kiss her at Zuma how seriously he prepared for his roles. Then again, he was an actor. He lied for a living.

"I'm going home for a few days," she said finally. "If you want to call me when I get back, *maybe* we can talk."

Trey reached out and put his hands on her shoulders. It disgusted her that the touch of his hand through the thin material of her cotton shirt sent a chill to her toes. "Don't go home." He smiled. "Come to Aspen with me."

"You're insane." She pulled away from him and headed out of her bedroom. She was strong. She was independent. She was . . . tempted.

"I need to be with you." He followed her to the door of the guest-house. "Please, give me one more chance."

Sophie didn't *want* to picture herself sitting in front of a cozy fire with Trey, drinking champagne and listening to Bing Crosby. She didn't *want* to imagine holding his hand as they skied fresh powder in coordinated snow suits. But the images flooded her brain.

"My friends would kill me," she stated, as if that ended the matter. "They think you're a complete asshole."

Harper, Becca, and Kate had made their feelings on the subject of Trey Benson quite clear. He was a liar and inconsiderate and several other unmentionables that had made her laugh aloud when she heard them.

"They don't know me." His brown eyes were drilling into her. The phrase "hot coals" came to mind. "You do."

Sophie hesitated. She had set aside her entire life to take a chance to move to Los Angeles and pursue her dream. The decision had been the definition of throwing caution to the wind. Now she had another chance to go for it, to live out a fantasy. Was she really going to say no because she was afraid of getting hurt? Sophie Bushell didn't *get* hurt. That wasn't her bag.

And wasn't it possible that Trey really was the great guy who'd taken her to his childhood home to show her dreams could come true? Wasn't it possible that he really was a fantasy come to life, and that they could ride off into the sunset, and have celebrity babies and star in movies together for the rest of their lives? She'd never forgive herself if she didn't find out.

"I'll go," she smiled, opening her arms and letting Trey hug her close. "But if you screw me over, I'll make you pay."

As Trey bent his head to kiss her, she thought fleetingly of her mom, dad, Becca, and Harper. She'd make them understand why she wasn't coming home. All they wanted was her happiness. Sam was another story. He'd say it was shallow to pass up Christmas with her friends to cavort with Trey.

But she wasn't living her life for him. Or for anyone else. This was her year. And she'd spend it exactly as she pleased.

△ **AOL** mail

From: herDivaness@aol.com
To: waddlewords@aol.com, katherinef@ucb.edu, rebeccawinsberg@middlebury.edu
Subject: Please Vote

Hey all,

Please cast aside previous notions that Trey Benson is an asshole. Okay.
Now that you've done that, consider the following question:
SHOULD I HAVE SEX WITH HIM?

To help make up your mind (and mine):

PROS:	CONS:
Scorchingly Hot	Can be ridiculously self-centered
Fairly famous (not that it matters)	Lies?
Could help my career by shoving me down his agent's throat	Could hurt my career if he decides fake boobs are where it's at after all
Makes me laugh	Pisses me off
Is probably WAY better than Barton in bed	Has probably done it with tons of girls
I really like him	Might lose interest afterward
I think he really likes me	
No visible ear hair	
Aspen = romantic	
Born-again virgin = frustrated	

TWENTY

Becca walked up the path to a lovely, brick colonial, thinking about rainbows. Because if she allowed herself to think about what she was about to do, she would drop her duffel bag and flee. So Roy G. Biv it was. Red, orange, yellow, green, blue, indigo, violet, she chanted to herself. A mantra for the ages. She'd been thinking of those seven colors since her plane landed in Kansas City. They had calmed her nerves for the entire forty-minute cab ride that had taken her from the airport's Midwestern fields into an unexpected metropolis, and beyond to the suburbs. They had gotten her this far. And she was not going to abandon them now.

Red, orange, yellow, green, blue, indigo, violet. Then she raised her hand and knocked on the door.

Red, orange, yellow, green, blue, indigo, violet, red, orange —

The door opened. Stuart looked at her.

. . . yellow, green, blue . . .

In the span of an instant, shock followed by happiness followed by anger flashed across his face. Then the hurt settled in, and he started to close the door.

But Becca *had* seen the flash of happiness, even if it had been fleeting, and that was enough.

"Wait!"

He waited. He wouldn't look at her, but he was there, standing in the doorway, and he was waiting.

Maybe, she thought desperately, if she said "forgive me," he might do that, too. And then this would all be over, and they could go back to being . . . whatever they were.

"Forgive me," she tried.

Stuart dragged his eyes to her face.

"No," he said, and started to close the door again.

Right. Then Becca stepped up and grabbed the door. Stuart looked at her like she was a life form from another planet.

"I thought I was in love with him. Please, listen to me. For five years I thought I loved him. But it was stupid and fake and a figment of my ridiculous imagination, and he started dating my best friend, so then it was this big unrequited thing, and it was a total accident that I even saw him in New York, I didn't plan it."

Stuart was watching her, unreadable. Becca plowed on.

"I thought about you the whole time, which sounds awful, but you need to know that. And that it was terrible, every second. But I was confused. I never . . . I never really believed you could like me, and maybe I was trying to push you away, to give myself a way to not be good enough for you, because I really, really like you, and I don't like people like that. I mean, I like a lot of people, from a distance, but I don't trust people, and I definitely never potentially love anyone. Guys I mean. And maybe I potentially love you, which I am completely incapable of dealing with, so I let myself get swept up in something I knew was wrong and bad and cruel. But I swear it was just as cruel to me as it was to you, because . . ."

She took a deep breath. Stuart waited, silent.

"I want to be with you. I added a stop to my plane ticket home, and I came here, because I have to tell you. You have to know. You're smart and funny and sweet, and your eyes make me melt, and I feel

350

something with you I've never felt before, ever, for anyone. Something *real*. And I'm so sorry I hurt you, but maybe that's good, too, in a screwed up way, because it means you might feel something sort of like that about me, too. And that would make me so happy, if you could learn to not hate me, because I want to play in the big game. No more practices and mistakes and —"

"Stop." Stuart held up his hand. "Just . . . come in."

Becca's whole body flooded with relief and happiness. It wasn't a declaration of love, but it was something.

"Are you sure?"

"C'mon." He opened the door wider. "You look cold."

Becca smiled, and stepped inside.

"That was lovely, dear," someone said.

Blanching, she turned toward the sound of the voice. A woman who could only be described as a sweet little old lady sat knitting in a chair not ten feet from the front door.

"Gram, this is Becca."

As Becca tried to physically sink into the floor, the little old lady gave her a long, assessing look, then smiled and went back to her knitting.

"I like this one," she said quietly.

Stuart turned to Becca. He reached out a hand for her bag. As she handed it to him, he looked into her eyes.

"Yeah," he said, "Me, too."

And, with those words, Becca got everything she wanted for Christmas.

"I just got really bent about it," Kate told Chantal, who was as elegant and dynamic as always, sitting across from her at Café Bazin.

"Well, he was your boyfriend for so long," Chantal said, waving her hand. "It's natural."

Chantal had a particular way of connoting complete understanding of all facets of a situation, and at the same time utterly dismissing their importance, that made Kate feel better about how angry she'd been at Becca. It really hadn't made sense. She and Jared had been broken up for months, and she was . . . okay, she was in love with Magnus. But she'd just started to feel like she understood how the world worked, and finding out Becca had not only had sex with Jared, but had been semi-in-love with him forever, had kind of rocked her already-rocked world.

That, and her conversation with Habiba, had led to her decision to spend Christmas with Chantal, instead of alone on a train halfway through Russia, or alone in a hotel room in China. Her plans were constantly shifting these days anyway, she'd realized, and Russia and China would still be there in a week.

"Plus," Kate continued, "it was really stupid and self-sabotaging. I mean, she just found this great guy, then she screws it up. . . ."

She trailed off, realizing she had done sort of the same thing with Magnus when they first met. Of course, she'd left Magnus because she had a mission to accomplish, whereas Stuart *was* Becca's mission this year — which was probably why she screwed it up, just like Kate had almost screwed up her mission by hiding in Paris for so long.

Lord, she shook her head, she was really going to have to work on the judgmental thing. Just one more flaw to add to the list. She wasn't generous enough, she was judgmental, she was self-centered. . . .

The flip side of learning her strengths, apparently, was a crash course in her weaknesses.

"Do you want to be with this Jared again?" Chantal asked.

"No." Even if she ended up at Harvard next year, and she never saw Magnus again, she didn't want to be with Jared. He wasn't remotely enough for her anymore, and his understanding of her had never gone beyond the surface, beyond the expected.

"So you have the problem half solved." Chantal nodded. "You

352

know what you *don't* want. That is just as difficult as to find what you *do* want, yes?"

As usual, Chantal had a point. Kate knew she didn't want to be with Jared, or be Perfect Kate anymore, or *always* have a plan and stick to it.

She knew now that she wanted to approach life from her heart *and* her head, and that she wanted to be judged by her actions — which meant she actually had to *do stuff.* All kinds of stuff. Stuff that challenged her, stuff she loved, stuff that made a difference in her life and the lives of others. Whatever her dream was, it rested somewhere in that most vague of directions.

As Chantal excused herself to go to the *toilet,* Kate took a sip of her tea and listened to the familiar sounds of the café. The cappuccino maker hummed as the two regulars at table eleven went over the final arrangements for the trip to Africa they'd been planning since Kate had first served them in October.

I feel at home here, she realized with a smile. Here, and at Chantal's apartment, and in Umbria, and anywhere Magnus was. . . .

By the end of this year, she hoped to have little spots of home all around the world. Habiba would like the sound of that, as well. Kate had never considered herself a globalist, or political in any way, but she had discovered that the more she grew, the more the world shrank.

"*Quand le puits est construit, nous devrions prendre l'eau autour aux villages environnements . . .*" one of the women at table eleven was saying.

Kate, lost in her own thoughts, hadn't been eavesdropping, yet the words made their way through the folds of her subconscious.

Take the water around to surrounding villages, the woman had said. *Take the water.*

Slowly, she turned toward table eleven. The two women were in their mid-twenties, tanned, and devoid of makeup in the manner of those who have more important things to think about than vanity. A month ago, Kate had found them intimidating. But since then she had screamed her name in the middle of the *Grand Place,* eaten blood sausage, driven a motorcycle, and chosen *not* to be with the man she loved.

Kate ignored the pounding of her heart as she stood up and approached their table.

"Excuse me," she began, in French. "I overheard you say you're going to Africa soon. Is that right?"

"*Oui.*" The taller woman nodded. A brightly printed scarf was layered several times around the length of her neck. "*Assis,*" she added, and held a hand out for Kate to sit.

The woman, whose name was Mira, explained that she and her friend, Dorothé, were volunteers with an organization that operated humanitarian projects in Kenya, Ethiopia, Chad, and the Sudan, depending on the evolving political situations in each country. They were leaving for Kenya and Ethiopia right after Christmas.

Ethiopia.

"Do you need more volunteers?" Kate asked in French, a nervous lump in her throat.

"*Oui,*" answered Dorothe, the rounder and friendlier of the two Frenchwomen. "*Toujours,*" she added. Always.

Mira, on the other hand, gave a Kate a long, assessing look, then explained that going to many countries in Africa was arduous, possibly even dangerous. There would be little food and water, limited access to Western medicine. She could develop malaria or cholera or any number of diseases. Before she could even consider going, she would have to get a visa and several painful inoculations.

Kate listened to every word, undissuaded. Chantal had once said that "Take the water" was the thing on the list that would get to the soul of her. Maybe it would, maybe not. But either way, Kate felt the hand of destiny at work, and that wasn't a hand she was willing to slap away. So many things had had to fall into place to get her to this moment — deciding not to go to the wedding with Magnus, going back to Athens, calling Habiba, coming back to Paris. Without even one of those things, she would have been a thousand miles away by now. She would never have been sitting across from Mira and Dorothe as they made their plans to dig an African well.

"I'm in," Kate said.

She'd had enough of plans. From now on, she was going to follow her gut. She was going to listen to her heart. She was going to take action.

And she was going to trust fate.

"You don't love me."

"I *do* love you!" Sophie insisted. She'd been having the same phone conversation with Harper since she arrived in Aspen two days ago. "Will you ask your mom what she puts in her turkey stuffing?"

"If you love me, how come you abandoned me?" Harper whined. "I think she adds celery, mushrooms, and croutons."

"You *wanted* to stay in Boulder," Sophie reminded her, turning her already full cart toward the produce aisle of the tiny, super expensive grocery store. "You didn't feel guilty when *I* was the one who was getting left behind."

"But it's Christmas."

"Is this about me or Mr. Finelli? Be honest."

"Can we *not* talk about him?" Harper asked. Sophie could picture her pacing back and forth across the basement, cell phone pressed tight against her ear.

She stopped in front of the celery and grabbed two bunches. Then a third, just in case. She wanted the dinner she was making for Trey to be perfect.

"You could come hang with us in Aspen," she suggested half-heartedly. "You'd love Trey."

Please say no, she added silently. For the last forty-eight hours, she and Trey had been blissfully happy. Harper's sour mood would *not* add to the party.

Harper snorted. "Trey's a dick."

"He was at Samurai training camp," Sophie informed her for the fifth time. "He takes his art very seriously."

As she headed toward the mushrooms, she heard Harper pop open a fresh Diet Coke. Clearly, this phone call wasn't going to end any time soon.

"Just don't have sex with him. That's all I ask."

"Why shouldn't I?" she dropped two boxes of mushrooms into her cart and headed toward the cashier. "By the way, when I asked your opinion on the subject, I didn't mean for you to e-mail me a hundred and six times."

"You never said we could only vote once," Harper pointed out. Then she groaned. "The whole thing is just *so* clichéd."

Sophie *wouldn't* be confiding to her that she'd decided to get up close and personal — in every way — with Trey after dinner tonight. So far, Aspen had been magical. They'd spent yesterday afternoon scouring the tiny boutiques downtown for a winter wardrobe for her that Trey had insisted on charging to his credit card. Soft-as-butter cowboy boots, a knee-length shearling overcoat. Cashmere sweaters in six different colors. . . . It had taken Sophie an hour to decide what to wear to sushi at Matsuhisa last night, where they'd ended up chatting with Lindsay Lohan and her boyfriend over saki after dinner. Eventually, the four of them had gone back to Lindsay's plush log cabin and soaked in a hot tub under the stars, nothing but snow as far as their eyes could see.

Tonight, though, was just about Sophie and Trey. They were going to hole up in their luxurious condo, kick off their shoes, and eat the traditional turkey dinner she planned to make in their state-of-the-art kitchen. If all went according to plan, she would end up naked and intertwined in Trey's arms while Bing crooned about chestnuts roasting on an open fire.

"Why do you like this guy so much?" Harper asked.

Sophie thought for a moment. "He's hot, he's smart, he's talented. . . ." She felt all warm inside just thinking about it. "And he makes me feel like I can do anything."

Maybe she would come out of the bedroom in her new shearling coat with nothing underneath. Or in her cowboy boots, and her cowboy boots only. Decisions, decisions.

"Since when do you need a *guy* to make you feel like that?" Harper asked. "I mean, this is *you* we're talking about."

"I think you should call Mr. Finelli," she suggested as she got in line, hoping to change the subject.

As Harper started a long monologue, Sophie glanced at the covers of the tabloid newspapers that were stashed next to the register. Two of them featured the same photo. A hot guy kissing a woman whose face was obscured.

Wait.

That wasn't any hot guy. That was Trey. And her.

"Ohmigod!" she exclaimed. She was in the tabloids!

Harper broke off mid-sentence. "What?"

Sophie looked closer at the photo. Wait. Trey wasn't kissing her. He was kissing some other beautiful woman.

"Sophie?" Harper's voice barely registered. "Sophe . . . ARE YOU THERE?"

"I'll call you back," she said, her voice wooden. "Uh . . . Julia Roberts is in the ice-cream aisle, and I want to see if she's got Hazel and Phinneus with her."

"Tell her Phinneus is a stupid name," Harper ordered. "Call me back."

Sophie moved like a robot as she shut her phone and picked up one of the tabloids. The magazine rack had hidden the headline but now she saw it in bold black-and-white: "Trey Benson Gets Cozy with Costar." Her hands shaking, she opened the paper and flipped to the article about Trey.

Heartthrob **Trey Benson** was caught kissing sultry **Pasha DiMoni** on a return visit to London several weeks after the two were in town to promote their romantic comedy, "In Love with Mrs. Granville." Strolling the streets, the pair looked madly in love. But don't tell DiMoni's husband, veteran actor **Ray Terrance.** DiMoni returned home to him last week, reportedly leaving Benson with a broken heart. Sources reached him in Aspen, where he denied reports of the romance and said, "I'm spending a quiet holiday alone, reflecting on the blessings this past year has brought." DiMoni declined comment for this article.

Sophie dropped the tabloid back in the rack and backed away from her grocery cart. Lies. It had all been lies. Missing her on his press junket . . . Samurai training . . . wanting to be with her . . .

Idiot! Sophie screamed at herself. Everyone had told her Trey was no good. . . . Why hadn't she listened? Because you always have to know best, she continued screaming inside. Because you wanted him to be part of the Dream.

Tidal waves of humiliation swept through her as she thought of what Becca, Harper, and Kate would say. *I told you so.* And Sam. She couldn't face him. Not after this.

Sophie didn't realize she'd started to run until she heard the cashier woman call after her. "Miss, where are you going? You're next in line."

But she didn't turn back. She's probably seen me gallivanting around town with Trey, Sophie thought, putting distance between herself and the cashier. She's probably laughing at me.

All she wanted to do was run and keep running. All the way home to Boulder, where no one gave a shit about Trey Benson or agents or auditions or going to a party just to "be seen."

Sophie knew she wouldn't be going back to Los Angeles. For her, the Dream was over.

Harper Waddle was evil. She was worse than evil. She was delusional. The admissions staff at NYU had obviously read between the lines of her essay and seen an evil, delusional human being. Accordingly, they'd rejected her.

Which had been the right thing to do, she realized. She hadn't read over the pages of her manuscript since the night in Mr. Finelli's apartment. Until now.

Harper read the last line and set the pages down beside her on her mattress. They were terrible. Sure, the sentences all made sense and there were some funny moments. But each of the characters sounded the same, and the dialogue was like something out of a Spanish language textbook. It was stiff and unnatural . . . and, well, *written*.

Mr. Finelli wasn't jealous. He was right. And so was Judd. Harper had known it all along. She just hadn't wanted to see it.

They'd both tried to help her, but she'd put up a brick wall, over which she'd thrown poison darts and hand grenades. She didn't blame them for hating her. She hated herself.

She stood up and walked over to a pile of her clothes. Under a pair of jeans she hadn't worn since September, she found a small paper bag, inside of which were a pack of Marlboro Reds and a yellow Bic lighter. She'd never smoked a cigarette, but she'd bought them during the worst of her writer's block. Lots of great writers had smoked, and she'd figured if she got desperate enough she'd try anything.

Tossing the paper bag and the Marlboro Reds aside, Harper held on tight to the yellow Bic lighter. Then she grabbed the metal trashcan from under her desk and dumped the contents on the floor. Kneeling over the empty trashcan, Harper took her pages and held them close to her chest for a moment.

I'm sorry, she told the pages, as if they were alive. As if they could hear her. She'd failed her story, and she'd failed Violet and Eva and Patrick and Phillipa and all the other characters. They deserved more than she'd given them.

The Moments in Between. The moments in between what? Debasement? Self-hatred? Lying?

Harper set down all but the first page of her book, then flicked the lighter with her thumb. The small flame lit, and she held it up to the corner of the page. As the first words of what was supposed to have been the next Great American Novel went up in flames, Harper's heart broke a little.

And it kept breaking as one by one she set the pages of her novel on fire. She set each one in the trash can, watched it burn, then moved on to the next. The process took almost half an hour, but finally her Dream was gone.

When it was over, she stared at the remnants, wondering where she'd gone wrong. Was it way back when she'd neglected to apply to a back-up school? In April, when she'd decided not to tell her friends and family the truth? Or maybe that day in August when she'd announced her so-called Dream Plan?

There were no answers. Just more questions. Well, one question mainly. *How would it be different if I'd gotten into NYU?* Harper shook away the thought. It was too painful.

Remembering *last* Christmas Eve was also painful, but she made herself do it. The memories were flooding in. She, Becca, Sophie, and Kate had all sneaked out of their houses and met up in the park near Kate's for a snowball fight. They'd laughed so hard that Harper's stomach muscles had ached for two days afterward. And after rolling around in the snow for an hour, the four of them sat in Mr. Foster's Volvo with the heat blasting and exchanged gifts.

Now it was three hundred and sixty-five days later. Kate was halfway around the world, Sophie had bailed, and Becca was . . . she didn't even *know* what was up with Becca. Which left Harper alone with a Christmas bush and the pile of ashes that used to be her Dream.

Merry Christmas. Fa la la.

I, HARPER ELLEN WADDLE, SWEAR I WILL NEVER LIE TO MY
BEST FRIENDS AGAIN. UPON PAIN OF DEATH. I, HARPER ELLEN
WADDLE, SWEAR I WILL NEVER LIE TO MY BEST FRIENDS AGAIN.
UPON PAIN OF DEATH. I, HARPER ELLEN WADDLE, SWEAR
I WILL NEVER LIE TO MY BEST FRIENDS AGAIN. UPON PAIN OF
DEATH. I, HARPER ELLEN WADDLE, SWEAR I WILL NEVER LIE
TO MY BEST FRIENDS AGAIN. UPON PAIN OF DEATH. I, HARPER
ELLEN WADDLE, SWEAR I WILL NEVER LIE TO MY BEST
FRIENDS AGAIN. UPON PAIN OF DEATH. I, HARPER ELLEN
WADDLE, SWEAR I WILL NEVER LIE TO MY BEST FRIENDS
AGAIN. UPON PAIN OF DEATH. I, HARPER ELLEN WADDLE,
SWEAR I WILL NEVER LIE TO MY BEST FRIENDS AGAIN.
UPON PAIN OF DEATH. I, HARPER ELLEN WADDLE, SWEAR
I WILL NEVER LIE TO MY BEST FRIENDS AGAIN.
UPON PAIN OF DEATH. I, HARPER ELLEN WADDLE,
SWEAR I WILL NEVER LIE TO MY BEST FRIENDS AGAIN.
UPON PAIN OF DEATH. I, HARPER ELLEN WADDLE, SWEAR
I WILL NEVER LIE TO MY BEST FRIENDS AGAIN. UPON
PAIN OF DEATH. I, HARPER ELLEN WADDLE, SWEAR I
WILL NEVER LIE TO MY BEST FRIENDS AGAIN. UPON PAIN
OF DEATH. I, HARPER ELLEN WADDLE, SWEAR I WILL
NEVER LIE TO MY BEST FRIENDS AGAIN. UPON PAIN OF
DEATH. I, HARPER ELLEN WADDLE, SWEAR I WILL
NEVER LIE TO MY BEST FRIENDS AGAIN. UPON PAIN
OF DEATH. I, HARPER ELLEN WADDLE, SWEAR I
WILL NEVER LIE TO MY BEST FRIENDS AGAIN.
UPON PAIN OF DEATH. I, HARPER ELLEN
WADDLE, SWEAR I WILL NEVER LIE TO MY
BEST FRIENDS AGAIN. UPON PAIN OF DEATH.
I, HARPER ELLEN WADDLE, SWEAR I WILL
NEVER LIE TO MY BEST FRIENDS AGAIN. UPON

TWENTY-ONE

"Harper." Sophie poked her in the ribs. "Wake up."

But Harper, who was wearing the same pair of red-and-green-plaid flannel pj's she wore *every* Christmas, just rolled over and kept snoring. At least one of them had gotten a decent night's sleep. Sophie leaned in close to her ear.

"Merry Christmas!"

Harper's eyes popped open, and she jolted up in bed. "What?" she demanded. "What's wrong?"

"Ta da!" Sophie exclaimed, spreading her arms wide. "I came home after all."

Harper squinted against the light. "You look like shit."

"Thanks." No shit, she looked like shit, Sophie thought.

"Nice coat, though," Harper added as she let out a huge yawn.

After Sophie fled the grocery store, she had gone directly to Trey's condo and packed her bags (cowboy boots and shearling included). He had grilled her about why she was leaving, but she refused to utter even one word to him. Asshole.

She'd ended up at the Aspen bus station, where she'd had to wait six hours to get on a Greyhound home. The bus had arrived in Boulder at six AM, and Sophie had taken a cab directly to the Waddles and climbed through the basement window. She wasn't ready to be psychoanalyzed by her mother.

Harper wiped the crust out of the corners of her eyes and glanced at the digital clock on the milk crate nightstand. So much for the three-month redecorating plan, Sophie assessed. But she managed to keep her mouth shut.

"What're you doing here?" Harper asked. "I thought you couldn't bear to be away from Trey."

Sophie plopped next to Harper on her mattress. She was still wearing the jeans/Uggs/black sweater combo she'd had on since yesterday and was starting to smell a little ripe. Based on the appearance of Harper's needed-to-be-shampooed hair, however, she doubted her friend would even notice.

"You were right," she announced. "It's much more important to be here with you guys."

Harper looked her over. "Okay, now tell me the truth."

"I dumped Trey," Sophie informed her. "It's over."

Sophie had spent her bus ride carefully planning how she was going to present the Trey disaster to friends and family. She figured she'd try to pretend like nothing had happened. If that didn't go over (which she knew it wouldn't), she'd at least manage a blasé attitude so that no one would feel sorry for her.

"I thought you were, like, in love." Harper reached for her glasses. *Uh-oh. Here comes the scrutiny.*

"He's a liar," she admitted. "Which I found out in the grocery store when I saw a picture of him kissing Pasha DiMoni on the cover of one of the tabloids."

"Ouch." Harper winced. "Does this mean you *didn't* see Julia Roberts with Hazel and Phinneus?"

"Sorry to disappoint you."

Harper threw an arm around her shoulders. "This is great. We can be single together."

But Sophie could tell that Harper was hurting for her. She *hated* it when people hurt for her. Sophie Bushell was not to be pitied.

"It's not a big deal," she insisted. "I was pretty much planning to leave LA, anyway."

Harper's eyes got big. "What the hell are you talking about?"

"I got some sun, met some cute boys . . ." She shrugged. "Los Angeles did me right."

"Hello?" Harper said. "Acting?"

Oh, right. Acting. Her Dream. Well, there was always Boulder's local production of *A Christmas Carol*.

"I did a national commercial," she reminded her. "I succeeded."

"Telling the world you've got a love-hate relationship with your hair isn't exactly winning an Oscar."

Harper was taking the knife and twisting it. But Sophie wasn't going to crumble. She hadn't cried in the fifteen hours since she'd seen that photo, and she wasn't going to start now.

"Can we talk about something else? I promise I'll let you torture me with questions later."

"Sure," Harper agreed. "What d'you wanna talk about?"

She gestured toward Harper's trashcan, which seemed to have housed a small fire. "What's going on there?" she asked.

Harper groaned. "Can we talk about something else? I promise I'll let you torture me with questions later."

Sophie laughed. God, it felt good. She hadn't done that enough the last few months. For several moments, they sat in silence, both wracking their brains for small talk.

"Sophe?" Harper broke the silence.

"Yeah?"

"I'm glad you're home."

Sophie grinned and wrapped her arms around Harper, hugging her friend close. "Me, too, Harp," she murmured. "Me, too."

Becca yawned herself awake, stretching. As her arms bumped her headboard, the tassel from her navy-blue eighth-grade graduation cap swooshed back and forth familiarly.

She was home. And it was Christmas.

She had spent only one day at Stuart's house in Missouri. They'd talked into the early hours of the morning, then Becca had fallen asleep with her head against his chest. His mother had found them a little after dawn, nestled against each other on the couch. She'd sent Stuart to bed, then shown Becca to the guest room.

"I don't know what happened between you," his mother had said, as Becca climbed into bed. "But he was very sad when he got home."

"That was my fault," Becca had admitted. "I did something really stupid."

"Well." His mother had smiled. "He seems happy now. I'd like him to stay that way."

"Me, too," Becca had answered. There was nothing she wanted more. And she'd told him so when he took her to the airport that afternoon. He had kissed her, and wished her Merry Christmas, and handed her a small, wrapped box.

"You got me a present?" she had asked, stunned. She hadn't gotten him anything. She'd been too wrapped up in self-hatred to even think about it. And he hadn't exactly adored her for the last several weeks.

"I got it a while ago," he said. "Open it Christmas morning."

"Okay." She smiled, thinking she would never be able to wait sixteen whole hours.

But, Christmas morning it was. Becca got up, pulled Stuart's box from her suitcase, and ripped the wrapping paper. She opened the box to find a sterling silver bracelet. It took her a moment to figure out it was a charm bracelet — the silver was thinner, more delicate, than the charm bracelets she was used to. But when she picked it up, something dangled from the silver links. Becca held up the bracelet in the dim light coming through her window shade, and laughed.

Dangling before her eyes was the tiniest pair of crutches she had ever seen.

Becca latched the bracelet around her wrist. Whatever was waiting on the other side of her bedroom door, she could handle it with Stuart's charm on her wrist. And no matter what, she only had to get through an hour of opening presents with her mom, Martin, Mia, and Carter. After that, she could escape to Harper's house for the rest of the day, where they would spend hours catching up on the progress of their respective dreams.

Her mom had actually been sort of normal the previous night, when she'd picked Becca up from the airport. But it had been late, and Becca was distracted, so she hadn't spent much time thinking about it — other than to mentally note that she didn't regret her Parents' Weekend outburst. She was slightly embarrassed, perhaps, but everything she'd said had been true. And, as far as she was concerned, it all needed to be said. Perhaps she could have been more polite about it, or more mature, but then they wouldn't have listened.

And they did seem to have listened, at least somewhat. When Becca had called her mom at the last minute to say that her Christmas travel plans were going to be slightly altered — which had required at least a bare minimum of explanation — her mom had said okay, and wished her good luck with Stuart.

"So," her mom had asked last night at the airport, "how did it go?"

"It was good."

"Does that mean he's your boyfriend?"

"Yep," Becca had answered.

"Well," her mom had responded, "then he's a lucky boy."

Which was about the sweetest thing her mom had ever said to her.

Becca took a last look at her new bracelet, threw on a robe, and opened her bedroom door. She could hear voices in the living room downstairs, but she was completely unprepared for what she found when she got to the bottom of the stairs.

Her *father* was there.

Becca stopped and stared. She couldn't help it. Her *father* was sitting on the living room couch. On Christmas. In her stepdad's house. And her mom wasn't skinning him alive. Quite the opposite. Her mom was passing out presents to Carter and Mia, who actually looked like she'd gained a few much-needed pounds. Her stepfather stood at the fireplace, acting as if he spent every Christmas morning with his wife's ex-husband.

"Here she is," her dad announced, looking up and seeing Becca. "We figured we'd let you sleep in."

He patted the spot next to him on the couch.

"Merry Christmas," her mother added. She was trying hard to seem cheerful, but Becca could tell she was nervous.

And then suddenly, everything made sense.

They *had* listened to her. *Really* listened. And they were making this very odd gesture to show her that they were trying.

Becca's eyes filled with tears. She sniffled, and went to sit beside her dad. He gave her a hug.

"Good to see you, sweetie," he said.

"You, too, Dad." She hugged him back. She decided not to ask where Melissa was. Hosting her father's wife was taking the gesture too far, she imagined.

Becca's mother handed her a large rectangular box.

"This is from your father." It was the first time Becca had heard her mother say the words "your father" without venom in over seven years. That, alone, was a better present than whatever was in the box.

Although the brand-new Spyder ski jacket her father had gotten her was pretty good, too.

"And I say, 'glor inte på mina barmar,'" Kate said, gripping the telephone tightly to her ear.

Her best friends — minus Becca, who was on the way — were at the other end, and she didn't want to miss a word. She would have given almost anything to be with them, in the same room, for just five minutes. But since she had yet to master time travel, Chantal's nineteen seventies rotary phone would have to suffice. At least Harper had a speaker phone.

"I don't get it," Sophie said. "Glor inte whatta?"

"It was *your* thing," Kate reminded her. Sitting on Chantal's vintage divan, staring at a framed sketch of Jean Paul Sartre, it was hard to believe that she could feel so connected to her friends.

"Yeah, well, I don't speak Swedish," Sophie laughed.

"I got it!" Harper shouted. "Don't stare at my breasts!"

"Exactly." Kate grinned. "But he kept staring, so then I said it in French, Dutch, *and* Italian."

"Well, if I ever see Trey Benson again," Sophie said, getting back to herself, "I'll just need English."

"I still can't believe you blew him off," Kate added in disbelief. From all of Sophie's e-mails, Kate knew she was semi-obsessed with the guy.

"I decided I need to be the prettiest person in a relationship," Sophie informed her after a slight pause. "Besides, the whole time I was in Aspen all I could think about was getting home."

Kate suspected there was more to the story. But before she could press for details, she heard a series of high-pitched screams at the other end of the phone, followed by a string of oh-my-Gods and you-look-amazings.

"Is that Becca?" she asked loudly.

"Katie!" Becca yelled.

"Becca has a boyfriend!" Harper hollered in the background.

"Yay! What happened?"

"I went to his house," Becca said. "I was like one of those insane girls you read about."

"But it worked," Kate said, thrilled. "A little insanity can be good."

Kate tried to picture her friends in Harper's basement. Becca was probably wearing a Christmas-themed sweater, and she doubted Harper had gotten out of her pajamas. If she had been there, she would have come bearing a batch of the elaborately decorated gingerbread cookies that Habiba made around the clock during the holidays.

"I'm a fan of all things crazy from now on." Becca laughed. Then, she added, obviously leaning toward the phone, "Thanks, K. I owe you."

"Anytime," Kate replied genuinely. "I have some news, too."

"What?" Harper immediately prodded.

"I figured out what 'take the water' means."

She was met with silence at the other end of the line. Then Harper said, "Huh?"

"*Huh?!* You're the one who put it on the list. I spent months trying to figure it out."

"It's just a line from a poem," Harper said. "By this guy Friedrich Holderlin. 'Sometimes a human's clay is not strong enough to take the water.' I thought it sounded cool."

Kate smiled. She should have known.

"How's the rest of it go?" she asked.

"Hang on," Harper said, "I'll find it."

"So what does it mean?" Sophie asked.

"Something different for everyone, I think." She could hear Harper rummaging around the basement.

"Don't be mysterious," Becca laughed.

"I'm not —" Kate began, but Harper was back.

"Here it is." Then she started to read:

"Oh, friend, we have arrived too late. The divine energies
Are still alive, but isolated above us, in the archetypal world.
They keep going there, and, apparently, don't bother if
Humans love or not . . . that is a heavenly mercy.
Sometimes a human's clay is not strong enough to take the water;
Human beings can carry the divine only sometimes.
What is living now? Night dreams of them. But craziness
Helps, so does sleep."

"The poem goes on from there," Harper informed them. "But it gets sorta depressing."

Kate's hand had risen of its own volition to her chest, "Oh, Harp, you have no idea how perfect it is. The only thing wrong with it is that it's *not* too late."

"Okaaay," Harper said. "I'll e-mail it to you. But I still don't get it."

"I can't even explain, exactly. But the upshot is, thanks to you guys, I'm strong enough to take the water. Literally. I met these two women who do humanitarian relief projects, and I'm going with them to Africa."

"You can't go to Africa." Harper insisted, having visions of Kate getting caught in the crossfire of local insurgents or being gored by an elephant tusk.

She hadn't bothered to change out of her Christmas pajamas, and she was lounging on her Harry Potter sheets with Becca, both of them leaning against a pile of throw pillows Harper had scavenged from upstairs. Sophie was stretched out on the floor, her head propped in her hand. The old blue sweats Harper had lent her were a few inches short, giving her the overall vibe of a female Huck Finn. Harper held up her cell phone with one hand so that everyone could hear Kate over the speaker.

"Why not?" Even from thousands of miles away, Kate had no trouble communicating her irritation.

"Yeah, why not?" Sophie asked, sitting up to pull on a faded purple hoodie that was lying on top of a heap of clothes on Harper's green plastic lawn chair.

"Because . . . Because . . ." The only reason Kate had embarked on this odyssey was because of Harper's lies. Because Harper had started this whole stupid Dream Train. If it weren't for her, Kate would be home in Boulder for Christmas, where she belonged.

"Africa's too dangerous," Harper persisted, reaching. "I don't think your parents would approve." As soon as the words were out, Harper knew she'd made a mistake. Kate's whole year was about bucking parent approval, not seeking it. "I mean, *I* don't approve," she added lamely.

Kate didn't speak right away, but when she did her voice was strong and clear. "Harper, I've been mugged, beaten, and nearly raped. I think I can handle a few months of helping people in Africa."

Becca had been playing with Sophie's cell phone for the past few minutes. Now her head popped up and she looked at Harper. Harper looked at Sophie. Sophie looked at Becca. Had they heard her right?

"You were WHAT?" Becca shouted at the phone, her brown ponytail practically vibrating from shock.

Kate sighed. "I didn't want you guys to worry. Or, worse, tell my parents."

"You said some guy stole your day pack," Sophie retorted, getting on her knees to be closer to the phone. "You said it wasn't that big a deal."

"Well, it was," she answered quietly. "It was . . . terrible."

Harper had visions of Greek thugs punching Kate's beautiful face, dragging her into some dark alley and ripping off her clothes. . . . The vivid images made her want to throw up.

"Katie, I'm so sorry." Becca's lips were trembling, and Harper knew she was going to cry. "What — what did they —" Her tears started to flow.

"They messed up my face," Kate admitted. "I didn't want to look in the mirror for a long time . . . but I'm fine now."

"And they didn't —?" Sophie began, her huge brown eyes even huger with worry.

"No," Kate stated emphatically. "A really nice couple chased them off. I didn't even know exactly what had happened until I woke up in the hospital."

"You were in the hospital?" Sophie shrieked. "How could you not *tell* us that?"

Harper imagined Kate hooked up to a dozen machines, getting shouted at in Greek by some sadistic Nurse Ratchet. It was unbearable.

"Shouldn't we all just be happy that I'm okay?" Kate asked. "I got through it, and now I've got to prove to myself that I'm not scared anymore."

Harper wanted to say something. She wanted to tell her that she loved her and that she'd never let anyone hurt her again. Only she couldn't utter a word. She was too ashamed. If it weren't for her, this never would have happened.

"Harp?" Kate's voice sounded a million miles away now. "Are you there?"

"I . . . I'm . . ." Harper's voice trailed off. *I'm a liar. I'm a horrible friend.*

"And I thought *I* was traumatized," Sophie exclaimed, saving Harper from having to finish her sentence.

"What happened to you?" Becca asked Sophie, sounding terrified. "I don't think I can take much more."

"I was totally and utterly destroyed," Sophie announced, pulling her black Gap tote toward her with one toe. "I wasn't going to tell anyone but Harper, but since we're *sharing* . . ."

She opened her bag and yanked out a newspaper tabloid, holding up the cover for everyone to see the photo of Trey kissing Pasha DiMoni.

"Ohmigod!" Becca screeched. "That's awful."

"What's awful?" Kate asked. "What am I missing?"

"There's a gigantic picture of Trey kissing Pasha DiMoni on the front page of a tabloid," Sophie explained into the phone. "I can never show my face in Hollywood again."

"Trey Benson's a skeeze," Kate stated from the other end.

"Yeah, but he was *my* skeeze," Sophie replied mournfully.

Looking at the photograph, Harper felt even worse for Sophie than she had before. At least her hell was private. Sophie's was out there for the world to see. And once again, it was all Harper's fault.

"So much for Dreams, huh?" Kate asked.

"My carpe diem speech really screwed things up." Harper forced herself to say it, even as self-hatred ate at her very bones.

Becca turned to her. "Worked out okay for me. I kicked ass on the ski team, I made friends. . . ." She grinned. "And, best of all, I've got Stuart."

"See?" Sophie said to Harper. "At least one of us is happy."

There was a levy inside of Harper, and it was about to burst. All the guilt, shame, and anguish were bubbling up to the surface, and she was going to explode. She couldn't stop it. She didn't even know if she wanted to.

"BECCA'S HAPPY BECAUSE SHE WENT TO COLLEGE!" Harper screamed. The levy had broken.

"Whoa, girl," Sophie admonished. "I think you just popped a blood vessel."

"Should I hang up so you can call nine-one-one?" Kate inquired. Harper couldn't believe she was so calm. So irritatingly buoyant. She'd had almost been raped!

"If it weren't for me, Kate would be *here*. The straight A's from her first semester at Harvard would be rolling in, and she and Jared would still be together."

"Harper, it's all right," Kate said. But Harper wasn't done talking.

"And Sophie would be starring in some awesome play at UCB, probably dating half her acting class and loving every minute of being worshipped." The words were tumbling out now. Everything Harper had feared had come true, and she needed to give voice to it.

"What about you?" Becca asked, pulling her ponytail tighter, her voice full of sympathy. "What would you be doing if you hadn't ditched NYU?"

"I'd still be sitting in this shitty basement!" Harper shouted. "Because I lied!" She was shaking, and her arms felt numb. "I didn't get into NYU! They *rejected* me."

Somewhere in Europe, Kate gasped. "What d'you mean?"

"I made up the whole Dream thing because I didn't want you guys to feel sorry for me," Harper confessed. "I never thought you'd join in!"

Becca and Sophie stared at her in shock. No one said anything. The enormity of Harper's lie — and all that had followed because of it — was sinking in.

Harper's muscles seemed to have seized up. She couldn't move. It was like she was looking at her life through some kind of eerie kaleidoscope.

"You're joking." Sophie finally broke the silence, the photo of Trey and Pasha DiMoni forgotten in her hands.

Harper shook her head. "I planned to tell you guys I didn't get in. But I was so humiliated . . . the days just kept passing by."

"Jesus, Harper!" Kate sounded pissed. Really pissed.

"I don't get it." Sophie looked perplexed. "You mean the whole speech about having something to express to the world and wanting to write the next Great American Novel was bullshit?"

"No. . . ." Harper wanted to defend herself, but how could she?

"I was ready to blow off Middlebury," Becca added, her voice low and dangerous. She was holding a pillow in her lap, and it looked like she might punch it. "You would've let me *do* that?"

"No!" Harper exclaimed. "Never! I promise."

"Hate to break it to you," Sophie pointed out coldly. "But your promises don't mean shit right now."

"We're your best friends!" Becca's anger was turning to hurt. "You couldn't trust us with the truth?"

"No, it's not that —" Shrinking. Harper was actually shrinking.

"Then what is it?" Sophie yelled. "You just thought, hey, since I'm sitting this year out why don't I drag everyone else down, too? Kate, yell at her!" she shouted at the phone.

"I've been living out of a backpack for four months," Kate responded, but she wasn't really shouting. "I could have been killed."

"I'm sorry!" Harper wanted to scream it at the top of her lungs. "You guys can hate me! I understand."

"Let me finish," Kate went on. "I've been living out of a backpack — which sucks — and I could have been killed. *But,* I'm also more myself than I've ever been."

"You are?" Harper squeaked. She felt like she was looking at a very tiny light at the end of a very long tunnel.

"I'm sorry you felt like you had to lie to us. I think I had something to do with that."

"That's it?" Sophie shrieked at Kate. "You're *apologizing?*" She looked like she was ready to grab the phone from Harper's hand and beat her on the head with it.

"I'm sorry," Harper repeated softly. She placed the phone on the end of the bed and pulled her knees against her chest, wrapping her pajama-clad arms around them. An upright fetal position seemed appropriate for the occasion. "I don't know what I was thinking."

"Harper, I did what I did for my *own* reasons," Kate stated. "You're giving yourself too much credit." She paused. "And I *am* going to Africa."

"Does anyone besides me care that our best friend *lied* to us?" Sophie asked in disbelief, her curls bobbing. "Not to mention, she got Kate and me to throw away our futures."

Becca looked at Sophie. "We all do things we regret. I know I did."

True enough, Harper thought. Having sex with Kate's boyfriend wasn't Becca's shining moment. But at least she hadn't sent the rest of them on a life-altering path while she was doing it.

"And it's not like going to college was *all* great," Becca went on. "I mean, most of the time I was a miserable heap of human flesh, cowering under my comforter."

"You were?" Harper asked. Somehow, the image made her feel better.

As Becca nodded, Sophie flung her arms in the air, sending the photo of Trey flying across the basement. "It's just . . . I thought everything would be like it was once I got home, but it all feels different."

"Because we've changed." Kate was the first to reply. "It doesn't mean we don't love each other anymore."

"*I* haven't changed," Sophie responded.

"Really?" Harper asked, glancing at her. "The prom queen I knew wouldn't have tossed aside her dream because some guy kissed another girl."

379

"The Dream was based on a *lie,*" Sophie countered. But she sounded slightly less outraged.

"I think we all need a hug," commented Becca, who was now holding Sophie's cell phone to her ear.

"Angela would say the whole thing with Trey was character-building," Sophie sighed. "She'd say it was one of life's little gifts that comes in a brown paper bag."

"Are you two really *related*?" Kate asked.

Oxygen returned to Harper's lungs. Her friends didn't hate her. They were mad, and there would be residual fallout, but they didn't hate her.

"I'll go back to LA," Sophie conceded finally. "But only because I know I'm destined to be a brilliant actress."

Harper couldn't help smiling. It almost seemed like . . . maybe they didn't think she'd ruined their lives. Maybe they were *glad* they got on the Dream Train, despite the derailments that had happened along the way.

Sophie turned to Becca. "What are you doing?"

"Listening to your messages," Becca answered matter-of-factly. "I want to hear Trey's voice."

"Delete, delete, delete," Sophie ordered her.

Becca looked concerned. "Have you checked these lately?"

Sophie shook her head. "I didn't want to bother when I was in Aspen — and once I left, I didn't want to hear his weasel excuses."

"You should hear this one," Becca pressed three to repeat the message and handed the phone to her.

In a weird way, Harper felt better than she had since April, when she got that letter in the mail. She'd thought telling her friends she got rejected from NYU would be the hardest thing she ever had to do. Turned out, lying to them had been a lot harder.

"OHMIGOD!" Sophie screamed.

"What?" Kate screamed back. "What happened?"

Sophie dropped the phone and stared at them. "I got a part. I have three lines in a movie."

"The casting director left the message a few days ago," Becca explained, because Sophie seemed to be having some sort of spasm. "Something Sophie auditioned for a while back."

Kate, Becca, and Harper erupted in cheers. Sophie jumped up and down. "Harper, I love you for lying!" she shouted. "I love the Dream Train!"

"Can I go to your Paris premiere?" Kate asked over the cacophony. "I'll make a special trip back from Africa for it."

"You're all coming," Sophie responded. She still hadn't stopped jumping.

"Good thing you decided to go back to LA," Harper said, breaking into a full smile for the first time since Kate had announced she was going to Africa.

Sophie snorted. "Like I'd ever let some stupid guy get in the way of my dreams."

"In one way or another, it looks like all of our dreams have started to come true." Becca looked at Harper. "Your carpe diem speech was right on — even if you didn't know it."

Harper nodded as she glanced toward her lonely pile of ashes. Maybe she hadn't written the next Great American Novel. But she'd finally owned up to her friends. And to herself.

For now, that was enough.

EPILOGUE

Typhoid," the Parisian doctor said. He pointed at the first in a long line of needles laid out on a sterile metal tray.

"Tetanus." He pointed at needle number two. Four more needles followed. "Hepatitis A and B, measles, meningitis, yellow fever," the doctor recited dully.

Kate wished she'd brought a bottle of water. Her throat suddenly felt exceedingly dry.

"I'll prescribe some anti-malarials, as well." He stuck the first needle into her arm.

"Okay," Kate flinched.

"You should avoid insect bites. And use sunscreen at all times."

"Got it." She gulped.

Finally, after the last shot, he said, "You must be one of those save-the-world types."

Kate thought about it for a moment, then, "Yeah," she said, smiling. She guessed she was.

Among other things.

"Don't take the 405," Sophie informed her cab driver as he sped out of LAX. "It's hell this time of day."

As the driver grunted something in Armenian, she rolled down the window in the cab and inhaled. It felt good to be home.

She'd had to cut her trip to Boulder three days short, because wardrobe needed her for fittings. When she'd gotten the news, she'd pretended to throw a diva fit about the frenzied life of an actress. But the truth was that as much as Sophie wanted more time with Becca and Harper and her parents, she couldn't wait to get back to her life.

Not that it was going to be easy. She knew she wouldn't be giving up her job at Mojito anytime soon. And she was still too broke to indulge in hot stone massages. Most of all, she'd accepted there was no knight in shining armor who was going to whisk her away from obscurity and open the doors to stardom.

But that was okay. She was ready to put on her fake Jimmy Choos and pound the pavement. She'd knock on every door herself, and she'd keep knocking until someone answered. Because Sophie Bushell didn't need a famous boyfriend or an Oscar to tell her she was a Somebody.

As long as she believed, the rest would figure itself out. It always did.

Becca lunged for the phone on her bedside table.

"Hello?" she said quickly. But she was too late.

"It's a guy," she heard Mia say — both through the phone line and through her bedroom door. "For Becca."

"A guy is calling *Becca?*" she heard Carter yell.

"Bec?" Stuart asked.

"Hang on." But before she could track down and murder Mia and Carter, she heard her mother shouting downstairs.

384

"Mia! Carter!" Her mom's voice sounded authoritative for once, instead of overwhelmed. "Get off the phone and quiet down!"

Instantly, there was a click on the line.

She and Stuart were alone.

"Hey," she said.

"Hey back." She heard him smiling. "I called to see if you want to go to dinner tomorrow after we get back."

"Like a big date?" She grinned.

"Nah," Stuart said. "I've learned my lesson. I'm thinking burgers and late night TV."

Becca sighed. Harper, Sophie, and Kate had given her a year to fall in love.

She was ahead of schedule.

Harper fluffed the cushions on her new sofa and stood back to gaze in awe. It was amazing what an orange seventy-dollar piece from the Salvation Army could do to change a room. Step one in her extended three-month redecorating plan was complete.

She walked to her desk and turned on her laptop. She realized now that living in ugliness had been a way of punishing herself. A college reject didn't deserve a nice place to live. A college reject didn't deserve to be happy.

Only that was total bullshit.

Harper knew why those fifty-one pages hadn't been what she wanted. Why nothing she'd written had been what she wanted.

Because she had been writing to prove something. She'd wanted to produce the next Great American Novel to show the world that she was worth something. That she wasn't just a waste of oxygen. The Dream Plan had been nothing more than a tool to hide her shame.

But all of that had changed when she confessed to Becca, Kate, and Sophie. Something had been released inside of her, and she knew now what she wanted to do.

Harper opened a new document and put her fingers on the keyboard. From now on, she was following her Dream for herself, not for anyone else. Maybe she'd write the next Great American Novel. Maybe she wouldn't.

Either way, she was ready to start.

ACKNOWLEDGMENTS

Deepest thanks to our ever-supportive editor, Cindy Eagan, and assistant editor, Phoebe Spanier. Without you we'd still be on page 10. Thanks to the rest of the team at Little, Brown and Time Warner Book Group — especially Alison Impey and Christine Cuccio. To Matt Solo, Richard Abate, and Eric Brooks — thanks for paying attention to the big picture. And of course we must acknowledge everyone at *The Shield*. We'd also like to thank our personal focus group: Sherry Carnes, Melissa de la Cruz, Karine Rosenthal, and Tracy Bellomo, who turned our proposal into a work of art.

EC: Thanks to my parents, Karen and Jack Craft, for teaching me to pursue my dreams, no matter how far-flung, and to my sister, Gretchen Rubin, whose blind faith and endless input I can't imagine living without. Thanks to Mindy Wilson and Caroline Suh for being there, always. And special thanks to Adam Fierro, who graciously sacrificed our weekends so I could write this.

SF: Coach Forest Carey of the Middlebury ski team, Cheryl at Americans for African Adoptions, and Evan Dumouchel — thanks for sharing your knowledge and expertise. Many thanks to Pamela Beccera, who mentored me just as much as I mentored her. And, of course, to all of my parents — Judy Strong, Bob Fain, Anna Fain, Jerry Carson, and Gordon Scholes — thanks for knowing that when it comes to dreams, tread softly.